GARDEN

OF

SECRETS

BOOKS BY SUZANNE KELMAN

A View Across the Rooftops

When We Were Brave

Under a Sky on Fire

When the Nightingale Sings

GARDEN OF SECRETS

SUZANNE KELMAN

bookouture

Published by Bookouture in 2022

An imprint of Storyfire Ltd.
Carmelite House
50 Victoria Embankment
London EC4Y 0DZ

www.bookouture.com

ISBN: 978-1-80314-059-9
eBook ISBN: 978-1-80314-058-2

To my bridegroom. Thank you for showing me daily your gift of fathomless love. I could never have believed in a love kept alive in someone's heart for seventy-five years if it weren't for the love you have shown me for thirty.
And in memory of Brian Ernest Wilson.

And the secret garden bloomed and bloomed and every morning revealed new miracles.

–Frances Hodgson Burnett, *The Secret Garden*

PROLOGUE

HATWORTH MANOR, NORFOLK, NOVEMBER
1941

Anya

Too dangerous to hide something during the day, she was grateful for the bleakness of the wartime blackout that swallowed her up in its gloom as she rushed out into the night. The evening air was as sharp as splintered glass as Anya hastened across the estate, her secret tucked under the layers of her clothing. Needled breath raced in and out of her lungs in jagged short spurts of frigid spiky air as she ploughed through the heavy, wet snow, attempting to muffle the thuds of her bulky work boots.

She cursed the weather. It was going to make it easier for her to be tracked and her footprints to be seen by the light of the full moon that toyed with exposing her. Large and incandescent, her adversary hung as round and as heavy as summer fruit, waiting to make an appearance from behind its billowy grey clouds. Anya forced her eyes open as she battled against the sleety snow that fell in icy sheets, dragging down strands of her golden hair from beneath her black knitted cap that then clung to her neck, freezing her to her core. Buffeted by a sharp east wind, the snow moved in rolling damp waves that found every gap within her clothing, trickling down her collar and sliding down the back of her saturated trousers. Already two sizes too big for her, they hung well below her hips. As she hurried, the soggy cuffs slapped against her ankles, leaving an icy trail of their own alongside her footprints.

She wouldn't have time to dry them tonight. As soon as her plan was in place, she would have to flee the estate in her wet clothes.

When she finally reached her destination, her trembling fingers pushed the heavy key into the lock, her red hands swollen and burning with the cold as she twisted it twice to the right, grasping the solid brass handle, jerking it hard to the left, pushing the whole weight of her tiny frame behind the oak door until it creaked open.

As she stepped inside, she breathed a sigh of relief. It was like entering another world. She forced the door back into place, and the aged wood groaned as it scraped a floury groove through the drifted snow.

Waiting for a second, Anya flattened her back against the wood, panting. She was safe for now. She couldn't be seen from here. As her breath slowed, she listened for anything out of the ordinary, any raised voices or muffled running feet following her. But all she could hear was the trickle of the fountain in the centre of the garden, its usual exuberant flow muffled by the mound of snow accumulating in its basin. Swiping curtains of wet hair from her face, she patted at her trousers. It was still there.

She was alarmed by a noise above her and her breath hitched at the sound of startled wings. As she stared up into the darkened sky, a sliver of moonlight drifted from behind the clouds, outlining the white flowing feathers of a majestic barn owl, silhouetted against the cushion of an inky black sky.

Allowing it to pursue its course over the red brick walls, she took a second to balance the beauty of this moment against the danger closing in on her from all sides.

Striding through the walled garden, air rushing in and out of her frozen cheeks, she got her bearings. Even in the darkness, even with the unfamiliarity caused by the blanket of snow that stretched out before her, she knew exactly where she was going, had memorized the whole garden as she'd been taught to do in her training for any environment she found herself in.

Her stomach tightened in its growing knot.

'Be brave, Anya,' she whispered to herself.

If all went to plan, it was her only hope of ever seeing Nikolai again. She brushed past the red painted swing that creaked as it rocked, showing its annoyance at being disturbed from its slumber in the depths of the night. She slithered across the slate-grey stepping stones, which were now nestled ankle-deep in snow, as she headed towards the place that had been selected. She could still hear Nikolai's whispered instructions in her ear.

'Here, just below the young willow tree, is the best place, my Mishka,' he had whispered, using his pet name for her. 'Underneath its weeping branches, it will be difficult to see a patch of disturbed earth.'

Pulling out the long piece of string dangling down the leg of her trousers, she took out what she'd been carrying and, dropping onto all fours, scrambled beneath the branches. Even in her heavy beige Land Girl trousers, the cold penetrated all the way through to her knees, chilling her to the bone. She was not deterred. There was more chance of the ground being less frozen farther under the canopy.

Reaching a good spot, she tore away at the undergrowth and dug into the soil with her bare hands. With only a tiny window of time to escape the house, there hadn't been the opportunity to pick up a spade in the rush to get away unnoticed. Already frozen, her fingers stung with the pain as she continued to claw through the icy mud, the smell of wet soil and rotting leaves assaulting her senses. She had no concern for either. The longer she was gone, the more chance there would be of finding her missing.

As she scooped away frigid earth, she distracted herself from the cold by her memories of the garden, memories of vegetables being planted in much finer weather and a lot less dire circumstances than this. Memories of loving Nikolai. The garden had been such a joy for her. Built to be functional in the 1800s, it had been recreated into a more ornamental garden as a wedding gift for Lady Sarah, the mistress of the manor in the 1920s.

'There is something magical about the world within the walls. It has a powerful alchemy of its own,' the gardener had told her, peering at her with such intensity she had been afraid to look away. 'Nature captured like a ship in a bottle. Remember, a walled garden keeps its own secrets and you need to respect it,' he had demanded of her.

More recently, its purpose had been to nurture the village with extra food it provided during rationing, but not this evening. Tonight, it would fulfil its destiny and would not only have to keep Anya's secret, but it would also provide a way out, an escape.

She laid down the tiny object and carefully scooped the wet earth over the top of it. As she sat back on her heels, a heavy clump of wet snow startled her, finding its way between the branches, and she felt the fear rise once again, now to her throat. She couldn't give in to it. She needed to be strong for both of them. Laying an extra covering of leaves and ferns on the spot, she waited for a second to catch her breath. The deed was done. It felt right to say a small prayer. She whispered a few words in Russian to her God under her breath as she felt the weight of her task lifting from her shoulders.

Crawling out from between the branches, she stood up as

beams of the full moon finally broke free from the stranglehold of the clouds and illuminated the thick snowflakes still falling. The moonlight warmed her. Was God answering her prayer, sending her his blessing? She doubted it. There was no blessing here. What she was doing was totally selfish, the only way to save the man she loved. If she was caught by the British or even her own government, she knew she could be executed.

Hurrying back to the garden door, she pulled it shut behind her and locked it once again. Moving back through the night, she made her way carefully to avoid the side of the house where people would hopefully now be sleeping.

Once inside the house, she closed the door quietly behind her and gathered her breath as she lay against it, enjoying its reassuring presence. Relieved, she took a deep, long, slow breath and marked the moment in time, etching it forever in her memory. Remembering what she'd done tonight, what she'd done for love.

1

HATWORTH MANOR, NORFOLK, PRESENT DAY

Laura

Laura banged 'enter' on her keyboard and, pushing back hard into her chair, clamped her teeth together and drew in the corners of her mouth to stop herself from crying. She was definitely not going to cry. He was not worth it. As the word 'undo' flashed up on her screen, she balled her hands into fists to stop from having second thoughts. But as the words 'Your mail has been sent' replaced the undo message, the flash of anger that had propelled her through the writing had gone and all that was left was sorrow. She had done everything in her power to make this relationship work, but she knew it was over.

Slamming down the top of her laptop before there was a chance of getting a reply, she left her bedroom feeling suffocated by the weight of sadness. The walls of the workman's cottage on the grounds of the Hatworth Estate where she was staying felt like they were crowding in on her. She had to get out.

She glanced out the kitchen window and drew in a welcoming breath. At least after three days of continuous snow,

now there was a break in the weather, and a foot of white crys-
tallization shimmered under a late winter sun. As she stood
staring out the window, the kitchen came to life around her
with the sound of scampering claws, as the two border collies
that also lived in the cottage appeared to be feeling restless as
well. With wet noses pressed against the latched cottage door,
they could barely wait for Laura to pull on her red anorak and
polka-dot boots. Glancing in a mirror, she pulled her fair shoul-
der-length hair into a messy bun and, noticing the dark circles
under her blue eyes, sighed. Getting some fresh air would do
her good.

She tugged on the back door, working against the accumula-
tion of age, grease, and snow as the impatient pets nosed their
way through the tiny gap and raced off to create haphazard paw
print trails through the snow. As she left, Laura reached up onto
the kitchen wall and pulled down an antique key from its brass
hook and placed it into her pocket.

Once outside, a shaft of bright late afternoon sunlight
bounced off the stark ground, causing her to screw up her eyes
as she tried to track the path of her rambunctious companions.
Bounding along, one echoed thud after another, she revelled in
the velvet crunch beneath her feet and marvelled at how beautiful the world looked under nature's blanket.

Tracking the dogs, she circled a path around the building
and took a moment to admire the manor under its winter overcoat. An attractive square grey-stoned building, with a multi-
tude of odd-shaped chimneys, it glistened in the morning sun,
like a cream-coloured cube dusted with icing sugar. Surrounded
by a tiny moat, the frontage was studded with numerous
windows, and six elegant Grecian pillars marked the grand
main entrance with its large oak doors. Above the threshold, the
family crest, toiled into the stone under the hands of craftsmen
centuries before, depicted a pair of prestigious lions reaching up
on hind legs, roaring a formidable warning.

With an impressive history, Hatworth Manor had stood here in one form or another since the 1500s and had barely changed for centuries.

Through a rough thicket, both dogs burst forth, their mouths open, noses and tongues wet, and tails wagging as they panted their joy at their ultimate freedom. Finding their mark, they bounded towards her and wet paws and weighty thuds stopped Laura in her tracks.

Ruffling their damp ears, she already felt better. Being outside made her feel alive again. It smoothed her feathers, helped her connect all the dots. She had friends who liked to run to the music on their iPhones, but Laura preferred to amble, enjoy the rhythm of nature as it unfolded before her.

She pushed away any thoughts of Liam receiving her email. His face clouded with the anger of his powerlessness. There was nothing he hated more than feeling he couldn't control a situation. Her body shuddered with that realization. It didn't matter. It didn't matter anymore how he was feeling, she reminded herself.

As clouds of frigid breath formed in front of her, she tucked her hands into her pockets and headed to the place she had been itching to inspect in more detail since she had arrived. The estate manager and longtime friend, Simon, had given her a brief tour two days ago before the snow had arrived. But she had always loved being able to survey her projects at leisure, allow the gardens to tell her their secrets. Under the gnarly branches of the old wisteria, she found what she was looking for. Its red brick walls, crumbling and ancient, welcomed her.

The secret garden was presently completely smothered with ivy that even in wintertime hung in long petulant strands. Tentatively brushing aside a snowy string of them, she located the door, now so weathered in places it had faded to a light grey, its iron studs staining the wood with black streaks.

Turning the round iron handle, Laura unlatched the door,

nudging it open carefully. Snow on either side of the door hampered her progress, but as she gently eased it forwards, it finally gave way at her insistence and groaned open. Both the dogs bounded in past her, excited for a new place to discover.

Inside, she kicked a trail through the snow and looked around her.

'Hello, my new friend,' she whispered into the air. Under its winter blanket, the world inside the walls felt hollow and spacious, and even with its white camouflage, she could still make out many of the structures and features of the garden.

A three-foot-high box hedge ran down either side of a narrow stone path in front of her. Clipped and kept in exact order by the estate's myriad gardeners in days past, it now looked more like an unkempt hairstyle. Single branches and stems jutting out at odd angles, covered in glistening nuggets of ice, strained to find their own paths to the sun.

In the centre of the garden was an elegant fountain. At the pinnacle, a cheerful cherub trickled water from a Grecian urn that dripped down into tiers of grey stone, and even though it was somewhat pathetic with lack of care and muffled by the snow, Laura was comforted by the gentle magical sounds of water as it whispered to her.

Closing her eyes, she was calmed by the feeling of solitude. The frigid air numbed her cheeks as she stood breathing deeply. All at once she remembered Liam's letter.

Simon had passed it across the table at breakfast, over the top of a pot of his wife Alicia's homemade marmalade, his eyes hinting at the knowledge of whom it was from.

'It came to the main house yesterday,' he'd informed her, exchanging a concerned look with Alicia. 'Someone from the trust dropped it here at the cottage.'

Laura had known instantly. The long business envelope, with the distinct looped handwriting – even though there was no return address, she knew it was from Liam, as her stomach twisted itself into a knot. Trying not to show the immense amount of pain she was feeling, she placed it down beside her plate as both Simon and Alicia eyed it curiously before continuing their tasks, he reading his paper and Alicia methodically buttering her toast.

'Don't you want to open it, Auntie Laura?' Simon's daughter inquired, staring at it with anticipation. 'It might have money in it. When I get cards, they always have money in them,' she added, biting into her toast and sending a splattering of golden marmalade onto her school tie.

Her mother quickly attended to it by dipping a napkin into a glass of water and scrubbing, then she filled Laura's silence as she sat paralyzed by the letter's intrusion.

'Leave Auntie Laura alone, Lucy. Older people's letters are different.'

Her nine-year-old honorary niece furrowed her brows thoughtfully before continuing through her mouthful of toast, 'Do you mean like the electricity bill, when Dad swears?'

'Exactly,' responded Alicia with a half-smile.

Simon peered over his paper, frowning. 'Do I?'

Lucy nodded.

'And the one that says "t-a-x,"' added Oliver, Simon's seven-year-old son.

'Enough talking, both of you,' responded their mother sternly. 'More eating or you will both be late for school.'

Once breakfast was over, both children raced off to grab satchels and winter coats. As Simon went outside to warm up the car, Alicia leaned forward and grabbed her friend's hand. 'Are you all right, Laura?'

Laura nodded, fighting back the tears. 'I will be.'

She knew she would need to tell them exactly what was going on with her soon, when she was ready to share her broken heart.

Laura, Simon, and Alicia had all been friends at university

together, and when Simon had offered her this project on the estate he managed, she'd jumped at the chance to get away from London. The estate he worked on had a modest walled garden that needed restoration work, and though the money wasn't great, it was her area of expertise and would be a lovely project for her that also meant she could save money if she stayed with Simon and Alicia in their cottage.

Since she had arrived, her friends had been very gracious, not asking questions when she avoided any mention of Liam.

'It will be lovely to spend time with you,' Alicia had reassured her on the phone. 'It will be like uni all over again.'

But up until now, they had not asked, and she had not wanted to share with them, what was going on in her personal life. Laura had just wanted to be comforted by their lovely home and be with people who loved her before she faced the fact that her life was shattered.

Laura took another deep breath and opened her eyes. She hadn't expected Liam to write to her. So, he had stopped emailing her now, she thought as she cleared a low-hanging branch of snow with a gloved hand. Now, her boyfriend – exboyfriend, she mentally corrected herself – was writing to her. First the texts, then the emails, now letters.

Stooping under the golden chain tree that framed the fountain, she noticed its branches fought for a place against a wild rose that had joined forces from another ancient arbour. It reflected much of the garden's neglect. But even in its current state, Laura felt the deep presence of the garden as it whispered its ancient story to her. It would be a big project to bring it back to its former glory, as the trust had commissioned her, but if she could get an early start, it could be in good shape by late spring, early summer, her favourite time of the year.

Continuing around the edge of the walls, set out in a long rectangle and spanning almost a half an acre, she passed one of the many weathered benches, grey and sun-bleached, placed in a convenient location for any nanny of the last century. She imagined them sitting there in black, in a rigid no-nonsense state, sharing manor gossip with the gardeners in whispered tones as they watched their young charges racing about within the safe walls of the garden. Now, a chain of leafy ivy had claimed the bench as its own, tumbling down from the red brick walls and crawling up its silver legs.

Hanging from the boughs of the magnificent apple tree that dominated the far north-eastern corner was the swing. Its greening ropes, threaded through a large wooden seat of peeling paint, appeared to be long enough to tackle a long slow arc. She pictured children of the past pumping their legs furiously to swing high enough to see over the red stone walls. As she approached the elderly tree, a light wind rippled through the branches, accelerating the melting snow, and some of the chilly droplets brushed her cheeks and caused a clump of heavy wet snow to fall beside her.

Shivering with the chill, she inspected the apple tree, still deep in its winter slumber. Its branches were weighted down with ice instead of apples. She was pleased to see it was unharmed. The blizzard that had arrived two nights before had been followed by a plummeting freeze that had created a weight of snow that would have tested any flat roof, or tender limb. But apart from its heavy frosting, it had stood up well to the test of the weather.

She brushed off the swing and tentatively sat down. It still seemed sturdy and strong, despite its age. All at once Bobby appeared and galloped up to her and placed his black velvety snout on her lap, encouraging her to stroke his soft warm head. His brother, Dylan, had completely disappeared. She could hear his distant patter far off, accompanied by heavy panting, his nose no doubt to the ground.

She realized all at once why she had been driven to come here this morning and what a wondrous and magical place it was. Even in midwinter, it had cast its spell on her. The soothing peace and quiet, the complete feeling of solitude, being hidden away from the world, made her feel deeply secure. But there was also something about being within these walls that created a feeling of hope. It had an enchantment all of its own, because just like nature all things can become new again.

From her new view on the swing, Laura identified other architecture in the garden. The blue treehouse, created with a Victorian theme, was frosted white, and the pond at the western side was frozen over, and the little stone bridge was missing brickwork and various stepping stones needed attention... There would be a lot to plan.

Though this was her expertise. Her job included researching and planting gardens of the past, restoring them to their former glory. She loved her work, which was a combination of research, gardening, and detective work.

Laura shivered. She should get back.

She called out to Dylan, who was still missing. An utter rascal, he loved to romp about the estate and could go for miles before even realizing he was alone, Simon had warned her. 'Dylan!' she called out again, more urgently into the silence, only punctuated by the dripping snow and a cooing wood pigeon far off. Bobby followed obediently by her side as she continued her long lap around the garden, his black tail wagging, his glossy eyes watching her intently, his wet nose rustling at her pockets in the hope of treats.

Even though it was barely midday, a winter mist was starting to creep over the tops of the walls, and Simon would wonder where she and the dogs were. She called out again, and again, more urgently, but all was quiet. No panting or pattering paws, just the silence of the day and the smell of the earthy cold as it crept down the collar of her coat and was now starting to make her ears numb.

As Laura lapped the garden for a second time, down in the

undergrowth behind the apple tree something much smaller than a dog scurried away to hide, but Dylan was nowhere to be found.

All at once, she heard something in the very far northwest corner, where there was an elderly willow tree surrounded by thistles. This part of the garden had been left very unkempt. 'A little bit of the wild,' Simon had informed her as they'd stood in front of the patch of overgrown blackberry bushes.

Laura continued towards the corner, following the scratching noises. She called out again to Dylan, louder. Whistled to him, even patted the tops of her legs, as she'd seen Simon do, but there was nothing. Just Bobby's head and wagging tail beside her.

Even though it was winter, there were still thorns on the blackberry bushes. Sighing, she knew she'd have to go in after him. She was sure now that this was the only place left he could be in the garden.

Using her gloved hands, she carefully moved through the thistles. They snagged her anorak, and the thick undergrowth tried to trip her under the snow. Bobby bounded ahead of her, making his way to find his brother, barking their arrival.

As she reached the corner, she drew breath. Instead of the aging willow tree that had dominated that far end when she had toured on arrival, there was a mountain of twisted branches in front of her. Roots ripped raw from the ground, a mangled nest reaching dark witchy fingers into the sky. The heavy weight of the snowstorm had just been too much for something this old. Beneath the weeping willow was a huge hole it had been ripped from.

Pulling herself free of the last bramble, she moved towards it, calling out to the dog. He was close to the hole, his black nose brown with mud and his paws digging manically. He ignored her, continuing with his task at hand.

Excited by the prospect of a find, Bobby joined him, sniffing and barking at the hole that the collie was digging.

Laura called out to him again. 'Dylan, come here. Come here now. Leave that!'

But Dylan got more enthusiastic rather than less. As he did, Bobby barked too.

As both dogs stopped to sniff the ground, she saw something on top of the mound of soil. He'd dug something up and beside it lay the blue shell of a robin's egg. All at once her worst memory from childhood came back to haunt her and she audibly gasped. 'Katie,' she whispered into the icy day and, closing her eyes, started to count backwards as her therapist had taught her as her body trembled violently. This was ridiculous. How could something so long ago still affect her so badly? She reassured herself everything was all right now, she was safe, and slowly Laura opened her eyes.

She refocused on the ground. As Dylan drew back and barked again, she caught sight of something silver-coloured and flat by the eggshell. She moved closer for a better look.

'What have you got there?' she asked the dogs, still aware of the quiver in her voice. They were both wagging their tails furiously and barking their encouragement. Moving to what had been the base of the willow tree, she bent down and picked up the object. It was a tiny metal cigarette case.

Dylan jumped up at her, pushing his paws against her, asking for a treat.

'I don't think you can eat this,' Laura informed him gently. She studied the small tin in her hand. It looked old and a little rusty but in surprisingly good condition. Brushing off the rest of the dirt, she slowly opened the lid.

There was something inside, something shiny at the bottom. Holding out her hand, she poured the contents into her mitten. It was a tiny silver key. But that wasn't all. As she looked back inside the box, she could see something else. She pulled off her glove and carefully pulled out a torn WWII ration card. On the back was written a short message, with a woman's name. 'PLEASE FIND ME! Grace Mere is our only hope.' And as she pondered the words and refocused on the tiny fragile eggshell still lying on the dark earth, her stomach clenched as the memory of her dead sister tore at her heart.

2

MOSCOW, NOVEMBER 1940

Nikolai

Nikolai Petroff pulled the collar of his new regimental green wool coat around his ears and moved out onto the streets of Moscow. It was raw with cold and the shock of it made his jaw ache as the frost winked at him from the icy ground and the frigid trees. He moved at a nervous trot, the echo of his feet in his rigid shiny new shoes competing with his fast-beating heart as he strode briskly towards the building that he knew could change his life forever. He was proud to be serving Mother Russia, even though he felt uncomfortable in the stiff fabric of his uniform with the red collars that marked him as a member of the NKVD. As he tightened the collars of his coat he mused how he couldn't believe he was now a member. The Russian secret service had been through so many upheavals in the last years. Primarily set up as the CHEKA after the revolution, now under Joseph Stalin it was more streamlined.

The clock on the front of the Lubyanka building chimed out into the square. He was an hour early. But he hadn't been able to stay in his communal apartment one minute longer.

Catching his breath, he joined a line for a newspaper, now wishing he could wear his thick woollen hat with the earflaps instead of this peaked cap, as his head throbbed with the chill. Even with the gloomy temperature, the mood in the line was jovial as people greeted one another. Still experiencing something relatively new and exciting, Russians queued early to seek the news of the day, even if it was curtailed by their own government. Handing over a few roubles, he nodded at the seller and made his way to the *stolovaya*.

The heat of the room stung him as the elderly man behind the counter with a day's worth of growth and a heavy moustache bade him welcome.

'Nikolai, you're early. You'll want your tea.'

Nikolai nodded his head, wiping a gloved hand down his face, which was already soaked with a mixture of sweat and the freezing dew from the outside. He removed his gloves and cap and picked up a tray.

'How are you today, comrade?' Nikolai asked of his old friend.

'I am well. The hospital is taking good care of my wife. Not having to pay the doctors who take care of our sick is a nice gift from our wonderful leader, don't you think?'

The man pointed at the portrait of Stalin that hung with pride on the canteen wall, as it did in many establishments. Even if people didn't always approve of Stalin's ideals no one wanted to be seen as not being supportive.

The man continued, interrupting Nikolai's thoughts. 'And now both my daughters have also been granted the chance at an education. Maybe one day one of them will be a doctor too, no?' The man chuckled as he strode off to get Nikolai food as he contemplated his words. It was true, the communist movement had its benefits and not worrying about doctor bills or an education was definitely a plus, but there was always this underlying feeling of being controlled that never sat well with Nikolai.

Even so he was proud to serve his country. Although he had his own agenda for what he was doing.

Opening the newspaper, he started his now-daily search. There was always the hope that there would be the clues he was looking for somewhere in some article. It had been two years since the death of his father, but he had never given up hope of finding out what had happened. He carefully scoured every inch, not allowing one word to be overlooked.

A steaming glass of tea appeared on his tray, and he barely acknowledged the tender as he continued his investigation and made his way to a table. Today he hoped it would be different. Today he hoped that he would find out what he'd been wanting to know for a long time.

After closing the final page, he sat back, disappointed, and lit a cigarette, with no new answers to the usual questions that haunted him. His father, Anton Petroff, had been a man of precision, a man of accuracy. The strange way that he had died still lay hard and heavy on Nikolai's heart.

At least after today he had a plan, if the Russian government was behind it as he suspected. Today he would have a chance to investigate that.

Now he would be allowed to enter the building that held all those secrets.

He crushed out his cigarette and went over his plan. He would look around, read documents that were classified. Of course, he would be careful. He wouldn't let on to anyone his ulterior motive for taking this job. As far as the government were concerned, he was excited to be joining the secret service.

As he drained his glass, the bitter tea leaves scratched his throat. He turned back to the front cover, which touted the news of the ongoing war in Europe. It was concerning that the Russians were siding with Hitler. He wondered if this was wise on Stalin's part. Hitler seemed like a madman to him, trying to control the whole of Europe. Why would Russia have any interest in that?

Handing the paper as a gift to the grateful canteen worker, he stepped back out into the cold, which seemed to sting even more now that his limbs were warmed. He had just completed his secret service training and now he was ready to start working as a transcription translator in the government building.

He had been conscripted straight from university because of his incredible linguistic abilities. The two darkly dressed men had approached even before his final exams. He remembered the clock ticking in the classroom as the professor, seeing the auspicious visitors, had clutched his files close to his chest and made himself scarce, scurrying from the classroom so that they could approach Nikolai at his desk. Nikolai had just been finishing an assignment when he'd looked up into the faces of the two men who stood before him.

'Nikolai Petroff. We knew your father. He was a good man.'

Nikolai felt his heart quicken, hoping he was finally going to find out what had happened.

The man took off his hat and put it on the desk. 'We hear you are very good with languages. You are top of your class.'

Nikolai nodded, a little concerned now. Where was this conversation going?

'We're looking for people like you right now. People who are good at speaking different languages. It says here...' The man pulled out a file, and Nikolai wondered where he'd received it from. But there were his grades in front of him. 'That you have the top score in English. I imagine your life in other countries gave you a good ear, no?'

Nikolai nodded. 'We were assigned to England for a few years when I was young. I went to a private school there. My father was a diplomat in London. I've always been able to pick up any kind of language.'

The men nodded there with satisfaction. 'Exactly. We want you to come to this address next week. We have a job for you, serving your country. We'll pay you well, better than anything you could earn as a teacher.'

Nikolai sucked in a breath. How had they even known that had been his desire?

'We look forward to seeing you there,' said the other man as they got to their feet and left the room.

Nikolai had gone the week later, only to find out that the secret service was recruiting him. With the war ongoing in Europe, Stalin wanted to be able to stay ahead and informed. He was assigned to listen in on incoming transmissions and translate them. He had worked there for a while before he had once again been recruited into the job he would be doing now. And though he wasn't sure of what the assignment was, he had been told to report for duty that very morning at the head-quarters.

Dressing in his hat and gloves, he got to his feet. Bidding the canteen worker goodbye, he made his way back out into the street. In the distance, the multicoloured onion-shaped domes that Russia was famous for now glinted in the light of an early morning sun, attempting to defrost the pavements to little avail.

He crossed the street and made his way towards the building. He would, of course, work for them. He would do what they wanted, but all he really would be doing was looking for anything he could find out about his father until the day he died. He would find out what had really happened and seek revenge on those who had perpetrated it, even if it meant going against his own government.

3

HATWORTH MANOR, NORFOLK, ENGLAND, PRESENT DAY

Laura

Herded by both collies, Laura pushed open the farmhouse door to be greeted by the cosy warmth of the kitchen. As both dogs clipped, panting, across the red-tiled floor, Laura pulled off her boots and replaced the garden key as Simon arrived in the kitchen.

'You're back! We thought you'd left with our dogs and were planning a ransom. Unfortunately, it looks like you brought them back. How did you enjoy the walk they took you on?'

Laura smiled and shivered as she made her way to the Aga that was well-stocked with coal and warming the whole kitchen. On the top she noticed that a huge cast-iron saucepan was now bubbling with something warm that smelt delicious.

'Alicia made some soup,' Simon noted, seeing Laura inhaling the rich aroma. 'She thought you might be hungry after your walk.'

'Looks delicious,' responded Laura, lifting then replacing the lid. 'Hey, I was just in the walled garden.'

'Could you see much in the snow?' inquired Simon, focused on his task of filling the dogs' water bowls.

'I was able to see the lie of the land,' she responded, holding her mittened fingers over the heat from the Aga as the smell of damp wool and wet dog filled the air.

'Is everything still standing?'

'Well, actually, not exactly,' said Laura, swiping at her cold dripping nose. 'Unfortunately, it looks as though the willow tree has come down.'

'The one in the northwest corner?'

Laura nodded.

'It just shows how much we've needed you to restore it. It has been so neglected for years.'

'By the looks of the ground, it was the weight of the snow and ice that just brought it down,' continued Laura.

'What a shame,' he commented absently as Alicia joined them in the kitchen.

'Cup of tea?' her host suggested in her usual upbeat tone as she glided up next to Simon and hugged him, her tiny, barely five-one frame lost against his large solid build. At six-three, Simon had been a jumble of lanky growing limbs when Laura had known him at uni, but now nearly a decade on with Alicia's organic home-cooked meals and days spent out on the estate, he had become quite rugged and handsome with his fair straight hair and grey eyes.

On the other hand, Alicia hadn't changed one bit since their university days and often joked about getting mistaken for a pupil from the local secondary school. Not really surprising with her being so petite with curious blue eyes, a pixie grin, and straight silky black hair that she often wore up in a ponytail.

As Laura watched the two of them interact, she thought, not for the first time, how fortunate she was to have such wonderful friends as these. 'I'd love a cup,' she responded.

Laura removed her damp clothes and watched Alicia bop about the kitchen gathering tea supplies as she chatted animatedly about her day, and once again Laura wished she were bubblier. Alicia always seemed to be having much more fun in her life than she did.

'PG or mint?' inquired Alicia as she pulled her nose out from inside a cupboard she'd been searching in.

'Strong PG,' responded Laura. 'I need something with a little body to warm myself up.'

'Laura was in the walled garden,' Simon informed Alicia, returning to their past conversation.

But before Laura could mention her find, the door burst open and in came Oliver and Lucy, who had been dropped home by a friend. They had the afternoon off school and, becoming bored quickly, were arguing about one of their iPads. Simon went into parental mode, admonishing both of them, and the room became heated with the electric experience of family. The dogs also joined in the fun, barking and jumping up at the table. Alicia, with one hand resting on her boiling kettle, continued to stir her soup, giving her own parental opinion over her shoulder.

The conversation moved on, and Laura momentarily forgot about the cigarette case she'd found, lost in the hubbub of family life.

Taking down a fresh loaf of Alicia's homemade bread, Simon started to cut it as his children whined about being hungry and he explained that lunch would not be long.

'They're always hungry,' continued Alicia jovially. 'They're either eating or arguing. There's only two modes for my children,' she laughed.

After lunch, Laura ambled into the main family room. A log fire was lit and both dogs had found their way there and lay dozing and twitching in front of it. Alicia's taste in decor suited her exactly. A farmhouse charm with a touch of the whimsy. A comfortable sagging sofa was brightened by a bohemian throw and colourful pillows, her shelves and bookcases filled with eclectic knick-knacks and treasures that competed with Simon's taste in antiques.

With the snow now settling, Alicia and Simon wanted to do a trek out to the supermarket before it got dark and possibly cold and icy. They asked Laura if she'd keep an eye on Oliver and Lucy while they were gone. She was happy to do it, as the children were pretty self-contained in their bedrooms, and she sensed her friends might appreciate a little time alone together, even just at the supermarket.

Standing at the window surrounded by the cottage's built-in bookcases, Laura watched her friends' Range Rover drive away slowly down the long winding drive to the gates. Checking her phone, she noted the last text from Caroline, who was not only Liam's sister but also one of her closest friends.

I know this is awkward, but just know that you can talk to me anytime. I'm always here for you as well as Liam, don't forget that. xx

Laura sighed again and shut off her phone. She just didn't know how to bridge this strange gap between them, and even though she missed her dearest friend, she just didn't know what to say.

Grabbing one of the woollen throws that Alicia always kept in a well-stocked basket by the fire, she sat on the little window seat and drew up her feet. As she did, something brushed against her leg and she remembered the cigarette case in her pocket, and the urgency she had felt in the garden returned.

'Grace Mere,' she mused, remembering the woman's name inside. The researcher in her wanted to automatically go and find out. Grabbing her laptop, she settled herself back on the window seat to see if she could find any references to her. But apart from a few Graces who had lived and died in different parts of the country, nothing of significance came up.

Laura took the cigarette case again and rolled the key around in her hand, looking at it more closely. She'd been taught in research that the smallest thing could lead you on a trail of great discovery.

She held the key up to the window. It was about two inches long with an ornate filigree design. It looked too small for a door, but maybe the right size for a box. A cashbox or a small writing desk, perhaps. She noticed that it was well worn, with a tiny chip in its barrel. *Probably well used*, she thought.

She then took out the torn ration card again. Though it was old, it was in good condition. Surely rations during the war were very important. Who would tear up a ration card to write on it? The words had been written in an elegant hand, with an unusual curve to the loops, not anything like the joined-up writing she had been taught at school.

It looked as if the words had been written quickly, as there was a little ink smudge at the top. Surely if somebody had wanted to take their time about it, they could have written it down on a different piece of paper, something that was clean. She looked at the paper itself. It had been torn quickly, as displayed by its jagged edges. Someone had definitely written it in a rush.

Laura then turned her attention to the cigarette case itself. Opening it up, she put her fingers inside. About three inches long and two inches wide, with a spring lid. It wasn't very ornate. Not something she would imagine an estate lord using. More likely a member of staff or, maybe if it had been placed there during the war, a soldier. She sniffed the inside hoping to detect even the faintest scent of tobacco but it was absent after so long.

She slipped the key in and then rolled up the piece of paper and put it back inside. One thing she knew from research: when someone wanted to convey information, certain things just weren't random. By the urgent feel of the note, Grace had been very important to someone. If only she knew who it was.

Slipping the case back into her pocket, she started to peruse Simon and Alicia's books for anything that might jump out at her. Surely if this had been buried in the garden, someone at the house would have known about it. They'd maybe even lived here or had been working on the estate during the war. Maybe there was some history of the manor on the bookshelves that would help.

Simon had a real love of books, as did Alicia, and a few years before, he had bought a lot of the estate books that had been sold to help pay for restorations to the west wing of the main house, which had been in much need of repair. The most valuable books had gone to auction, but there had been a few books that were too worn to be of any great value, which Simon had rescued.

'They're like little pieces of history,' he had said when he had shown them to her on her arrival. 'Think of the people who have read them. It's like they've left clues telling you about the taste and desires of the ancestors of the manor. Special passages that are marked, books that fall open at a well-loved quote, the stains from flowers that were pressed between pages. Just an echo of the presence of the people who have lived there. For example,' he said as he pulled out a book, 'look at this edition of Charles Dickens's *The Old Curiosity Shop*. It's so worn you know somebody loved it. I wonder how many times this was read.'

Laura scanned the bookshelves for that book. She wanted to look at it one more time herself. She found it on the third shelf up in the Dickens collection. Pulling it out, she was careful to handle the tattered binding and spine that looked as though it would fall apart at any moment. She opened the front cover, noting the manor's stamp marking its ownership. She ran her fingers down the page, in awe of its age.

Simon found her a few hours later, after she had pulled out every book about the manor she could find from the bookshelf. Being the researcher she was, she had books spread out across the coffee table, stacked in piles according to importance. Her laptop was open as she recorded any findings. Simon smiled at her.

'So, this is where you are.'

Laura looked up. 'What time is it?' she asked, yawning absently.

'Five,' he answered.

'Five!' she repeated incredulously as she stretched her tired body.

Simon scanned the books she had piled up. 'What's all this?'

'Research.'

'Research for the garden?'

'Kind of.'

'Huh,' said Simon as he picked up a rather tatty volume of *The Lords and Ladies of England*. 'Thinking of studying estate heritage, are you?' he asked, cocking one eyebrow.

'Not really, I actually have a little bit of a mystery I'm trying to solve. Have you ever heard of a person called Grace Mere? Would you know if she was someone who lived at the manor or was here working?'

Putting his hands into his pockets, Simon walked to the window and looked out as he thought.

'The name doesn't ring a bell, but there are more books in my bedroom.' He disappeared out of the room, reappearing about ten minutes later. 'How about this?' he said, pulling out a book that somebody had written about the estate.

He laid it on the coffee table. It looked as if it had been

written in the '80s. Across its glossy cover were the words '*The History of Hatworth.*'

She started to look through it hungrily, looking for the name that she had found just hours before. She went to the back of the book and ran her finger down the contents list, stopping at the letter 'm,' but there was nothing of interest, then moving to the letter 'g,' but there was no 'Grace' either. Disheartened, she flicked to the front again and started to make her way through the book itself.

It opened with the short history of Hatworth Manor and how it had been standing in one form or another since the sixteenth century. It documented all the refurbishments over the years with pictures and blueprints. There was a double page of a complete family tree. Then after that some pictures of the gardens, and then short stories about some of their most notorious or newsworthy ancestors.

She glanced through them, knowing that she would read it more thoroughly later for anything that would be of significance, particularly the pictures of the gardens.

'Would you like a cup of coffee?' suggested Simon, heading towards the door.

'Yes, that sounds wonderful,' she mumbled as she continued reading through the book. The stories were what you'd expect of any upper-class family, about the ancestors and their heirs.

Then, she turned the page and there was a story about how the estate had served the community during WWII.

A group of Land Girls stood shoulder to shoulder, smiling with ruddy cheeks and hair whisked up under spotted headscarves. They were comfortably dressed in light-coloured trousers, and dark-ribbed jumpers. In their hands were a myriad of gardening tools.

She turned the page and two girls laughed into the camera as they dug a deep furrow in the ground. She scanned the description, which talked about how the whole estate had been used to plant vegetables for the war effort. And Land Girls had lived and worked at the manor during WWII.

Over the page were some more pictures of the women, in the walled garden, planting lettuces.

Simon arrived back with her cup of coffee and placed it on the table in front of her. Looking over her shoulder, he noticed the picture.

'I see you found all the uses for our secret garden over the years. A lot of it was used to grow crops during the war, anything that needed more shelter from the east winds this area is famous for.'

'Do you know much about the girls who worked here?' inquired Laura.

'Not much more than I've read in what you have open, courtesy of Mr Walter Bartholomew.'

Laura turned back the page again and looked at the picture of the young women, their expressions strong and defiant.

Something about this whole story intrigued her. Had one of these women perhaps been Grace? Whoever had placed that key there, it must have been important. Surely no one would tear up a ration card unless it was in desperation. She breathed in a long heavy sigh as she closed the book, and hearing her stomach rumble, she decided she was hungry. Simon heard it too.

'Why don't we go and get something to eat? Maybe you'll get something before the young thugs I call children arrive and demolish everything.'

Laura nodded and smiled. Shutting the book, she stood and stretched and looked out towards the walled garden. Had the secret garden been locked during that time like it was now? If so, there were only so many people who could have hidden that key. Perhaps it'd been someone from the house. Visitors probably wouldn't have been privy to where the garden key was kept, so someone had walked across the lawns through the old wisteria and hidden that box. She shook her head and made her way to the kitchen, where the smell of spaghetti Bolognese and the squeals of excited children awaited her. One thing Laura knew in her gut: this had been important to somebody, and because of her sister, she was determined to find out why.

4

MOSCOW, NOVEMBER 1940

Anya

Just a mile away from where Nikolai Petroff was starting his first day for the NKVD, Anya Baranov stared at herself in the mirror, carefully studying her face to see if anything was as visible as the bruises that were now darkening the top of her swollen arm. As she studied her face in the glass, her emerald eyes squinting back at her, the humiliation and anger burned as furiously as the ache in her jaw, and she couldn't shake the memory that still lingered on her skin, an indelible impression, as if his hands were still on her.

She held up her long blonde curls from the side of her face and there as she turned her head to the light were four dark circles running right along her jawline where his fingers had dug into her skin, a forceful reminder that her stepfather planned to have his way.

She fought back the tears as she looked in her wash bag. She couldn't take too long in the communal bathroom that was shared by all the residents on their floor, but she hoped that she could quickly find some powder to cover them, noticing that her hands were still trembling from the altercation.

Even after a year, it was still hard to believe that she was in this situation.

She still missed and loved her sweet-mannered father, who had died so suddenly the year before. Her mother had been so consumed with her own grief that she had been an easy and vulnerable target, for someone with the right words and a soft shoulder for her to cry on. Ivan, a distant relative, had swooped in to fill the gap left by her father's passing. So attentive at first, he had vowed to rescue both of them from their fathomless gloom.

So preoccupied by her own pain, neither Anya nor her mother had seen the telltale signs that may have alerted them to his real character. The fact that he seemed to have no close family or friends to vouch for him didn't matter. He had presented himself as well dressed and well spoken. It was only for them to find out after the marriage vows had been exchanged that it had been merely an act, instigated with the use of a small inheritance. He had used every rouble he had to clean himself up and marry someone he'd thought was a woman with money. When it turned out that neither of them had enough money to pay the rent, the pressure and expectancy had been transferred to Anya to marry well instead.

That had been what her stepfather had been reinforcing that morning. His boss's son was single and Anya's age, a fine catch with a good-paying government job. Although under the communist movement everyone was supposed to be equal, it was known that people who worked directly for Stalin were treated well.

But she had been disgusted by her potential suitor. Even though there had not been a lot of money when she was being raised by her English mother, she was used to a level of decorum and delicateness, and Egor had been crude and uncouth. From the minute they met, he had treated her with little respect. Invited by her stepfather to dinner, he had looked down his nose at her as though assessing her in the way a farmer would the potential purchase of a milk cow. Later, when they'd been given some time alone to get to know one another, he'd made it very clear what he expected of a wife – someone to take care of him and bear his children.

When she'd voiced her opinion to Ivan this morning, he had reinforced that she was to marry Egor, and as her mother cowered in the corner, he had screamed at Anya, smashing her grandmother's porcelain vase in a show of strength. Then she had tried to storm out of the room, but he'd grabbed her, squeezing her face with his fingers and digging his other hand into her arm.

'You will do as you're told, Anya. You will marry this man, otherwise I will throw you out into the streets and you will have to become a whore.' From the corner she heard her mother whimper.

Looking defiantly into his eyes, she spat back, 'I would rather be a free whore than Egor's slave.' It was then that Ivan had lifted his hand and backslapped her, knocking her clear across the room.

Anya studied the other cheek now. The red welt was only starting to dim where four red finger marks could clearly be seen.

She drew a bowl of warm water and held a soaked wash-cloth to her cheek in an attempt to ease the pain.

Thank goodness she had secretly applied for a job, knowing if her stepfather found out he would demand all of her pay. She had started the week before after hearing that working for the government was a good prospect. She planned to save as much money as she could and somehow get away from here, taking her mother with her.

She had informed her stepfather she was doing some

charity work, assured that Ivan would start drinking early and would be waiting for her when she got home. But at least during the main hours of the day, she could be away from him.

She washed her face and applied the powder heavily, the plan in her mind becoming more and more clear. It wouldn't take long with the money the government was paying her, which was good. Because in the pit of her stomach she felt a rising fear that there was a need for urgency.

5

HATWORTH MANOR, PRESENT DAY

Laura

Later that evening, as the family were tucked in Simon's cosy front room, Laura pulled out her iPhone and did another search for Grace with no success. She then searched for Walter Bartholomew, the man who had written the book about Hatworth. Maybe he knew more about the Land Girls who had been here at the manor during that time. But he seemed as elusive as Grace herself. No Facebook or Twitter page, nothing on Google. She looked up the book on Amazon. It was out of print, but it did have the name of the publishers on it. So she wrote a quick email to them, saying who she was and that she was interested in getting in touch with Mr Bartholomew about research. She knew it was a long shot but had to try.

Later, once the children were in bed, Alicia came to join her in her bedroom for a chat. They often sat there in the evening while Simon was watching the news or a football match. They loved to sit top to tail on the bed, sharing all the nuggets of their day. It was very reminiscent of their time at uni, and Laura loved that. As they moved towards the bed, Liam's letter on the side table made her hitch her breath, as she remembered her pain again.

Alicia must have caught the look on Laura's face as she cringed inwardly.

'What's going on, Laura?' she asked as they settled on the bed. 'We've wanted to give you some time and space, but it is clear that things between you and Liam aren't great. Did you want to talk about it?'

Laura drew a pillow close to her for protection and sighed.

'It's complicated,' she whispered.

Then, seeing Alicia's expression and knowing her oldest friend was not going to be satisfied with just that, she began the story of what had happened. Explaining how she had come home one day unexpectedly from work and heard him talking on the phone to another woman.

'He stood with his back to me in the kitchen looking out the window. But I could tell by his body language, the tone of his voice, and the way he was talking that this was something more than just a casual conversation. I was honestly paralyzed with shock as I listened.

'He was telling someone that he loved them, that he would do anything to be with them, and that they would be together soon.

'At first, the information didn't filter through my logical mind. He had to be talking to his sister, Caroline. It couldn't possibly be another woman, could it? I stood there with a Sainsbury's shopping bag filled with chicken and wine for tea, just stood there helplessly listening, as my life quietly crumbled around me. Two minutes before, all my thoughts had been about paying the gas bill and a favourite recipe I needed to download to make dinner, and now the life I thought I had was gone. Just like that, in an instant, it had changed forever.'

Alicia reached out and took her hand, and, very unlike

Alicia, she didn't give an opinion. She just listened, allowing all of Laura's story to spill forth.

'Liam turned then, and noticed my expression – that must have communicated everything I was feeling. He hung up quickly, becoming flustered, overcompensating by walking towards me and hugging me hard, but I was just frozen. We didn't talk about it right away. He had some work to finish and I wasn't able to believe it, let alone articulate my feelings about it. So robotically I started to prepare dinner, allowing the reality to slowly absorb into my consciousness as I mashed potatoes and stirred gravy.'

Alicia's eyes widened with disgust as she listened.

'Finally, when he came back into the kitchen to open the bottle of wine, I confronted him.

'"How long has it been going on?"

'By then he was cool and collected and I couldn't believe that he then lied to me. He told me the relationship meant nothing, that I had misheard. She was a colleague, she was friendly, they got on. He tried to make it sound as if I were being unreasonable and insecure, even though I'd just heard him tell this woman how much he loved her and how much he wanted to be with her. He continued to plead his innocence as I stood staring at the fridge, with the magnetic calendar of activities we had planned together as a couple mocking me.

'After a number of hours of us arguing, he finally confessed to me he'd met her at a work dinner three months before. I remember that ringing in my ears. *Three months? He'd been having sex with another woman for three months?* I remember staring at the wall, thinking about all the things we'd done in that time, all the times we'd made love, all the times we'd gone out together or just sat on the sofa watching a movie. I hadn't suspected a thing. I couldn't believe that I'd been so naïve.

'We didn't eat that night, because apart from the fact I burned the chicken, neither of us was hungry. He spent the rest of the night apologizing and explaining how he was having some sort of midlife crisis. But something clicked in me, even with all we had been through, including my breakdown, and I knew I could never go back to what we had, no matter what he said. I no longer trusted him.'

Laura paused in her story to take a breath, then she pulled a discarded jumper from the bottom of the bed and started to stroke its soft wool for continued comfort.

'It's so embarrassing, Alicia. Even though I know I did nothing wrong in my mind, there's a side of me that's so ashamed that I didn't know, and what is wrong with me that he didn't want me?'

'Bastard,' Alicia finally spat out and squeezed Laura's hand. 'I know you know this, Laura, but it's true this is not your fault. This is on him, not you. And honestly, you deserve better. You deserve to be loved. What did his sister, Caroline, say? Aren't you really close with her?'

Laura felt fresh tears prick her eyes, not just with the loss of her relationship, but with everything else it had affected.

'We are.' She nodded, drawing in her brimming feelings. 'That has been really hard. I told her the next day and she was completely supportive and so angry at him, but they're close and he's her brother and it's made things difficult between us all, as he is constantly texting her. It created this weird triangle of stress between us. Which is why coming away was the best decision. I told Caroline I was coming to be with you both and would be really busy. Also, I needed some time and asked her not to call me for a while. Just until I can figure out how to go forward in our friendship.'

Her voice finally cracked with the emotion. She hadn't cried about Liam for a few days. There had been a lot of tears in the first week, a lot of heart-wrenching sadness, but since she'd come to Norfolk, she'd been able to lay her thoughts aside, put her heart on hold while she cocooned herself in a world that felt safe. Here with her best friends, the country-side, and the world of the garden, all the things that comforted her.

Laura wiped at her eyes and, slipping off the bed to grab a tissue, noticed his letter on the table and, grabbing it, ripped it into shreds and threw it into the bin.

Alicia stood up and slipped her arms around Laura's neck and hugged her for a long time as she reassured her, 'You are welcome to stay as long as you need with us, and you didn't need to have a job to do that. You could have come any rate. You will get through this and we are here to help you.'

Laura pulled away and nodded. Now that it was out, she desperately wanted to change the subject. Seeing the shock and anger in Alicia's face as she had told her story made it all so much more real and more painful somehow. When it had been her secret, she could pretend for a few days that she was just visiting and when she got back to London everything would go on the same, but confessing it made her pain so much more present. And the world of illusion she had been creating for herself in the interim was now gone.

'I don't want to talk about him anymore,' she finally stated, forcefully blowing her nose, 'and besides I have something to show you.' Laura swallowed down the quiver in her voice and crossed the room. Thrusting her hand into the pocket of her anorak, which was hanging on the back of her door, she pulled out the silver-coloured cigarette case and handed it to Alicia. 'I found this buried in the walled garden.'

Alicia looked down at the antique in her hand in awe.

'Open it.'

Alicia lifted the lid and the elderly springs creaked a little. She tipped the contents into her hand.

Laura continued, 'It's a name on a ration card, so it may have been written during the war. And I think that little key must open a small lockbox or something.'

'This is very exciting. I wonder who this Grace is,' Alicia said, reading the scrap of paper.

'Do you know if anyone by that name lived at the manor during that time?'

Alicia shook her head. 'Simon knows more about the history than me. I do know there were a lot of Land Girls here during that time, but there was a fire in the '60s that destroyed a lot of the earlier staff records. What a mystery. Who do you think it could be? This was obviously a message from one person to another. "Our" must mean they were connected somehow. Partners in whatever this was. Maybe a soldier with a secret message for his one true love? And maybe the key opens a gift for her?' Alicia speculated. 'Their love sounds so urgent.'

'You're such a romantic,' Laura chuckled.

Just then, from somewhere in the house, the sound of children arguing filtered into the room. Alicia rolled her eyes. 'And I wonder why?' she sighed. 'Living through other people's romances is the closest I get to that right now. Those two little monsters are supposed to be asleep.' Squeezing her friend's hand, Alicia excused herself to deal with them. 'You're going to be okay, Laura. I'm glad you came to us.'

Laura nodded, taking in a threaded breath.

After she left the room, Laura closed the cigarette case and laid it on her bedroom table. And down there in the bin, torn into pieces, Liam's letter taunted her.

Heartache was so odd. Sometimes she would forget for a moment, and then something would remind her and it was as if something heavy came crashing down on her, making her feel hopeless. She hoped one day soon all this would be behind her so she could finally move on to live the rest of her life.

6

MOSCOW, 1940

Nikolai

Nikolai couldn't help but be impressed by the establishment as he entered the building. Its high ceilings, marbled stone walls and cornices, and high banked windows commanded attention, a powerful statement of the Russian secret service known as the NKVD.

Marching to the office that he'd been told to report to, he climbed the elegant staircase and knocked on a huge mahogany door. It was so solid his knock was muffled. From inside, somebody grunted something that sounded like, 'Come in.' So, he made his way inside.

As he strode through the length of the vast room, his footsteps echoed on the polished wood floor, the sound bouncing around the austere walls and up to the ceiling.

Behind the desk at the end of the room, a serious-looking man in full military uniform sat writing into a ledger. The desk was neat but with many files piled high and nothing but a name plate with the words 'Commandant Trajesnski' to distinguish the occupant.

Even though it took Nikolai a couple of seconds to get across the room, the man still made him wait at his desk for at least two minutes before he spoke. Then, sitting back, he looked Nikolai up and down before asking, 'What can I do for you?'

'Nikolai Petroff,' he stated confidently, though it was hard to disguise the slight tremor under his tone. Just the flicker of the nervousness that he felt, knowing he was here for a very different reason than what he had been recruited for. 'I was asked to report today to you for my new assignment here. I'm supposed to be translating foreign documents.'

The man merely quirked an eyebrow before he nodded and, picking up the telephone, mumbled into the receiver.

'You will wait,' he informed Nikolai with a tone of disinterest as he plucked up a lit cigarette that had been nestled in an ashtray. Then, sitting back in his leather chair, he blew smoke out from a clenched jaw and surveyed Nikolai with obvious disdain. The acrid blue smoke ballooned between them. In response, Nikolai smiled awkwardly and then nodded, before letting his eyes explore the room and study the large portrait of Stalin on the wall. Anything rather than meet the steely gaze of the man in front of him.

The door opened and another person clipped to the desk, and only then did the commandant stand to his feet to walk to the large bank of windows. He didn't turn and face him as he spoke to Nikolai.

'You have been chosen for a special mission,' the man said with a measured low tone.

In response to his words, the man who had arrived opened a file and handed Nikolai an envelope.

'You will train in the fifth department, foreign intelligence, and will report to section seven, where you will be trained.'

Nikolai felt his heart sink. The whole idea of him coming to work for the NKVD in the first place was so he could get into this building and find out more about his father's death. This sounded like it would be taking him away from the very thing he was trying to do.

'Forgive me, Commandant, but I understood that I would be working here.'

The man swivelled on his heels, his eyes conveying a thunderous expression, as though he had never been crossed or questioned before. 'You are working for the NKVD. And you will do as you're told. What I have told you to do is to report to section seven.'

The man beside him stared at Nikolai, his desperate expression willing him to take the envelope from him and leave the room.

'May I know anything about this mission?'

'Not at this time. Things will be revealed to you while you are in training,' snapped the commandant as he walked back to the desk and ground out his cigarette with another waft of smoke that stung the back of Nikolai's throat.

Nikolai was determined not to be intimidated. What he had to do was too important. 'How long can I expect to be in training?'

The man sighed as though this was tiresome for him and his tone became highly irritated.

'Probably six weeks. Less if you are not very good at what you do. Then we will just give you a simple menial job here filing papers. If you turn out as you have been recommended, you will be assigned to a vital mission. Mr Morozov here will be available for you if you have questions.'

Taking it, Nikolai opened the envelope. He started to read down it before realizing that the man was signifying by his look of disgust that the meeting was over.

Morozov nodded his head and left the room, and Nikolai felt he had no choice but to follow him. As he walked the length of the room, his feet echoing all the way, he felt his heart sink.

How on earth would he do what he needed to do now? He had to go on some ridiculous training mission.

He looked at the details on the paperwork once he'd left the room. He had to report the following day. There was nothing but a time, and a person he was meeting with. He folded it neatly into four and dropped it into his pocket. At least there was some hope. The commandant had insinuated if he failed, he would have to come back here and file papers. Which was exactly what he planned to do. Hopefully sooner rather than later.

On the outside of the door, Morozov made it clear he wouldn't be needed for the rest of the day. He wouldn't even have a chance to be in an office, let alone do any looking around. Feeling frustrated, he strode back out into the street, angry that he was so close yet was being driven away from solving the mystery burning a hole in his heart. Nikolai made his way despondently back to his communal housing. And when he reached his rooms, two of the family were already preparing food. They asked him if he wanted something to eat, and he shook his head, heading to his bedroom. The way the houses were set up was very common in Russia. People shared kitchens and bathrooms but had their own living rooms and bedrooms. Everyone being on equal footing, as with communal housing, was a vital element of the communist way. Throwing himself down onto his bed, he sat and remembered the last day he'd seen his father. He had been young, just finishing college, only a few years before. He had seen worry etched on his father's face for weeks. And when Nikolai had asked him about it, the man with the dark thick hair, short goatee, and piercing blue eyes had just tapped his son's hand and said, 'I think it will all work out. Don't worry, Nikolai.'

Nikolai had known that Anton had not wanted to share too much with him of concern since his mother had died three years before of influenza. It had been a hard time for the pair of them after her death. After years of travelling as a diplomat where their life had been very different, returning to Russia, they'd found Joseph Stalin's vision of the country challenging. Everything had changed, some things for the good, but also their leader insisted on total loyalty, and people like his father, who had been loyal to his country rather than a person, found himself having a few run-ins with his superiors.

Even so, Nikolai had never seen his father's mood as dark as he did the last day he saw him.

Nikolai had woken up early, and when he saw his father staring out of the window, something had tightened in his stomach even then.

'Are you okay, Father?' he had asked as he got ready to prepare breakfast. Anton had seemed surprised, so far away in his thoughts, and the smile that he gave his son at that point was wistful, almost as if he knew his fate that day, almost as if he knew that he wasn't coming home. Nikolai had pressed him, but his father had shooed away his attempt, placing a hand upon his son. He had always been very demonstrative with Nikolai, even though that wasn't really the way in their culture. He wasn't ashamed to hug his son. And Nikolai loved the bond that they had.

'You have far too much to think about yourself with your exams.' His father's words had broken his thoughts. 'Do not worry about me. I'll be fine.' He'd seen the tiredness around his father's eyes then, the despondency in his tone. Nikolai decided then that he would cook something special for the both of them when he came home, something to cheer his spirits. He remembered arriving home that evening, deciding on the meal he would cook and then waiting for his father, waiting for hours.

When his father never returned, he'd gone to the authorities. No one seemed to want to help. When he did not return the next day, Nikolai was beside himself, so distraught, but no one would tell him what was going on. He eventually went to his father's workplace, where somebody pulled him into an office and told him in a dry matter-of-fact manner that, unfortunately, his father had had an accident, and they were very sorry. Even as the man had spoken to him, Nikolai had known that something else was going on, and he would never forget the fear, the sadness, and the crushing heartache he'd felt. His beloved father was gone, and he decided in that moment that he wouldn't stop till he found out exactly what had happened.

———

The next day, Nikolai arrived at work with his overnight case, still oblivious of where he would be going. In the hall, waiting with Morozov, was a rather dour-looking man in army clothes who barely acknowledged him before he ordered Nikolai to follow him. As he complied, he felt a creeping dread. He knew he couldn't say no. People didn't act that way with the NKVD. But it wasn't unheard of for people to disappear once they had been taken away. He was driven out in an army van, a long way out of the city, with many twists and turns. And even though he tried to memorize his route, he quickly gave up. After about thirty-five minutes, they reached their destination. The driver pulled off the main road onto a back trail, and he started to seriously be concerned he was being taken out to be shot, though for what he didn't know.

Was this how it'd been for his father? Had his father been told he was going somewhere and then been driven to a location like this before they had killed him? He felt every muscle in his body tense and tried to imagine ways to escape.

All at once, they came to a large field. At the end of it, there were high gates with the words 'Military. Do Not Enter,' and his tightening stomach muscles relaxed a little. The driver probably wouldn't be taking him anywhere military if he was just driving him to the woods to shoot him.

They rolled up to the gate. Pleasantries were exchanged between the two military personnel, gates were opened, and they drove inside. It was indeed some sort of training compound.

Lines of men in identical outfits were doing exercises on the lawn. Another group raced past him as a supervisor yelled instructions. Farther down the field, far off, he could see trainees practising shooting at targets as they raced from one location to another. Nikolai suddenly felt apprehensive. They were training them for combat. As much as he'd wanted to get into the NKVD building to find out more about his father, the work he had been trained for was all about translating British letters, correspondence, a desk job. He'd never been trained for war.

His driver continued towards a large army building. Perplexed, Nikolai tried to understand what all of this could mean. Of course, the war in Europe was in full swing, with Hitler, the madman, calling the shots. The fact that Russia was siding with him was ludicrous in his mind, but Russia had its own army and soldiers to go and fight. Why would he be brought here? And what kind of job did they want him to do as a spy? If that was what this was.

As soon as they got out of the vehicle, everything changed. The man who had greeted him gruffly, almost indifferently, now started to yell at him to run. Taken by surprise, Nikolai did as he was told and sprinted towards the building. Nikolai hadn't realized he was in such bad shape, but he was entirely winded by the time he got inside the building. Entering another office, he needed a minute to catch his breath as a new commander eyed him wearily.

'Nikolai Petroff?'

Nikolai nodded stiffly, but still wasn't able to speak, gasping for his breath.

'Seems like you need a lot of work. I'll let you know that not

many people make it out of here and onto the circuit. I have my
doubts about you already.'

Nikolai wanted to say, 'Look, I didn't sign up for this. I don't
even know what this is. I'm not interested in any circuit.' But he
couldn't get a breath.

'Take him to his barracks,' the man commanded to the
driver who had brought him in. Nikolai was taken away to
another room, with dark windows, and a small bunk bed, on
which sat blue-striped sheets, stacked in a neat pile. In one
corner was a clean but unattractive sink, and in another corner,
a small wardrobe was squeezed. On the bed, next to the sheets,
lay the same grey outfit he'd seen all the other men here
wearing.

'Unpack your things, get on your exercise clothes, and I'll
meet you outside so we can get started,' the soldier grunted
at him.

By now, Nikolai was starting to catch his breath.

'Please,' he rasped. 'Tell me, what is this?'

His driver gave him a crooked satanic grin. 'What is this?
This is hell,' he chuckled.

Nikolai shook his head. Dressing in his exercise outfit, he
observed himself in the mirror above the sink. He was still red-
faced and sweating. He reminded himself most people didn't
make the grade, and he wasn't interested in whatever mission
they had planned. He tried to look on the bright side. Perhaps
he'd get some exercise, learn a few skills, and he would make
sure that they didn't keep him. All that remained to know was
how long it would take for him to be out the door, ready to file
papers at the Kremlin.

7

HATWORTH MANOR, PRESENT DAY

Laura

Over the next couple of weeks, Laura found herself settling into a comfortable routine. In the early morning, she'd work on the garden plans. Scouring through old photographs of the walled garden in its heyday and researching the plants available at the time. For the rest of the day, she worked in the garden. And in the evening, she would continue her research on Grace.

The garden was coming together much better than the research. The search for names of Land Girls at the manor during that time was fruitless, especially because of the fire that had happened in the '60s.

However, the garden had started to take shape even though it had been a while since anyone had really worked its soil. Built in the late 1800s, it had lived many lives in its over one hundred years, Simon had informed her. A place of relaxation and reflection for the young married couple in their early days, a wonderland to explore for their children in the growing-up years, and even a thriving victory garden during the war. It had been well loved right until Lady Sarah's death in 1991, with her returning to it after a busy public life to lovingly tend the plants in the winter of her life. However, with her death, her daughter Rebecca had finally ordered the garden closed at the turn of the new century, unable to be reminded of her mother and her own grief. It hadn't been until Rebecca's death and when her son, Edward, had taken over the running of the estate in the past year, that opening the garden back up for the public had even been contemplated. Over the past twenty years, some work had been done on it from time to time, just to keep it from falling into a total state of disrepair. But it hadn't really been loved since Lady Sarah's death and it showed everywhere.

So, it was with great joy that Laura set about tackling this rewarding project. She had managed to cut back all of the old blackberry bushes and turn over some of the flowerbeds softened by the melting snow, adding a rich, dark mulch. She'd pruned the trees. Simon helped her repair the wooden bridge, re-rope the swing, and re-screw the hinges on the door of the little treehouse. She'd trimmed the box hedges and cleaned out the water fountain, reattached an elderly hawthorn bush to a post, and added new water to the pond, which was already showing signs of life.

On one of her many trips to the garden centre, she'd bought new plants to replace the elderly herbaceous border and ordered a new willow tree, as well as adding three new fragrant roses popular in the nineteenth century to the gazebo, which would bring about a nice splash of colour alongside their elderly companions.

Then she got to work doing what she loved. It was Laura's favourite part of her job: really getting her hands into the soil. There was something so stimulating about working with nature. As she ran her hands through the damp cool earth, she would remember why she started the work in the first place. After Katie's death an elderly neighbour had taken her under her wing at a time when acute pain was ripping their family apart.

The older woman never talked about the tragedy, but every time she saw Laura struggling, she would invite her into her garden to help her. Show her how the gentleness and the enduring nature of gardening could be a great healer. Laura was young at the time and didn't realize what the woman was doing. But she remembered with great fondness the joy of turning soil or watching something grow and bloom when everything in her own life seemed to be about death and dying.

One afternoon in mid-March, she stood back to admire her handiwork. Her face and hands were covered in mud, and even though she had her hair piled up in a messy bun, strands of it had escaped and clung to her neck in a damp mess. She didn't care how she looked because there was something therapeutic about working in the garden. Whenever she felt overwhelmed by her personal life, she would stride out into the fresh air and plant a tree or a new tray of annuals. It was a world she could control, unlike her own. There was also something magical about this particular garden too. Something she couldn't quite put her finger on, as though it were waiting, waiting to tell her something important.

Laura looked up towards the sky. It was turning an angry grey and the heavy clouds were threatening rain. As much as she was disappointed to cut short her time working, in a way their foreboding presence was a welcome sight. After a string of unusually dry days, she had been working pretty hard and her back was letting her know about it.

She closed the door to the garden just as heavy droplets of rain scattered all about her and an ominous crack of thunder rumbled overhead. Racing through the estate, she was soaked by the time she reached the cottage. Pulling off her work boots, she padded across the kitchen and to her room. Everyone else was out. The children at school, Alicia working in the local village library, which she did three days a week, Simon in his office in the main house working on estate business. Stripping off her clothes into a wet heap, Laura jumped into the shower and allowed the water to warm her aching body.

After her shower, she rubbed a towel through her damp hair and moved into her bedroom. On the way in, she glanced over at the research now piling up on her desk. She had copies of birth and death certificates and grainy photocopies of parish records of anyone with a name remotely similar to Grace's. Encouraged by Alicia's input, she had started to warm to the note being part of a love story. Laura knew her idea was pure fiction, but she liked it, as she envisioned a fairy-tale ending. Laura saw herself handing the key to a grandchild and it would all make sense to them and there would be this happy ending. She liked creating happy endings for other people. Especially as they seemed to elude her in her own life.

Dressing in clean dry clothes, she grabbed a padded envelope containing the latest parish records, which had arrived the day before, then she settled herself down in the family room with a cup of boiling-hot coffee and felt her body relax.

Out the window, the rain was still falling in long harsh streaks, and puddles had formed instantly along the cobbled stone path up to the cottage, swirling into tiny pools all over the garden. Shivering, Laura lit a fire in the fireplace to take away the chill from the room, then she returned to the window seat and picked up one of the bulky envelopes. Pulling out the wad of paper, she focused on the faded spidery text of the parish records, scrutinizing the details. When her phone rang, she absently picked it up. She'd been talking to the local garden centre about some plants she had on order. They'd called her back several times the day before, and she had left a message for them to call her about a particular lilac bush she was interested in. But as soon as she answered she realized this wasn't the call she'd been waiting for.

'Hi, Laur,' said a familiar voice.

The blood felt as if it had drained from her body, and sitting back against the rugged stone wall of the window seat, she started to shake as she swallowed down hard.

She berated herself. She had been fastidiously monitoring her caller ID and not answering any of his calls.

'Liam, I told you not to call me again,' she spat out, wishing she'd taken a moment to look at the number before she'd picked it up. But it had been weeks since he'd last called, and somewhere in her mind, she had pretended that he no longer existed, that somehow the old Laura and her past life in London weren't real. Just the life in the garden, or with her hidden in the past tracking down a lost love.

'Please don't hang up,' he urged her quickly. 'Just give me one minute.'

She took a deep breath. She needed to get this over with. He needed to know that she wasn't coming back once and for all, even though she thought it was evident from her lack of response to him. But before she a chance to say all this, he spoke.

'Laura, I know I did a terrible thing, but we need to figure this out, even though I know you have no right to forgive me, but before you throw our relationship away after eight years, think of all the history we have together, all that we've been through. Weddings, births, life events... Katie...'

She caught her breath, and suddenly she was transported back to the neat therapist's waiting room that still smelt of new carpet, with its basket of tatty books and well-used toys. Her freezing-cold stiff hand resting in his as they waited for her first appointment. The room inside where the overly welcoming man in a slightly creased white shirt and beige sleeveless tank top greeted them. His cheerful upbeat tone attempting to create an inviting space for someone going through a breakdown. Then the days when she hadn't wanted to go on and couldn't even get out of bed. Liam had been a rock for her then, sitting with her for hours in the middle of the night when she couldn't sleep with the pain.

Gathering herself quickly, Laura shook away her feelings of pain and nostalgia and found her voice. Even with what he had done for her in the past, she wasn't going to let him manipulate her.

'Put this right?' she hissed at him. 'You make it sound so insignificant. You lied to me, Liam. You cheated on me, and it broke my heart. And people knew, which was humiliating.'

'I know, Laura. You are so right and you have no idea how much that truth haunts me. But you have to understand. You're the only person I've ever loved in my whole life. There will never be anyone else but you. I admit it. I got swept up. Jane was visiting from our Australian office, and that accent, and she was so tanned and happy. She just caught me at a low moment, otherwise I would never have had an affair. You know how hard it's been at work for me over the last few months.'

Laura attempted to swallow down the dry rock that seemed to be lodged in her throat. This was the first time she'd known the girl's name. It was also difficult having him confirm that there had been a real affair. Up until this point, he had played it down as a weak moment of passion, nothing much. But now he was admitting it: he had confirmed to her there had been an affair and it sounded so real, not a fling, not a one-night stand, but a real affair.

'Laura, I swear to you I will never do this again. I've learned my lesson, I promise. We've been together for so long. Sometimes, I forget what this is. You're like my sister or something, like you'll always be there, my best friend, and these last weeks have been horrible without you. You have no idea.' His voice started to crack with the emotion. 'My life has no meaning. My life is so empty.'

His words slurred, and she realized he'd been drinking, even though it was early in the day. No doubt one of his business affairs and probably an attack of guilt after his third whisky. Someone shouted to him over his shoulder, and he answered back that he was just coming.

'Laura, please, I'm begging you. Just think about what we've had. Don't just throw this away. Please don't hold this against me, this one tiny indiscretion.'

'*Indiscretion*?!' Laura shouted back in disgust. 'You slept with her for *three* months. Now when I look back, I realize how distant you were during that time. All those late-night meetings you had to attend, then you came back smelling of alcohol. Where is this Jane now?'

'She flew back to Sydney a few weeks ago, and I promise you we will never see each other again. Please, Laura. You owe it to us to at least try. I can't believe you would give up so quickly. Every relationship goes through ups and downs. Mike here at work had something like this happen last year, and it changed his marriage, which is now stronger than ever. How will you know what we could have been if you give up before even trying? Now I know what I could lose, it has scared me, really scared me, Laura. I can't even sleep. It has changed me, I promise you. I will do anything to get you back. Anything, and if you would just give me that one chance, I will work every day to make you happy. Please, you can't do this to us.'

Laura felt angry and heartbroken. Why was he making her feel like she was the one being cruel? She stood up and marched up and down the room, swallowing down all of the pain, anger, and hurt rising from her stomach in acidic waves as she balled her fists. She tried to force the tears from rising, but they stung her eyes and ran down her cheeks anyway. Damn him for making her feel this way. How could he emotionally hook her back in like this? She wanted to shut off her phone and tell him to get lost, but there was also a side of her that still loved him, had loved him for so long, loved the life they had created together over eight years, and the thought of having to start again, to try and find someone new, overwhelmed her. Her eyes blurred as she looked through the droplets of rain running down the window. She was in absolute turmoil. Hearing his heart break, her own heart was saying one thing, but her head was telling her that she'd be a fool to take him back.

Laura suddenly felt very alone. More than anything, she wanted to feel the arms of someone who loved her around her. Someone to tell her it was all going to be all right. She girded herself. 'I think I've made it clear,' she finally said, not sounding very convincing. 'Liam, please do not call me again.'

On the other end, Liam's voice began to crack.

'Don't do this, Laura. Don't do this to us. Please, I'm begging you.'

She knew she had to stay strong.

'What about our home and our life together?' he continued.

'You should've thought of that before you jumped into bed with someone else.'

That seemed to smack home as she heard a sob in his voice. 'Okay, if that's what you really want,' he whimpered. 'But please let me talk to you again, please. Let's not finish it this way, over the telephone. Let's have a coffee or dinner or something. Let me just see you one more time, I'm begging you.'

She hitched her breath. Her stomach was now a tight ball. 'I'm sorry, Liam, I've got to go. I've got a life to start building and I mean it: do not call me ever again.'

She shut off her phone and threw it down on the window seat, then her legs gave way and she flopped into Simon's favourite leather armchair and sobbed. Why was her life like this? Eight years in a relationship with Liam. She'd wasted eight years. How was she ever going to feel happy again?

8

MOSCOW, 1940

Anya

Anya pressed her chin, which was still very tender from her stepfather's violent grab that morning, and hoped that the powder she had applied would keep it covered for the day. As she arrived at the NKVD building, and even though she had been working there all week, she still felt a sense of terror entering the door. The fact that she'd signed documents of secrecy was the least of her concerns when other employees would remind her daily that she didn't want to find out what would happen if she defied her superiors in any way. She just kept reminding herself that she was doing this for her and her mother. She was going to find a way, no matter what it cost, to get her mother away from her stepfather and maybe even back to England, even though she knew doing such a thing could be dangerous.

'You're over at section seven for a while,' her stern supervisor informed her before she even had a chance to get her coat off. 'You'll be teaching etiquette,' the supervisor snapped before she closed the door, parting with the words, 'Be ready in ten minutes.'

Anya sighed and moved to her bookcase, where she pulled out the appropriate materials that she'd need that day. It had been a stroke of luck that she had met someone at one of her mother's parties before her father had died who had also worked for the NKVD, though Anya had not known that at the time. At her father's funeral, he had slipped her his card after complimenting her perfect English.

'If ever you need a job, Anya, I know somewhere where you could work. You have the perfect skills for it.'

At the time of their meeting, Anya had been heartbroken and preoccupied by the death of her father and had just slipped the card into her bag, not thinking about it, not until the first time her stepfather had lost his temper.

'It was just a slap,' her mother had tried to play down later. 'He was just angry. It was my fault. I should've listened to what he was saying.'

Anya had known then; she had known she had to start looking for the way out that they both needed because she had a feeling. She sensed this wasn't going to end well for either of them.

About two weeks later, she had been in a tea shop when she had run into the same man and remembered his words. He had nodded his greeting in her direction, and Anya had approached him, asking if the job offer was still open. He had looked hesitant then, shifting his gaze as he surveyed who was around him.

'Come tomorrow to my office at ten,' he told her in a low tone. 'The address is on the back of the card I gave you.'

She nodded, and when she went home, she searched through her things till she found his card. She was not surprised at his hesitancy. Russia was in a strange time. No one trusted anybody after what had happened to the tsar and his family years before, even though he had been quite unpopular.

Nothing was cemented yet in a new way; the country was still adrift, trying to find its sense of balance.

When she'd arrived at his office, he'd invited her in, then asked her many questions: why she spoke such good English, where she'd learned everything. He'd talked to her in English the whole time, and she'd answered, explaining that as her mother was born in England, she'd always intended for Anya to go to school abroad to finish her education. So she'd only ever spoken to her daughter in English for the first ten years of her life.

She'd been aware of Russian but had treated it as a second language, something she had to speak if she came out onto the street or was entertaining people at a party. The rest of the time, she was as British as a British person. They drank English tea; they ate English food; they spoke of literature, Byron, Tennyson. They studied the classics, and her mother taught her every kind of etiquette, from how to place a tea napkin to how to greet strangers.

'One day, Anya, even though you are from a humble background, it is possible that – especially with impeccable manners – you will go to England and marry well. I know it is a lofty dream, but a mother can hope. It would be better if you didn't stay here, Anya, in Russia. It has no future for the young. You need to go and find your life somewhere else.'

Anya had listened to her mother's words but hadn't taken them too seriously. England seemed a long way away and the thought of her making her way up in the world seemed a remarkable dream. Besides which, she would never ever leave her mother.

After the family friend had questioned her that day, he had told her to report to the NKVD headquarters. It was only then that she'd realized the scope of the kind of work he was asking her to do. She'd be working for the secret service. She wasn't sure about all of it, but once she'd been to her appointments that he'd made for her there, she had felt heavy persuasion to do as they asked.

It also hadn't been too difficult to make the decision once they had offered her such a good wage. All she had to do was train agents in the way of English, teach them correct pronunciation, teach them just what her mother had taught her, how to take tea, how to greet people. What to say in social situations. It was so familiar to her. She'd been doing it her whole life. It seemed ridiculous to get paid for something that she could do with her eyes closed, but if that was what they wanted...

And now, she was sent from building to building to try her best to work with what they gave her. Most Russian spies, she noted, were cold and steely eyed, good at combat or building bombs, not the finery of how to take tea. It was hard work, but at least she got paid well for it.

Section seven was the farthest away. She trundled along in the truck they provided for her, the grey figure of her escort picking and sucking at his teeth as they went. He barely spoke to her, so she looked out the window and dreamed of escape.

Just a few more months of putting money away and she would have enough for two tickets. She would go to England as her mother wanted – she'd heard there were ways out via the coast – but she would not be going alone. She knew the most challenging part of her plan would be convincing her mother to also take the trip.

Her stepfather could be so charming when he needed to be. It was as though he sensed any time her mother started to pull away, and as she began to stretch from him like an elastic cord, he would snap her towards him, saying the exact thing to tempt her back in a seductive dance of charm and compliments. Making her feel like a princess, making her question every single time he had gotten drunk, sworn, or broken things. But Anya wasn't drawn in. She knew who this man was; the puppet master did not deceive her.

They pulled into section seven, and she made her way inside. She'd travelled here two or three times before, and she headed to the large room that she worked in.

She had set the room in mini areas in all the ways she needed to teach them. A table set for tea, a dance floor where she would teach dance, vocabulary books, etiquette books, all the tools of her trade to help hard-headed spies sound barely passable as English gentlemen.

Arriving in her room, she placed the stack of books she had brought with her down on a table and started to collect the tea things. Whenever she started back in a different area, they would send her a new spy. Tea would be his first lesson. She would spend it assessing him, seeing what he needed to work on. They all spoke English, though not many understood the nuances of it. She understood the way English people connected. That was what was harder to teach.

She'd barely finished setting out the tea table when the door opened, and standing in the doorway was a tall broad-shouldered man, looking very handsome in his green NKVD uniform. He had wavy sandy-blond hair with just the hint of gold flecks on the tips, defined cheekbones, and eyes of the lightest blue. Not the usual type. He appeared well toned but didn't have bulging muscles or a ruthless expression. He looked kind and thoughtful, somebody who could be a teacher or a poet. Anya caught her breath as she met his gaze. There was something about his eyes that was mesmerizing. They seemed to draw all the colour to him from the room as though everything around him disappeared into greyness. Her heart started thudding in her chest as she quickly averted her gaze. She was being ridiculous. Knowing from the heat in her cheeks, she was probably blushing, and didn't want to come across as unprofessional.

Oblivious to the effect he was having on her, he strode

towards her and introduced himself, thrusting out his hand and speaking to her in Russian.

'Hello, comrade. I'm Nikolai Petroff.'

Anya swallowed down her brimming attraction at the sound of his voice, which was deep and warm but with just a hint of mirth. As he stood so close to her, his presence took the air from her lungs as he waited for her to respond, his curious blue eyes studying her own intently. In response she fixated on a tiny scar above his left eyebrow, to divert from the power his close proximity was having on her whole body. Coughing to clear her throat and discomfort, Anya began with the first lesson. 'You never stretch out your hand to a woman, as you have just done. You wait for her to offer you her own.' She noticed her voice was tighter and more matronly than she wanted it to be as she compensated for her physical attraction. A look of curious surprise crossed his face as the corners of his lips twitched slightly in apparent amusement. She continued in English. 'And from the minute you come through the door, you will speak English, not Russian. That door is your door into England.'

Nodding his understanding, he dropped his hand, and removing his peaked cap, said in perfect English, 'Nice to meet you. My name is Nicholas Peters. Will that do?'

She offered her hand, introducing herself, and she couldn't help but return the smile that now lit up his face. Taking his own hand, she found that it was soft and warm and just his touch sent a rush of sparkly excitement through her body, which she attempted to swallow back down into her stomach. This was her job. She needed to get control of herself.

'It's a start,' she responded and signalled for him to join her at the table, noting there was a slight tremor in her voice and realizing that navigating this heightened awareness she suddenly felt was going to make this a much more challenging lesson for her than just teaching a spy how to take tea.

Standing in front of the chair, she waited nervously until he realized he was supposed to pull it out for her in order for her to be seated. He stood bemused for a moment before a look of understanding crossed his face.

'Ah, I remember this now,' he said with obvious recollection, 'from boarding school, all of the English etiquette.' She nodded and thanked him; as he stood behind her and held out the chair, she tried not to shudder as a whisper of his warm breath rippled across the back of her neck before he joined her at her side. 'What do we talk about now?' he asked, eagerly seating himself and pulling his own chair closer to the table. 'The weather and the state of the roads?'

Placing her napkin on her lap with a slightly trembling hand, she responded, 'It is polite for you to wait for me to initiate conversation,' then added with a laugh, 'which will probably be about the state of the roads or the weather.' Nodding towards the teapot, she continued, 'Why don't you pour the tea to practise?' Agreeing, his hands lifted the teapot and moved it towards her cup; instinctively she covered his hand with her own to stop him pouring, and quickly removed it again as another small shiver ran up her arm. She spoke quietly. 'You need to ask me first how I take it.'

'Ah, right,' he said, with an expression that conveyed he was adding it to a list he was making in his head.

'Miss Baranov, may I inquire of you, how you take your tea?'

'A little milk and sugar,' she responded with a nod.

Finding the milk jug, he started to pour and as she sensed his eyes boring into her, waiting for her to signal the amount, she focused on the cup, not wanting her heart to race again if she met his intense gaze. She nodded when he reached the right amount, and he then held up the sugar bowl and was about to use the tongs to add sugar when she gently shook her head. Then taking the tongs from him, she added two cubes of sugar into the teacup, before nodding her satisfaction. He was about to do the same for himself before she stopped him.

'Finish pouring for me first,' she coaxed him. Understanding, he lifted the teapot and started to fill her cup. With his eyes focused on his job, she took a moment to study his face without his intense gaze and noticed that close up she could see that across the bridge of his nose and around his eyes were a delightful cluster of tiny freckles that gave his face a boyish charm and stood out in comparison to the hint of dark stubble that shadowed his strong chin. Finishing pouring, he looked at her for approval and, avoiding his gaze again, she nodded her head as she stirred her tea.

They started to talk about everyday things and when she asked him about his young life in boarding school, he spoke with enthusiasm about the country he had loved. The beauty of the green fields and the timeless beauty of the villages and cities. As he spoke, Anya felt the same sense of nostalgia she sensed so often from her own mother. Because what he spoke of was so familiar to her, he was so easy to talk to and it was not difficult to forget this was a lesson. It also took all of her concentration to not get drawn in by his eyes or keep her mind from wondering what his body might look like beneath his green NKVD uniform. The hour went so fast Anya couldn't believe when the next spy was at her door ready for his dance lesson. She groaned inwardly. She had worked with this spy before and he always trod on her feet. Nikolai also looked a little disappointed their time was over and his gaze lingered on her as if not wanting their time to end. He finally whispered with great intensity, 'Thank you, Anya, this was very...' He drew in breath and searched her face as he attempted to find the right word in English. He settled on 'enlightening.' The way he said it was just a little seductive and it made her catch her breath again. In response, she jumped to her feet and moved away from the table before she blushed again. Following her, he stood in front of her, waiting for her to offer her hand before he bade her good-bye. Not daring to meet his gaze again, she placed her hand gently in his own. She may have been mistaken but she was sure he lingered a little longer than necessary, his fingers dragging gentle lines across her palm and fingertips as their hands parted, forcing her to withdraw her own, quickly, accompanied by that now familiar burn in her cheeks. As she watched his tall athletic frame stride out of the room with a brief look back at her as he exited the room, she suddenly felt a little lost and cold, as the warmth he had brought with him to the room was now gone. And, in its place, a beaming, short, slightly greasy-haired comrade now stood waiting for her to offer her hand.

9

HATWORTH MANOR, PRESENT DAY

Laura

Laura wasn't sure how long she sat there crying and was glad to have the house to herself. But when she finally slowed down to a hiccupping sob and blew her nose, she was exhausted.

Out of the window, the rain was starting to slow, and the sun was making its way through the clouds, highlighting a watery rainbow. A terrible fear of never being loved again gripped hold of her chest and stopped her from breathing for a second. She couldn't think like that, she told herself. Automatically picking up her phone, she contemplated calling her best friend for the first time in weeks. She missed Caroline so much and hated that this separation from Liam had put a wedge in their friendship. Caroline would know exactly what to say to help if this hadn't been about her brother. She would make her laugh and send her funny photos and memes. Laura pulled up some earlier texts from Caroline and smiled nostalgically at the fun that was always between them. All the nights out they had been on. She found a set of photos from when they had both dressed as witches on Halloween and they had left London and gone out into the countryside to a party. Then the taxi had broken down and they had had to walk for what felt like miles in the rain in nothing but sagging witch hats, thin dresses, high heels, and black-and-white stripy tights. They had both shivered through the rain as their dresses had become obscene. When they got home they had howled with laughter at what frights they both looked. As she stared at the photo they had taken when they arrived back at the flat, with heavy makeup running in black streaks down their faces, she remembered how much her stomach had ached from laughing, and now how much her heart ached with the void her friend's absence left in her life.

Making a decision, she pulled herself out of the armchair and gathered up the research files. She decided the cure was to bury herself in the garden work. It was a thing she could do something about. The garden gave her hope. Yes, it needed a lot of work, but little by little, day by day, things could be restored to beauty. All it took was time and love, and that was going to be her gift to herself as well. As Laura put the kettle on, her phone buzzed and bounced along the kitchen table. Leaning forward, she snatched it up to give Liam a final piece of her mind.

'Yes?' she spat out sternly, and waited for him to speak, but instead of his response there was a long silence.

She quickly looked at the number on the screen and noted that it wasn't Liam at all, but a number she didn't know.

'Hello?' she said again, now more meekly. The other voice answered. It was steady and slow, as if belonging to somebody who liked to order his words very carefully.

'Hello. Is this Miss Thomas? Miss Laura Thomas?'

Laura rubbed her red eyes and grabbed a tissue from her pocket and blew her nose. 'Yes. Yes, it is. How can I help you?'

Maybe it was the garden centre call she had been waiting for. The caller paused, apparently taking time to formulate his

words. 'My name is Walter Bartholomew. I believe you have
been trying to contact me.'

Laura screwed up her eyes and tried to think for a minute.
She had been doing so much research on so many names. She
knew this name was important to her. Who was it? Then she
suddenly remembered.

'Of course,' she said. 'Yes, I have been trying to get a hold of
you, Mr Bartholomew. Thank you so much for calling me back.'

'I was intrigued,' he said in his slow even manner. 'I don't
get many calls from fans. Well, at least not fans of the buildings
I have written about,' he said dryly. 'Have you visited it?'

'Actually, I'm staying here at the moment. In one of the
tythe cottages, working on a garden project for the National
Trust.'

'How marvellous,' he responded, and it sounded as if he was
smiling on the other end. 'How can I help you, Laura?'

'Well,' she said, clearing her throat and trying to move her
thoughts away from her horrendous love life, noting her voice
still sounded a little husky from the crying. 'I have a little bit of
a mystery that I hope you can help me with.'

'A mystery. Now who could resist something like that?' he
stated, sounding intrigued.

'And I was wondering if you'd be willing to talk to me about
the people who lived here, especially during WWII.'

'Aww, the Land Girls,' he reminisced, as if he knew them
personally. 'Fascinating time in the manor's history. I would be
happy to share with you the files I have about that time. And I
will be over in that area doing some more research on another
project in a couple of days if you would like to see some more of
my research.'

Laura felt hopeful. She wasn't sure why this mystery
seemed so important to her, but it was wonderful to finally have
a break, someone who might be able to shed more light on the
girls and their work.

Walter was speaking again. 'I can stop by the manor about two p.m. on Wednesday if that is convenient?' he offered. 'I really enjoyed researching Hatworth. It is such a wonderful building with a wonderful history.'

'Perfect, I look forward to seeing you then,' she responded and they hung up.

———

On Wednesday afternoon, Laura watched a restored Morris Minor wind its way down the driveway towards the manor. She'd positioned herself in the window seat where she knew she'd get a good view of her visitor.

It rolled to a stop and a thin-framed man stepped out with dark curly hair that was balding at the front. The hair he still had was wild and woolly and it lifted from the side of his head in the breeze. He looked friendly, with a pleasant face with lively eyes behind wire-rimmed spectacles. Looking around him, he didn't seem to be someone in a hurry. He took his time to stretch, yawn, and then gather a notebook and a file from the front seat of his car.

Laura walked to the door to meet him. He entered the hallway and took a long, almost embarrassing time to take in the architecture around him.

'I do love these old workman's cottages,' he finally said. 'So beautiful.'

'A little chilly without double-glazing though,' she commented in return.

'I'm sure it is,' he affirmed as he thrust out his hand. 'Walter Bartholomew at your service.'

'Laura Thomas. I thought you might be comfortable in the front room. I have a fire going in there.'

Following her into the main room, he beamed. 'I'm always comfortable with books,' he commented, instantly drawn to the overflowing bookshelves as he entered the room. 'Do you mind if I take a look?'

'Simon would insist,' she affirmed. 'Can I get you a cup of coffee, maybe?'

'That would be wonderful.' He nodded, his glasses now on his forehead as he stared closely at the spines of the books. She went to the kitchen to get two cups of coffee and found him a few minutes later with a small pile of books in his hand, looking through them all. 'A marvellous collection,' he mused. 'I always loved the library at the main house, and it looks as if some of those treasures have found their way here,' he said, showing her a book and noting the stamp marking it as belonging to the manor.

'My friend Simon is the estate manager here. This is his house. Anyway, he insisted on buying a lot of the books in a sale a few years ago. He says it's like a treasure map of the past. All the ancestors, who they were, we learn so much by what they read.'

'Absolutely, it's a shame that more people in stately homes don't take that seriously.'

She handed him his coffee, and, nodding, he settled himself down on the brown leather sofa.

She went back to the kitchen and brought in and placed a small plate of chocolate biscuits on the coffee table.

He helped himself to one and dipped it in his coffee before inquiring, 'Now, how can I help you?'

'I don't really know where to start. I'm trying to research something. A mystery of sorts that I found that I was hoping you could help me with.' She relayed the story to him and gave him the small metal case with the key in it to look at.

Handling it with the care of a newborn baby, he gently took the cigarette case and, looking inside, pulled out the roll of paper. 'Grace Mere.' He rolled the name around on his tongue, but looked none the wiser.

'I was hoping you could help me with her. Was she one of the Land Girls, do you know? Does that name mean anything to you? I've been on the internet and couldn't find anything there and the records of people here during that time were destroyed.'

He nodded. 'The office fire in the '60s, no doubt,' he reaffirmed.

'To be honest with you, I don't know what else to do to find out.'

Cupping his chin and tapping one finger on his lips, Walter stared into space and sat thinking for a moment before pulling out a small file of papers he'd brought with him.

'I brought my research with me. I wasn't sure what this was about, but I thought I might need to refer to my notes. There was a lot that I wasn't able to put in the book. Publishers want nice glossy photographs of elegant rooms and gardens. Long dry histories of people are not what sell books, but that's what interests me. Grace Mere,' he repeated. 'I know the name from somewhere but I can't quite place it. I've only been living in Norfolk for a short time. Before that I lived in the north. Unfortunately, the name doesn't ring a bell to do with the family tree.'

He started to pore methodically through his own notes, and through the names in particular, and then handed them to Laura.

'Here are the names of the family tree going all the way back to William the Conqueror. The photos I put in the book were strays from the family albums taken during the war. Unfortunately, no one had taken the time to add names to the backs. Besides, if my research is correct, many of the girls who were here during that time were from all over England.'

Laura started to feel despondent again. Maybe she should just let this go. What did it really matter? Then she thought of that robin's egg. If that had been a message from Katie, she owed it to her sister to find out.

Walter suddenly jarred her from her thoughts as he turned over a piece of his research.

'Ah, this may be of interest. There was one mystery that happened during that time, a Land Girl who just disappeared overnight. I jotted it down here in my notes, but I don't think her name was Grace. This looks like...' He placed his glasses back on his forehead to stare down at his scribble. 'Anna or Amy, I think? I can't remember for sure. It was a side note in a conversation I had with the old gardener of the manor. He was a young boy during the war when his father was the head gardener, but he remembered the girl because she was...' He thought for a moment to get the words right. 'So unusual. Yes, that's what he said. But she just upped and left overnight. That might be a lead worth following.'

The old gardener. Why hadn't she thought to contact staff who had lived at the manor? They were sure to know more about the people from that time.

'Yes, I should do that. Do you have his address?'

'At home in my address book,' he confirmed.

And it made her smile. No one she knew had address books anymore. It sounded so quaint.

'I will call you with it when I get home.'

'As long as it's not too much trouble, I would be so grateful. I know it seems strange, but I just feel so drawn to this story, as though me finding out about Grace has huge importance, somehow.'

'Ah, nothing strange about that,' he said, his eyes twinkling. 'Fate has an unusual way of taking us on paths of discovery that end up leading us back to a new truth for our own lives. It's all part of the marvellous experience we call life. You wouldn't believe the things I've uncovered about myself since I've researched other people's families.' He nodded, polishing off another chocolate biscuit.

They talked for a little while longer before Walter had to leave.

'One thing I do remember in my research,' he said as he stood up and stretched, 'is that in thanks for their ongoing service, the owner at the time gave the girls free range of his library. These shelves probably house books they were reading in the '40s.'

Laura's eyes widened. She hadn't even thought about looking through the books for clues. But anything was worth the effort. 'Yes, thank you for that idea.'

'I bet that Dickens was very popular,' he mused, pointing out the shabby copy of *The Old Curiosity Shop* still on the desk. 'Do you know The Old Curiosity Shop itself still exists? In London, somewhere. Isn't that just wonderful?' His eyes danced with the joy of it all. 'I should get off. I have a new project I am working on that will take me to the north and I have to prepare. But please call me, and if anything else comes up about Grace, let me know. A very intriguing story,' he repeated.

'Thank you,' Laura responded, escorting him to the front door. 'And thank you so much for your time today.'

'Yes, yes, my pleasure.' He nodded.

As she watched his Morris Minor leave the driveway, she felt reassured. He had validated her curiosity and hadn't played down her need to pursue the truth about what she had found. She revisited his words about finding out more about himself through his research and wondered if that was going to be her experience. More than anything in her life right now, she badly needed some clarity about her way forward at this time. Was this little mystery going to do the same for her, perhaps?

10

MOSCOW, 1940

Anya

As soon as Anya arrived home that evening, she knew something was wrong. There was a lot of activity all along the corridors of the communal building she lived in. Police officers were coming and going and all of the residents were out in the hallway talking amongst themselves. When they saw her, she noted the sadness in their eyes, the shaking of their heads, the nodding towards her in collective sympathy. Oh God! What had happened?

She rushed up the first two flights of stairs that took her to the last flight and the communal rooms they had on the top floor. At the end of the corridor a policeman tried to stop her.

'You can't go up there.'

'I live here,' she responded desperately. 'These are our rooms! My mother is inside.' The policeman's eyes softened, and she knew whatever she was about to face was going to be of the worst kind. He stepped aside with a gentle tap on her shoulder. But instead of feeling reassured, it filled her with dread.

She raced towards their rooms. In the hallway at the bottom

of the final flight of stairs a group of men all stood around talking in low earnest tones. A doctor with a stethoscope around his neck was upon the floor; another man knelt by his side in a black suit as they conversed between themselves.

'What is it? What has happened?' she cried out.

They all turned in surprise and then she saw her stepfather, standing up on the stairs. He looked terrified and wouldn't meet her gaze. Anya saw the guilt in his face. Whatever had happened, he had done it.

The doctor stood up and moved towards her. 'I'm afraid you must prepare yourself for a shock.'

'What happened?' she whispered again, the quiver in her voice pronounced.

The officials stood like a wall in front of her, not allowing her any farther forward.

'I'm afraid your mother has had an accident,' the doctor said in an even tone.

Anya stared at him, trying to understand the words. 'Then I must go to her and help her,' she cried, trying to push past him.

'I'm afraid it's not that simple,' he said, taking her shoulders gently. 'Your mother has broken her neck.'

Anya sucked in a breath. Her mother would have to go to the hospital straightaway. So why was everybody standing around?

'Then we need to get her to the hospital,' she demanded of the doctor.

Then behind him, she saw it, just the tiniest glimpse of pale skin, a limp hand lying across the bottom step of the stairs, with a spray of cream lace at the cuff, almost the same as her mother's dressing gown. She caught her breath as she put all the pieces together. It wasn't just *like* her dressing gown; it was her. Anya's mother, who was lying at the bottom of the stairs. Anya pushed past the doctor before he could stop her. And there she was, her wonderful mother, her body in a strangely contorted position, her face as beautiful as ever. Anya would've thought she was sleeping if she hadn't been bent in such a strange fashion.

'I'm afraid she's dead, Anya,' said the doctor, placing his arm on her shoulder.

Anya couldn't believe the words. She rushed to her then. Some of the men tried to stop her, but the doctor waved them off. 'Mama,' she said in English, taking hold of the limp hand. 'Mama, it's me. Open your eyes. Show everyone that you're not dead. Show everyone that you're fine, that you're alive.' But as soon as she took her mother's hand, she knew something was wrong. It was so cold and limp, like a doll's hand.

She stroked her frozen cheek, looking into her mother's face for anything, to see if she could see her breathing, but her mother was so still and so pale, almost grey.

'What happened?' she spat out at her stepfather.

He bumbled, 'It was an accident... She fell... down the stairs.'

'An accident?' screamed Anya, jumping to her feet. 'An accident?!'

Police officers around her became agitated, as did her stepfather.

'Yes, an accident, Anya,' he responded acidly. 'They happen every day. Don't you know that? Your mother was at the top. I heard her scream, and then she toppled down the stairs. By the time I got to her, she was already dying. So, I called for the doctor. But unfortunately, by the time he got here, she was gone.'

'You killed her, didn't you?' Anya accused him brazenly. She saw it on his face then. He must've pushed her. There was no way her mother had fallen down the stairs. She had a great sense of balance and always moved slowly and carefully.

A policeman put his arm on her shoulder. 'Come away. You are distraught, which is understandable. But your stepfather is also grieving. So, it doesn't help to accuse him that way.'

'But he did it,' she shouted. 'He killed her. I know he did.'

Apparently thinking she was hysterical, they took her to the neighbour's room, where she started to sob with the shock and the anger, and as comforting arms of other people surrounded her, Anya knew she would never be able to stay. She would have to find a way out now that her beloved mother was gone. She would never be safe here.

———

Anya took a week off from work to grieve the loss. She was heartbroken and received people in their tiny rooms. People spoke so highly of her and brought gifts for Anya and flowers. But in response she could think of nothing. Everything in her life was empty and hollow. A hundred times a day, she thought of something she needed to tell her mother or ask her. And then it would come back again, that she was no longer there.

Finally, on the morning of the funeral, her stepfather stepped into her bedroom for the first time. Since the death, he had kept well away, drinking till all hours and coming home after Anya was asleep, and she'd kept her door firmly locked and only used the communal kitchen when the other residents were around. Now he stood behind her, glaring at her in her looking glass as she sat combing her hair, preparing for the funeral.

'It's just you and me now, Anya,' he said. 'You must marry well, so we both have money to live on.'

'So *you* have money to live on,' she sneered. 'Isn't that your plan?'

She saw it on his face. The one thing about her stepfather was that he couldn't hide anything he was truly feeling.

'Don't speak to me like that, Anya. You are my daughter.'

'Only by marriage. Now not at all. I am nothing to you now.'

'You're just full of your grief. You must marry well. Working for the government, he has better benefits and we will be taken care of. I will contact Egor this week, and we will settle your betrothal.'

'I don't want to marry Egor.'

'That's the last of it,' he snapped, balling his hands into fists, trying to keep his temper under control. 'Do you hear me, Anya?' he growled furiously. 'You will marry Egor, and that will be that. That way, we can have a good life.'

'I will not.'

He started to laugh in a hollow way. 'What are you going to do then? You cannot stay here with me, unless maybe you want to make another arrangement?' he said, running a finger along the back of her shoulder.

Anya snapped at him, 'Take your hands off me.'

He gripped her shoulder, pressing his nails into her soft skin. And brought his face close to hers in a very menacing fashion. 'You will do this, Anya. Do you hear me?' he spat into her face. 'Do not defy me. If you choose another route and embarrass me, I will not rest until I find you. I would punish you, and believe me, you'd not like my punishments for bringing shame to my name.'

After he left the room, Anya felt desperate.

11

HATWORTH VILLAGE, PRESENT DAY

Laura

Laura located the little green gate with the swirling, black letters that had faded to grey nestled under a plum tree at the end of a row of workman's cottages. The gate creaked its welcome as she made her way inside and was pleasantly surprised to see a well-tended garden. A haze of spring flowers waved in the breeze, marking the way up a slight slope to the cottage door.

To the side of the house, two sturdy cold frames sat flanked by an ancient rusting watering can and a pile of terracotta pots. As she sauntered up the stone path, mauve and pink tulips nodded their heads in welcome to her. And even though everything was crystallized with the early frost, it looked lovely and dewy, sparkling in its morning glory.

The cottage was small but had four large windows and a door painted in the same green as the gate. On the front door, a rather impressive-looking knocker made of brass in the shape of a lion looked almost a little too austere for such a humble dwelling.

She gave two large raps on the door and waited. After a few minutes, she was concerned that maybe nobody was in. But it was such a cold day, Laura couldn't imagine an older man going too far. All at once, she heard the sound of slippered feet on a tiled floor, accompanied by a low rumble of a man's voice, who apparently was talking to a pet.

'Just a visitor, Percy,' she could hear him saying. 'Just somebody to see us.' She waited patiently on the doorstep, and when the door creaked open, in front of her stood an older man. The clothes he wore looked as though he'd shrunken down into them, as if maybe a few years before he'd been bigger, more strapping, and that they had fit him then. Now he appeared to be disappearing into his green knitted V-neck jumper. Underneath a white shirt, his collar showed slight frayed wear and the edge of a cotton vest circled his sagging neck. Sleeves were rolled to the elbows, and muscular sinewy forearms gave way to well-knuckled hands that looked as though they had worked hard for a living. Standing to attention at his side was an elderly pug, who stared up at her with concern and attempted a half-hearted bark. The smell of earth and Old Spice drifted out to meet her as she planted a smile on her face, hoping to look friendly.

He blinked up at her with the same wary expression as his dog; his droopy, red-rimmed eyes settled into lids that crinkled at the edges.

'Can I help you?' he said, his voice almost apologetic, as though he were the one knocking on someone's door.

Laura gave a brief explanation about Walter giving her his address and why she was there. As soon as she mentioned the manor's name, it was as if the man came to life. As if she'd woken him from a trance, his eyes seemed to dance with the memory of a world that was still alive to him. He beamed, opening the door wide to her; he was now all warmth and light.

'We don't get that many visitors,' he said, nodding towards

his dog. 'Do we, Percy? Lovely to have a little bit of company,' he informed her as he shuffled down the corridor towards his front room. He took his time, and Laura slowed her pace to keep in step behind him.

As she ambled, she took in her surroundings. Everything was clean, but also a little shabby. As though twenty years before, it would have been impressive. Now it was just waiting to become dust, and the rooms echoed with the man's loneliness.

As he opened the door into the front room, the dog rambled ahead and, grunting, curled itself into a ball in front of a tiny electric fire whose three glowing orange bars didn't seem to cut through the chill of sadness that hung in the room like cobwebs. Without being told, she knew this man lived alone. It wasn't just the lack of newness. Everything seemed clean and practical, but there was nothing that gave it warmth and hope. Nothing that gave her the impression of him being looked after.

She was dragged from her contemplation by the man's words.

'I was just going to make a cup of tea.'

'Oh, I don't want to be any trouble,' responded Laura brightly. 'I really won't take much of your time.' She instantly regretted her words. She could tell he'd been looking forward to a visitor. Even someone he didn't know. She hastily changed her tack. 'But of course, I'm not in a rush or anything, if you do have some time with me.'

His face lit up as he shuffled back into the kitchen. 'You make yourself at home, my dear. If you are from the manor, we have a lot to talk about.'

Laura entered the empty room and looked around her. On the mantelpiece stood three lone Christmas cards, even though it was March. Above it, a large mahogany clock ticked away the hours and the minutes. At the base of the electric fire, a beige-tiled fireplace betrayed the fact it had once been a common coal-burning fire. Probably had been converted in the '60s, as many had been, to electricity.

In one corner was a bookshelf, mainly well-thumbed gardening books and a stack of magazines. On a table by the side of one of the chairs was a picture of a child playing. A grandchild or a nephew, perhaps? She couldn't see a resemblance, but the photo looked old, like it had been taken in the '70s, maybe even earlier.

Her host arrived back and shuffled towards his chair. 'The tea will just take a minute,' he informed her. 'What a lovely surprise to have a visitor. Please sit down. Are you a gardener, my dear?'

She nodded and explained her job as a garden restorationist and how she also consulted on her past work, and his face brimmed with the excitement of sharing his love of plants.

How could Laura rush or not spend time with this man? He settled himself by the fire, in a sagging well-used chair, and the dog automatically leapt onto his lap and curled itself into a ball. Laura started to tell him about the manor, and he asked her many questions about the gardens. She explained she was restoring the walled garden, and he beamed.

'I have so many memories in that space, my dear. If you have any questions, you have to let me know. I'll be more than happy to help.'

He then went into a long rendition of all the plants that he had planted there. Laura didn't have the heart to stop him. So much of her research had already uncovered so much of what he was telling her. He seemed to take so much joy in telling her about it.

She asked about the willow tree.

'Oh yes, my father planted that in the 1930s. I can't believe how long it's lasted, can you? They're only supposed to last about eighty years, but that's been there a while now. The old thing will probably last another hundred years.'

Laura hadn't got the heart to tell him that it'd come down in the snow. He seemed so happy about the fact that it had been so rigorous over time.

A kettle whistled in the kitchen, and, slowly lifting himself up, he shuffled from the room. He was back in with a tray, balancing it in trembling hands. She wanted to jump up and grab it from him, but he seemed a proud man and she knew that that would have embarrassed him.

He placed the tea tray carefully on a table between them, and she noted the dirt under his fingernails as he lifted the teacup towards her. Its daintiness looked so out of place in his garden-worn hand, and she wondered if there'd been a wife to whom this tea set had belonged.

'Would you like milk and sugar, my dear?' he said as he lifted up a tiny jug, his hand shaking slightly as he moved it towards her.

'That'd be lovely. Milk, thank you, but no sugar.'

He poured the tea and a couple of splashes of milk into the two teacups.

Once they were both settled with their tea, she told him the story about the cigarette case that she had found. And he was fascinated, at times closing his eyes to concentrate on her words.

'Ever remember anybody called Grace Mere? Maybe someone during the war?'

The gardener settled back in his chair, his eyes raised as if the answer were written in the corner of his ceiling. Eventually he spoke.

'It was a hectic time during the war. Many people were coming, and even the Land Girls only came for a while. Until they'd have to go back and take care of a parent or get married or have children. I was a young boy then – my father was the head gardener – so I don't remember all the names, and unfortunately I don't remember a Grace.'

She felt her heart sink, but asked him her second question.

'Do you ever remember somebody called Ann or Amy? She disappeared during that time?'

Now his face lit up with recognition.

'I do remember an *Annie*,' he said. 'She was such a strange thing. She was a lovely young woman, petite, with white-blonde hair and green, childlike eyes. I remember her because I have to admit to having a little bit of a crush on her. She was like a perfect china doll to me, but she was also very strong. Worked hard in the walled garden mostly. It was a strange thing. She disappeared one night without a trace. Being so young, I don't remember all of the details at that time, but I know there were whisperings because she disappeared overnight not long after one of the other footmen left. And there was speculation about babies out of wedlock and such.'

Laura felt encouraged by his recollection. 'Do you remember when that was?'

'I believe close to the end of 1941, I remember thinking it would be sad she wouldn't be around for Christmas. In fact, I think I have a photograph of her somewhere. My father was asked to take photographs, to help document the gardens, so they could put them back as they were after the war. There was a photograph of her, I believe. Let me see if I can find it.'

Placing bent tortoiseshell spectacles onto his nose, he shuffled to the side of the room and pulled out a photo album. Sitting back down, he thumbed through it carefully until he came upon the photograph he wanted to show her.

'Here she is!' he announced, and, peeling back a piece of plastic that held it in place, he handed it to her.

Turning to the window, Laura peered at it. The photo had been taken in the walled garden; she recognized the stone bench. In the background behind the rose bush that was being captured, there was the face of a woman, her white-blonde hair lit up by the sun, which made her look almost angelic. The expression on her face was a mixture of shock and anger, as though it was the last thing she wanted to happen.

'She's so beautiful,' Laura commented.

'She was striking,' he agreed. 'Looking at this brings back all those memories, such an unusual young woman. I couldn't quite place her accent, as though her heritage had been stripped out of her. And sometimes, she did things that were just a little odd. She seemed to struggle with humour, not always understanding the jokes I told her. Though she would laugh, but you could see a lack of understanding in her eyes, as though she was desperately trying to fit in. A lovely person though. I was sad when she left. She just had a way about her that drew you in.'

'Do you mind if I take a photo of this with my phone?' asked Laura.

The man's face lit up. 'All the mod cons, hey?' he said, nodding his agreement as Laura took a quick picture. She wasn't sure if Annie's disappearance was anything to do with Grace, but somehow documenting it felt necessary. She wanted a record of it.

They talked easily for a little while longer about the garden while she finished her tea. When she finally bade him goodbye and left, she had promised to come back again once the restoration was finished, even take him for a tour of the garden. He showed great joy at this.

The elderly man waved to her from the door as Percy stood by his side, and she pushed through the gate. Getting into the car, she pulled out her phone and looked at the photo of the young woman. Could Annie be a part of this mystery? She pondered this thought as she drove back to the manor.

12

MOSCOW, 1940

Nikolai

In the second week of his training, Nikolai found out what the NKVD had in store for him when he met his partner, Olga. She was a tall angular woman with sharp edges and a disapproving glare. She scowled when she was introduced to him.

'He is to work with me on the mission in England?' she spat out to their supervisor with obvious disgust. 'He is so scrawny.'

Doubly shocked by what she had revealed and what she had insinuated, Nikolai pulled himself up to his full height and broadened his shoulders. He knew he wasn't hefty like many of his counterparts he had been training with, but he had never thought of himself as particularly scrawny. This wasn't a good start. The contempt on her face was as if he were an insect to be crushed.

'His English is exceptional and his training is passable,' informed the supervisor flatly. 'He will be fine.'

On his way out to the field for their run together, Nikolai weighed heavily what Olga had inadvertently revealed. There was no way he wanted to leave Russia right now. England hadn't been a terrible place when he had lived there – he actually had some very good memories of his boarding school days there when his father has served as an ambassador – but he was on a mission to find out all he could about his father's death and that would be impossible from another country. He had to find a way to be rejected from this programme soon so he could get back to what he was here to do.

Out on the field, he shook out his arms and legs to warm them for his run, just as he had every day of his training so far. Though running still wasn't his strength, he did feel he was getting better, something his new partner squashed before they had been together for an hour. He hadn't even finished stretching when Olga bolted past him, barely acknowledging him as she went.

'Come on, scrawny,' she shouted back over her shoulder. 'I will be amazed if you can even keep up.'

Teasing out a long stream of frustrated air and determined to prove her wrong, he sprinted to catch up with her, but she took off like a gazelle and was impossible to reach. Before long, he had over-exhausted himself and had to stop to catch his breath, cradling the pain in his side and fearing if he didn't stop he was going to throw up with fatigue. Looking over her shoulder, she sailed off away from him with a condescending laugh as she made her way down a dirt path into the woods surrounding the training area.

Working with her was going to be very annoying, he decided. Hopefully he would be rejected soon, preferably before he killed her.

The whole time they were together, he woke up dreading the day ahead and went to bed aching and infuriated. Everything she did was antagonistic and belittling, and just looking at her made his blood boil. How could he hate someone this much so quickly? There was no way he would ever be able to spend time with her on an assignment. Yet the NKVD thought it was possible for them to work together. Thank goodness Nikolai had plans of his own about that. Olga was also incredibly competitive. She had an enormous chip on her shoulder and wanted to win at any cost. She almost stabbed him at one point during hand-to-hand combat.

'I'm just trying to make you better,' she spat out when he complained loudly. 'My life is at stake and in your hands. I don't trust you if you don't know how to take care of yourself.'

He began to dislike her so much that he'd go to bed seething, where he would lie looking up at the ceiling, thinking of all the ways he could maim her. Surely that would get him kicked out of this programme.

He could trip her up, nothing fatal, just so that she twisted her ankle or something.

But every day he would get up and she would taunt him. Finally, at the end of their first week, they had to go to survival camp together. This included rock climbing and camping. It was an icy cold day, and even with all his winter training clothes on, Nikolai was freezing. As usual, she ran ahead, and when he approached the rock face they were to climb, Olga was already putting on her climbing equipment.

'Now it will help that you're so scrawny,' she jibed him, 'if you slip and I have to pull you up to the top.'

Turning from him, she started to climb.

'You are supposed to wait for me,' he shouted after her as he continued to secure his climbing gear. 'I need to check all of your harnessing.' They had only practised this a couple of times and their supervisor had reminded them to do this before they climbed.

'I don't need you,' she sneered as she climbed the surface of the rocks like a monkey.

'Wait, Olga, you have got to wait,' he screamed up to her in frustration.

'Not for you. I can do this on my own.'

'Oh, do it on your own, then,' he shouted back. 'See if I care if you fall and break your neck.'

'Say all you want. All that does is make me want to go faster and show you how much better than you I am,' she laughed down at him as she continued to climb higher and even faster.

He was fuming. He knew he'd have to go up after her, but there was part of him that hoped she fell and hurt herself.

Then, all of a sudden, as if the gods were reading his thoughts, he heard a rumbling noise above him, accompanied by the sound of stones crumbling and bouncing down the rock face.

It was a slide above them at the top of the cliff. Dropping to a squat, he cradled his head with his hands as rocks rained down upon him. Then, as soon as it had started, it was over. As he sat slumped forward on his knees, catching his breath, coughing with the rock dust, he heard it, heard her lose her footing. First, a scrambling sound above him on the cliff, then a slight whoosh of air from her lungs as Olga tried to pull herself up with her hands, then the next thing she was falling down the cliff, bouncing, rolling, scrambling, clawing, her face set in shock and fear as she tumbled headfirst to the ground and crumpled face down into a heap at his feet.

He had a terrible feeling as he stood in shock for a second, looking over her limp still body. A huge gash was on the back of her head, from where blood was starting to ooze, and it looked as if she had broken one of her legs.

'Olga?' he asked tentatively, approaching her. But she didn't move. Slowly, he turned her over, trying desperately to remember all of his emergency medical training so far. He felt for her heartbeat in her neck. It felt odd being this close to her and touching her. He kept waiting for her eyes to snap open and for her to yell at him, but she remained so still. He had to be doing this wrong because he couldn't feel a heartbeat. Could somebody die that fast? He must have missed it. He put his hand lower to her chest. There he felt it, just a feather of a beat but she was alive.

And slowly, the reality sank in, along with his guilt. Had his loathing wished this upon her? If he hadn't provoked her about breaking her neck, would she still be alive? Surely it wasn't his fault; she was so wilful. So why did he feel so bad?

13

CROMER, NORFOLK COAST, PRESENT DAY

Laura

At the end of March, the temperatures warmed up a little, and one particularly nice day, Laura decided she needed a day off to go to the beach. She hadn't been there long when she got a call. It was Jeannie, the woman in charge of the last restoration project that she'd been working on in London before she'd left.

Laura stood on the street, looking out over the water as she listened to the call. Jeannie was a kind gentle soul, and Laura always had it written into her contracts that there was a willingness to revisit clients as things started to bloom through the seasons in case they had questions. Jeannie outlined a particularly difficult problem they had been having with one of the plants not taking, and she could easily read the panic in her tone.

'Do you need me to come back to London?' she inquired as the woman on the other end finished the list of her concerns. As she said those words, Laura's stomach lurched at the prospect. She'd felt so safe here, hidden away in her secret garden, so cared for by her friends. Was she ready to go back home and face her fears?

'We have a guy coming out to look at it tomorrow, but if he can't figure it out, we might need you, Laura. We have an open day next week.'

'No problem,' responded Laura, somewhat reluctantly. 'I will drive down on Friday to look at it if you are still having issues, how about that?'

Jeannie sounded relieved. 'That would be brilliant, thank you so much. Hopefully we can get it fixed, but it's good to know you're available if we need you.'

As she shut off her phone, Laura sighed and was drawn to walk to the shore. She noticed her body trembled slightly as she moved. The thought of even being in the same city as Liam again filled her with dread. As she reached the beach, she drew in a long salty breath of air. Tipping her chin up to the sky, she closed her eyes, allowing the light of the sun to redden the inside of her eyelids with its rays as she soaked in the lovely sunshine.

All at once, her eyes sprang open, with the sound of a flock of seagulls that swooped above her head alerting her to their distress. Fighting over a mussel one of them had in its beak, they became a jumble of feathers as they screeched into the air, flapping their wings, angrily in confrontation with one another. Their high-pitched squawks a perfect frantic soundtrack for Laura's thoughts. She felt a little bit like that mussel; everybody seemed to need her. She never seemed to have much time to gather herself. She was always in demand. Liam needed her, the garden that was about to burst into spring craziness needed her, and her business needed her. She felt she never had time to think about what she wanted for herself.

With a sigh, Laura walked to the local coffee shop on the beachfront and ordered a latte to go. The rich aroma of freshly brewed coffee stirred her senses, reminding her of why she loved being close to the water. Coffee, a beautiful beach to walk on, the sand, and the smell of fresh clean salty air. She would miss this if she went back to the smoke. As she walked along the shore, gentle waves washed up onto the beach. She thought about Annie and felt some compassion for a woman disappearing overnight like that. Maybe she had also had her heart broken and was being pulled in a million different directions. And to top it all, she'd been in the midst of a war.

After what had happened to her sister, Katie, the story of Annie and Grace had compelled her to get to the bottom of it. If she could somehow put this right, maybe she could finally bury her own ghosts. She knew logically that Annie and Grace, by all accounts, must either be dead or very elderly now. But what if they were alive and still went to bed with similar questions, and Laura had the power to help them by delivering this part of their puzzle?

With a sinking feeling, she realized she didn't know where else to look. If she needed to go home on Friday she would have to figure out what she was going to do about Liam. But that felt so overwhelming. She'd felt so sure on leaving London that she wasn't going to go back to him. And the fact that he had slept with somebody else still stung her, but she'd also started to have second thoughts. And she hated herself for it. But this thought had started to run in a loop in her head. What if Liam was her last chance? What if she never found love again?

A young mother stopped next to her on the beach and asked her if she had change for five pounds. By her side, a little girl with flaxen plaits explained they needed money for the sweet machine. Laura smiled and dug into her handbag and, finding the change the woman needed, passed it across to her.

'Thank you so much,' said the little girl buoyantly, as she bounded off down the beach, dragging her mother behind her. Laura watched her with a knot in her stomach. That was another reason to consider a life with Liam. She wanted children.

No, she shook her head. She wasn't going to go back to him just because she wanted a child. Definitely wasn't going to go back to him just so he would marry her.

They had talked about marriage in a roundabout way. Or she had, anyway. Then he always seemed to shut her down on the subject, pat her on the arm, saying, 'We'll get around to that one day, won't we, sweetheart?' Nothing concrete. No commitment. Just a vague assurance that that was the direction they were heading in. He also often introduced her as his fiancée when it suited him for a business deal or with other associates who were married. He had never officially asked her, but assumed that it was some sort of agreement between them when it worked in his favour. She thought about that now, how everything was always on his terms. Engagement when he needed it and no commitment behind it for her own need of stability. Why had she allowed that?

The reality was, she did want to settle down. She did want to get married. She wanted to have children. She couldn't help the yearnings of her own heart.

She watched the girl move from the beach to the street and skip along the kerb, and even from where Laura was close to the water, she heard her giggling out loud and her mother making reassuring tones, probably about the great day they were going to have together.

Laura finished her latte and fought back the tears that suddenly started brimming in her eyes. She wished she could be clear. Why did she go back and forth like this? She knew what every one of her friends would say, especially Caroline. She thought about her close friend then. She knew she owed her a call and felt guilty about not being in contact.

But it was hard to separate Caroline from her brother. That was how she and Liam had met. Since Laura had left London,

Caroline had left a couple of carefully worded messages on her phone. But still, Laura found it hard to pick up the phone and dial her number because she really didn't know what she wanted to say.

Laura shook her melancholy thoughts from her mind and looked at her reminder list on her phone and noticed she had wanted to buy some more books while she was here. She googled 'bookshops' and some reviewers informed her there was a wonderful little independent shop with a great inventory.

Finishing her coffee, she made a decision. If she was still in this emotional place by the end of the week, she would go and check on Jeannie's plants and also face the music at home.

Laura entered the quaint little bookshop. A silver bell tinkled above the door to announce her arrival as the smell of wood, paper, and leather welcomed her in.

Moving around the room, she scanned the travel section. Mmm, Italy sounded nice, or maybe Spain. She wished she could just go on a holiday and never come back. Though she knew that was a silly idea, what was to stop her taking a couple of weeks off after the garden was finished? The thought of the sun warming her body sounded so good.

She continued to scan the bookstore when a perky little woman from behind the counter inquired in a strong Norfolk accent, 'Can I help you, love? Are you looking for anything special or just browsing?' She was a short, dark-haired, stocky woman with a rosy complexion.

Laura smiled. 'I'm just looking for your gardening section.'

The woman nodded and, pushing her spectacles up, she smiled. 'Follow me.' She nodded, walking to the back of the store, Laura in tow.

Thirty minutes later, Laura was back at the counter, a small stack of books in her arms. Two more garden research books, and on top the travel book to Italy. The woman was very chatty as she rang up Laura's purchases. She chatted about the weather, the lack of tourist trade, how hard it was to run a bookstore in a tourist town. In her own thoughts, Laura phased out much of the conversation, just nodding, saying 'Yes,' or 'Ah,' in the right places as the sweet little woman packed a paper bag for Laura with her purchases.

'What brings you down here?' she asked as she added the receipt to the bag.

'I'm staying at Hatworth Manor. I'm a garden restorer and I'd wanted to see if you had any books I don't already have about plants of this area.'

'Ah,' said the woman, raising her eyebrows as though she knew something about it. 'Did you find any?'

'I found one,' said Laura.

The woman nodded. 'You might want to try the library or even online. People want everything delivered instantly from Amazon now.' With a smile, the woman snapped the bag handles together and handed them to Laura.

Laura sauntered through the shop and cradled the bag with the pile of books in her arms.

The woman continued chatting as she walked Laura to the door. 'It's so sad, not the same as it used to be in my trade, you know.' The shopkeeper opened the door, adding in an offhanded manner, 'The days of Grace Mere are long gone.'

Laura stopped dead in her tracks. 'What did you say?' she asked.

The woman stepped back, surprised at Laura's sudden interest.

'I said these trades are long gone,' she said. 'You know, now we have all the iPhones and the iPads. You can order lace from China right online and have it delivered the next week and—'

'No,' said Laura, interrupting her, almost rudely. 'You said something about Grace Mere.'

The woman started to chuckle. 'Oh, I'm sorry. It's just a

local expression for being industrious. *As busy as the weavers of Grace Mere.'*

Laura almost dropped the pile of books she was carrying. Her heart was pounding in her ears, and she suddenly felt hot. The woman, who appeared to have only set herself up for a customary conversation, looked a little taken aback by Laura's dramatic reaction.

'You know something about Grace Mere?' asked Laura urgently.

The woman cocked an eyebrow. 'Well, yes, of course. Everybody knows the story about Grace Mere.'

'Tell me. Who was she?'

The woman started to chuckle again, 'Gracemere is not a person. It's a place. One of the cottages down on the waterfront. It was one of the many cottages weavers used to create their cloth. You know, cottage industries. You must have heard of them. The Cottage of Gracemere had one of our most notorious and well-known weavers of the area. You can read a little bit about it in the library if you want to—'

Laura stopped her again. 'You say it's down by the water, the cottage?'

The woman nodded her head slowly. 'Yes, but there's no weavers there anymore. I think the cottage is rented out.'

'I just need to know as much about that cottage as possible,' Laura blurted out, sounding almost ridiculous.

'Of course,' said the woman, frowning. 'Take a right out of the shop, walk down the hill and around the corner. About three streets across you'll see a row of cottages all facing the water near the little harbour. Gracemere is about the fourth cottage along. You can't miss it. It was a handy place because they used to be able to take their trades easily from the harbour—'

Laura cut the woman off. 'Thank you so much,' she said

and, rushing out the door, left the woman looking very bewildered.

'Enjoy the rest of your day,' the old woman mumbled, shutting the door, and Laura noticed she shook her head as she moved back to her counter. She must have thought that Laura was mad.

Laura stood for a moment and collected herself. She couldn't believe it. She couldn't believe it was this simple. Walking quickly towards the harbour, she was filled with excitement knowing she might be about to find out the next piece to this puzzle.

———

Laura stood on the street and her eyes filled with tears. Such a small, unassuming cottage that she had spent so much time trying to find.

The black wrought-iron gate gave way to a simple blue slate pathway and a stone step that had been whitewashed. But it was what was above the door that caught her attention, and held it. On a large blue circular stone plaque was the word 'Gracemere.' It was all one word. No wonder she had been unable to find it. Could this be it? Could it be this simple? The answer to her questions could be just beyond the small blue door with the gold letterbox?

Pushing open the gate, she strode up the pathway and knocked at the door. It was instinctive. She did it without even thinking about it. But as she heard someone coming to answer, she wondered exactly what she was going to say: 'I have a seventy-five-year-old mystery that I'm hoping you can solve.' Or, 'Do you have a clue hidden somewhere under a floorboard that might be to do with a runaway during WWII?' She froze with the fear. Nothing of whatever she could come up with sounded sane.

14

MOSCOW, 1940

Anya

Anya couldn't believe what she saw as she looked out of the windows. Stumbling across the grounds was Nikolai Petroff, in his arms, the crumpled body of another agent, Olga. His face was contorted with pain and shock. It was Anya's first day back after her mother's death and she stiffened, her heart starting to race with her memory of her mother, that one limp hand and her pale face.

Rushing from her room, she ran out of the double doors where many of the other agents had started to congregate, some at a distance, everyone in shock. As he arrived at the building, he dropped onto his knees breathlessly and carefully laid Olga's body down on the ground. All at once, there was a frenzy of activity as people bustled around, trying to assess if she was alive or not.

Nikolai continued to say over and over again breathlessly, 'I told her not to climb, told her not to go up alone, but she wouldn't listen.'

Anya couldn't help herself. He looked so vulnerable, so

devastated, his lovely blue eyes clouded with deep sorrow. She walked over to him and instinctively placed her arm on his shoulder. Then, their supervisor took charge.

'Anya, take Nikolai inside and give him something to drink. Our doctor is on the way. The rest of you give this woman a chance to be looked at.'

By the look of her, Anya knew Olga was in a bad way. Carefully, she helped Nikolai to his feet and held his arm, feeling the warmth of his body next to her own and trying to control the feelings rushing through her. He didn't shake her off, allowed himself to be taken into the building. He was filthy, mud-caked with sweat matting his blond hair, even though it was so cold. She took him into the room where she worked and sat him down. He slumped forward, his hands cradling his face. She thought about a hot drink. Though maybe he needed something more substantial. She poured a vodka. She held it out to him, and he just shook his head.

'I could do with some water,' he mumbled through his fingers.

When she handed that to him, it took a minute for him to realize that she had it before his face. Then, slowly, he sipped at it.

'I tried, Anya. I tried to tell her. She just wouldn't listen.'

'Hush now,' reassured Anya. 'Looking back isn't any help. What is done is done.'

He looked up into her eyes then, and she saw deep into his soul, not the man who had walked into her room the week before buoyant and full of confidence, but the little boy, the little boy who was hurting. It was instinctive. She took his hand and squeezed it. Once again the attraction she felt on their first meeting returned, but she pushed it away; he needed her, but not in that way, and they were work colleagues.

With her touch, the intensity of his expression softened a little and he looked at her with such gratefulness in his eyes.

Ignoring the waves of attraction that were rippling up her arm and making her stomach flip-flop, she continued talking to him. 'These things are going to happen. It is dangerous what you are doing. You can't blame yourself when things go wrong.'

He nodded his understanding, but still, it didn't seem to appease any of the guilt on his face.

It didn't take long for his superiors to find him and summon him to the office. He got up to leave. But as he walked to the door, he turned around and his eyes met hers again with real sincerity.

'Anya, thank you. I appreciate your kindness.'

She smiled and whispered, gently, 'I'll see you tomorrow. We have a class together.'

He nodded but looked unsure, as though not convinced he was still going to be there. And as he shut the door, Anya felt that now familiar stir of attraction in her heart. She would be glad when this particular spy was in the field; this distraction was not good for her. She was in limbo right now and still had to figure out her own life, though she knew falling in love with anyone about to leave the country would definitely not be a part of it.

———

That evening when she arrived home, the other people in their communal rooms were gone and only her stepfather was waiting for her in their own, and for once was not drunk enough to not be aware of her presence.

'Where were you?' he sneered in a low rumble. The tiny room was dishevelled and so was he, his shirt unbuttoned to his navel, his boots cast off on the floor. She caught her breath with the sight, and felt her stomach tighten as he ran his eyes over her body.

'I was doing some charity work,' she stammered.

'Don't lie to me,' he growled, knocking back another shot of his vodka. 'No one gets all dressed up like that for charity work.'

He leapt to his feet, and, roving towards her, his agility surprised her for someone who was drinking. She turned quickly to head for the door, but he reached it before her and, slamming it shut, threw his weight against it.

'You have a lover, don't you? That's why you won't marry Egor. You little whore.'

He grabbed a handful of her dress and drew him to her before she could get away.

Close to his face, the smell of tobacco and alcohol made her stomach wrench.

'If you are giving it away for free, I think you might owe me something for your home and board.'

She felt sick, as once again he ran his eyes over her body. She had to think clearly. She had to get away. Their room was high away from the others in the building. Even if she screamed, she wasn't sure anyone below her could hear her.

'Maybe something can be arranged,' she forced out, controlling the quiver in her chest from sounding in her throat. She smiled as suggestively as she could manage. 'But I need to change. I have been gone all day,' she whispered.

He nodded and released her from his grip. She waited in front of the door, and finally he stepped out of the way. As soon as the door was open, she rushed to her room with him shouting after her, 'Don't take too long.'

Closing and locking the door, she paced her room. She had to leave, but where could she go? They had no relatives for her to run to, and besides, she was fearful he would find her and drag her home from any of their friends. She made a decision. Taking the money from her job she had been saving under the floorboards where she had hidden it, she counted it. There was just enough for her to get a room for a couple of days. Then she would have to disappear. And in a way he could never find her.

Gathering a few of her clothes, she waited for him to move down the corridor to use the communal bathroom and then crept out of their rooms and back down the stairs and fled the building before he even realized she was gone. As she raced out into the night, she felt afraid but also free for the first time in months. She had nothing to keep her here. Her mother was gone and now she had to find her own way.

15

GRACEMERE COTTAGE, CROMER, PRESENT DAY

Laura

Laura's heart started to race and her mouth felt dry as she awaited the door opening. Maybe it would be a nice elderly lady, someone with a cat and tapestry chairs, someone who would invite her in for a cup of tea and listen to her tale. But as the door opened, all those visions diminished, as filling the door-frame was a tall dark-haired man.

His rich mahogany-brown eyes and dark eyelashes were striking and the first thing to catch her attention. He wore a cream jumper, a pair of faded jeans, and his feet were bare. On opening the door, his expression went from distracted to surprise as he took in Laura on his doorstep. In response, she became even more tongue-tied and found herself just smiling. How on earth was she going to broach her subject?

The dark-bearded man with the curly brown hair saved her.

'Can I help you?' he said as his face broke into a gentle smile.

'I'm not sure,' Laura blurted out. 'Are you the owner of this house?'

Nonchalantly, he leaned against the doorpost, slipping one hand into the pocket of his jeans. 'You're not about to sell me double glazing, are you?' he asked, a look of amusement dancing across his face. 'You see, it all depends on what you want.' His tone was playful and carefree.

Laura shook her head fervently.

'Oh no, nothing like that,' she said. 'But what I have come about is a little... unusual. A bit of a mystery, actually, one you might be able to help solve.'

'A little unusual and a mystery?' he echoed, lifting one dark eyebrow. 'I'm intrigued. Maybe you should come in and tell me about it. Unusual is what I specialize in. By the way, my name's Jamie,' he said, outstretching his hand.

'Laura,' she said, taking it warmly.

'Well, come in, Laura, and you can tell me all about your mystery.'

Laura followed him into his tiny front room. The miniature cottage was no more than a two-up two-down terrace, but she loved the charm of it. In his living room a large comfortable sofa had been draped with various blankets and covers, maybe Mexican or Spanish. Around the room too, she could see trinkets and souvenirs from distant lands.

Jamie heaved a rather large tabby cat from what seemed to be the only area to sit on his sofa.

'Come on, Mr McTavish,' he said, 'make space for our guest.'

The tabby did not look happy about being removed from his spot, with the only shaft of sunlight. But once lifted, he pawed at the carpet and stretched catlike and trotted off towards the kitchen, meowing.

'Sorry about the mess,' said Jamie as he ran a hand through his dark hair. 'I don't get many visitors,' he added with a smile. Pulling a stack of travel books from the sofa, he moved around the room, trying to find a different place for them. Eventually, he just stacked them on the floor by the fireplace. 'Please, make yourself at home,' he encouraged airily. 'Would you like a cup of tea or coffee?'

'Coffee would be wonderful.'

As he disappeared to busy himself in the kitchen, Laura heard the clatter of a kettle and the sound of water running.

She took a moment to wander around the room. Although it was cluttered, with a slightly bohemian feel, the choice of décor and pictures reflected that a great deal of time and energy had been put into choice and placement. Maybe he was a photographer or an artist.

On the fireplace was a row of photographs. One was obviously Jamie wearing sunglasses, beaming with some sort of Moroccan headgear. His arm was around the shoulders of another man, who looked very similar to Jamie. *Maybe a brother?* she thought. In the background behind them, a camel. She also noticed a picture in a silver frame of an older woman, a beautiful woman, with the same very dark eyes and very dark hair. She guessed it was probably his mother.

Continuing around the room, she moved to the window and looked out. He had a beautiful view of the cobbled street and she could see the tiny boats bobbing in the harbour.

'Must be nice to live so close to the water,' she shouted back through to him in the kitchen.

'Yes, it is,' he responded. 'It can get busy during the summertime, but the winter's very pleasant.' He arrived back with two cups of coffee on mismatched saucers.

'Sorry, as I said, I don't get many guests, and unfortunately I'm out of sugar.'

She smiled and took the cup from him. 'No problem, I don't take it anyway.'

'The view is lovely, but it isn't why I rent this house,' he added, taking a sip of his own drink.

'Oh?'

'It's the light.'

'Light?' She looked out of the tiny windows. It wasn't very bright.

'Here, I'll show you. Follow me.'

He took her cup off her and placed it on the table, and he padded up the stairs and she followed him.

It suddenly struck her. She was walking up the stairs behind a man she'd just met. Should she feel fearful about that? Something about his disarming manner made her feel very relaxed. But couldn't an axe murderer do that? She was glad she had taken self-defence classes years before, and she was reassured that she did have pepper spray in the bag she was grasping.

Fortunately, her fears were dissuaded when he opened up a door and instead of a bedroom she walked into the most marvellous-looking studio. All around the room were huge canvas paintings, depicting beautiful scenes from all over the world, and also here in Norfolk. But what was so enchanting about the room was one wall was practically a whole window.

'Wow,' she gasped, 'this is incredible.' The window was open and a soft breeze stirred in from the outside, bringing the sound of the gulls and the scent of sea air. She felt like she was actually floating on top of the water. It was so incredible, like being on a boat or a ship.

'You see?' he said. 'Another artist had the house before me. His mother owns it, but he did all the hard work, all the renovations, to encourage the most amount of light. This is where I do my work.'

She looked around the room. An easel with a palette of vibrant paints was set up facing the window, a charcoal outline waiting to be filled in on a new canvas. The walls were stark white, helping reflect the ripples of sunshine that bounced off a honey-coloured wood floor that creaked as she moved. He encouraged her to look around, and, moving from one canvas to the next, she was drawn in by the mixture of colours and brush techniques. They were all so exciting and alive. It made her feel as if she were right there.

She paused in front of a picture of some Spanish flamenco dancers in the throngs of their routine, the mixture of pleasure and passion caught perfectly on their faces. The picture was so vibrant she could almost feel their feet moving and their skirts swishing by the way that he painted it.

All at once he was by her side and a hint of a fresh-smelling shampoo drifted between them.

'My mother is Spanish, you see. I painted that in Malaga. We went back last year for the flower festival. It's a beautiful celebration. They really know how to party in Andalusia,' he noted wistfully.

'These are incredible,' enthused Laura.

'Well,' he said coyly, 'they keep the wolf from the door, but that's about all. They are available in a small gallery here in town. I do pretty well through the summer, but in winter, it can be a very hungry time.'

They headed back down the stairs. Once back in the front room, she picked up her coffee, and they continued their conversation.

'I've always wanted to paint,' she mused as she sat down, 'but I'm not very good.'

'I'm sure that's not true,' he responded, picking up his own cup. 'Everyone, I believe, has an undiscovered artist just waiting inside to be found. Maybe you just need the confidence to express yourself that way.'

She felt uplifted. He had an encouraging way about him, as if he really meant what he was saying. Not unlike a favourite teacher whose words had weight, meaning, and importance. Her thoughts were broken by his voice.

'Now, tell me, what is this mystery that you were talking about?'

Laura had felt so comfortable with him she had almost forgotten why she was there. 'Oh, yes,' she said, suddenly feeling a little self-conscious and maybe a little silly, the rusting cigarette case and scrawled note seeming insignificant. 'I'm trying to figure out where to start. It's kind of a strange story,' she began.

'Take your time,' he encouraged. 'I love a good story.' He beamed, and she relaxed instantly, feeling as if she could sit with him all day and share anything with him.

As she grappled for the right words, she was suddenly aware of how different he was to Liam. Liam, who constantly looked at his iPhone, a life under some perpetual deadline. His mind always somewhere else, planning his next deal. He always had a plan and a purpose for everything that was said and done. Jamie was so... laid back, open. That was the word, 'open.'. She started her story.

'I've been following a kind of mystery.'

'I'm intrigued.'

'I'm actually staying at Hatworth Manor. Do you know it?'

'Of course, I've heard of it though not had a chance to visit it yet. Do you know the family that owns the estate?'

'No, nothing so grand. I'm sorry I didn't introduce myself, properly. Laura Thomas,' she said. 'I live in London but I'm staying in one of the tythe cottages. I'm staying there for a few months, doing some restoration work on a walled garden.'

'Jamie O'Brien,' he responded, tapping his chest.

'O'Brien?' she echoed.

'My father is Irish. I'm half Spanish and half Irish.' He raised his eyebrows with a half-smile. 'An interesting combination, don't you think?'

She nodded, taking a sip of her coffee. She could talk to him all day, never mind get lost in those large brown eyes. She pulled herself together.

'Yes, well, the thing is, in the 1940s a Land Girl went

missing from the manor.' She looked at him, hoping that maybe something was going to trigger something, but he just nodded his head encouragingly before he responded.

'Okay...?'

'I was out in the garden earlier in the year and I happened to come across something that had been hidden. Something in a cigarette case.' She slipped her hand into her pocket, pulled it out, and handed it to him. He opened it and looked inside. Seeing the key, he dropped it onto his palm and then pulled out the piece of paper and read it slowly.

'Gracemere is our only hope!' His voice lifted with interest.

Laura continued, 'For a long time I thought Grace Mere was somebody's name, and it wasn't until today when I was in the bookstore that I found out about the weavers... I mean it may just be a coincidence, but it's kind of interesting that your cottage has the same name.'

'Yes, and it's been called that for many years,' responded Jamie. 'I know a little bit of the history of the cottage, but not much.'

'I'm aware this is going to sound ridiculous,' continued Laura, 'but I've been trying to track this down and for some reason, I think it's really important that I understand what happened to Annie, the girl who went missing, and see if this was somehow connected. Gracemere was obviously important enough for her that she wrote it down. So, I'm wondering if there's something here that the key belongs to.'

Jamie listened intently to her story as she continued to lay out everything she knew so far, ending with the experience she'd just had in the bookstore.

'I know this is a long shot,' she continued, 'but you're the only clue that I have right now.'

Jamie turned the key over in his hand as he listened. Finally, taking a deep, reluctant sigh, he spoke.

'I wish I could help you more, but the reality is, as I said, I just rent the cottage. It has been renovated a couple of times and I'm afraid there is nothing lurking in the attic or any cupboards this would fit for you to investigate. However, I do know that the owner of this house is still a member of the same family that owned the cottage back at the time you're talking about in the 1940s. If you like, I could see if she's available to talk to us. I'm not sure she would accept you if you called on spec, as she's a little fearful of strangers, but obviously, she knows me and maybe if I went with you...' He trailed off then, as if he didn't want to appear to be coming on too strong.

But the reality was, as he made the offer, Laura's heart leapt. She'd enjoyed spending time with him. He was easy to be around and he seemed to be taking this as seriously as she had been. She relished spending another few hours in his presence. After years with Liam's intensity, it was pleasant to spend time with this easy-going mild-mannered artist.

'Of course,' she answered. 'That would be great.'

'How about I give her a call,' continued Jamie, 'and then call you back if I hear anything? Sorry I can't be of more help.'

'You've given me the best lead I've had so far,' responded Laura buoyantly, handing him back her empty cup. 'I should probably get back to the manor, but I look forward to hearing from you again.' She wrote down her phone number and then, slipping her hand into his, shook it to say goodbye.

As she left Gracemere, she suddenly felt a wave of relief. Something was finally happening. Suddenly, she was closer to being able to get to the bottom of the mystery of Annie. A quest that had been so important, helping her reconcile her own ghosts.

———

It was the next day, midmorning, when she got the phone call from Jamie. She'd been out in the walled garden digging up weeds, allowing the tulips and the daffodils that were starting to push through the ground the space to grow. It was as she was loading the weeds onto a tarp that her phone had rung.

'Hi, it's Jamie.'

She felt her heart skip just a little. She had found herself thinking about him in free moments when she hadn't been trying to figure out what she was going to do about her and Liam. Not with any potential relationship in view, more just the awareness of being with another human being, another man, who was helping her see that the world wasn't just full of Liams, but there were kind honest hardworking people out there whom she could connect with.

'I have some good news,' he continued. 'Mrs Dunfreece has agreed to see us later this afternoon at four. Does that work for you?'

'Absolutely,' said Laura, pulling off her gardening gloves and swiping a sticky strand of her hair from her forehead. 'What time shall we go?'

'How about two o'clock, then we don't have to rush? And, hey, why don't I come to the manor and pick you up, so we can go together?'

'I'd love that,' responded Laura eagerly.

'Great, I'll be over then.'

16

MOSCOW, 1940

Anya

The day following her escape from home, Anya strode into the office of the leading commander of section seven. He looked up in surprise.

'What is the meaning of coming in here like this?' he demanded.

'I will go,' she stated in a very commanding tone.

'Sorry?'

'I heard this morning Olga will take a long time to heal so I will go with the agent to England. I have all the qualifications.'

He sat back in his chair, not understanding. 'What are you talking about?'

'Nikolai Petroff. I know you were training him for a mission to England. But now as his partner is injured, you can send me instead. It would take you too long to find a new female agent in time, but I am already here. You can train me. I speak good English. I know the etiquette. I can help him. I can do this job. Trust me.'

'But you have never done any spy training. Yes, you might

be able to make tea, make polite conversation, but how will you know how to tackle a gunman, operate a radio, plant explosives?'

'Train me, and I will learn. I'm a fast learner. I know you want to get him there soon.'

She studied his face and could tell, by the fact he hadn't thrown her out straightaway, that the idea tempted him. She'd heard that they were all under a time constraint and hoped that would be the deciding factor.

He signalled to his second-in-command and whispered to him, and the man left the room.

'Miss Baranov, I don't think you realize what you're asking. This isn't some tea party assignment. There'll be a lot expected of you. The training is hard. You would be under a great deal of pressure.'

'I know that. I know what I would be under, but I have to go. I cannot stay here.'

He quirked an eyebrow. '*Cannot* stay here?'

'My mother is dead. She was my only family,' she said. 'There's nothing for me here in Russia. But this way, I can serve my country. I can do some good, and I promise you I'll work really hard.'

Nikolai appeared in the doorway. He still looked crest-fallen. He'd aged so much in the last day; his guilt seemed to weigh heavy on his shoulders.

'Mr Petroff, we have a proposal for you and maybe a new partner.'

Nikolai looked up, surprised and with a momentary look of disappointment. 'I didn't expect you would still be sending me,' he mumbled. 'Not after what happened.'

'These things occur from time to time. It is a dangerous job you are doing. Olga knew that, and unfortunately, she paid the price. But that doesn't mean that we scrap the whole mission. We still need you in England, working for us. I have already agreed to it with the Germans, and I do not want to let them down. It will make us look weak and disorganized. You will go as scheduled in five weeks.'

'Go? But with who?'

'Miss Baranov.'

Nikolai turned then to stare at Anya, and he burst out laughing.

Anya felt livid. How dare he judge her without even really knowing her?

'But she teaches me how to make tea. What use would she be to me?'

'She speaks excellent English, and she has agreed to get trained.'

'How can we train her in five weeks?'

'This is all part of being an agent, Mr Petroff. We will often ask you to do the impossible. Anya, you will move into the barracks today and Nikolai, you'll work day and night with Anya until she's ready. And if after time she doesn't make the cut, then we'll think again, but starting tomorrow morning, you and Anya shall be training together.'

'Please, no,' he implored. 'I'm not going to put anybody else's life at risk.'

'You will do as you're told,' growled back the man, standing up. 'Tomorrow, you and Anya will start working together, and that's the end of it.'

———

The next day, they both arrived early on the grounds. Anya was out waiting nervously, pacing in the exercise clothes that she'd been given, which were way too big for her. She knew she wasn't that strong, but she was determined to make this work. Nikolai strode up to her.

Gone was the flirtatious expression she had seen at their first meeting; now he seemed angry.

'What do you think you're playing at, Anya? You know you can't do this.'

She felt her own anger flash up inside her. 'Who are you to tell me what I can and can't do?'

'You don't understand. I can't do this again. It's too hard. So, please, I'm begging of you, step down. Let them delay the mission or whatever, but please don't make us do this.'

Anya ignored him, her mind set. 'Where do we start?' she said. 'On the assault course?'

He glared at her. 'You are very obstinate.'

'My mother called it single-minded,' she answered defiantly. 'You can call it what you like. No matter what happens, I'm going with you. So, you had better start to like me.'

Then, for the faintest of seconds, a laugh danced in his eyes.

'Better start to like you?' he echoed back at her and for a minute that attraction she had sensed the first day was back. Then his face clouded again with concern and he spoke quietly. 'Look, Anya, I'm not trying to be awkward, but this is so dangerous. I just don't want to put either of us in that position again.'

'I am not Olga. I worked with her a few times,' she spat back. 'I am not stupid and proud like she was. Yes, I'm single-minded, but I'm not self-serving. I will learn, and you are going to teach me. Just give me a chance. I know I can do this.'

His eyes roved her face slowly as he seemed to be making up his mind and she tried not to be drawn in again by his eyes as her heart started to thud in her ears once more. 'Okay,' he agreed reluctantly. 'We'll start with a run, shall we? Ten miles is what Olga and I normally do.'

'No problem,' she said, brighter than she actually felt. *Ten miles?* She could barely walk that.

He started to jog. 'I'll set the pace, shall I?' he shouted over his shoulder as he ran off at a clip.

She followed behind him, tugging up her trousers on the way, which dragged on the floor. He ran at quite a lively pace, and she kept up with him most of the way, trying not to stare at his broad back and well-defined shoulders that were much more obvious in his tight exercise outfit. It didn't take long for her unfitness to catch up with her and she had to stop at about two miles to catch her breath. He came jogging back to her and circled her.

'Do you give up yet, Anya? Want to go back to your tea set?'

'Never!' she spat out. 'I just need to catch my breath for a second.' And as he was taunting her, she raced off past him, hearing him laughing behind her.

'Okay, then,' he said as he raced to catch up with her. 'There is some life in you, after all.'

They continued to jog side by side, and she finished the ten miles.

Then she went on to learn hand-to-hand combat. Even though her hands were small for the weapons, she found the fact that she'd taken dance classes a real help and easily jumped out of the way as they practised the knife combat. And once she'd learned how to throw him, she was quick in learning how to get Nikolai onto his back. When she'd done it for the third time, he looked up at her in surprise.

'You are determined to go, I see,' he said breathlessly as he held up his hand to her from the floor and she stretched forward to grab it. But instead of getting up, he pulled her down next to him and, rolling over her, pinned her to the floor. 'But never let your guard down, Anya. I learned that in the first week,' he whispered. 'Even to somebody who seems weak and vulnerable.'

He hovered over her, his thighs pressed against the sides of her body holding her in place, his hands pressing down on her shoulders and his face so close to her own his panting breath warmed her cheeks. An involuntary shudder rolled through her body. And even though he infuriated her at that moment, the attraction she felt was at great odds with her anger.

He seemed to feel it too. She swore she could sense it as he met her gaze. He lingered longer than was necessary. His eyes drifted to her lips for a second, as though he was contemplating kissing her, and then as if he too was shocked by his own brimming emotion, he jumped up and looked away. 'Come on,' he said gruffly, 'we have more to do.'

They worked all day. And by the end of it, she was exhausted but content. Her whole body ached, but she had kept up with everything. She knew she didn't have long, and there was no way she could ever go home.

Before they finished for the evening, they were practising their fighting skills and, losing her footing, she fell onto her back in the mud and he roared with laughter.

'Look at you,' he said. 'With your face covered in mud, and with your hair like that' – she had placed it roughly up in two buns on the side of her head an hour before – 'you look like a little bear. So that's what I'm going to call you. Mishka. The little bear.'

Jumping up, she was tired and frustrated not only with the exhaustion of the work but with navigating her feelings towards him. Without thinking, she shoved him hard in the chest, and he toppled backwards into the mud as well, looking up at her in surprise. 'Don't forget this bear can roar,' she snapped back, a little surprised at her own reaction but, wiping the mud from her face, she walked off not looking back, leaving him lying there.

17

HATWORTH MANOR, PRESENT DAY

Laura

Viewing her phone, Laura couldn't believe it was already after twelve. She looked down at herself. She was a mess. It had rained the night before, and the garden was very muddy. As she'd spent the morning moving rocks to build up the pond, she was covered in dirt. She would have to go back to the house to clean herself up before Jamie arrived.

Back in her room, Laura got a glimpse of herself in the mirror. She had a huge smear of dark earth across her forehead and cheek. Her hair was wild with fallen leaves and twigs. Her jeans were mud-caked and her T-shirt filthy.

Stepping tentatively out of her clothes, she jumped into the shower. Drying off, she dressed in fresh clothes, applied a little makeup, and blowdried her hair, more to give her confidence than to impress. As she did, she thought about Jamie's disarming and quiet manner. She was looking forward to spending more time with him. He was such pleasant company.

Laura arrived downstairs just in time for the barking dogs in the driveway to alert her to his car's arrival. Concerned he

would be bowled over with their enthusiasm, she rushed outside
to find him petting them and enjoying himself immensely.
Awkwardly, she managed to wrestle both the collies into the
kitchen and brush herself down before greeting him properly.

'Jamie,' she said breathlessly, appearing back in the doorway, 'I'm so glad you could make it.'

He stood in the driveway with his hands in his pockets,
surveying the main house and gardens. As he did he whistled.

'Wow. The manor is impressive,' he said, beaming. 'I have of
course heard of it, living here, but this is the first time I have had
a chance to see it for myself. So many beautiful areas to paint.
We have some time before we need to leave. Any chance I
could have a quick look around?'

Laura smiled. 'I can't see why not. There are not many visitors this time of year so there's just us here on the property. I'm
sure Simon – my friend who's the estate manager – won't mind
us looking around the grounds.'

Slipping on a cardigan and her boots, she walked him out
towards the main building. He towered by her side, and she
realized he was taller than Liam, well over six feet. As they
rounded the corner of the manor, Laura pointed out architec-
tural details and talked about what she knew about the history.
All at once, Oliver appeared with a model airplane. He stopped
short when he saw a stranger and looked up coyly through his
blond fringe. Then, apparently remembering his manners, he
extended his hand.

'Hello. My name is Oliver Graham.'

Jamie seemed delighted. He crouched down to Oliver's
height and shook his hand. 'Nice to meet you, Oliver, and look
what you've got.' And then he named the plane that Oliver was
holding.

Oliver looked really impressed. 'You know about planes?' he
asked, his eyes shining.

'Absolutely. Living in Norfolk with all this wind, you've got to be able to know how to fly a kite, sail a boat, and pilot small aircrafts,' enthused Jamie as he handed the airplane back to Oliver.

Laura smiled to herself. It was sweet. It was sweet the way that Jamie interacted with everyone. From the dogs when he'd arrived, whom he'd fussed to death, to now Oliver. She once again felt that twinge and difference between him and Liam. Liam was Jamie's opposite. Everything was an inconvenience to him that wasn't about work or himself.

'Would you like to go back to the cottage for a cup of coffee?' she asked.

'I'd love one,' said Jamie as she took him back to the house and led him through to the main room.

'Wow,' he said as he took in full sight of the bookcases. 'This is incredible.'

'I know. Feel free to browse while I go and make us drinks. Do you take sugar?'

He shook his head and smiled, heading towards the vast book collection.

On her return ten minutes later, Jamie was engrossed. 'Look at this,' he said, flashing a cover towards her. It was a book about artists of the eighteenth century. 'Look how beautiful it is,' he continued, turning it over gently. 'It has gilded edges and is leatherbound. I could get lost in a book like this.'

Laura placed his coffee on the table, and Jamie settled himself down in Simon's leather armchair as they got into an easy conversation and he continued to flip through the book.

'Tell me about Mrs Dunfreece.'

'Ah,' he exclaimed thoughtfully, putting the book aside and taking a swig of his coffee. 'Now, there's a story. She is quite a character. Her family's been here for years, living in this area, mainly fishermen that go back for generations. Her son, William, is the person who I mainly deal with, but his mother, Mrs Dunfreece, likes to keep her hand in. She feels a real connection to the cottage, which was her mother's, her grand-mother's, and her great-grandmother's before that. It's unusual to find a family that's still so connected to one place.'

Laura nodded as she took a bite of a chocolate biscuit she had arranged on a plate.

'Why don't you tell me more about this Annie,' he asked. 'What's the fascination?'

Laura's heart caught in her throat as a picture of Katie's smiling young face passed through her thoughts. But she wasn't ready to share this part of her life yet. It was too intimate and painful to tell him. Maybe if their friendship developed, and she felt safe enough. She looked up at his expectant eyes as he took another sip of his coffee. He was just making small talk and had no idea how deep that question was for her.

'I have always loved solving a mystery.' She told him a half truth, making her explanation sound lighter than it felt, with her heart hammering. 'And you never know how it can impact a person. It may all be nothing, but I may be able to hand this to an ancestor whom it could mean the world to...' She trailed off, taking a swig of her own drink to disguise the fact that there was a slight tremor in her voice.

He nodded listening, without judgement. Liam would have picked at this like a scab, reading something in her eyes, but Jamie seemed happy to take her at her word. And that felt like a breath of fresh air.

'Well,' he said, finishing his coffee and looking at his phone. 'It's a long shot that there will be anything at her house that can help you. But let's see what Mrs Dunfreece has to say. Maybe she can help you out with your mystery.'

'I'm ready,' said Laura.

'One thing,' said Jamie as he got up and followed her to the door. 'You should know about Mrs Dunfreece. She's a little' – and he searched for the right word – 'eccentric, and so is her home.'

'Oh?' said Laura, her eyes widening. 'In what way?'

'Why don't I just let you see for yourself? And... I hope you're not allergic to cats.'

'Not at all,' said Laura. 'I love cats.'

'Good, because you're about to meet a lot of them.'

'Ah,' said Laura. 'I'm beginning to understand.'

He chuckled. 'That's only the half of it.'

She put on her jacket and followed him out to his little car. Inside his Mini it was as cosy and cluttered as his home. Hanging from the mirror, an assortment of museum passes, a dream catcher, and a compass. In the back, there was a windbreaker, a picnic blanket, a small easel, and a box of paints. She liked the way it felt as if they were going on a day out.

The sun was shining, even though it was early in the year, so he opened up the sunroof as they drove away.

'Tell me more about yourself, Laura,' Jamie asked as he turned out onto the main driveway.

Laura felt a cramping in her stomach. She didn't really want to talk about herself. All the conversations led back somehow to Liam. And right now she wanted to be spared the experience of going through the memory of that trauma all over again.

'I normally live in London,' she answered, trying to find things that skated around the truth. 'I'm basically a historic gardens specialist.'

'Interesting. What kind of gardens can you tackle?'

'Everything and anything,' she said, smiling. 'I'm trained in the knowledge of a range of sources, including horticulture, architecture, and garden design. Mainly I have learned to really appreciate the study of garden history. It's fascinating to learn all about garden-making over time and in different countries. I've restored gardens from the sixteenth century all the way up to present day. But what about you?' she said, quickly moving the subject from herself.

'Ah,' he said. 'Well, mine's a pretty simple story. I've lived all my life in Norfolk, and I'm a painter, so I'm very poor, and very happy.' He smiled. 'And I sometimes work at a local bistro a friend of mine runs. Just to supplement my income.'

'Interesting,' she said. 'What do you do there?'

'I'm a chef,' he said with a wry smile. 'Well, that's what my mother encouraged me to train as after leaving school. But I soon realized that it's very high-pressured and I'm not really suited to that kind of career. So, I just do it occasionally and part-time now.'

'Chef,' she said, her eyes twinkling. 'I've never met a man before who's a cook.'

'Let me put your expectations to rest right away,' he chuckled. 'Most people who are chefs don't like to cook at home. My ex-wife was very disappointed about that one.'

Laura drew in a breath with the reference to an ex-wife but, not wanting to pry, kept her face in an amicable smile. She would have loved to know more. Maybe they would have more in common than she'd first realized. He didn't elaborate and went on to talk about the countryside they were passing and some of his childhood memories.

As they turned from the main road onto the coastal road, she stole glances of him when he was unaware. She found him very attractive, with his thick, dark, curly hair, his eyes almost black with his long lashes, the way his whole face lit up when he laughed, and the enthusiastic way he talked about his life, as if he was on one long adventure. If she weren't feeling so raw in her own emotions, she probably could find herself falling for him. But right now, she didn't need to risk her heart, and that was what she really liked about him. He made her feel comfortable, and at this moment in time that was exactly what she needed, a friend.

18

FRANCE, 1941

Anya

Five weeks to the day that Anya started training, the two of them moved swiftly through the streets of Le Havre at daybreak. Nazi soldiers were everywhere and from every government building flags emblazoned with swastikas billowed in the breeze. Anya's mind was buzzing with the last-minute instructions about their contact once they arrived in England. Anya couldn't resist looking around. She wanted to pinch herself. She was in France. Well, German-occupied France. Even though she had desperately wanted it, she had never in her wildest dreams imagined ever being in Western Europe.

The locals who were up that early eyed them warily from their sidewalk cafes and their shop doors. When they arrived at the port, the smell of briny water and engine oil greeted her. Even this early in the morning, the port was alive, bustling with German soldiers in their smart grey uniforms and German naval officers too. Seeing so many of the fighting forces brought it home to Anya exactly what she was doing and whom she was fighting for. A member of naval personnel met them and ushered them down steep concrete steps to the submarine pens.

The high-pitched sound of her stilettos echoed, bouncing off the concrete walls as she strode alongside Nikolai through the tunnel that housed the submarines. As she clipped along, a cold wind blew through the passageway, making her shiver, even though the morning sun danced on the lapping waves, reflecting rivulets of water across the stone tunnel. With each step, her stomach tightened with the mission she was to embark on. For the past five weeks, she'd had one focus: leave Russia and her stepfather at any cost. It had kept her determined, through every rock climb, night of deprived sleep, and intense mock interrogation. She had worked really hard, day and night, to get to the point where she was ready, despite the reluctance of her partner.

Nikolai had continued to protest to his supervisors about their lack of readiness. Even insisted it would be safer for them if he went back to the job he had been doing before. But the people in command were having none of it and were determined to meet their deadline of dropping Russian spies on British soil as soon as possible.

Now, as she'd managed to get through all of that, the weight and cost of what she was doing filled her with an impenetrable doom that seem to deepen with each step.

Turning a corner, they approached the submarine they were to sail on, its gunmetal grey body glinting in the morning sun. A long cylindrical vessel, it was a lot smaller than she'd expected. This was maybe two hundred feet long and no more than twenty feet wide. A gun was mounted on the front to remind her she was going into a war zone, and the group of sailors that were already assembled to meet their captain stood to attention along the deck. From the port, other members of the crew were lowering huge torpedoes that hung on thick metal chains onto the vessel.

As the only woman, she drew a few low whistles and crude comments from the men around her as she passed them, but she responded by clenching her jaw and not allowing her determined stare to waver. Stepping onto the narrow gangplank, she felt her senses assaulted by the smell of mildew and salty water. On the way onto the deck, she saw a crewmember welding one of the panels, and she had to jump out of the way of the hot bright sparks that flared up in front of her. Responding to her reaction, he spat into the water and gave her a look of great contempt, making it very clear he didn't like the idea of a woman onboard.

She swallowed the hard lump bobbing in her throat, realizing how potentially difficult it was going to be on a submarine with thirty men.

Anya felt every eye upon her as she made her way down onto the deck. Onboard, the captain was there to greet them. He was wearing a black uniform and a peaked black-and-white cap, a gold emblem around his neck – the silver cross informing her he'd done well in battle. By his side, two of his officers were also wearing black. He nodded towards them and greeted them in their own language.

'*Zdrastvooytye*! I am Captain Danson. This is my first officer. He will help you while you are aboard.'

As she and Nikolai nodded, she noted he had a contemptuous tone, and though he didn't show his disdain for her openly, he made it obvious by the lack of eye contact he gave her.

Once they were aboard, the captain ordered the men to man their stations, and they jumped into action – securing the torpedoes being loaded, pulling in rigging, dragging in the chains as they prepared the craft to sail. She stood on the top deck next to Nikolai as they moved smoothly out of the tunnel towards the sluice gate that led to the open water. Lined along the banks of the port, dockworkers and other military personnel cheered and applauded, and even a brass band played to encourage them on their way.

People called to them as if they were heroes, shouting, 'Sink them all!' 'Go get them!' It felt unbelievable.

As the wind whipped her skirt around her knees and her hair across her face, she caught sight of Nikolai, and he looked as terrified as she felt. It was one thing to be training at a camp; it was another to be totally alone aboard a submarine of rough German sailors. Once they had cleared the port, they were instructed to climb down into the submarine. Nothing could have prepared Anya for what was waiting for her. It was a hot, dark, cramped space, and as her eyes adjusted, it felt almost as if she could stretch out her arms and touch both walls at the same time. Men were squashed in together like sardines with no chance for privacy.

Pipes ran along the ceiling, lit by intermittent lights, and every available space was taken up with provisions. Low-hanging baskets dangled from the ceiling filled with bread, sausage, cheese, like the inside of a cramped shop.

She stayed close to Nikolai as they walked carefully through the long metal tube. The smell was intense. A mix of sweat, food, and gun oil. The first officer seemed oblivious to it all as he escorted them through the different areas. First the control centre, where blinking panels of dials and switches, listening devices, and charts took up every conceivable space. In the same area was the periscope, and she was so transfixed by all that she saw. Anya nearly tripped over a sack of rice on the floor and just caught herself in time.

'It's tight down here,' the first officer confirmed. 'Even the captain doesn't have privacy,' he added as he walked them through the officers' room. Men sat eating at the table. 'In there in the evening, the captain sleeps here, but in the day we eat,' he said, shoving one of the men jovially.

'This leads to the sleeping quarters,' the first officer was saying as he moved them through the sub. Just flimsy curtains separated the bunks that were high up on the sides of the submarine. She had to walk sideways to get through them. How did men survive like this in such a cramped space?

In front of her, she could see that Nikolai was concerned.

'Where will we sleep, sir?' he asked.

'We'll have a bunk for you. Everybody's bunk is assigned to two sleepers. One sleeps while the other works his shift. Hopefully, we'll find one for you at night. It may be different each evening, depending on who's on duty.' He took them to a supply closet and pulled out two gas masks. 'These are for you,' he said, throwing the masks toward them, 'in case of a gas attack. You should keep them with you at all times.'

He then led them through the main engine room. It was incredibly loud, as valves and pushrods pumped up and down with a clatter. It was stiflingly hot, and the diesel smoke choked her throat and stung her eyes as they moved through it.

'You shouldn't need to come down here often,' he yelled to them. 'But if we dive quickly, we all have to rush to the front of the boat to help us get down quicker. Do you understand? If that alarm goes, you will have to join us. Everyone who is not in the control room has to do that.'

Anya didn't like the idea of being squashed up against thirty men and hoped they would never have to dive quickly.

As they made their way out into open water, Anya found a relatively uncluttered spot and sat on her luggage, leaning her head against the submarine's hull. She closed her eyes, and the cool metal seemed to pulse with life beneath her temple. She could hear the faint sound of water swishing past the craft as they cut a course through it and also the distant hum of the propeller. As she listened, she ran through all the instructions their handlers had given them before they'd left.

A sympathizer with a job in the British government had assigned her a place to join the Land Girls on an estate where the lord was very influential. Nikolai was to become a footman in the same manor. Because of the war, there was a lack of able-bodied men in England, so it had been easy for the British contact to arrange for Nikolai to be in service there. Though it had been made clear he had limited experience, she hoped that her etiquette preparation training with him had been enough for him to pass without being uncovered as a spy. His job would be to listen to important conversations and pass information back; hers was to observe and report troop movements and activities on a very local airbase, called Coltishall.

The submarine lurched, and, opening her eyes, she caught a glimpse of Nikolai, who was talking easily with the crew in German farther down the cabin and had challenged one of them to a game of chess. Anya understood very little of what was going on around her. She allowed the weight of what she was doing to sink in, and she suddenly felt so alone. She desperately wanted to see her mother again. Inside her shoe she had stuffed her mother's lucky British penny and as she felt it pressed against her skin it was the only tangible thing she had left of her.

She'd been so single-minded about getting away from her stepfather, she hadn't really had time to think much about her mother since her death, and suddenly she felt so homesick for her life. With stark realization, she acknowledged she was utterly alone in this world, on her way to a strange country, where she would probably be uncovered and shot for being a spy. What had she been thinking?

As the evening wore on, a scruffy-looking seadog whose breath stank of garlic sausage came up to her and grunted, beckoning for her and Nikolai to follow. He led them to the area filled with the bunks and, slapping his hand on the top of one of them, he scattered crumbs from the bread hanging in nets above it.

'This is where you will sleep.'

Anya looked at Nikolai as he translated.

'This is where I'll sleep? What about Nikolai?' she asked.

As Nikolai continued in German, the man roared with laughter.

'This is where you will sleep, both of you,' he said.

Nikolai stumbled on the translation, looking across at Anya nervously as she sucked in a breath. The bunk was tiny. Even though she was petite and slender, it would still be cramped for both of them to be on it.

'Do you need help up, princess?' he grunted in crude English, as many of the crew in the cabin began to laugh. 'I would be happy to help you,' he added, and Nikolai answered him sharply. And though she didn't understand Nikolai's response, she heard a protective tone in his voice, which surprised her. They had gotten on amicably during training, but he had always seemed very distant, preoccupied with his own thoughts. This was the first time she'd seen him show any genuine concern for her.

'I can take care of myself,' she spat back in Russian, and Nikolai translated with a smile as the members of the crew hooted their response at her put-down.

She put a foot on the bottom bunk and swept herself up onto the top bunk as the crew cheered. She perceived a few off-colour comments that Nikolai declined to translate for her.

Once in the bunk, it felt even smaller on top. With the rough beige canvas moulding around her body, there was no way she would be able to avoid contact with Nikolai. But as scratchy as her British clothes were, she decided she would keep them on, as she put her head onto a flat grubby pillow. She wondered how much sleep would be possible.

Nikolai gingerly climbed up next to her and sat on the edge of the bunk. 'I can sleep this way,' he said, signalling he would sleep with his head at her feet, and, pulling off his jacket, he created a pillow for himself at the end of the bed. She nodded, quickly averting her gaze from his shirt and the fabric that was pulled taut across his chest. She turned her head to the wall, not wanting to see him or look at him, and tried not to show the fact that tears were brimming in her eyes from the fear of what lay ahead.

It took her a long time to get to sleep with Nikolai's body next to hers, his legs pressed up against her, his back under her feet. She had never been this close to a man, and she was hyper-aware of every movement. She tried not to think about his calf muscles nestled into her back, which felt well developed from all the running, or the fact her toes were just inches away from touching his well-toned back.

Before long, she could tell that he was asleep, his breath coming in long, low, smooth waves. And with her eyes adjusting to the reduced light, she took a snatched moment to watch him. Her stomach contracted again with the attraction. He was lying on his stomach, his broad frame filling the bunk, one of his hands tucked under his head and his eyes, brushed by his long fair lashes, were closed and a lock of his dampened golden hair had escaped from where it had been combed and fell across his forehead. She felt angry with herself. She needed to get control. This was her partner. He didn't need a love-sick woman mooning over him. They needed to have their wits about them as they held each other's lives in their hands.

When she finally did fall asleep, she had a nightmare. She was kneeling over her mother's body, and her mother was crying out to her that she was still alive and she needed Anya to help her. Anya tried to call out to the doctors and police around her, telling them she was alive, but she had no voice. She could not cry out. Suddenly her mother was being taken from her, and she screamed for them to leave her and to let her stay in her home. Anya tried to go after her, but her legs wouldn't move, and she turned to see her mother had not gone and was gripping her shoulders.

All of a sudden, she was awake. Someone did have their arms upon her. She turned quickly, still in her dream state, thinking it was her mother, and for a split second, she thought everything that had happened in the last few weeks had been the nightmare, not the other way around. But when she looked up into the darkened face hovering above her, she saw it was Nikolai, his hands gently holding her, his blue eyes filled with concern.

'Are you okay?' he whispered into the darkness.

Anya hitched her breath with the closeness of him. Her throat was dry from yelling in her sleep, and sweat was beading across her forehead and trickling down the back of her neck. She nodded slowly, trying to focus. The submarine was dark, apart from a few dim lights, and she could only just make out Nikolai's form above her.

'I was dreaming,' she finally croaked.

'You are hot. Let me get you some water.'

Her instinct was to say she could do it herself. But she wanted to get him to move away from her. Quickly. His close proximity was making her heart thud in her ears and she was afraid he would see how much it disturbed her. As he ran his hands down her arms in a comforting way, she felt his warmth, and a ripple of what felt like electricity ran through her body, once again.

Breaking the moment of tension between them, she nodded, speaking quickly. 'Thank you. I would like a drink of water.'

As he moved off the bunk in search of what she needed, she felt her whole body quiver with the experience. They had been close in combat training many times, but nothing had ever felt quite like that when they had been trying to defend themselves. Again, she willed away any attraction that was making her heart quicken and her limbs feel weak. She could not become close to Nikolai. They had a job to do, and she didn't want to complicate her life any more than she already had.

19

NORFOLK, PRESENT DAY

Laura

Jamie and Laura pulled into the small town where Mrs Dunfreece lived. It was one of those little seaside towns with plenty of little cottages in bright pinks and yellows. The view from the hill looked down to the water as he slowly drove his car down the cobbled street.

'Mrs Dunfreece lives at the bottom of this hill, the last cottage. We need to park farther up though, because there's very few places down there.'

Pulling the car into a parking space, they both jumped out and he locked the doors.

'This way,' he said and started to amble down the road. She joined him by his side. It felt good to walk on this lovely sunny afternoon.

As they got to the bottom of the hill and to the last cottage, she got a glimpse of what he meant by eccentric. The rest of the houses were neat as a pin. Well maintained, some with early window boxes of spring flowers and little squares of cut lawn.

The cottage at the end of the row was a mass of overgrown bushes, and the weeds had already started to grow with the early spring rains. At a window, with a crack in the pane, four cats sat, staring out at the world.

He opened the rickety gate with peeling paint and ushered her in. When they arrived at the front door, Jamie knocked loudly.

'She's a little bit deaf,' he informed her as he also shouted through the door, 'Mrs Dunfreece, it's me, Jamie.'

A high-pitched panicked voice floated back. 'Who is it, did you say?'

'Jamie, your tenant over at Gracemere.'

'Jamie,' she said again. Suddenly her face was at the cracked window, looking out at him with great apprehension. She stared back and forth from him to Laura. 'And who is that?' she said. 'Your girlfriend?'

Jamie smiled, and did he blush? Laura thought she caught a little reddening of his cheeks.

'No, just a friend, Mrs Dunfreece. Remember, I told you? This is Laura. The lady staying at Hatworth Manor?'

'Ah,' she said. 'Well, there's nothing of the likes of Hatworth Manor in here,' she said with a sniff, looking at Laura through the window warily. 'Not sure it will be up to your standards.'

Laura smiled, recognizing the woman was half joking. 'I'm sure I'll be fine,' she answered.

She moved from the window and they listened to her shuffle down the hallway towards them until she undid several large bolts and then opened the final latch as the door swung free and three cats escaped.

The smell was the first thing that hit her. The smell of cat urine, stale air, and old food. Laura quickly started breathing through her mouth and tried not to react to the unpleasantness. They followed the frail bent-over figure of the woman, who leaned heavily on a stick as she moved down the hallway that was packed to the ceiling with boxes.

'Jamie, put the kettle on, love. You know where it is,' the old woman sang out.

'Oh, I'm fine,' said Laura. 'I don't really need a drink.' She dreaded what the kitchen might look like.

The woman stopped and peered at her. 'Don't be so contrary. I will serve you tea. Whether you drink it or not is up to you. But still I know my manners, particularly for someone who lives up at that manor. You're all posh up there, I know. I'm sure you serve tea, right?'

'Well, yes,' Laura continued with one last-ditch attempt, 'but I just didn't want to put you to any trouble.'

'No trouble for me. Jamie's doing it,' said the older woman as she sucked on her teeth.

Laura looked towards Jamie, who raised his eyebrows, signalling their mutual despair, but disappeared towards the kitchen anyway, chatting to one of the cats that followed him.

As she entered the room, Laura tried not to react to the clutter. The hallway had been practically tidy compared to the amount of belongings in the front room.

It was dark and dismal. Most of the curtains were closed, apart from the one with the cracked pane. All the lights were on, even though it was sunny outside. In every available space there were even more boxes, accompanied by stacks of books, trinkets, clothes, all piled in towering circles around the front room.

'Grab a chair,' said the older woman as she settled herself onto a rather large sofa that looked like she sat in it every day, the way it was compressed. Three more cats jumped onto her lap as she sat, and two more paraded the room around Laura's legs as she pulled a box from one of the seats and sat down. She suddenly wanted to have a wash and didn't really want to touch anything.

Jamie arrived back. 'Well, the kettle's on,' he said. 'I just wanted to introduce you two so you could get to know each other.'

'We can do that on our own,' snapped back the woman. 'Why don't you go back to the kitchen? Us girls might want to talk about you.'

Jamie looked with concern over at Laura, who shrugged her shoulders. 'Okay,' he said, wandering back out, 'I'll go and continue chatting to my new friend, the white cat.'

'That's Joshy,' the old woman shouted after him. 'And he likes being tickled under the chin. So, he's a nice young man, isn't he?' the old woman said, getting straight to the point as she gave Laura a tight-lipped smile. 'I hope you're not going to break his heart.'

Laura reddened at the directness of the woman's comment. 'Oh no, honestly, we're just friends. We literally just met yesterday.'

'Ah,' she said. 'You might be just friends now, but there's something about the two of you I can sense. When you're as old as I am, you can sense couples that are meant to be together.'

'I can assure you,' said Laura, feeling her stomach cramp as Liam's face flashed through her mind, 'really, we are just friends.'

'Well, we'll see about that,' she said wistfully, jutting out her chin and running her tongue along the front of her top teeth. 'But don't you come here from wherever, breaking his heart. He's a nice lad. I'm very fond of Jamie. He already had his heart broken a while back and I wouldn't want to see that happen again. You seem like a nice young lady, but I sense... a reluctance in you.' She paused, screwed up her eyes then and said the next words very pronounced, as if she was reading something in Laura's face. 'I can see you are about to come to a cross-roads in your life where you will have to make a difficult decision. Don't be afraid of loving again. Not every man is like him... the one you are thinking of.'

Laura shifted uncomfortably in her seat as the truth of this woman's words struck her heart. Was she psychic or something?

Jamie arrived back in with three cups of tea on a tray. Surprisingly, the cup he handed to her looked spotless. Maybe the kitchen was better than the rest of the house. Or maybe Jamie had spent the whole time in there cleaning.

'Ah, here he is,' said the older woman with a smile that showed the gaps in the side of her mouth where there had once been teeth.

'Did you finish talking about me?' inquired Jamie. 'I could feel my ears burning.'

'No,' she said, 'we weren't talking about you, we were talking about Laura.'

As he handed out the tea, the three of them settled.

'Now, what can I do for you both, now you're here? I'm sure you weren't just passing and wanted to visit an old lady.'

Laura looked over at Jamie and he spoke. 'It is kind of a strange thing, but we're wondering how much you remember about the time when your father lived in the cottage during the war.'

'Oh,' said Mrs Dunfreece, drawing in a deep sad breath. 'That was a long time ago and an unfortunate tale. My father was... let's say, a little disillusioned during that time. Went a little crazy after my mother was killed in an air raid. Though he went to jail for what he allegedly did...' She drifted off then, as if the memory was just too painful to continue, as she sipped absently at her tea.

They both waited for a moment, not wanting to intrude on her reflection.

Finally, Jamie broke the silence gently. 'Allegedly did...?'

Mrs Dunfreece batted away his question with her hand.

'Nothing I want to go into now. What has all that got to do with your visit?'

All at once, two more cats appeared at the door and distracted her as she called to them to join the others on her lap.

Realizing she wasn't going to go into any more detail about her father's past, Laura picked up the conversation. 'I found a cigarette case in the walled garden at the manor, with a note in it, which we believe was written during wartime. And it led me to Jamie, because there was a reference to Gracemere, which, of course, is your family cottage.'

'Been in my family for generations,' she said proudly. 'Made famous by a cottage trade there. There is even a saying about it. "As busy as the weavers of Gracemere,"' she said with great fondness. 'That was about my great-great-grandmother. She started her very own cottage industry from that little house. It's a nice little place but too small for me and the cats. I've got seventeen of them, and they all need their room. It works for Jamie though,' she said, pointing her stick at him.

Jamie nodded. 'You know I love it, Mrs Dunfreece.'

'Well, yes,' she said. 'Anyway, carry on, young lady.'

'I just wondered if there was anything your grandfather left or kept from the war. You see, a Land Girl went missing during that time, and I have a feeling this box is something to do with her. But whoever it was, they wrote about Gracemere. Might you know anything about that mystery?' By the way the older woman's eyebrows were knitted together, nothing seemed to be ringing a bell. So Laura continued. 'Or maybe something that would fit this key?' Laura pulled out the little key from her bag and handed it to the woman, who picked up her reading glasses and examined it carefully.

'I don't think so. I did keep a few things from that time when my father went away. I don't like to throw things out – you never know when you might need them. I have the odd thing.'

Laura thought that was an understatement.

'But nothing that would fit this key, I don't think. Although, if there's anything from that time, it would be in the attic. I haven't been up there for years, so you would have to be careful. But you're welcome to go up and have a look if you think there's anything up there that might help you with your mystery.'

Laura did not relish the thought of going through this woman's attic. It was bad enough walking through her house. She could only imagine what an attic would be like.

Jamie nodded, sensing her reluctance. 'I'd be happy to go into the attic. I love a good rummage.'

Mrs Dunfreece nodded. 'That would actually help me out. I have some photo albums up there I haven't seen for years, and I keep asking William to go up and get them but for some reason he's a little resistant. So maybe while you're up there you could get those down for me. They're in a wooden chest near the hatch.'

'Great,' said Jamie, 'more than happy to help. Where do we go?'

'Up the stairs, to the left of the landing you'll find the attic door. There're some ladders in the back garden and there's a torch in the kitchen, second drawer. I keep it just in case the electricity goes out,' she said. 'I do pay my bill, but you can't be too prepared.'

Jamie trotted off, and Laura gathered up the cups and nodded to the older lady. 'Thank you so much.'

'Like I said, I don't think you'll find anything up there, but you may as well have a look. My father's stuff is up in the far left-hand corner.'

Jamie arrived back with the ladder from the garden as Laura eventually found the torch under an assortment of clutter. The ladder looked rickety at best, and Laura looked at him imploringly. 'Are you sure you want to do this?' she hissed.

'Absolutely,' said Jamie, his eyes shining. 'This is the most excitement I've had in weeks.'

They made their way up the stairs, where they found the opening to the attic. Carefully climbing the creaking rungs, Jamie pushed on the attic door. It took him a while to move it. It obviously hadn't been opened for a long time.

Laura hung on to the ladder as he stepped inside. He shone the torch about, and then looked down. 'It's actually not too bad,' he reported. And then in a whisper, 'It's actually tidier up here than down there.'

Laura nodded and slowly followed him up the ladder. When she got inside, she was pleasantly surprised. Not only was the floor finished, she could actually stand up in the attic. The rafters looked fairly new. Maybe a new roof had been put on the house not long before?

They studied the attic. It was full of boxes and chests. Following Jamie to the corner that Mrs Dunfreece had indicated, she moved about and looked around. There was a lot.

'Do you think we're going to find anything here?' said Laura despondently.

'We won't know if we don't try.'

They started to search through the boxes. It looked as though nothing had ever been thrown out. Bed linens, tea towels, serviettes, tablecloths, a silver service, plates, dishes, spoons. Laura shook her head as she pulled out box after box and started to gently, carefully go through it.

They found the WWII box and started taking out item after item. An old gas mask, a stack of newspapers from that time. Blackout curtain fabric, a wartime cookbook, and then Jamie found a nondescript green canvas kit bag. It looked about the right period. He pulled out all the contents, some old clothes, but there was nothing obvious.

But Laura noticed something as he shone the torch around the bottom. She took it from him and, holding it up, looked at the outside. She had read about this in a book once. She turned to Jamie.

'Look,' she said, placing her hand inside and her other hand under the bag, 'this is a lot less deep than the bag itself. See, if you hold it up, there's another couple of inches.'

Jamie examined it. 'Oh yes, what does it mean?'

'I think it has a false bottom. There's room to hide something in a compartment.'

Jamie's eyes lit up. 'You're right, Watson. Do you think the murder weapon is concealed in there?'

Laura laughed but was carefully feeling around the bottom of the bag. 'Here,' she said. And Jamie shone the torch down to where she was insinuating.

Laura's heart skipped a beat as it lit what she had felt: a tiny hole just big enough for a thin screwdriver.

'Do you have anything that would fit that hole?'

He checked his pockets and pulled out his keys. Picking a slim key, he manoeuvred it in the gap. It took a couple of tries, but suddenly something shifted and the whole panel of the bottom of the bag lifted, revealing a flat metal tin nestled in the bottom.

'I believe we have found the treasure,' he whispered to Laura, so closely she felt the warmth of his breath on her cheek and for a moment it made her tingle.

She pushed down her brimming feelings and pulled out the little metal square tin. On the bottom were some words she couldn't make out. She turned it around in her hand until she found the keyhole. She beamed as she pulled out the key in her pocket and it fit perfectly into the lock. She could hardly stand the anticipation as she turned the key. Would there be another letter and more clues, or maybe the engagement ring her heart yearned for? Why had this all been so secretive? But she could hardly contain her disappointment when inside was only a battered hardback book.

'Oh,' she said, the disappointment obvious in her tone.

'Not exactly what I was expecting,' stated Jamie, voicing the words she was thinking.

Quickly, she flicked through the pages, then shook the book upside down, looking for a letter, a clue, something more. But it just seemed to be a nondescript copy of *The Old Curiosity Shop*.

20

NORTH SEA, 1941

Anya

Arriving at the rendezvous point, the submarine waited offshore in a remote part of the Scottish Isles. Nikolai and Anya paced nervously in front of the periscope, waiting for the code sign from the boat they were supposed to meet. When it came, the submarine glided to the surface, and Anya and Nikolai stepped out onto the deck, seeing the outside world for the first time in two days. The fresh air smelt so sweet to Anya. After being in the belly of the submarine with all its foulness, it felt luxurious to draw in a deep slow breath with all its cool crispness.

It was just before four o'clock in the morning and a long way from sunrise. Gathering their coats around their ears against the sharp North Sea wind, they peered out towards the black expanse of rugged shoreline as they steadied themselves on the rocking deck. A light flashed, two long sweeps from a beam to inform them that the boat to take them to shore was on the way.

It was cold, and Anya shivered and felt awkward in her new English clothes. Somehow, they didn't fit as well as her Russian ones. She wore a dark suit, and wool coat and leather gloves that matched the colour of her leather handbag and felt cloche hat.

Nikolai turned to her nervously. 'Here we go then, Anya.'

She looked over at him, thinking he looked handsome in his new British clothes, which included a grey fedora and trench coat, underneath that a dark suit, white shirt, and red-and-blue-striped tie. Feeling inside of his coat, he checked the travel papers they had been given to get to their handler in the south. They had spent the last night on the submarine going over their paperwork, counting out their money, and remembering their cover story to get them to Norfolk, where they were to be stationed. Their first contact should have travel tickets for them already purchased and any last instructions. They also went over their map, which would aid them from getting to the drop-off point to the train station. To divert suspicion, as they travelled together, they were to pretend to be a married couple on their journey, which with several changes would take them from Scotland to Norwich, where they would then change trains and head to Cromer and their contact. As they had sat on their bunk going over their plan, Nikolai had pulled out a thin band of gold from the packet that he had been given. Anya swore she saw his cheeks redden as he placed it on the third finger of her left hand.

'You should put this on now, so we don't forget,' he told her as she avoided eye contact as her own cheeks matched the colour of his.

She looked down at her fake wedding ring now and fiddled with it, trying to swallow down all the fear churning in her stomach. It had been one thing to make the decision and be brave enough to leave Russia. It was a different kind of braveness to walk into another country and spy for their enemy.

Before long, a tiny rowing boat made its way out to the submarine, and a tired-looking man in a worn fisherman sweater and a tight knit cap nodded to them.

'You'll be my passengers, then,' he croaked, showing blackened and broken teeth as he smiled. 'Didn't realize you'd be so pretty,' he said, nodding at Anya.

She swallowed down her anger at his forthrightness. Nikolai stepped in front of her and helped her down into the boat. The boatman nodded at the crewmember from the submarine and started to paddle towards the shore, slowly.

'Hopefully, you will put this right,' he murmured as he moved through the water. 'Stupid bloody war. Got to get Hitler over here fast so we can stop all this fighting. I don't really care who is in charge. Do you?' He seemed to be talking to himself more than asking them questions. Struggling to understand his strong Scottish accent, Anya sat staring silently at Nikolai, who just nodded in the man's direction to placate him.

As they got towards the shore, the dark rocks crowded above them as the white spray of the water rolled in, breaking at their base. Even in her coat, the wind, which was cool and sharp, began to penetrate straight through her clothes, and she wished she had more on her legs than just stockings.

It wasn't long before they arrived on shore, and the man gave them an envelope and wandered off before Nikolai and Anya had time to ask him any more. Nikolai opened the envelope. Inside were two train tickets, and a coded message about the train station. The message said it was about three miles away, so they started walking. It was hard, in the cold and dark, but Nikolai had his compass, and she had the map and a flashlight as they set off in the way they were meant to go, keeping away from the main roads, making their way across farmers' fields and through woodland. After a long walk, they finally made it to the station, just as day started to break.

Nervously, they played with their tickets as people around them glared at them with suspicion. Anya realized this was a small place, and seeing two strangers here was probably quite a curiosity. She and Nikolai had started speaking English before they'd left Russia, and as he guided her to the platform his hand pressed protectively on her back they slipped into their role. As they waited, they nodded and said good morning to people as they passed; Anya tried not to stare at the propaganda poster that warned about loose talk and also at the young British servicemen waiting to board the train.

When one old man approached them directly, she kept her head down and surveyed her shoes.

'Are you on your honeymoon?' he asked with a strong Scottish accent, looking warily at the pair of them.

Nikolai answered quickly before Anya could say anything, and, slipping his arm around her waist, he pulled her in close. 'How could you tell?' he said in his best Oxford English. 'We've been staying up here in a family cottage. All we've wanted to do is be together, didn't we, darling?'

She smiled nervously as the man nodded his understanding. When Nikolai kissed her gently on the cheek, she tried not to react with surprise. Even though it was the gentlest brush of his lips on her cheek, it felt so intimate and instantly caused her stomach to tighten. As much as she knew he was acting for this man, having Nikolai do that without warning sent a shudder down her spine. She had never even been kissed before, and even this fleeting intimacy heightened all of her senses.

He continued to hold her close, keeping his arm around her as people seemed to acknowledge their situation and relax. All the while she tried to fight the awareness of him being so close to her. She could smell his shaving soap, feel the strength of his arm around her, the edges and heat of his body pressed against her own and his breath warming her cheek.

'Good luck to you both. It's a nice time in your life. Shame you have a war to spoil it,' the man continued. 'So, I won't disturb you.' And as he walked off to the other end of the platform, the train arrived, screeching to a stop, steam rolling in billowing waves of acrid smoke.

They both got on and slipped into an empty carriage. Looking all around him, Nikolai let out a sigh of relief.

'That was close,' he whispered into her ear. 'I thought for a minute they'd figured us out. I'm guessing they don't see many strangers.'

She nodded, wondering if he'd felt any of the same sensations that she had. She wasn't about to tell him he'd been the very first man to kiss her, even on the cheek.

Anya settled herself down to look out the window as the train started to move towards the south. She was in awe of the beauty of the world outside, so different from Russia. She thought back to all the stories her mother had told her about England, the picture books, and the literature she'd read, and it all came to life beyond the window of the train. Anya realized at once that she'd never really believed that it really looked this way. It had been some sort of wonderland in her mind. But here it was, beautiful rolling hills, green grass, tiny cottages, burbling streams, and heather everywhere.

They didn't talk much on the way. Both were preoccupied with their own thoughts and nervous about speaking out loud. Even though they were in a closed carriage, they didn't want to be overheard. He had all their maps with him, and she sat nervously playing with the strap of her suitcase with all their important documents under a flap inside.

When they finally arrived in Norwich, the place they would change trains, the platform was heaving with British servicemen, and tearful wives, girlfriends, and family members. And her stomach tightened again with what they were there to do as they stood waiting to board another to Cromer, the place they had been told their contact lived. The next train was very crowded, and they sat opposite one another eying each other wearily as everyone chatted amongst themselves. It made her so homesick for her mother, hearing them use the exact phrases she remembered from her childhood.

Arriving at the station, they went to the seafront and looked for the name of the cottage they had been given, *Gracemere*. They eventually found it and, opening the little gate, they walked down the pathway and knocked on the door.

It was opened hastily, and a scruffy nervous-looking man peered out. 'Ah, yes,' he said in a clear tone. 'You must be the young couple coming to look at the room. Come in, come in, and I'll tell you all about it.'

They quickly moved inside, and once the man shut the door, his friendly tone disappeared and he turned out the hall light.

'Were you followed?' he hissed.

Nikolai shook his head. 'I don't think so. We were very careful. We followed all the instructions the way we were taught.'

'Come in, come quickly,' he snapped, moving swiftly down the hallway. 'I have all your papers here.'

The house was dingy, dark, and messy, and Anya had an uncomfortable feeling. When they'd left Russia as spies, she hadn't expected it to be like a novel. But this somehow felt amateurish; between the crazy boatman talking to himself and this man who was intense and angry, she was concerned for both her and Nikolai's safety. They stumbled into a room, and their host lit another dim light.

'Here are your fake birth certificates. From now on, you'll be known as Annie Stone. And this is for you, as Nicholas Brown. You are not serving in the army because you have been listed as having flat feet. Here is a story created about your lives in case people ask questions. You should read it, memorize it, and then destroy it.'

He continued, staring at the pair of them intently.

'Your handler runs a photographer's shop in the closest village to the manor and his brother owns a bookshop there. You will pass information through the bookshop. There will be a book by Charles Dickens called *The Old Curiosity Shop*. Tell him you are looking for Charles Dickens's most unpopular book and he will take you to it. If it is safe to drop and receive messages, the book will be out of place on the shelf below. If for any reason it is not safe, it shall be placed in its rightful place in alphabetical order. Do you understand? Each week you will receive instructions from your handler in the photo shop, and each week you will pass on information through the bookshop. Is that clear?'

They both nodded.

'Annie, we have two big airbases here that have been gearing up since before the war. Your main job will be to count planes and keep an eye on their coming and going from one of those airbases, especially Coltishall, which is very close to the manor. You will record the total number of planes you spot weekly and update us. This is why we want you outside working as a Land Girl. It is a large base for Hurricanes and we want to know the extent of their forces and if you see any escalation of activity, which could signal an invasion is imminent. Nick, your job is to work inside the house. As I'm sure you have been briefed, Lord Sinclair is a member of the House of Lords and great friend of Mr Churchill and supporter of the government. He often has meetings and dinner parties, which members of the cabinet attend out here at his manor, which is seen to be a safe space away from London. Your job is to listen to what is being said carefully and also, whenever you get a chance, to take photographs of any important documentation in Sinclair's office. Dates, times, and relevant information. He is away three days a week in London, so it should be possible. Here is a new microfilm camera to use. Have you been trained in how to use one?' Nikolai nodded and slipped the camera into his pocket. 'Be very careful and only take photographs when you feel it is safe. We don't expect the cabinet to be talking about top-secret missions over the dinner table, but there is a lot that can be gleaned from conversations about where they think we are in the war and the odd comment from friends when tongues have been loosened by wine and brandy. You will both do a weekly drop at the handlers'. Photographs at the camera shop and any information from the dinner parties and troop movements at the bookshop.'

He stared at them both for a moment before nodding and giving them their papers. Teasing out a breath he must have been holding, he lit a cigarette, offering them one. They both shook their heads.

'Well, you're not exactly what I expected – you're much younger – but hopefully that will stop you both from arousing suspicion. Now, you'll go separately to the manor so as not to attract attention. Our contact in the office of the Land Girls has secured your placement, Annie, and you will leave here soon. And, Nick, you'll stay here and go to the house a couple of days after that. Have you got all of that?'

She looked across at Nick, fingering her case. It would be the first time they had been apart since they had started training and it made her nervous. Could she do this alone? She wasn't sure, but girding herself with a deep breath, she prepared for her mission ahead, though she wasn't looking forward to the experience in the slightest.

21

NORFOLK, PRESENT DAY

Laura

Removing their haul from the attic, including the requested stack of photo albums, Jamie and Laura made their way downstairs. Mrs Dunfreece was eager to see what they had found, but turned up her nose when Jamie revealed the kit bag and the battered Charles Dickens book.

'Oh, *that* old thing? That bag has been knocking around for years.' The older woman sniffed, eyeing their find. 'And what's this?' she asked, taking the book from Jamie and turning it over in her hand. She didn't look very impressed. 'Well, this is just an old book,' she added. 'I've been meaning to get rid of stuff like that, but life always seems to be just too busy,' she concluded, picking up another one of her cats and stroking him as he kneaded her lap and purred his content.

'Would you mind if we took it?' asked Laura. 'I would be willing to pay you for it.'

Mrs Dunfreece's eyes lit up for the first time since they had arrived.

Laura gave her a price, which she was sure was much more

than the bag was worth, but knew, because of the key and the book, this had to be an important part of the mystery.

'Well, of course, if you love it that much, you are welcome to it. It's not cheap, taking care of my little furry family. I would welcome the money. Is there anything else you might like?' she asked enthusiastically, nodding to the piles around her.

'No, this is all I want,' Laura replied. 'Perhaps it can help solve the story of why someone hid the key. Just as long as you don't need it?'

'No, I don't need it.' Mrs Dunfreece sniffed dismissively as she attempted to pick off the many cat hairs that clung to her clothes.

'Great, thank you,' Laura said, handing the older woman some crisp new banknotes from her purse.

Jamie placed the book back in the bag and pulled out his car keys. 'We really should be going. Is there anything I can do for you before we leave?' Jamie asked.

'No, dear,' she said, tapping the albums he had just brought down. 'I'm just going to sit here and visit with some of my older relations for a while.'

He nodded. 'Take care of yourself and all your little family.'

'Oh, I will,' said Mrs Dunfreece, struggling to her feet to see them out and shooing away Jamie, who attempted to help her up. 'And you make sure you take care of my house.'

'Yes, I will.'

'And don't forget to pay me on time,' she added, with mock sternness.

'I will try my best.'

The two of them left the house, followed by two more cats that came out the door with them.

'They're okay,' she shouted after Jamie. 'They like to have a walk about now.'

As Laura made her way back to the car, she wanted to go home and have another shower, order her mind, sit in the garden, and watch the frogs in the pond. Anything to get away from the feeling generated by such prolific clutter.

When they got back in the car, Jamie paused for a moment. 'I wonder what secrets that book holds.'

'I don't know, but someone went to a lot of trouble to make sure it was where it was at a given time.'

Now outside in the light, Laura examined the book more closely too. It seemed barely read, some of the pages not even cut correctly and still joined together. Only the middle seemed to have had attention. There were a couple of pages in there that showed some wear, creased in places that warped it slightly. 'It is a little disheartening. This is the first breakthrough we've had and I feel none the wiser.'

'Do you think it was Annie's?' asked Jamie as he started the car.

'There's no way to know for sure, but at the same time, I can't see why it wouldn't be. It's not from the manor, I don't think. As there is already a copy of this book from there on Simon's bookshelf, and that one has the manor's stamp in the front. But if she wrote the note before she left and then placed this key in the cigarette case, the book has to be significant.'

'Maybe a birthday present for a friend who liked mysteries, perhaps?' Jamie suggested as he pulled the car out onto the road.

'I don't think so. The fact the note says "Gracemere is our only hope" sounds a little more desperate than that. As though this book held the key to something that would give someone else the hope they needed. That doesn't sound like just a birthday gift.'

'So maybe there used to be something else in the book that isn't there now?' asked Jamie as he turned onto the main road and started to head towards the manor.

'Maybe,' said Laura. 'Here in the middle, where there's some use. But if the key was always buried in the manor garden, this book would be just as it was left. Unless someone had another key? Otherwise, there must be something about the book itself.'

'*The Old Curiosity Shop?*' Jamie said wistfully. 'Have you read it?

'No, have you?'

Jamie shook his head.

'But I intend to.' She beamed. 'In fact, I intend to read this copy and see what jumps out to me.'

Arriving back at the manor, and reluctant to say goodbye to Jamie's company, she suddenly had an idea. She turned to him. 'We need to celebrate.' He looked surprised, but enthusiastic, as she continued, 'If it wasn't for you, I wouldn't have found this. I want to make a picnic and watch the sunset, if you'd like to join me? Though I don't have anything to drink.'

'I would love to,' responded Jamie. 'I'll run out and get us a bottle of wine if that's what you would like.'

She nodded as she got out and he started the car. She felt a twinge of joy for the first time in a long time. Waving to him from the door, Laura followed the sight of Jamie's little car beetling off down the driveway. Feeling excited, she went inside to prepare the picnic.

In the kitchen, Alicia was piecing together some cracked china with glue on the kitchen table. 'Don't look,' she said, with great drama. 'It will probably break your heart.'

Laura smiled. She loved being around her friend again.

'What have you done, Alicia?'

'Only broken some old china. It's probably four hundred years old or something, knowing the pieces that Simon likes to collect. I was up in the dining room getting some cleaning done, and I just happened to knock the shelf and down came this ornate beautiful plate, and now I'm sticking it back together before Simon sees it.'

Laura started to laugh. She suddenly remembered their

university days and how Alicia often broke things. 'I think he's going to notice, Alicia,' she said, looking at the terrible job she was doing of it. 'There are people who can repair this. You don't have to do this.'

Alicia sighed. 'You're probably right. I'll call someone, later. You seem very happy,' she added as she looked up at her friend and placed the china into a box.

'I think I found another clue about Annie and I'm very excited about it.'

'Oh, the disappearing Land Girl? Are you sure she didn't just run away and join the circus?'

'I don't think so,' laughed Laura.

'Are you sure this is the way you want to be spending your time? Wouldn't you rather be on a dating app, trying to find some gorgeous man to have a fling with so you can put the memory of that rat of a boyfriend behind you?'

'It's a good distraction for me, like a hobby. You know, like yours is breaking plates. But I also feel compelled to get to the bottom of this...'

Alicia looked across at her friend, and her eyes grew serious. 'Is this a little bit to do with Katie?' Her tone moved from playful to tender.

Laura looked out of the window, not wanting to meet her friend's gaze; that would only encourage the pressure in her chest, which was bursting with the pain she still felt.

'I know I'm being silly, but what if this is a solution? What if solving this can somehow set me free, from the guilt. Maybe I will feel a little better about what I did...' Her voice trailed away and Alicia pulled her in for a hug.

'Then you must do it. Fate has a way of bringing things into our path that are important.'

'I agree. This might sound dramatic, but this feels like part of my destiny, something I am supposed to do.'

Alicia nodded and moved to the kettle. 'I think it's time for a cup of tea. And then, I think we should get you on that dating app.'

'You might not need to,' said Laura with a coy smile.

'Really?' said Alicia, looking intrigued.

'Because I already have a date.'

'*A date?*' asked her friend incredulously.

'Not really like a *date* date. I mean, just, I have a friend coming over. We're going to go and have a picnic in the garden.'

'The friend?'

'Jamie.'

'The artist you met at the beach? I wondered about him. You didn't say very much about him at the time.'

'Yeah, I like him.'

'Like him? Or "*like him*"?' interrogated Alicia, adding air quotes to her words.

'I'm not sure yet,' she chuckled. 'My heart is way too broken to think about that. It's just too early. We're just going to have a picnic in the garden, that's all.'

'A picnic in the garden at sunset sounds romantic,' said Alicia thoughtfully. 'That sounds as if it is "*like him.*"' She did the air quotes again.

'You're incorrigible,' replied Laura. She swept towards the fridge to look for something to eat. 'What have we got that I can take with me?'

'It depends on what your plans are,' responded Alicia with a smirk. 'We've got chicken, but maybe you're looking more for oysters,' she said, grabbing her friend's waist playfully.

'Stop it, otherwise I'm not going to tell you any more.'

'Okay,' said Alicia. 'I'll stop as long as you don't spare me any of the juicy details!'

The two of them laughed together as they assembled a picnic basket: the chicken, a beautiful French baguette she had bought the day before, some pâté, a little wooden chopping board, some vintage cheeses, and apples. Alicia gave her a jar of her homemade pickles, and they finished it up with some salad and two slices of cheesecake.

'Well, that looks good,' said Alicia as she added cutlery and plates to Laura's basket. 'Do you want to take the dogs with you?' she said, smiling. 'Or will they kill the mood?'

Laura shook her head. 'You're killing the mood right now,' she said sarcastically.

Suddenly the bell rang to the main door.

'That will be your potential fling,' said Alicia, her eyes shining with anticipation as she poured herself a cup of tea. 'I'd pour you one, but I suppose you want to get going.'

Laura hugged her friend. 'Thank you, you will always be my most favourite friend in Norfolk.'

'I also happen to be your only friend in Norfolk,' Alicia shouted after her as Laura left the kitchen and walked to the front door to meet Jamie.

22

NORWICH STATION, 1941

Anya

'So, you're going to Hatworth, then?' a breezy voice said behind her. The whole of Anya's body became rigid as she turned to face another passenger standing on the platform. The woman was curvy, a few inches taller with brown eyes, dark curly hair and the sweetest smile. She was young, about the same age as Anya, with a friendly demeanour that was warm and inviting. She repeated her words, obviously thinking that Anya hadn't heard her. 'You're going to Hatworth, right?' Anya still didn't answer but gave her a nervous grin.

The girl started to laugh. 'I suppose you're wondering how I knew that. I'm not a mind reader, in case you were worried. All your secrets are safe.' She pointed at Anya's luggage. 'You've got a label on there as I have, look.'

Anya looked down at the young woman's suitcase, and there, indeed, was the label, identical to her own, which her handler had given her, with the words '*Hatworth Manor*' written on it. Anya let out the breath she'd been holding.

'Are you going to be a Land Girl as well?' the young woman asked.

Anya nodded, relieved. For a minute, she thought she'd done something unpardonable, something that had stuck out. The one thing she had learned as a spy was she didn't want anyone to know what she was doing, even if it was innocent. She had to keep herself to herself, which was difficult for Anya, as she'd always been a warm person who loved chatting and being with people. But here, it was different. She was the enemy.

'My name's Millie, by the way,' said her new acquaintance, offering her hand. Anya remembered her etiquette: she should shake hands gently, but not for too long. She smiled as she did.

'Annie.'

'Looking forward to being a Land Girl, are you?'

Anya nodded, now relaxed.

'Doing our bit,' Millie added.

Anya felt confused. She'd never heard her mother use an expression like that.

'For England, you know?' added Millie, finishing her sentence.

'Ah, yes,' said Anya. 'Doing our bit,' she repeated, memorizing the expression.

The train puffed into the station and screeched to a halt. Plumes of smoke and the acrid smell wafted out onto the platform to greet them.

'Come on,' encouraged Millie. 'We may as well sit together if we're going to the same place. We can get to know each other. I don't know anybody there, and I'm guessing neither do you.'

Anya shook her head and felt her chest tighten. This would be the first time she would have to lie about who she was, and she was worried that she wouldn't get all of her cover story right. She'd hoped to have her own thoughts to go over it before she got to the manor. But, she realized, she was going to be thrown right into it.

Millie stepped up onto the train, moving through it until she found an empty carriage.

'Here we go,' she said in a singsong way over her shoulder, 'nobody in here. Means we can have a good natter.'

Anya's heart sank. The last thing she wanted to do was have a natter, whatever that was. She realized straightaway that it would be very different talking English here than the way her mother had taught her to speak it. She would have to go with her intuition on what things meant, and she really didn't want to have to talk about herself much. She had her story memorized, but she was worried that somebody would ask too many questions to something she didn't know.

She needn't have worried though, as Millie took up all the air in the carriage once they settled themselves. She was quite a talkative person, and Anya was relieved, smiling and nodding in the appropriate places, or what she thought were the appropriate places. Millie seemed oblivious. She seemed quite a simple soul. She loved her family and her brother had already signed up, and she also wanted to do something for the war.

'I helped my dad a lot in his garden, and I did love being out there, so I thought the Land Girls were for me. Never been over this way though. Have you?' she asked, looking out of the window at the view. Anya shook her head and tried not to fidget in her clothes. The skirt she'd been given was very tight and she wasn't used to being this warm. Even in February, she felt warm. The hat on her head felt peculiar, and this shirt just felt as though it was buttoned up too tightly. She missed her own clothes. Everything about this was awkward. She just hoped it didn't show on her face.

Millie had said something, and she'd missed it.

'Well, do you?' she said.

'I'm sorry. I was miles away,' responded Anya.

'I said, "Do you want a sandwich?" My mom packed the basket before I left. I've got meat paste, country pickle, and Scotch eggs. I think she was worried I was going to starve. She thought I was going off to a work camp or something. Did you want anything?'

Anya shook her head. Then added, remembering British people were always overly polite, 'I'm fine, thank you.' She must admit she was starving, but she didn't like the sound of any of that food, not remembering any of the names from her mother's table, and she was frightened to sample them for the first time with someone watching her.

It wasn't long before they got to Hatworth, and a young man in baggy work trousers and a flat cap was there at the station to meet them.

'You two will be coming with me.' He smiled. 'Can't get the petrol coupons, apart from for the lord's Daimler, of course. So, I'm afraid it's a horse and cart for you girls,' he said, winking at Millie, who blushed. She seemed to like the look of this young man and he was obviously flirting with her, Anya noted.

'You the lord of the manor, then?' joked Millie, with a bob of her head.

'Nothing so grand for me,' he responded, grinning. 'My name's Charlie. I just take care of the horses.'

'I love horses,' Millie added with a coy grin. 'Are you all set, Annie?' Millie called out over her shoulder as Anya climbed in the back of the cart and sat on the old sacks piled up there.

'Yes,' she responded, tugging at her uncomfortable wool skirt again.

Charlie helped Millie onto the rig, placing her by his side.

As they trotted along, Millie continued talking, telling Charlie all about herself; Anya found it very helpful without the pressure to answer. Millie was from a place called Birmingham, and the same age as Anya, twenty-two. Anya was intrigued by the way they bantered back and forth, teasing one another. And she enjoyed the singsong cadence of both their accents.

She was also awestruck by the beautiful countryside around her. England was breathtaking even with the constant presence of the war all around them.

'Did you hear what he said?' Millie asked, breaking into her thoughts. 'Charlie thinks we'll be bunked together. That would be great, wouldn't it, Annie?'

Anya smiled, nodding, noting the word 'great' in Millie's sentence, but had no idea what 'bunked' meant.

Millie seemed oblivious to Anya's lack of understanding. And Anya felt relieved. As long as she remained quiet, she could be perceived as shy. Fortunately, Millie was exactly the kind of person she needed in her life.

Arriving at the manor, Anya was stunned by the sight of it as the cart bounced down the long driveway towards the beautiful Regency building. Millie echoed her thoughts. 'Wow, this is a bit posh,' she said. 'Didn't realize we'd be going so upmarket. I hope they've got the blue room ready for us.'

Charlie grinned, 'Not for you, my dear. You'll be in the red room, I'm afraid. That's where we put all the naughty duchesses.'

Millie punched him playfully on the arm. 'Get away with you. But, seriously, will we be staying here?'

'I think so. It's been tough to get the staff, and there's a lot of room available right now in the servant quarters. They talked about putting the Land Girls in there. There's some more arriving next week. Not quite the blue room, but I think it's clean and dry. And if you have any problems, I can always pop over there and tuck you in.'

'Oh go on with you!' Millie said, nudging their new friend playfully as she blushed again.

As Charlie drew the horse to a stop outside the door, a young woman was waiting at the entrance. She was willowy and tall and moved at a clip as she swished towards them. Her blonde hair was cut into a fashionable bob and her lively green eyes were warm and inviting. In her hand, she had a notebook and pen. She greeted them enthusiastically.

'Welcome to Hatworth! I'm Rebecca Sinclair. I'm the daughter of Lord and Lady Sinclair; we own this property. It's been in our family for eons. It's all very grand, but you'll find we are very down to earth. We are not really into all the pomp and ceremony, so feel free to call Mother and Father by their first names, Sarah and Thomas, and you can call me Becca. My father is very busy in the House of Lords at the moment with the war and everything and my mother is often in London tied up with war work too. Which leaves me here to keep things ticking over.

'We're so excited to be providing food for the village, to help out with the rationing. So we are grateful to get your help with all the extra planting that will need doing.'

Getting down from the cart, Millie shook her hand tentatively, and so did Anya as they introduced themselves.

'I hope you really enjoy it here,' Becca enthused. 'It is tremendous for us to see some new faces. We've seen so many people leave because of this blasted war. It makes a nice change. Now, let me get you settled in. The local office for the Land Girls has me in charge of you both, so you can come to me with any questions. Our head gardener is going to help you out with what your daily duties will be. But I'm here to help in any other way.' She strode away, her long arms swishing by her sides as she pressed forward towards the manor.

She took them in through the back door, where she introduced them to the cook, Mrs Barton, a rotund woman with rosy cheeks, and two of the kitchen girls. They all wore crisp white aprons and caps and were busy working around a large wooden table and nodded to them as they entered. The food they were preparing smelt delicious, and Anya's stomach growled in response. She still hadn't eaten since some greasy sausage and bread at the safe house.

'I'll get you settled in,' continued Becca, and then, as if hearing Anya's thoughts, added, 'and then please come down and get something to eat if you're hungry. I believe there's some cheese and bread in the refrigerator for you both that Mrs Barton put aside, in case you hadn't eaten.'

Anya breathed a sigh of relief. Bread and cheese, she understood.

Becca led them along a dark hallway and up a long set of stairs that creaked with age. 'Our maids are normally up here. We're now down to just four, so we have so many rooms spare that it seems silly to put you out in the stables or somewhere else. You might as well stay in the house with us.' She moved down the corridor until she came to a door. 'We thought we'd put you two together in here for company. I think it's friendlier when there's two of you, don't you?'

Millie nodded enthusiastically, and Anya sighed reluctantly. She had been hoping for her own room, but she wasn't going to make a fuss.

Becca opened the door. The room was relatively small with two beds, but there was a lovely view of the gardens. It was clean, simply decorated with a small wardrobe in the corner and a dark brown chest of drawers with a mirror squeezed between the beds. A pile of crisp white sheets and a grey woollen blanket were folded up on the end of the grey mattresses. On the beds were a pile of clothes.

'Here are your outfits,' Becca said. 'They're quite strict about the Land Girls' outfits, so you need to wear them, I'm afraid. Not that attractive, but what can I say?'

Millie held up the dark olive-green rib jumper.

'Very stylish,' she said sarcastically.

'I know,' responded Becca, wrinkling up her nose. 'You haven't even seen the trousers yet.'

'We have trousers?' said Millie with excitement. 'I have never ever worn trousers.'

'You might not be so excited when you see them.' Becca held up a pair of beige knickerbockers and long fawn-coloured socks. 'You have to wear the socks and the trousers together tucked in, I'm afraid. Not the most flattering. I have a picture somewhere I'll sort out and show you, and there's a tie and a hat too.'

Millie began to laugh. 'We'll be done up like a dog's dinner, won't we, Annie?'

Anya smiled. Another expression she didn't understand but guessed it meant something funny.

'I'll let you get settled in,' Becca said, bounding out of the room. 'You can call me anytime if you need to chat about anything. My room is on the second floor, but I'll be around most days in the library, as I also help manage the estate for my dad. Oh, and by the way, we have a dance next week to raise money for the Spitfire fund. Everybody's invited, including you, of course. I can't wait to see you there.'

Millie glowed. As Becca left, Millie turned to Anya, throwing her brown felt hat down onto the bed and unbuttoning her heavy wool coat. 'Not bad, hey, girl? We seemed to have landed on our feet, and a dance as well. Hopefully, I'll get a chance to meet that Charlie again, maybe get to dance with him.' She nudged Anya with a giggle. Anya was taken by surprise by the gesture but nodded. 'So now, unless you've got a sweetheart hiding somewhere you haven't told me about, all we've got to do is find you a nice chap as well.'

Anya shook her head. 'No, no sweetheart at the moment,' she commented flatly. But as they started to unpack, she thought again about Nikolai, and how she actually missed him, and how kind he had been to her on the submarine.

23

HATWORTH MANOR, PRESENT DAY

Laura

Jamie stood on the doorstep with a smile, holding up an icy bottle of Pinot Grigio. Grabbing a blanket, the basket, and some candles, Laura headed out onto the estate, Jamie by her side.

'Have you got anywhere in mind?' he asked, looking around in awe.

'I'm going to show you what I've been doing for the last few months.'

'Perfect,' he murmured.

At the walled garden, she ducked under the wisteria and, taking the key from her pocket, pulled back the ivy, revealing the door in the wall.

'A secret garden!' exclaimed Jamie in a fascinated whisper as she nodded.

Turning the key and pushing open the heavy door, she gave him a little history of its past, finishing with, 'I've been working for the last two months to restore it. Unfortunately, it's been rather neglected for a long time.'

Jamie stepped inside and looked around. She could tell he

was impressed. And she had to admit, it did look at its most lovely in the twilight. The peonies were just starting to push up through the soil and the early spring roses were beginning to bud.

'This is breathtaking,' he finally said. 'You've been doing all this?'

Laura nodded and led him past the fountain to the scalloped lawn. She unfolded the blanket close to the pond so they could get a central view while they ate. Around the lawn, tulips and crocuses were just finishing, but the scent was sweet and intoxicating, along with the evening primroses and the lilac trees that surrounded the area. The whole garden was awash with the smell of spring.

Jamie sprawled out on the blanket and looked around him. 'I'd love to paint in here, Laura, if you would let me.'

'Of course, you can keep me company, along with all the furry creatures that share this space with me.'

She unpacked the picnic basket and they settled down to enjoy the food and the beauty all around them. But their conversation soon turned to the book, which Laura had brought with her.

'So, what are you going to do now you've got it?'

'I'm not sure,' responded Laura. 'I know it's important, but I don't know why.'

'Can you check for anything else in it?' he suggested. 'A folded page, an underlined word? Something highlighted?'

'I wish,' she responded as she flicked gently through the pages again, then examined the cover, which was a greyish blue with a red and blue spine. The only unusual feature she could see was that the inside cover had a lovely pen and ink drawing of a church. 'Unfortunately, there's nothing that stands out.' She tipped the book upside down once more to demonstrate. 'I have already done a lot of research, but until just a few days ago I was looking for Grace as a person – it was no wonder I couldn't find her. Now we don't know who the note and the key were for, but think it may have been Annie the Land Girl who disappeared. I'm going to start to read this book tomorrow and also want to learn everything I can about the Land Girls and start a new search. I do have this photo of her.'

Laura scrolled through her phone until she found the photo she had snapped at the old gardener's house and showed it to Jamie.

He peered at it.

'She's quite lovely, isn't she?' Laura noted.

'She is,' he agreed thoughtfully as he tilted his head to the side. 'She doesn't look totally English though, maybe has some Slavic roots? I have some Czech relatives. They have a similar look.'

Laura studied the photo again. She hadn't thought about it before, but now that he mentioned it, Annie did have a slight Eastern European look to her features, around the eyes.

She handed him a slice of Brie, and he pulled off a crust of the French bread and then poured them both two glasses of golden-coloured wine.

Laura sighed with contentment. It felt good to just be enjoying the garden, sharing it with someone. Far away, an owl gently hooted and the frogs began their nightly ritual. She looked over at Jamie, who had his eyes closed to enjoy the last rays of sunlight that stretched across his face. Laura noted again how handsome he was and wondered about the ex-wife he had mentioned.

As if reading her mind, he responded, 'This is so wonderful. My ex-wife would have hated this. She wasn't really into nature. She preferred an expensive meal out to a picnic. But this is so much more me,' he added, taking a sip from his glass.

'Was it a recent split?' asked Laura, trying to sound nonchalant and not convey her eagerness to know every detail.

'A few years ago,' answered Jamie. 'Apparently being

married to an artist can have its drawbacks.' He spoke the words without malice, in a matter-of-fact way. 'We were just two very different people,' he added as he stretched out on the blanket and grabbed a drumstick from the basket, his eyes meeting her own in an intense gaze. 'What about you, Laura? Is there someone in your life right now?'

Laura swallowed down hard a piece of cheese she had been chewing. Was there someone in her life right now? How would she talk about Liam? She decided she didn't want to tell him about her past just yet, and besides, it wasn't lying to say there wasn't someone in her life. Hadn't she finished with him before she left London?

She shook her head. 'No one at the moment,' she confirmed, and hoped he didn't hear the unconvincing undertone in her voice. It felt uncomfortable saying that for the first time to somebody new. She and Liam had been together for so long. To say that out loud to him made her feel lonely all of a sudden, adrift somehow.

A curious robin hopped across the grass looking for worms. Jamie threw a few breadcrumbs, and it greedily snatched them up and flew away. 'What made you decide to restore this particular garden? You're a long way from home.'

She hesitated for only a moment before answering. 'I needed to get out of London for a while and it has been wonderful to spend time with two of my dearest friends, who live here.'

'That's nice. You have a lovely job.'

She agreed.

They took a break from eating, and before it got too dark, she took him on a tour of the garden, leading him past the apple tree and around to the new herbaceous border she had planted. A lazy bee seeking spring nectar hovered past and she showed Jamie her work on the little bridge and the pond. Now it was warming up, she would get fish for it the following week. They finally headed to the corner where the willow tree still lay on its side, roots roughly splayed into the air. She had cut back the brambles but hadn't had a chance to remove the willow or replace it yet with a new one she had ordered. Laura showed him where she'd found the key.

'There may have been a connection with this tree,' Jamie said thoughtfully as he smoothed his hand along the upturned trunk. 'Willow trees have always been a fascination for me. They're a wonderful hiding place and are symbolic of overcoming adversity,' he continued wistfully. 'Even the weeping willow grows upward.'

She reflected on his words. 'They're also a symbol of new life,' Laura added. 'A cane from a willow tree can be placed in the ground and a tree will grow up from it.'

'So its story can continue, but rooted in new life,' he added, and she nodded. Jamie continued, 'There must have been some understanding between Annie, whoever the person that the message was intended for, and also Mrs Dunfreece's father, who lived in my cottage at the time. It's strange to think that Annie could have visited my home that has kept her secret for all these years.'

'Do you know what happened to Mrs Dunfreece's father, during the war years?' Laura asked. 'She hinted at it, but didn't elaborate.'

'Only bits and pieces that I've picked up in snippets of conversation. Apparently, he did something illegal during that time that sent him to jail. Something quite shameful, as neither her nor William, her son, will talk about it. She had been sent away to stay with an aunt after her mother had been killed in an air raid, and he lived at Gracemere alone when it occurred. Apparently, it was very hard for her after he was convicted. She was an only child with no mother or father and only an indifferent aunt to take care of her. She told me once in a moment of vulnerability that her childhood had been painfully lonely. It's no wonder she likes to hold on to things and feels so close to her cats.'

They finished their tour of the garden, and, grabbing the basket, he followed Laura up the rope ladder into the little tree-house to eat their dessert. She lit vanilla candles and the light bounced off the eaves, waltzing their shadows across the walls of the little Victorian-styled building, sheltering them from the evening chill as they continued to talk into the evening with ease. He told her all about his brother and the many adventures they'd been on together. And she talked about her own family, being very careful to sidestep anything about Katie or Liam. She wasn't sure why she didn't want to tell him about these parts of her life. But she knew she just wanted to enjoy this precious moment in time without the hundreds of questions that always followed whenever she opened up about Katie's tragic death. Also, her heart was still raw about Liam and she didn't want to spoil this lovely evening by potentially spending the rest of the night sobbing on his shoulder about it all.

All at once, the wind gusted through the tiny room, flickering the candles and rattling the little blue shutters. She shivered and he slipped off his jacket and placed it around her shoulders. It felt the most natural thing in the world to let him wrap it around her, still warm from the heat of his body and carrying the scent of his aftershave. She breathed in the mixture of leather and orange with an undertone of spicy ginger. She felt such ease around Jamie that she wasn't even sure if this was a date. It was as though they had known each other for a lifetime. He was already so familiar to her.

They got down from the treehouse and as they arrived at the gate, she turned to say something to him, and he bumped into her and his lips brushed against her cheek. He stopped short, his face inches from her own. Then, ever so gently and slowly, he caressed her cheek with his fingertips, then, holding her chin, drew her in for a kiss.

His lips were soft and warm and the kiss so sensuous it felt like it enveloped her whole body. Long and lingering yet heartfelt and deep, the experience lit her up inside, making her head spin. Trying to regain her equilibrium, Laura drew a breath and the whole experience was enhanced by the scent of his gingery orange aftershave mixed with the warm, sweet, evocative fragrance of an early flowering honeysuckle that was planted by the gate. She had never experienced a kiss so slow and gentle that had drawn such a strong reaction from her. It was so different to kissing Liam, the only man she had kissed for almost as long as she could remember. Liam's kisses were active, sometimes passionate, but all about moving things to the next level, as though their lovemaking was on some sort of deadline. Jamie's kiss was the opposite. She could feel him giving himself completely to the experience. It was all about the richness and deepness of this moment in time. Laura just wanted to melt right into him and live there for the rest of her life. As he finally pulled away from her, her knees became weak and she reached out and steadied herself against the door. Instantly she felt alone, wanting desperately to be close to him again.

He looked over at her a little sheepishly. 'I'm sorry, I don't know what came over me. It just felt right.'

Laura shook her head. 'No, don't apologize. It was lovely. I wasn't expecting it, so it kind of took my breath away.'

'I know what you mean. It was meant to be just a friendly *"thank you for the picnic"* kiss, but I felt it too, something unexpected. I think it's some sort of garden magic.' His face lit up with that thought. And she believed it.

Hand in hand, they made their way through the estate and back to the cottage.

He lingered on the doorstep. 'You know, they say the weather is going to be nice over the next couple of days. If it's not inconvenient, I would love to bring my easel over and maybe paint in the walled garden, tomorrow?'

'That would be wonderful,' she said. 'I'll check that's okay with Simon – he's the estate manager – but I can't see why it would be a problem.' She tried to sound casual, though her insides were screaming 'Yes!'

Just then the front door opened and both dogs flew out into the garden. Light poured out of the house towards them, and Alicia was silhouetted in the doorway. She stepped back into the light and looked a little taken aback but delighted by the scene of the two of them so close together.

'This is my friend Alicia,' Laura said, quickly stepping away from Jamie, now awkwardly aware she was still wearing his jacket.

Alicia leaned forward and shook Jamie's hand. 'Very nice,' remarked Alicia, drawing out the words as she scanned him up and down.

Jamie blushed with her apparent reference to his looks and centred on fussing with the dogs, who were giving him their full attention.

'She doesn't have a lot of subtlety,' responded Laura bluntly as she handed him back his jacket.

Jamie laughed nervously. 'I should go. I need to get home. Maybe tomorrow, Laura?'

'Yes, tomorrow sounds wonderful. Just come by any time around ten. I should be in the garden by then.'

Jamie got into his car, and they both watched him drive away.

'Not bad, Laura, and he's going to come to the garden tomorrow?' Alicia said, raising an eyebrow.

'He wants to do some painting.'

'*Painting?*' echoed Alicia, with emphasis. 'Is that what it's called now?'

'You are the worst tease in the world.'

'I could always pop over and do some weeding. Do you need a chaperone?'

'No, we'll be fine, thank you,' she laughed.

As Laura went to bed that night, her thoughts ran over and over in a loop, reliving all of their conversations, his smile, that kiss. All enhanced by the intoxicating experience of the garden in the early evening light. She thought about the willow and new life. Everything fragranced by the scent of his spicy orange aftershave, which still clung lightly to her skin. As she drifted off to sleep, she wondered if finally she was ready to put the past behind her and move on into her future. She didn't have the slightest idea that by the next morning the whole of her life would be in turmoil.

24

HATWORTH MANOR, FEBRUARY 1941

Anya

Anya woke with a jolt and tried to remember where she was. The room was dark and smelt slightly damp. There was only a chink of light coming into the bedroom from underneath the blackout curtains, and she could hear somebody else breathing next to her. She knew she needed to be on heightened alert, but she wasn't sure why. Then she remembered she was in England. She was actually going to spy on Russia's enemies, and it felt terribly real now she was here.

As her eyes started to acclimate to the dark, she realized her throat was dry and her mouth parched. She would creep down and get some water from the kitchen. Slipping on her dressing gown and slippers, she made her way out of the room and down the stairs.

The hardest part of this mission for her so far was just how friendly everyone had been. When she'd been preparing in Russia, there'd been so much propaganda about the enemy. But now she was here, everyone reminded her of her mother. These people were kind and sweet to her, thoughtful, looking out for her. And her stomach started to cramp with fear about what she had to do.

She also felt incredibly lonely without Nikolai. As much as they'd had their disagreements during their training and she had been so preoccupied with her home life, she had come to rely on him, the only person in this country who knew who she was and why she was here. And it felt isolating and lonely without him.

Finishing her glass of water, she looked out of the window. The sun was starting to rise, and the garden was beginning to come into view. A hazy blue dawn made everything look cool and beautiful. It was such a lovely estate. She thought about her home in Russia in communal housing. It was so stark and cold compared to the beauty of this land.

She made her way upstairs. And as she opened the door, she must have awoken Millie because she turned over in her bed and yawned.

'Morning, Annie,' she said in a cheerful tone. 'You're awake early.'

Anya slipped back into bed and nodded. 'I just got some water. I needed something to drink.'

'You should have put the kettle on,' she said with a smile. 'Mrs Barton told us to help ourselves. I'm desperate for a cup of tea. I'll pop down and get us one in a minute,' Millie said as she sat up in bed and bobbed the curlers in her hair. 'I can't believe I'm here. So exciting, isn't it?'

That was the last thing that Anya felt. But she nodded her agreement. Millie slipped out of bed, putting on slippers and her dressing gown. Popping to the kitchen, she made her a cup of tea and brought it back up to their bedroom. Even though Anya didn't ask for it, she was grateful for the warm drink as she dressed. First, she washed in the cold bowl of water that had been left out for them with a jug. And then, pulling out the clothes, she tried them on.

She had a tiny waist, and even the smallest size of knickerbockers Becca had found for her were two sizes too big. So, she slipped on the thick brown leather belt and tightened it as far as she could, even though her trousers pleated with the extra fabric. The beige shirt was warm, made of cotton. And then there was a tie. She had never had to wear a tie before. She had no idea how to make it work. Millie must have noticed her confusion and came over to help her.

'Didn't you have to wear a tie for school, Annie?'

Anya shook her head.

'You were lucky. I had to do it every day. Here, I'll show you.' Millie stood behind her and used her hands in the mirror to show her. Anya watched as her new friend pleated the tie over and over, smelling the fragrance of Millie's flowery shampoo behind her, watching her warm, kind eyes as she showed her.

It was going to be so much more challenging than she'd thought. Being a traitor to her country was going to be nothing compared to being the enemy to these people who had greeted her so warmly.

She finished tying the tie and smiled. 'It suits you, Annie.'

Anya tried on the green ribbed jumper and the socks and looked at herself in the mirror. It was a strange kind of uniform, masculine but also quite flattering on her waist and hips.

As soon as Millie was dressed, they went down to the kitchen. Becca had told them to meet there for breakfast. The family ate on a different floor, but all the servants ate together in the morning. They went down, and as they entered, a group of the male servants around the table whistled and cheered at their outfits.

'You won't be keeping that very clean,' said Charlie as they passed him. 'Once you get yourself in that dirt, those nice beige knickerbockers are going to be black.'

'You can help me wash them then,' said Millie, nudging him playfully in the back.

The butler introduced himself; Anya noted Nikolai hadn't arrived yet. Even though she understood it to be a couple of days, she still was looking forward to seeing him.

'This is James, one of our footmen,' the butler continued. 'We should have another one coming, though there seems to be some problem with the arrangements. Unfortunately, that isn't uncommon in these times.'

Anya felt her stomach tighten. He was talking about Nikolai. Had something already gone wrong? Had he already been uncovered as a spy? She nodded, trying not to show the anxiety on her face that was churning in her stomach as she seated herself at the breakfast table next to one of the other servants. There were eggs and ham on the table. Mrs Barton had baked fresh bread. One of them explained that they hadn't had too much trouble with rationing because they had their own farm nearby.

'And once you get the gardens going,' said another one of the maids, 'we'll all be able to have a few greens as well.'

At ten o'clock, the gardener came in to find them and took them out to the gardens. But first, he showed them where all their equipment was. 'One of you is going to have to learn how to drive a tractor on the land when you are not in the walled garden.'

Millie looked mortified. 'Not me because I'm terrible with anything mechanical.'

'Then I guess that means you then, Annie,' the gardener stated.

Anya swallowed down a hard lump. She didn't even know how to drive a car. How would she know how to drive a tractor?

He took them out and showed them the field they'd be ploughing later that day. 'But first, I want to show you where we're going to start the greens.'

He took a key from the kitchen and walked out towards the back of the estate. The two of them followed with a fork and spade in their hands, as he'd told them to do. He slipped the key into a wooden door in a red brick wall. And when he opened it, Anya gasped with surprise. It was like a wonderland inside, magical. Beautiful roses and flowers and trees, a fountain, a red swing, and a lovely Victorian treehouse. It was exquisite.

'Now, don't get your hearts all set on how pretty it is. You're going to be changing a lot here. We're going to grow things in here that don't do well in other areas of the estate. We have a sharp east wind that comes in off the sea. So, this will keep them sheltered. Follow me, and I'll show you where you're going to start.'

He walked them to the back of the garden, where there were two beautiful herbaceous beds.

'I know it seems sad to dig them up, but we've got to think about doing our bit for our country. Then, of course, we'll replant these plants somewhere else, but right now, you're going to put some lettuces in here. So the first thing you've got to do is dig out all the plants, turn over the soil, and get planting. Is that clear?'

Both the girls nodded as they got to work; Millie loved to talk and continued to keep then entertained till lunchtime. A plane roared overhead and Millie wiped the back of her hand over her damp forehead. 'Blimey, they're loud, aren't they? That's about the third that's gone over since we started working.'

It was actually the fourth Anya had counted, but she feigned disinterest as she briefly glanced at the sky and Millie continued. 'I don't know how my brother does it, being up in the sky in one of those. Do you think they are Spitfires?'

Anya shrugged her shoulders, knowing full well they were Hurricanes, having studied before she left Russia all the planes she would be looking out for.

25

HATWORTH MANOR, PRESENT DAY

Laura

Laura was woken early by her honorary niece tugging on her arm. 'Auntie Laura, you have a visitor,' she said, her voice bright with the excitement of it. 'He's waiting in the front room for you.'

Laura lifted an eyelid and peered at the clock: 8.30 a.m. She couldn't believe that Jamie had come back so early. He'd only left her hours before. He was eager. Maybe he was going to drive her to the village for a coffee or something. She yawned and sat up. That sounded nice, though she would have liked more notice. She wasn't sure if they were at the *'This is what I look like bleary-eyed and with bed hair'* stage yet. She also had mixed feelings. It felt as if the relationship was moving to the next level, and she wasn't sure she was ready for that. Having him turn up so early this morning didn't give her much chance to process her feelings. Nevertheless, on the whole she felt happy.

After getting dressed, she made her way to the front room, realizing she couldn't wait to see him again. She opened the door and he had his back to her and was shadowed by the early morning light. Though, as he turned, she realized it wasn't him at all but...

'Hello, darling,' Liam said, bounding towards her. He took her in his arms before she had time to even think and kissed her brutishly on the lips.

Laura staggered back. 'What are you doing here?' she spat out, the shock and anger obvious in her tone.

She blinked as she tried to come to terms with the vision of the person in front of her. He had on a steel-grey-coloured suit, ice-blue tie, and a crisp white shirt. His white-blond hair was newly cut and washed, and the expensive aftershave he liked to wear was now scenting her cheek, overpowering the last strains of orange spice that had still lingered.

His blue eyes appeared silver grey in the morning light as he continued to rove about the room, taking in everything, as was his way.

'Well, that's a nice way to greet your boyfriend.' The anger and surprise of rejection was obvious in his tone. 'I haven't seen you for months and that's the best you can do? I know you needed some space, but Laura, don't you think you are overre-acting to all this? It wouldn't be the first time, now would it.'

She hitched her breath. Surely, he wasn't referring to her breakdown, was he? She knew that during that time her mind had distilled the world into a dark and fearful place that he had felt was his job to guide her through.

She shook the notion from her thoughts; no, she wouldn't even entertain what he was insinuating. It was obvious he had hoped to swoop in and bowl her over with his charm. And though, as always, she was taken in by just how good-looking he was, she wasn't in a place to be swept away by him, in any form.

'Remember, we talked about maybe having a coffee or lunch.' Then he dropped his voice to a patronizing whisper. 'Did you forget?' He looked at her with real concern, as a young person might do dealing with an elderly forgetful relative. He was trying to confuse her. He continued without giving her a chance to respond with the fact she was sure she hadn't actually agreed to that. 'But as it happens, I am here about something completely different.' He looked at her then and his whole demeanour changed, his vulnerability palpable. It was something she didn't see very often, so it intrigued her.

As she watched him trying to find the right words, she suddenly felt a stab of familiarity that made her sad for where they were with each other. After years together, she could read him like a book. Whatever he had come to tell her was big and it had taken the wind from his sails. She could see clearly on display the insecure little boy he spent so much time hiding behind his flashy exterior.

He bounded to the window, his hands in his pockets. 'Are they ever going to develop this land?' he asked, looking out at the acreage. 'This would be a great place for an Airbnb. You could rent out all these little cottages.'

Laura knew it was a deflection, so she spoke again. 'I asked you, Liam, what you were doing here.'

'I had to come and see you...' He paused. 'It's about Caroline.' His voice quivered.

So that was it. His love for his sister had always been the Achilles heel to his bravado.

Laura felt her chest tighten. As much as she was angry right now with Liam, she adored his sister and they had a very special relationship. Caroline was creative, beautiful, thoughtful, and kind. They had become very good friends over the years especially since Liam and Laura had been together.

'What about Caroline?' asked Laura, now feeling guilty she had not really spoken to her friend in weeks.

He paused and looked crestfallen, apparently unable to answer.

'What about Caroline?!' she asked again, now more urgent.

'She was taken into hospital yesterday,' he said quietly. 'She collapsed at work. They're not sure what's wrong with her. She knows that you and I are working through some issues right now and didn't want to bother you while you were taking some space. But it's quite serious and I think she's really scared and needs to see her best friend.'

Laura tried to take in the information, horrified that her closest friend was in hospital, but her thoughts were conflicted as the second half of his statement sank in. So even though she knew Caroline knew the truth, that's what he was telling people: that they were having some issues. He obviously hadn't wanted to let anyone know they were over. He still wasn't facing that reality and she knew it.

'Does she know we are completely over?' she asked, starting to feel hot. She had wanted to tell Caroline the finality of that as it had become more and more clear to her but had been putting it off. She was afraid of how it would affect their friendship. Caroline had always been so excited about her and Liam's relationship, and even though she would joke about his roguish ways sometimes and stand up for Laura when they had fought in the past, he was still her brother and she loved him.

He shook his head. 'Look, I know that you've had some issues, and I guess you needed to paint me as the bad guy as you dealt with them, but you need to put that aside. Caroline really needs you, and I would so appreciate it if you would come and see her. I spoke to her yesterday and said that I was coming to get you and that I'd bring you back to London today.'

'You shouldn't have promised her that,' said Laura sharply, her brimming emotions turning to anger. 'How do you know that I didn't have something going on?'

Liam looked out at the estate again and balked, as if she couldn't possibly have anything going on in the country.

All at once there was the unmistakable crunch of car wheels grinding to a stop on the driveway. She was still processing the information and trying to figure out what to do when Simon poked his head in the door. 'Laura,' he said quietly, 'you have another visitor, a friend.'

Laura spun around. Jamie stood looming in the doorway behind him. As he walked in, Liam strode defensively to Laura's side.

'A *friend* of Laura's?' he echoed, not even trying to hide the sarcasm in his tone. 'How wonderful.' Jamie looked taken aback for a second. Before he had time to regain his balance, Liam reached forward and grabbed his hand powerfully. 'Liam Rand,' he said, shaking it harshly. 'I'm Laura's fiancé.'

Laura felt sick. Though they'd never officially got engaged, there had been times that saying that had been acceptable in his business dealings. People felt more comfortable dealing with somebody who was settled. It made them not fear for their wives or their girlfriends around him, made him look as though he was a happy settled man. Right now, this was the last thing she wanted Jamie to believe.

Jamie echoed the word back. 'Fiancé?' He looked to her for confirmation.

She shook her head. 'Not officially, we are—'

But Liam interrupted her impatiently. 'Where did you meet my fiancée?'

Jamie responded, his tone careful but assertive, his eyes searching Laura's for any kind of answer. 'I live locally. We met two days ago.'

'Really?' said Liam. 'I'm surprised you guys found a place to meet in this area.' He slipped his arm around Laura's shoulders as she stood mortified to the spot. She felt so embarrassed. Why hadn't she told Jamie about Liam last night? At least he would have understood what was going on here. With him turning up like this and finding them together, it looked as if she had been deceiving him, and that coupled with the waves of emotions that were wracking her body right now, dealing with Caroline and this early morning intrusion, she felt paralyzed to clarify it all.

'When I was here last night—' said Jamie.

Liam cut him off. 'You were?' His voice now rose in frustration as he attempted to pull Laura closer to him.

'He was my guest, we had something to celebrate,' Laura finally managed to stumble out, pulling herself away from Liam's hold and wandering to the window, her stomach tying itself into a knot. This was horrible. She wished she could get him alone to clarify with Jamie what this was all about.

But when she looked over at his face, he looked shocked, hurt, and betrayed. She couldn't even imagine what this must look like.

'You actually left this in my car,' he said flatly, handing Laura the handbag he had in his hand. 'I know you said ten o'clock, but I was concerned you would be worried about it, or need it this morning.'

She instantly felt her heart go out to him. He had cared about her not having it and had driven over to make sure she was okay.

She took it gratefully, and her eyes looked up pleading with him to understand, but he just looked away.

Jamie continued, 'I was also going to see if you had spoken to Simon about me spending time painting in the garden with you today unless you have now made other arrangements...?' His voice petered out.

'Afraid she won't be able to, mate,' stated Liam, answering for her. 'She has needed some time to sort out her thoughts, but now I've come to take her back to London.'

Jamie finally sought Laura's eyes for confirmation, and she found words. 'A friend of mine is very sick and in hospital. Somebody who's very dear to me. Liam came to tell me,' she whispered, wanting to go into more detail, but not with Liam in the room. He had a way of making it sound like she was crazy somehow.

Jamie stepped back and his eyes narrowed with wariness, and she felt sick.

Liam thrust out his hand, as if he was ready to end the intrusion. 'Well, it was nice of you to pop by, mate. I'm sure Alicia and Simon will be glad you did. I assume that is how you met Laura?'

He shook Liam's hand stiffly, then Jamie stood staring from one to the other awkwardly for a second before turning to walk towards the door.

Her heart followed him as she watched him get into his Mini and leave. Everything in her being wanted to go with him, but one of her favourite people in the world needed her and it made sense to go with Liam and finally convince him they had no chance together. Besides, she could grab the rest of her stuff from their flat. She would text Jamie later, when things were straighter with Liam, clearer, when she'd made sure Liam understood the breakup was final. The last thing she had wanted was to put Jamie through anything like what had just happened. She felt so ridiculous and wished more than anything that this had not been the way she had had to say goodbye to him before she left for London.

Liam seemed to need to gather his energy for a second. Pulling himself up to his full height, he sniffed in deeply, as if to embolden himself. Then there it was, his game face. She knew it well.

'Well, Laur, we should probably get going,' he said, striding towards the door. 'It's quite a trip and visiting hours aren't very long.'

Laura nodded. 'I'll go and pack a few things,' she said. 'I've also got to figure out where I'll stay tonight.'

'You'll stay at the flat, of course,' stated Liam, irritated. 'It's your home. Why wouldn't you stay there?'

'Because we split up, Liam,' she wanted to say, but with all the emotion swirling around her mind, she just didn't need the confrontation right now, not here in Simon and Alicia's home. *Oh God, Caroline is sick.* Her heart wrenched again. She went upstairs and quickly put together an overnight bag and told her friends what was going on.

At the top of the stairs, Alicia pulled her aside.

'Are you okay, Laura? Seriously? If you want, I'll come with you.'

Laura tapped her friend's face. 'Thank you,' she said. 'You're like a big sister, always taking care of me.'

'You don't have to go back with him if you don't want to,' continued her friend defiantly.

'I know, but maybe it's time to put this right. It's a good opportunity.' She kissed her friend on the cheek and ruffled the heads of the dogs, who were padding around the landing. 'Hopefully I'll see you soon.'

Alicia nodded. 'If he mistreats you in any way, I'm coming down to London to punch him on the nose.'

Laura smiled at this, picturing five-foot-nothing Alicia punching Liam on the nose. It would be worth it just to see it. But for now, she had to finally deal with this once and for all, and then she would have to see if there was any way to rescue the budding relationship with Jamie.

26

HATWORTH MANOR, FEBRUARY 1941

Anya

Anya passed her days working in the walled garden, identifying and counting planes and listening to any information about the war she felt could be of help to their government. She wrote down everything in code while Millie was sleeping. She was due to connect with her contact at the bookshop on her day off at the end of the week, but until then she worked long hours turning over soil and planting vegetables. There was a lot to do to get the garden established, and they were soon joined by two more Land Girls, Jennifer and Christine. Jennifer was a slender pale-looking girl with fair hair and white eyelashes, and Christine was tall, broad with black hair and a ruddy complexion. They were both great girls, and the four of them got on really well. Anya continued to keep herself to herself. Sometimes she even forgot what she was here to do. This was the first time she'd really had friends, and Millie had turned out to be the kindest of people. Bringing in little vases of flowers to cheer up the room, sneaking cakes from the kitchen for her to eat, and telling her stories about her life at home, late into the night before they went to sleep. Anya felt so heartsick for her own home and her mother, and this little family was fulfilling a deeper need in her.

She waited with anticipation for Nikolai, but when he didn't arrive on the day he was scheduled to, she worked hard to hide her anxiety.

On the day of the dance, Nikolai had still not arrived. He was days overdue, and Anya started to get a creeping fear. Should she go to her handler in the photographer's or leave a note at the bookshop? They had been instructed to carry on regardless in their training, but it didn't feel right that she didn't even know what had happened to him.

That afternoon, the head gardener let them all finish their day early so that they could prepare for the dance that night. All four girls crammed into Millie and Anya's tiny room as Christine hummed big-band tunes as they got ready together. Anya had never worn makeup before, but it didn't take long for Christine to show her how to put it on, making her eyes large and catlike and rouging her lips with crimson lipstick. Anya couldn't believe the difference in herself as she watched the application in the mirror. All her features looked so accentuated.

'You really should do something with your hair as well,' suggested Christine, studying Anya's reflection in the mirror. Pulling up Anya's hair from her shoulders to the nape of her neck, she curled it up under her chin. 'A bob would look really good on you. They're all the rage in Paris.'

Anya stared at the woman who looked back at her. She did look modern and Parisian, the short style flattering her pixie chin and large eyes.

'I could do it for you,' stated Christine matter-of-factly. 'I trained as a hairdresser. I didn't stick to it, but I did all the cutting classes. So, I know how to give you a bob.'

Anya found herself nodding her head before she had time to say no, and the next thing she knew, she was sitting in a chair in the middle of the bedroom as the other girls watched with glee as Christine pulled out a pair of scissors and got to work. Waves of golden hair fell around her shoulders onto the floor and she suddenly felt so daring. She'd never had short hair, but she'd never done half the things she was doing now.

She hadn't had anything to wear either, but when Becca had found out, she brought her something of her own. A lovely red dress made of satin that accentuated her tiny waist and showed off her shapely shoulders.

'You look so gorgeous,' all the girls gushed when she was finally ready. She stood and looked in the mirror and didn't even recognize herself. She tried to imagine what her mother would say if she could see her, and she didn't think she would believe it.

Nervously, Anya went down to the dance, looking surreptitiously around for any sign of Nikolai in case he had finally arrived.

'Let's get a drink,' Millie shouted in her ear to be heard over the loud band that was playing a lively rendition of *'Kiss Me Goodnight, Sergeant Major.'* Millie pulled her friend's arm and dragged her towards the bar.

As Anya waited for a drink, she took in all the decor around her. The dance was taking place in the manor's main ballroom, which had very high ceilings and ornate furniture; it had been moved to the side to make way for the dance floor. Floor-to-ceiling windows glinted with the last rays of twilight and strands of lights had been hung everywhere to enhance the beautiful wall lights. At the one end, a makeshift stage had been erected and a band was already in full swing. Behind them on the wall, a huge banner announced that this event was to raise money for the Spitfire fund, and it had been decorated with dozens of flags and strands of lights. The room was packed with service members, servants, Land Girls from all around the area, and men and women from the local village whom she'd seen occasionally in passing.

The atmosphere was lively, and a group of soldiers at the bar were raucous. Millie and Anya grabbed their drinks and made their way to a table, when Becca approached.

'How are you both?' she asked in a chirpy upbeat tone, also shouting to be heard over the band. She was wearing an emerald-green silk dress with a full skirt and a glittery hair slide in her curly hair. She was obviously part of the organizing committee, as she still had her notebook with her. 'I have someone I want you to meet,' she continued.

But before she could get any further, Charlie appeared at the table, looking eager. His hair was washed and combed and he was wearing a worn, but smart, suit.

'Want to dance, Mill?' he asked, holding out his hand with anticipation.

'Yeah, all right then.' She beamed enthusiastically as she jumped to her feet. And, placing her drink on the table, she swished out onto the dance floor with her partner.

'Oh!' said Becca, impressed by Charlie's forthrightness, before she turned to Anya and smiled. 'I'll introduce Millie later,' she mused. 'What about you, Annie? There's a nice young man. He seems quite shy, like you. Maybe you'd be a good person to cheer him up.' She pulled her across the room, cooing about how stunning she looked in the red dress with her new haircut, and flung her towards Nikolai, who looked as shocked as she did.

Anya was so relieved to see him and in the same breath taken aback by how handsome he looked in the dark suit and tie he was wearing. So different than his uniform or the exercise outfits she had seen him in for weeks. His blond waves were combed back and there were those blue eyes with their long lashes that always made her heart skip a beat.

'Here you are, Nick. I told you I would find you a dance

partner, didn't I?' enthused Becca. 'She's new here too. I'm sure you'll get on like a house on fire.'

Nick nodded at Anya and waited for her to introduce herself as Anya had taught him.

'Annie,' she said, putting out her hand.

'Nicholas Brown,' he said quietly, shaking her hand. 'I go by Nick.'

And as he touched her again, there was that feeling of excitement that ran through her body. Was it because she was just so glad to see him after so long? Or was it that attraction she had been fighting?

'Good,' stated Becca with a nod, obviously pleased with her matchmaking abilities. 'I'll let you two get acquainted and have a dance.' And she strode off to organize the buffet.

Removing his hand from hers, he stared at her in surprise, taking in her madeup face and short haircut, before glancing down at her outfit. He then looked nervously around him before asking, 'Would you like to dance?'

They had been told not to draw attention to themselves as a couple while they were there, but both of them seemed to recognize that, by not responding to Becca's introduction, it would actually draw more attention than just dancing with one another. Besides, it was important that she found out what was going on.

'I'd love to dance,' she said, loud enough for people to hear.

On the floor, he held her tightly in his arms against his taut chest so he could whisper in her ear. 'I have something I need to tell you. Is there somewhere we can meet?'

Her body shuddered with the feel of his breath on her ear and the clean fresh smell of his shaving soap. She forced an even tone. 'I know where to get a key to the walled garden. It's away from the house and secure, straight through the garden beyond the roses,' she whispered back, trying to fight the feelings rushing through her body of being so close to him, mingled with the relief of seeing him at last.

'I will meet you there in half an hour,' he responded before she threw back her head and laughed as though he'd just told her a joke.

As he moved around the dance floor, his eyes flicked around the room, taking in everything around him, and she enjoyed the smooth way he moved; he was a good dancer. When they swung in front of the band that were blasting out 'In the Mood,' made famous by the Glenn Miller Orchestra, she leaned in to speak to him again without any chance of them being heard. 'I was so worried about you.'

He looked down at her with a thoughtful expression, apparently touched by her sincerity, before whispering in her ear again, 'There's a lot going on I need to tell you about.'

She nodded again as he continued to lead her around the dance floor. He looked as nervous as she felt. But, once again, she couldn't get away from the fact every part of her was electrified by his presence. The occasional brush of his cheek against hers, the feeling of his body close to her own as he twirled her around the dance floor, one hand of strong fingers clasping hers and the other splayed across the middle of her back, guiding her to the music.

Once the dance was over, he nodded at her and moved away, and she felt breathless. Did he feel the same, or was it just her heart that was stirred? She didn't know for sure, but she knew she had to get past this. This could so easily cloud what they were here to do. She'd seen a genuine fear and concern in his eyes when he had told her he needed to speak to her. So she would wait for a little while, then slip out to meet him in the garden.

Twenty minutes later, Anya paced the garden, waiting for Nikolai to arrive. She'd managed to leave the dance, telling Millie she'd got a headache, and Millie, distracted by Charlie, had barely acknowledged her departure. Changing her clothes quickly, into something darker, she'd rushed out into the garden through the kitchen, which was now empty, everybody at the dance. Inside the garden walls, it was cool with the night air. It was still lovely, even though many flowers had been replaced now and vegetables planted in their wake. She paced the lawn listening to the flowing water in the fountain and the sounds of frogs in the pond. Then, all at once, she heard the creak of the wooden door. She strode towards him and locked it behind him. Beckoning him to the north-western corner, where there was an established willow tree, she parted the branches and stepped underneath it. It was farthest away from the house, and if someone had another key to the garden, they couldn't be seen from the door beneath the branches and there was nothing behind the wall at that point except for dense bushes.

Her heart skipped a beat when she looked up into his face.

'I'm so glad to see you,' he said, his face close to hers, the feeling of safety under the tree making the space feel more intimate.

'What happened?' she hissed. 'Why were you so late?'

'The day after you left, there was another drop. A Russian agent came in that night and was intercepted and taken away. As he was part of the same cell, they had to be careful. They weren't sure if we'd been compromised. They wanted to wait a couple of days to make sure there was no backlash.'

She looked at the fear in his eyes and thought about what she'd been doing over the last few days. At any time she could have been exposed. She suddenly felt guilty for all the fun she'd been having with the other girls while he had been lying low in hiding, fearing for his life. She had been acting as if she was on some sort of English holiday. Inwardly she scolded herself. She had to remember why she was here and what she was here to do.

'Everything is all right now?' she asked.

'They think so,' he stated, then drew out a long slow breath, looking across at her, a smile creeping across his face, his deep eyes penetrating hers. 'I like your new haircut,' he said coyly.

She smiled. 'The girls did it. I thought I had better get on the right side of our enemy.'

He placed his hands on her arms, and she could feel the warmth of them through the sleeves of her sweater. A look crossed his face. 'Anya, there's something I need to tell you.'

She looked up.

'It's only fair that you know. I don't want to put your life in danger.'

Her heart skipped a beat.

'What?' she asked. She was trying to listen but was totally distracted by the warmth of his body next to hers.

'I'm not exactly who I said I was.'

Her heart started to thud. What did he mean?

'I'm not really a spy,' he continued.

She furrowed her brows. What was he talking about? She'd trained alongside him.

'I mean, I know I am a spy, and I wanted to serve my country, but I had no intention of being one. I only joined the NKVD because I was trying to find out what happened to my father, who was murdered. So, the fact they have sent me on assignment is an accident. That's why I was desperately trying to get out of it. I wanted to be at the NKVD headquarters to do some more exploring, find out what happened to him, and I never intended to come abroad, never intended to work for Russia like this.'

She breathed a sigh of relief, if that was all it was.

'Nikolai, I have something to tell you too.'

He looked at her, questioning.

'I didn't want to be a spy either. But I had to get away from a situation at home, a potentially dangerous one. My stepfather was, let's say, getting a little too friendly, and I had nowhere I could go.'

He looked angry then. 'What do you mean, a little too friendly?'

'The night that I joined up, he was trying to take me to his bed. That's why I had to get away, to be able to live in the barracks. I didn't have enough money to go anywhere else.'

He looked horrified and automatically pulled her towards him and held her for a second, then, realizing what he was doing, let her go.

'I'm sorry. I didn't mean to do that.'

She hitched her breath as she felt the energy between them intensify. He searched her face then, as though he wanted to say something but was unable to vocalize it. Surely, he could feel the attraction and now this confession had brought them closer. She realized part of the reason she'd been holding back was that she did not want to get involved with somebody who was very pro-Stalin, as so many of the NKVD were. Her mother had never been very enamoured by their new leader, and now she realized that that was the opposite of what Nikolai was.

'Anya,' he whispered. 'My little Mishka,' he joked, his face close to hers. 'I'm not sure how this is going to end for us, but I am committed to making sure that you're safe, no matter what happens. I could never go through what I went through with Olga again. So please do not take any risks, and we'll both try to get through this the best we can.'

'Is that why you were being so indifferent to me before?' she asked.

'I didn't want to compromise our mission,' he whispered, his eyes scanning her face, 'but I find that I am feeling...' He was trying to find the right words as he stared down at her, his gaze drifting to her lips.

All at once, there was a sound out on the estate. A group of people had moved out from the dance and were roaming the grounds.

'We need to go,' he whispered. 'Let's meet here late when we can.'

She nodded. 'I'll try and get away in the evenings after Millie is asleep.'

They slipped back out the wooden gate, and ducking under the wisteria they parted. Each headed off in the opposite direction, he to his side of the house and she to hers. As she crept away, she thought about his words. *I find that I am feeling...* What would have been the end of that sentence? A confession of his attraction towards her, maybe? She felt excited with the thought but also apprehensive. If only she had met him in peacetime. A relationship under this kind of pressure felt impossible no matter how much they were attracted to each other.

27

HATWORTH MANOR, PRESENT DAY

Laura

Kissing goodbye to her friends, Laura strode out onto the driveway, where Liam was pacing, waiting for her. He watched her approach with a grin.

'You look gorgeous, Laur,' he said as he opened the door to let her in.

She rolled her eyes. She wasn't even wearing makeup and her hair was swept up into a messy bun.

He got in and started the car, but he didn't move. He just sat there staring at her. 'God, I've missed you, you have no idea.'

Laura sighed. It was going to be a long trip.

As they drove away, Liam's tone was intense. 'Laura, I know I did wrong.'

'I don't want to talk about this,' she snapped back, staring out at the countryside rushing by outside the window.

'But we have to talk about it right now, because I can't believe how I have felt in the last few months, completely empty and lost without you.'

She was surprised at how sincere he sounded as he continued.

'I know I've been an arsehole. I know what I've done. It took this separation for me to know, Laura, for me to know that you are the one.'

She turned towards him and couldn't keep the ice from her tone. 'What exactly are you saying?'

He paused, then looked at her intently. 'This time away has made me sure of one thing, Laura. You're the only woman for me in this world. I want you to marry me, Laura. I want us to put the past behind us, and I want us to move forward into the future. I know I can be a good husband and a father. I can be the person you want me to be. We're so good for each other.'

Laura couldn't believe the words she was hearing. In the eight years they'd been together, whenever marriage had been broached, he'd always changed the subject. Now here he was proposing to her in the car?

He reached into his pocket and gave her a black velvet-covered box.

'I wanted to do this right, with a meal, flowers, and wine, and some sort of a romantic violinist or something. But with the situation with Caroline, I just don't know what is going to happen in the coming weeks and I just couldn't wait.

Her stomach lurched as she looked down at the box he had placed in her hand. As she tried to will herself not to open it, tears misted her eyes. Then before she could stop herself, she lifted the lid and caught her breath. Years before, she had seen this incredible sapphire ring in the window of an antique shop, and when they had gone inside, the owner had told them an amazing romantic story about its history. She had fallen in love with the whole package, but it had been way too expensive. Now here it was in a box in front of her.

'I found it, Laura, the exact ring you wanted. Don't ask me how I tracked it down and how much I paid for it. But I wanted you to know not only how serious I am about all this, but also that I know you. I know who you are and what you need.' He grabbed her hand. 'Don't leave me, Laura. You would break my heart. I'm asking you just to give us one last chance. I know what I've done, trust me, and I know that I've messed up. It took this – it took this time apart for me to realize what a terrible boyfriend I've been to you, and what an incredible and amazing woman you are. But, God, I know now, and I promise to treat you the way you deserve to be treated. I have work to do, and I know this is all me. I will even go for couple's therapy or something if you want me to. I will do anything to get you back. I have started looking for a house with the garden you have always wanted. We could have the wedding of your dreams, go on the honeymoon we have always talked about in Tahiti. I won't even take my phone, so we can spend all day together as I thank my lucky stars that I have this amazing woman by my side.'

Laura felt her heart race as the air rushed rapidly in and out of her lungs as she tried to take in all he was saying. Her mind spun with the beauty of the ring and the words he was saying. Words she had wanted to hear from him for years. He had just proposed. She tried to grapple with that reality as she clutched the box. As he continued to describe the beautiful life they would have together, having the family she had always wanted, she could feel her resolve starting to crumble.

His eyes pleaded with hers. 'Don't give up on me, Laura. I need you so much. I'm nothing without you.'

Were those tears in his eyes? Laura felt sick as he continued.

'Will you promise me that you'll just think about it. You don't have to make a decision too quickly. You can give me a chance to prove what I'm saying is the truth. Spend time thinking about our wedding and what it will be like to have a family together. Please, don't give up on eight years without at least doing that.'

Laura folded her arms as tears pricked her eyes. She forced herself to look outside again. She couldn't answer him, afraid of what she would say. It seemed so easy to just say yes, and so much harder to hold her ground. But she needed to be strong; she needed to fight this. But all at once she was tired, tired of the pain, tired of being alone in the last few months. The magical evening in the garden with Jamie the day before swam into her thoughts, and she suddenly felt guilty for being so happy then. What if she and Liam were meant to be together? Everyone she knew went through difficult times. What if this was the time she was supposed to recommit, dig in, and give herself back to this person who had been part of her world for as long as she could remember? Didn't all happy married couples talk about taking the rough with the smooth? Was this what people were talking about when they had spent thirty years together? They had somehow managed to bridge these kinds of gaps with forgiveness. As she tried to work through her feelings, with every mile they moved closer to London, Jamie felt further away.

28

HATWORTH MANOR, MARCH 1941

Anya

After that first night in the garden, Nikolai had backed off from Anya, but they had increased their surveillance on those whom Russia and Germany had sent them to watch. Never again had they broached the subject of their feelings. Instead, keeping a distance between them in the garden, Nikolai averted his eyes as they exchanged information and she responded by doing the same. No matter how Anya felt about her partner, they had a job to do and it was terrifying. She remembered vividly how she'd felt during her very first drop. She had walked into the village, telling Millie she needed to post a letter. Then, with her heart pounding, she made her way towards the bookshop. Signs of the war were everywhere in the village. Ration restrictions posted on shop windows, posters about digging for victory, and a group of off-duty airmen from the nearby base whistled at her as she searched for the right shop. Finding it and drawing in a deep breath, she placed her shaking hand on the brass doorknob and willed her trembling knees inside. A bell tinkled as she put the door back in place, and the man behind the counter barely looked up from a ledger he was writing in. She noted he was about fifty years old, with a heavily lined brow, sharp chin, and thin mouth. His beady brown eyes, round and glassy, hardly acknowledged her as she stepped inside. And she couldn't help thinking he looked so ordinary. How could she be sure that this was the man supposed to be taking care of her messages? After all, her whole life depended on him. Nervously she gave him the coded message and he smiled and pointed to the shelf, whispering, 'The book you are looking for is called *The Old Curiosity Shop.*'

She started to glide around the room, glancing across the bookshelves as though she were just an average shopper, hoping he couldn't hear the sound of a heart that was beating so frantically it sounded like a bass drum to her. He looked over and gave her another dry smile.

Finding the correct section, she glanced quickly along the shelf until she located books by Charles Dickens. Holding her breath, she looked for the book. *A Christmas Carol, Great Expectations, A Tale of Two Cities... The Old Curiosity Shop* was not there. She released her breath. This was what she had expected. She scanned the other shelves around her, trying not to draw attention to herself. Finally, Anya located it sandwiched in with the Jane Austen novels two shelves up. Reaching tentatively forward, she plucked it out and turned her back on the rest of the shop and opened the cover. Her hands were shaking so hard she could barely turn the pages. But eventually, she found what she was looking for towards the centre of the book, a blue slip of lined paper, and on it, a coded message that looked like a shopping list. Slipping inside the coded message she had, she pulled out the note inside and placed it in her handbag before jamming the book back into place with the Austens.

'Can I help with anything?' the man asked as she moved

back towards the door, pretty sure that now her face was bright red.

'I have what I need,' she said, trying to sound a lot more confident than she felt.

Then he raised his eyebrows, understanding, his thin lips forming a tight smile. 'See you again, my friend,' he said.

She nodded as she made her way out of the shop.

As soon as she returned to the manor, she went straight upstairs and into the toilet. She locked the door and began to decode the message. She was to go to a nearby airbase, where they were expecting an influx of new Allied planes. And she was to report on how many there were and send them the information back through the book to her handler.

———

Nikolai had his first experience the next day. His contact was in the photography shop. Walking into the cool dark shop with the cameras in the window, he moved to the counter and looked around.

'Can I help you?' the man asked.

'I have a camera,' he said nervously, looking over his shoulder to make sure no one was on the way in. 'I think I need some film for it.' And then he gave the code words he had been told. 'As long as it doesn't rain, I think Sunday would be the perfect day for a picnic.'

The man's eyes rose in interest. 'Welcome, my friend. I've been waiting for you. Follow me.'

He ushered Nikolai into a back room, turned the sign on his front door from 'open' to 'closed,' and pulled the curtain that separated his private room from the shop.

'We heard about the little scare last week,' he hissed in a whisper. 'You are both okay?'

Nikolai nodded his head.

'Tomorrow night, we have a job for you at the manor. Lord Sinclair has some significant people coming to dinner. We want you to gather any information that is swapped there and bring it to us. Have the female agent place it in the bookshop with my brother. Do you understand?'

Nikolai nodded.

———

The next evening, he was very busy with the dinner in question, and he still had a lot to learn training to be a footman, but he was grateful for all Anya had taught him. The butler had been patient with him, and nobody had complained when they were so desperate for staff. The room filled up that evening, and many people in military uniforms appeared. And as he moved around the table, serving and removing plates, he listened carefully to the conversations.

There were a lot of concerns about the new weapons the Germans were rumoured to be developing. There was also talk about the need for experienced pilots, as so many had been lost since the Battle of Britain. He listened carefully, memorizing everything, and then put it onto a coded note that he gave to Anya in the garden the next night.

This was both of their lives for the next few months. Nikolai gleaning information from meetings and whisperings from the staff, Anya monitoring the base activity, taking herself off on long walks past the bases to keep an eye on the activity and counting planes daily. It was intense work, and neither of them really enjoyed it.

Though the most challenging thing for Nikolai over these days was not the work nor the spying. He actually found he had quite an aptitude for serving and listening at the same time. What he found increasingly hard was he was becoming more and more attracted to Anya, his thoughts turning to her whenever he was about his work. Cleaning the silver, he would picture her eyes. Preparing a table, what it would be like to touch her, hold her in his arms, kiss her, even though he tried desperately to push the thoughts away, knowing they had a job to do. Instead of it getting easier, the feelings in him just seemed to become stronger, and he didn't know what to do with them. He wasn't sure if she felt the same way. Sometimes when she looked at him, he thought he saw something in her eyes. But she was fiercely independent, and he didn't want to approach her unless it was something she wanted as well. Then came the turn of events that neither of them could have predicted. It threatened not only their ongoing undercover work, but also their lives.

29

LONDON, PRESENT DAY

Laura

When they arrived in London, Laura's emotions were still in a turmoil. Her head seemed to be saying one thing and her heart another. As she looked at Liam, her heart was telling her to at least give him a chance. Maybe he had changed. Whereas her head was telling her this was the same old Liam, just working the crowd, working his magic, as she knew he could. On the way to the hospital, Liam received a text message saying that Caroline had taken a turn for the worse and had been moved from St. Thomas's Hospital to the National Hospital for Neurology and Neurosurgery over in Holborn. Liam rushed to his flat, parked the car, and they got the Tube to Holborn.

It was so strange for her being back in London. It was as though her life in Norfolk didn't even exist. As if it had been some sort of dream. She sat next to Liam as they rattled along together on the Tube, the clatter of the train on the track and the sound of air whooshing along outside so familiar to her. The Tube was packed. The smell of sweat, coffee, and cheap perfume was almost overpowering with so many people crushed together. All around her people stared at their iPhones on their way to work and appointments.

Even in the few hours it had been since she had left Norfolk, Jamie was starting to fade, becoming a beautiful memory, like a holiday romance, and she felt so confused. Jamie didn't deserve that. He was a decent human being, and in the short time they had gotten to know each other, she had grown very fond of him. She closed her eyes as her body swayed back and forth with the movement of the underground train and she relived the kiss from the evening before. It had been garden magic, that's what he had said.

She was pulled from her reverie by Liam taking her hand. Laura forced herself not to pull away. Behind all of his bravado, she could detect something she'd never really seen before, fear. Caroline was his only sibling, and he loved her dearly.

'Thank you for coming,' he whispered sincerely, the fear now evident in his eyes.

She shrugged her shoulders. 'It's Caroline.'

He squeezed her hand. Then just like that, the vulnerability was gone and he went on to complain about the Tubes and how dirty and crammed they were, and Laura sighed.

As they exited the Tube twenty minutes later, they made their way into the hospital, where they were greeted by a very grave-looking doctor, who updated them on her progress.

'I'm afraid your sister had a difficult night and they have brought her here, where we are more equipped to deal with this sort of situation. We think now she may have experienced a severe brain haemorrhage brought on by a stroke. We have managed to stem the bleeding, and right now she is stable. But the next forty-eight hours will be critical. We have done some more tests and will know more in the next hour. She is conscious but very weak, so you can't spend much time with her, but she has been asking for you.'

Liam was grey and Laura felt sick. They entered the dark-

ened room. Caroline looked so tiny in the bed. Usually a vivacious bubbly character who talked nonstop, she was now lying
there like a broken doll, so still and quiet, very pale. Her curly
blonde hair was scattered across her pillow. Different tubes and
machines monitored her every function.

Tears sprang to Laura's eyes as she sat down next to her and
took her hand. It was limp and cold.

Liam went to the other side of the bed and called out her
name. 'Caroline, Caroline, look who's come here to see you.'

For a long moment, there wasn't any movement. He
appealed to her again, and finally, her eyes slowly fluttered
open. She focused on Laura, and a smile crept across her face.

'You came at last. I've missed you so much.' Her eyes misted
over.

'You will clearly do anything to make me come and see you,'
Laura joked quietly, with tears in her own eyes.

And Caroline smiled wanly, croaking out, 'I see my plan
worked.'

The doctor came in and needed to speak to Liam, who
slipped out of the room, leaving the two of them together.

'You look happy, Laur,' she whispered stiltedly. 'You look
really happy... I haven't seen you look that way for... a long
time.'

Her words shocked Laura. Was it that obvious? She
couldn't bring herself to tell her friend the truth. Laura knew
she'd be heartbroken about Liam and her, and if he wasn't
telling anybody the truth, Laura didn't want to be the one to
break it to her. So, Laura just squeezed her hand.

'You've got to pursue happiness. It's all that matters, really.
Find what makes you happy and do that. You don't owe anyone
anything... remember that.' Her voice trailed off then and her
eyes fluttered shut and she slipped back into a deep sleep.

Laura was transfixed. Had she been hinting to her about her

and Liam's relationship? Had she been telling Laura to follow her heart?

Liam came back into the room and signalled for Laura to come outside. His expression was grave. His voice quivered as he conveyed the news. 'It looks really bad, Laura. They just got the tests back. They were able to repair some of the damage from the clot, but they're not sure if she will make a full recovery. They just don't know. The only chance is for them to go in and operate again, but they're only giving her a thirty per cent chance of survival. But they say if they don't operate, there is a good chance she will die anyway.'

He crumpled then, falling into her arms and sobbing.

He cried out in his distress, 'What shall we do, Laura? What shall we do? I don't want them to operate again. She may get well. People do.'

She held him in her arms, the arms that felt so familiar to her, and rocked him. With both of their parents dead, Caroline was all the family he had, and as upset with him as she was, her heart went out to him.

She spoke gently. 'You have to let them operate, Liam, if it's her only hope.'

He pulled away from her, blowing his nose. She could see he wasn't able to believe this, unable to take all this in. 'But what if they screw up like they did with my dad? She's my only family.'

The doctor came out to see them both and needed Liam to make the final decision, but he was still living in his denial, looking adamantly opposed to another operation, and Laura wasn't sure what he was going to do.

30

HATWORTH MANOR, JUNE 1941

Anya

All of the Land Girls were invited to eat their meals with the staff of the main house. They would congregate in the kitchen in the morning to eat together. It would sometimes be the only time in the day that Anya would catch sight of Nikolai, at the other end of the table. She would steal surreptitious glances in his direction as he sat with a butler and the other footmen, trying not to draw attention to him. It was imperative that no one connected them.

One morning she arrived in the kitchen as usual with Millie. They had been discussing planting the turnips for the autumn when they noticed the room was unusually quiet as they walked in. One of the footmen was reading from the paper, and they silently made their way to their end of the table and settled down to listen.

'What I don't understand,' said one of the maids, 'is why Hitler would want to invade Russia. I mean, it's a huge country. What is he thinking?'

'He's a madman, isn't he?' said one of the other footmen. 'He's not really thinking. He's power-hungry. He wants the world.'

Anya felt the breath tighten in her throat. Had he just said that Germany had invaded Russia?

'Well, that's really going to mix things up,' added the same maid. 'I mean, wasn't Russia on Germany's side? Weren't they working together? So, what will that mean for the war?'

Anya glanced over at Nikolai. His eyes were staring down at his breakfast, but she could just see the concern furrowing his brow. She knew neither of them wanted to ask any more questions and draw attention to themselves, but if Russia was no longer fighting for the Germans, what did it mean for them? What side were they now on? She thought back to the training school where she'd heard rumours of the authorities killing their own agents when it suited them, when things weren't working as they wanted. Would the Russians now come after them, their own people, their own government?

The conversation continued. Anya had a strong feeling of foreboding about this turn of events. There had been no warning about it. She couldn't wait to talk to Nikolai later in the garden, and her stomach tightened with a fear that was now creeping into every aspect of her being.

When she arrived at the gate that evening, he was already waiting for her, pacing up and down under the wisteria. They hurried inside.

Rushing to the willow tree, they moved under the canopy to where they always sat now.

'Oh my God, Nikolai, what does this mean?'

He shook his head, still in obvious disbelief. 'I will go and contact our handler and find out what he knows.'

———

She saw the look of concern on Nikolai's face as he entered the garden the following evening.

'What is it?' she demanded.

'It is a mess. Nobody knows what is going on. They are hearing nothing from Russia and all of the agents and networks here are on high alert.'

'Because the Germans know about the network and the fact we are here as spies.'

He nodded. 'I knew that madman Hitler was not to be trusted. What was Stalin thinking? I asked the handler if we should give ourselves up now we are Allies, and he was adamant about us continuing our work for Russia, and in no way should we give ourselves up. He stated it was highly unlikely we will be pulled out of the field and sent home.'

'But surely, this makes us really vulnerable. Do you trust him?'

Nikolai let out a ragged breath before continuing, 'Honestly no. I am worried we are now expendable, especially if we are caught. I have a feeling they would just cut us loose rather than us being an embarrassment to our own government.'

'We have to make a plan,' said Anya decisively. 'That's potentially three factions, including the Brits, who already would want to get rid of us if they knew who we are. So, you and I have to protect one another. What happens if we get separated?'

He pierced her with his gaze before saying, 'Okay, I have an idea.' He outlined it to her and explained how it would work. It was ingenious. 'And then, if we do that, all you have to do is leave me a note,' he said. 'Here, just below the young willow tree, is the best place, my Mishka. Underneath its weeping branches, it will be difficult to see a patch of disturbed earth. Dig a hole under the branches of the willow tree – nobody will see it – telling me where you have gone. Do you understand?'

She nodded her head.

'Then, with the plan I've outlined to you, we will follow one another until we are reunited again. This is just a precaution, but I feel very fearful of where we are right now. I feel we need to protect one another.'

31

LONDON, PRESENT DAY

Laura

Laura sat holding Liam's hand as they wheeled Caroline into surgery. He had finally agreed to the operation when the doctor had warned him that her blood pressure was dropping and, if they didn't go in soon, the window available to operate would start closing. Laura had taken his chin in her hands and looked deeply into his eyes. 'Liam, you've got to say yes. You've got to do this. I know you distrust doctors because of what happened to your father.' He flinched. His father had been misdiagnosed years before and had ended up not being treated for a heart attack that had finally killed him. 'But just because of what happened to your dad doesn't mean that this is wrong now. On the contrary, this might be your only chance to save Caroline's life. How would you feel if she died because you didn't let them try and save her?'

Her words seemed to shock him, but she knew she had to get through all that fear controlling him. He appeared to understand then and nodded numbly, and she knew that he would agree to let them take his sister into surgery. She just hoped they'd made the decision in time.

After Caroline had been taken to the operating room, she turned to him. 'I think I'll go and get a cup of coffee. Would you like one?' He nodded absently, not even looking up from the floor where he had been staring since they had wheeled his sister away. She felt a massive pang of compassion for him. Laura had never seen Liam look so defeated. This was really hard for him. As someone who prided himself on always being on top of every situation, this was something that was entirely out of his hands, and he was powerless to control it.

Finding the cafeteria, Laura put in an order for a couple of lattes. While she waited, she quickly pulled out her phone to text Jamie. Scrolling down, she found his number from a couple of days before, then hastily tapped in a message.

> *I know how this must've looked to you, and I'm deeply sorry you had to walk into that, but you need to know that Liam and I split up before I left London. But as you can see, he is having trouble coming to terms with this truth. Contrary to what he said, you need to know Liam and I ARE NOT ENGAGED!*

She suddenly felt a pang as she wrote the words, thinking about earlier in the car when Liam had asked her, apparently genuinely wanting to marry her.

She looked down at the ring now; he had insisted she try it on to make sure it fit. She had not placed it on her left hand, not wanting him to think she'd said yes, but had put it on her right hand so as not to lose it, and it fit her perfectly. It was so gorgeous as it glistened and shimmered under the coffee shop's ambient light. A small part of her had been tempted to say yes after wanting to hear the words for so long, but something that tugged on her heart had told her not to jump into this decision.

Right now, all she needed to focus on was getting through this time with Caroline.

She continued to punch the rest of her message into the phone.

> *I really enjoyed last night and would love to see you again. I realize now I should've told you about Liam. I just didn't want to spoil our evening.*

It sounded a bit pathetic, but it was the truth. She read it over and added a kiss to her name. Then, holding her breath, watched it go. Finally, she saw that he was reading it but she felt deflated when he didn't respond. She hoped she hadn't spoiled their new friendship. She had really enjoyed his company the previous few days, but now she felt even more conflicted. Was fate lending its hand? Had it steered her back to Liam for a reason? She thought she owed Liam at least a little time to contemplate his proposal. They had been together for so long, and he'd been amazing when she'd gone through everything with Katie.

A young woman from behind the counter called out, 'Liam and Laura,' and the words stabbed at her heart. They had been Liam and Laura for as long as she could remember. Picking up the coffee cups, she took them back to the hospital corridor to find him.

'It brings it home to you, doesn't it?' he contemplated flatly as she handed over the hot paper cup. 'All the things you're trying to achieve in life, all the things you think are important. Sitting here waiting makes you realize none of it's of any value.'

Taking the lid off her cup and blowing to cool the heat of her own drink, she thought about his words as the smell of fragrant earthy coffee swirled around her. Having life and death hanging in the balance did help make it straightforward for her. But maybe not in the way he was insinuating. It made her more adamant to make sure she made the right decisions for her own happiness. Though she was still struggling to know what that was right now.

All at once, he grabbed her hand, his watery eyes meeting her own.

'I'm so glad you're here, Laura. You're the only person in the world who truly cares about me right now. The only person who I can rely on. The only person who loves me.'

Her stomach twisted as she gave him a placating smile. This wasn't the time to correct his perception. He was on the lowest ebb, and she knew there was so much fear, fear of him losing his sister and of being left alone.

As they sat in the stark corridor, watching people come and go, the passage of time as she knew it ceased to exist. Sometimes they talked and shared favourite memories about Caroline. Sometimes she watched the large clock on the wall at the end of the hallway tick away a whole minute that seemed to last forever; then, thirty minutes had passed in a blink of an eye. The doctor had informed them that the procedure could take up to three hours.

When it hit the fourth hour, Liam started to pace the corridor, frantic. She watched him, her stomach tightening a new knot with the fear of what this could mean.

When the doctor finally came out to see them, his expression was grim. Liam stalked towards him, but the doctor shook his head before he even reached him.

'I'm so, so sorry,' he said in a calm and thoughtful tone. 'We did everything we could, but the damage to her brain was just too severe.'

Laura came to Liam's side, where it was evident from his expression that he could not retain the information.

'So, what are you saying?' he spat out, his anger and frustration evident.

Laura touched his arm. 'They're saying that Caroline's gone, Liam. She's gone.'

'No,' he screamed, 'not again! I don't believe you. I want to see her.'

The doctor looked resolute but not shocked. 'Of course you can see her. We're just finishing, preparing her. We'll bring her out into one of the rooms, and you'll be able to spend some time with her then.'

He lowered his head, then tapping Liam's arm, he walked away. Laura took hold of Liam as, for a minute, she thought he was going to pass out; he was so pale and seemed to be spinning on his feet.

He looked up into her face for confirmation, his eyes wild. 'What does it mean, Laura? What does it all mean?'

'She died, Liam. She's gone,' she said again.

He collapsed into her arms then, sobbing as she held him tightly, feeling distraught herself. Her best friend was dead. As Liam sobbed on her shoulder, she was suffocated by the memories of all the times they had spent together: birthdays, Christmases, holidays. She closed her eyes as she pictured her beautiful, vivacious, bubbly friend whose voice and laughter she would never hear again. Caroline had been so alive, it was unfathomable to contemplate that she was gone. But as she looked at the man sobbing on her shoulder, she realized she had more significant problems ahead of her.

———

They arranged the funeral for ten days later. And as Liam's parents were both dead, only Laura was there and their friends. She helped with all the arrangements, making so many of the decisions. It was strange to be around Liam in this way; he was always so decisive and enjoyed controlling every situation. However, to see him so empty and vacant behind his eyes was frightening for her. She feared for his mental health. He was walking so close to the edge that it occurred to her that he might be tempted to take his own life.

The day before the funeral, she managed to get a minute to herself to talk to Alicia on the telephone.

'I'm so sorry you are going through this, do you need me to come and be there, I can figure something out with the kids if you do,' said Alicia as Laura reassured her friend she would be okay. 'And I feel terribly sorry for Liam, but I know you, Laura. Please don't get caught up in all this. Don't feel responsible for him. It will only make it worse for him in the long run if you don't really want him.'

Laura felt the usual stab in her heart. The big problem was that she wasn't sure of anything. Her feelings were all so mixed up. Coming back to London had only confused her more. Everything around her here was so familiar. She had moved back into the flat, only after Liam had assured her he would sleep on the sofa.

'I'm not sure I can stand to be alone,' he had pleaded with her.

And honestly, she wasn't sure she wanted to be alone either, or on a friend's couch attempting to make pleasant conversation or in an unfriendly hotel. Her mind was going crazy with all of her thoughts. But since she'd moved back in the flat, it had only got harder to resist slipping back into her old life. There were all of her things around her and the familiarity of their long-established routines. The first night after Caroline's death, the two of them had shared a bottle of wine and remembered her. All the good memories they'd had with his sister, looking through tons of photographs, laughing at the time when they'd all been together on holiday in Cyprus the year before.

As she had watched him recall a particularly wonderful story, his eyes had paled to an icy blue in the dim lighting, and she had remembered why she had been so attracted to him for all these years. The longer she stayed with him, the harder it seemed for her to hear her heart. She also felt compelled to take care of Liam. Just as Liam had done when she'd had her breakdown about her sister's death. How would it be if she walked out on him when he needed her the way she had needed him? Surely her own plans could wait a bit longer.

The day of the funeral was horrendous. Not only was it a dark day outside, but the atmosphere inside the church was heavy and ominous. The feeling with everyone was of shock and disbelief. Someone in their prime, taken so quickly, made everyone fearful that they could be next. People came over to the flat after the service, and Liam said very little. As she handed out plates of food, she was unable to shake the look of his distraught face, his terrified eyes unable to meet hers. Earlier he'd stood next to Laura, his ice-cold hand gripping hers at the graveside.

At the wake, a colleague from Liam's office came over to talk to her in hushed tones as he nibbled on a sausage roll. 'I'm so glad you're here for him,' he whispered. 'Liam has been so lost without you. Having you here is everything he needs right now.'

She smiled weakly, feeling like the fraud she was.

After everybody left that night, she felt so lonely it was painful. When Liam approached her and put his arms around her, it felt like the most natural thing in the world to turn her face towards him and kiss him gently on the lips. When he attempted to deepen the kiss, she had pulled away. 'I can't do this, Liam. It wouldn't be fair. I'm not sure what I want, and I don't want to complicate this situation.'

He looked at her, the pain evident in his eyes. 'Does it need to be complicated? Can it not just be comfort for us both? You look as lost as I feel. I just thought maybe it would be nice to have this night, just a moment of closeness when we both seem to need it most.'

She didn't say it, but she desperately needed to be as close to someone as much as he did. She needed a break from all of her own grief too. Liam was familiar, he was known to her, and he was offering her some love. They made love that night in their bed, on the understanding that it couldn't mean anything more than what it was, and with that freedom of expression, it felt so poignant. But afterward as he slept fitfully by her side, she felt overwhelming sadness. So much had changed in her heart towards him. It wasn't just the affair, she'd realized with absolute clarity for the first time in months, but it was the fact that she had moved on, and she no longer belonged in his arms. Making love to him had only reinforced that realization.

The following day, she got up early, and, slipping the ring back into its little velvet box, she left a note for Liam saying she was going for a walk and that she'd bring back coffee. She needed to clear her head. Now she knew exactly what she needed to do, she just had to find the strength to do it.

32

HATWORTH MANOR, JULY 1941

Anya

It was the height of midsummer and the Land Girls had been out ploughing one of the upper fields, Anya driving the tractor, which she had become quite adept at, and the rest of the girls gleaning and harvesting the vegetables. It was already baking hot, though it was barely 10 a.m., and the girls were stripped down to their shirts, sleeves rolled up, no socks, and they had their hair bound up in knotted headscarves, sweating, when Becca approached them. 'Okay, you lot,' she said as Anya brought the tractor to a stop. 'I'm officially giving you the day off.'

They all looked at her in disbelief. 'It's far too hot to work, and you girls haven't stopped since you arrived. I think it's time you had a break. So, I've organized a trip to the seaside for you all today.'

Christine whooped, and Millie threw the pile of radishes she had in her arms down on the floor and dusted off her hands. 'I'm game,' she said.

An hour later, they all climbed into the horse and cart that

Anya and Millie had arrived on months before, Charlie at the reins. Mrs Barton had packed them a large picnic basket, and the girls laughed with one another as they prepared for a day out. They started their journey to the beach and Millie began to sing a roaring chorus of 'Oh I Do Like to Be Beside the Seaside,' and everyone except Anya joined in. She just smiled as she listened.

Millie nudged her. 'You don't know "Oh I Do Like to Be Beside the Seaside"?' she said as they came to the end of the last chorus.

'I guess we didn't sing it growing up,' responded Anya, trying to find a reason she wouldn't know what seemed to be a popular song.

'Annie, you must have lived a very sheltered life,' she said, and they started the chorus again, forcing her to join in until she got all the words.

Once they arrived at the beach, Anya was in awe. She had never been for a day out on the beach in Russia; they were just too far away from Moscow. Now, she couldn't wait to get out onto the sand. Even though the shores were all mined and wired near the water, some areas of the beach, farther up, were open, where they could sit and relax and have fun. Charlie had also been given the day off to get the girls there and back, which kept Millie very happy.

Walking onto the beach, they all lay out on the hot sand to enjoy the weather.

'I bet I could find a way through that barbed wire to get us a paddle in that water,' said Charlie, eyeing it curiously, a white handkerchief knotted on his head to keep the sun off.

Millie grabbed the handkerchief from him and ruffled his hair. 'And get ourselves blown to kingdom come? No, thank you.'

He tried to snatch his handkerchief back, but she threw it over to Christine, who caught it and then threw it to Jennifer.

Then, continuing the game, she passed it to Anya, who joined in the fun. They all laughed as they watched Charlie, trousers rolled to his knees, shins burned from the sun, rushing from one girl to another, shouting out, 'Here, give that back!'

After they ate their lunch, they went for a walk, and all bought ice creams. Then they found a children's paddling pool farther up the promenade to wade in, much to all their relief. After that, they went for a walk on the pier and enjoyed all it had to offer. Charlie bought some saucy postcards, which made Millie blush.

'I'm keeping these in case I get called up later this year when I'm of age. Then I'm going to send them all to you, Millie,' he joked, grabbing her around the waist and tickling her.

'I'll send them right back,' she said defiantly, 'and write on them, "Never heard of him!"'

They stopped at the end of the pier to look out over the water, staring out towards occupied Europe.

'Do you think the Jerries will make it over?' asked Jennifer thoughtfully as she shared a cigarette with Christine, the wind ruffling all their hair.

'No chance,' declared Charlie, his forearms and face already burned red from the sun. 'I can't wait to join up. Until then, the lads will do their job, and we will do ours.'

'I don't think planting potatoes will stop an invasion,' said Millie with a giggle.

'Oh, yes, but Annie can drive her tractor over a few of them, can't you, Ann? You could take on this enemy, right?'

Anya gave a tight smile and shrugged her shoulders. She felt her stomach tighten as it did when they talked about the enemy, every day. She feared being found out, and she couldn't imagine how it would feel to be ostracized from her little family here.

'You seemed distracted,' stated Christine.

'Well, our Annie has a secret. Don't you, Annie?' Millie said.

Annie looked across, not sure where this conversation was going.

'Shall I tell them?'

Anya hitched her breath. Her whole body turned ice cold.

Millie didn't wait for an answer. 'I think she's in love, though I don't know who with, but she is definitely in love.'

Anya stared at her friend, her face growing hot.

'Is it me?' asked Charlie, playfully hooking his arm around her shoulders as Anya shook him off.

'There is no such person,' she stammered, though her tone was unconvincing.

'Right,' said Millie, 'but she walks into the town to post a letter once a week and never tells me who it's to, and she often has that dreamy look about her.'

'It is just an elderly aunt,' she lied, rebuking herself to be more careful. She took a letter into the village every week but destroyed it before she got back to the manor. It was a ruse to do her drop at the bookstore.

She did have a secret, and one that would be deadly if it was ever uncovered.

After they finished the last of the picnic, Charlie, Jennifer, and Christine went off to play on the pinball machine in the penny arcades, and Millie and Anya walked the beach to collect shells. They had already filled their pockets when Millie stooped down and plucked one from the sand.

'Here, Annie. Look at this one.' Anya looked down into her friend's hand. It was a beautiful white, pearlized shell, and it was in the perfect shape of a heart. 'You should have it,' she said. 'Keep it for your sweetheart, the one you are pretending you don't have.'

Anya blushed again.

'What about you, Millie?' said Anya, changing the subject quickly. 'What about you and Charlie?'

Millie shrugged. 'We'll just have to see about that, won't

we?' she said. 'He is younger than me. Though I do have to admit he is so fun to be around and I am a little bit smitten.'

The girls giggled and walked arm in arm back to join the rest of the party. On the way, Millie, as always, talked about her life, her family, her brother, who was in the skies flying for Britain, and her parents back in Birmingham. It was like the perfect day, if only Anya hadn't been living such a lie. On the way home, she felt the loneliest inside that she'd ever felt. She wasn't sure how long she could keep living this double life. She hated deceiving these people that she was growing to love, hated what she was doing. The worst of it was that she feared they would find out at some point, and the thought of that brought her so much sadness.

33

LONDON, PRESENT DAY

Laura

Leaving the flat, Laura caught the Tube to the hospital that had cared for Caroline; they had called the day before to say there were still a few of her personal items waiting to be picked up. Laura decided to save Liam from the heartache and go herself.

A nurse handed to her an envelope, which she slipped into her bag without even looking at the contents. She didn't want to burst into tears at the nurses' desk if there was something heart-stirring inside.

Outside the hospital, the day was fresh and crisp, and the streets around this area were quieter than the bustle of central London, so Laura decided to walk part of the way back to the flat rather than catching the Tube all the way.

Turning a corner, she couldn't believe what she saw in front of her. A shopfront with the words '*The Old Curiosity Shop*' emblazoned above it in an Old English script. *That's right*, she reminded herself. *Walter said it was still here*. She was instantly drawn towards it. Looking in the window, she noted now it housed handmade shoes.

Laura had to ring a bell to enter, but as she stepped inside, she could sense the history that seeped from its walls. This building had been here since the 1500s, and it had that antiquated feel of Old England and the timeless smell of highly polished wood and leather. The floor was uneven and creaked and groaned as she made her way across it, feeling as if she had fallen into an endearing copy of 'The Elves and the Shoemaker.' The walls were painted a stark white and the wooden fixtures a slate grey. The shop was an odd shape with strange angles, apparently made with timber from salvaged ships, the owner informed her. There was even a fireplace set in one of the brick walls. As she wandered the room, she thought about her mystery again. It had barely crossed her mind since leaving Norfolk. But now she recalled reading somewhere that the Charles Dickens Museum wasn't far from here, and once she left the shop, she pulled out her phone to search for it.

She thought about Annie again as she strolled the ten-minute walk and remembered the book she hadn't even had a chance to read that was still in her handbag. Then, turning a corner and onto an unassuming street, she found the museum in a grand Edwardian house behind a blue door. Inside, she took the time to absorb everything. It felt good to be somewhere else, doing something different, not thinking about Caroline or Liam, or feeling the heaviness of the past weeks. She enjoyed the freedom of mingling with people as though she was just an average London tourist.

She stopped in front of a highly polished desk, where a plaque informed her *Nicholas Nickleby* and *Oliver Twist* had been written in this very place. How wondrous to think the author had sat there writing words with quill and ink. She drifted through all the rest of the rooms, enjoying the history. There was even a display of the many editions of Charles Dickens's books. On one of the shelves was the exact copy she had in her bag. Next to it was the information about its publi-

cation, including the date of its release in the 1930s. It was
protected by a plastic cover but was opened to the front page,
and she decided to take a photo of it in case the information
was significant. Reviewing the photo on her phone, something
seemed different from the copy she had in her bag. She
couldn't think what it was but knew something wasn't the
same. She didn't want to get the book out in the middle of the
museum but made a mental note to compare her copy as soon
as it was possible.

On the Tube back to the flat, she pulled out her phone and
expanded the photo. With the book in her other hand, Laura
scrutinized them both together. Then, all at once, she saw it,
and she couldn't help but gasp. Could it be this simple? She
closed the book with growing excitement. Maybe this was the
key. As her sense of adventure brimmed, it felt so foreign to her
after her nearly two weeks of heartache and pain, and she
couldn't wait to get back to Norfolk and Jamie and tell him
about it – if he was still speaking to her.

It was then that it hit her. Laura was already thinking about
her and Jamie as a potential couple, wanting to share things
with him. Even though she was feeling such a responsibility
towards Liam, her heart had truly moved on. She no longer
wanted to share herself with him anymore. This thought hit her
with sadness and joy all in one go. She had thought when she'd
first left London that it was over, because of the affair, but the
truth of it was, that had only been the beginning of the journey
of saying goodbye. Over the years their life together had gone
from something she had seen as solid and long-lasting to being a
house of straw, and the wind of indifference and change had
snatched it from her. Not, as she had thought, by his affair in
one fell swoop, but one piece at a time. Until now, when there
was nothing left.

Liam was part of her past. However, now she had the more
complicated task of convincing Liam of that. Though she felt he

knew it too, deep down. He had just been holding on desperately to her as an anchor, the only family he had.

'Oh, Caroline, what shall I do?' she whispered out to the universe. She sighed deeply and put the book back in her bag, her fingers grazing the items from the hospital. Slipping her hand inside the large white envelope, Laura pulled out the contents that had been in the drawer next to Caroline's bed. She smiled wistfully at the small tube of her friend's favourite moisturizer, a couple of her chunky rings and colourful bangles, and on top was her small journal. On the cover were the words, embossed in silver letters, *'Follow Your Heart.'* Laura's breath caught in her throat. Was this some sort of a sign? She opened the cover, and in her friend's large scrawl were the words 'Do what the book says!' punctuated by a smiley face. And it was then that she knew. If Caroline were here, that was precisely what she would have said to Laura; she could hear her saying it, the sense of adventure in her tone, and the sense of wonderment dancing in her eyes.

When Laura arrived back at the flat, Liam was dressed and ready for work. She was surprised as she handed him the coffee she had bought on the way.

'Are you up for work, Liam?' she asked with concern.

He swirled the coffee around his cup and shrugged his shoulders. 'I left them all in the middle of a couple of big deals, and only I have all the information that they need. They've been managing over the last couple of weeks, but I got a call this morning. They're struggling. Besides, also, I think it'll be good for me to go in.'

The sadness was still in his eyes, but she saw this decision as a good sign. She saw a little bit of the old Liam. A desire to take on the world.

'Did you enjoy your walk?' he asked.

'I picked up the last of Caroline's things from the hospital.'

He nodded sadly. 'Thank you for doing that. I will probably be gone all day. We can talk more when I get back if you want.'

He was subdued but genuine. Over the last weeks, the pain and the heartache of the loss of his sister had changed him, opened him up. She knew this would be a good time to talk to him honestly when he got home that night.

Laura spent the day going through the flat and gathering everything that was hers, and packing it up in bags and cases. She realized with a heavy heart that she'd never really felt part of this home, even though she'd lived in it for six years after they had decided to move in together. It had been Liam's place when she'd met him, and she'd just moved in. It had been the best option at the time for both of them, but everything was really his taste. And even though she'd left her mark a little with some of her furnishings and curtains, etc., it still had the feel of the cold stark sophistication that he loved.

And as she pulled her things from their places, it slowly went back to what it had been when she'd met him, as if she'd never even been there.

Laura had left her car in Norfolk, so she would need to come back and collect everything at a different time when she'd decided on where she was going to live. But at least it would be a quick trip, and she could take some of it with her now on the train. So after she finished packing, she placed her bags in the hall cupboard and called Alicia and told her she was coming back, asking if she might stay a while longer. Alicia was over the moon.

'I know it's been a tough week for you, Laura. But I know you're doing the right thing.'

She knew it too, but it didn't make it any easier. That evening, she decided to cook dinner for herself and Liam. They'd been eating out or grabbing takeout for the last week. And it just felt right to do something together on the last night that they would be together. She searched through her phone for a recipe. And the last one that she'd cooked popped up. The chicken recipe the night that she had found out he had betrayed her. She shook her head with the irony of it. Why not? It was one of their favourites.

She went to Sainsbury's and bought the food she needed. And when he arrived back at six, the dinner was already cooking. His eyes lit up as he came into the house.

'Smells good, Laura. It's nice to come back to dinner cooking.'

She felt the twinge in her stomach with the conversation that was ahead. But first, she would feed him, and they'd enjoy a nice meal. So, they sat down for dinner, and he poured her a glass of wine, and they talked. He told her about his day, and she listened. There was still a sense of sadness, but there was definitely an energy to him now. Being at work had been good for him. When he finally came across her bags in the hallway cupboard, he looked across at her questioningly.

'What does this mean, Laura?' he said in an even tone.

Gone was the anger and the desperation. Now he just seemed deflated. He walked into the front room and looked out of the window. As she approached him, there was no point beating about the bush.

'Look, Liam, this is not right. If I married you now, I'd be marrying you for all the wrong reasons.'

He looked devastated.

'Look at us,' she continued. 'We're completely different people. And I know you don't want to face that. Your affair isn't the reason that we split up; it was a symptom of what was already going on.'

He peered at her then, confused.

'We'd grown apart from each other, and it was no one's fault.'

'I just wanted to hold on to something. I wanted something

that I could count on in my life. And, Laura, I want you to know, I really do love you.'

She smiled sadly. 'And I love you too. I'd forgotten that with the hurt and the betrayal of your affair. So, in a way, I'm glad I got to come back and remember again,' she said. He looked hopeful for a second, but then she continued. 'But the love I feel for you isn't the kind of love we could build a life on. We have history. We have memories. We grew up together through my sadness and the awkwardness of our twenties. But then we grew up *into* different people. I don't think either of us wanted to face that. But we're so different now.'

'Don't they say that opposites attract?' he said despondently.

'They might attract. But I don't think they can build a life together. Not realistically. Not the differences that we have. My life is all about simplicity, about being in nature, about sunrises and sunsets. You like the glamour of life. You deserve something better. So do I. You deserve someone who wants to go to Paris at the drop of a hat and have an expensive meal at the top of the Eiffel Tower with you. And I deserved the joy of sitting on a beach under a homemade knitted blanket and watching the tide. That kind of gap between us is just too big. This probably would have ended years ago if it hadn't been for me losing Katie and the death of your parents. After my breakdown you were wonderful, Liam. I'll never forget that. You were strong for me, exactly what I needed at the time. But as I started to heal and move past it, I didn't need someone to make decisions for me anymore. Didn't need that kind of strength. You deserve somebody like you. What about the woman that you met? She sounds like she was more like you.' He then looked over at her dubiously. 'Wasn't she?' She felt a twinge of hurt, but she also knew she needed to get this point home to him.

'I guess so. She likes living the good life. She even invited me to Brisbane. At our office over there, they're looking for someone with my skills. But of course I said no, because of us.'

'But you don't have to do that now, Liam. That can be a choice. So why don't you take a chance? There's nothing for you here, now. So why don't you go and see what Australia has to offer?'

Liam looked hopeful for a moment. 'What about you, Laura? Will you go back to beard and jumper?'

She laughed at his reference to Jamie.

'I don't know,' she said. 'That was only at the beginning. And after the way that you spoke to him, I'd be surprised if he'd be interested anymore. But at least there's the hope of someone else. Even if there isn't anyone right for me right now.'

He nodded and reached out to her. She moved into his arms, and they held each other there. He kissed her gently on the lips, saying, 'I hope you're happy, Laura. I really hope you're happy. I know I can be overbearing sometimes. I know I can be thoughtless. But you've always been amazing to me. And I've always known, even with my huge ego, I've known what a special person you were.' The tears came then for both of them, not tears of sadness, but tears of understanding that this was over and at least they were ending this in a good way.

When she kissed him on the cheek the next day and made her way to the train station, she didn't know what lay ahead, but she finally felt released.

34

HATWORTH MANOR, AUGUST 1941

Anya

Anya heard the scream even though she was in the garden and recognized it straightaway as Millie's. Dropping her spade where she'd been planting potatoes, she raced out of the walled garden towards where she had heard the sound. As she sped across the estate, it was undeniable what was going on. Millie was in the arms of Mrs Barton, and a man in an RAF uniform stood in front of them, his cap in his hand. This had to be bad news. As she reached her side, Anya looked over at Mrs Barton for an explanation.

'It's her brother,' she whispered. 'He was killed yesterday.'

Anya's heart hurt for her friend. Millie was beside herself, sobbing on the shoulder of the older woman. When she saw Anya, she turned and threw herself into her friend's arms. 'Oh my God, Annie. Oh my God. I can't believe it.'

Anya felt the weight of her body as she sank into her, the heat of her friend's face warming her shoulder as Millie's tears saturated her blouse.

'Take her upstairs to her bed,' encouraged the cook. 'Get her settled down. I'll get her a cup of tea.'

Anya nodded and helped her friend carefully up the stairs. She got her into their room and sat her on the end of her bed. As she pulled off Millie's work boots, Millie's whole body was wracked with her sobs. She sounded like a wounded animal.

Laying her down on her pillow, Anya smoothed out her hair and pulled up the covers, cooing to her as her own mother had done when she was a child and had been hurt.

'It's all going to be okay,' she whispered. 'You need to rest.'

Millie grabbed her arm, her eyes wild with her pain.

'I hate the Nazis. All those enemy bastards,' she spat out, her tone something Anya had never heard before. 'What kind of a person does this?'

Anya was stopped dead in her tracks. *Me*, she thought. *I am that kind of a person.* The pain of that thought tightened her throat. How could she be part of something so evil? Her mind started to whirl as she continued to nurse her friend, but she felt all the same anger and frustration and absolute pain deep down. Later that evening, as soon as Millie was settled, Anya made her way out to the garden, where she was alone, and that's where she sobbed, for her part of this web of evil, and what would happen if her now dearest friend found out who she really was.

———

Nikolai found her there later, crying in the garden. She was crouched beneath the willow tree, her head in her hands, trying to muffle the sound. He watched her for a second. He ached with desire for this woman who was so beautiful and held his heart. Then, moving towards her, he called out gently, 'Anya?'

She started and looked up, quickly wiping the tears away, and then seeing that it was Nikolai, she released the breath she'd been holding and looked embarrassed. She tried to get to her feet. He put his hand on her arm. She couldn't seem to look him in the eye.

'What is it?'

She just shook her head in response, and, pulling a handker-chief from her pocket, she blew her nose and wiped her eyes.

'I can't do it, Nikolai,' she sobbed. 'I can't do it anymore. I can't live this lie.'

His heart went out to her as he knelt beside her.

'What happened?' he asked quietly.

'Millie's brother was just killed. Shot down by the Germans. And you and I came here working with them. How do you stand it, Nikolai?' she hissed at him in frustrated anger.

His stomach twisted with his own conflicting emotions. He, too, was having second thoughts about what they were doing. He was tired. He was tired of all the secrecy and so damn tired of this war.

She continued in a spluttering whisper. 'I'm not even sure what side we're on. Somebody's going to end up shooting us for being spies, and it could be either side. I'm lost. I don't know who I am anymore. My life was complicated in Russia but at least I knew who I was. There's no hope for us here. No way out of this where we can stay alive that I can see.'

As she looked up at him, her face red from crying, the heartache obvious in her desperate eyes, he couldn't stand it anymore. His attraction to her was just too strong and his need to comfort her overpowered him. He had to hold her, had to feel her body close to his own, had to make it better somehow, as though if he didn't something inside him would snap. An ocean of desire overtook him, something akin to animal instinct. He saw his arms reaching out as he pulled her close to him, holding her so close he could feel her frantic heart beating in her chest, smell the fragrance of her hair. As her tiny body filled the space that had been yearning for her for so long, for a second he thought he had just imagined her in his arms as he had so many times before. But with great surprise, when he looked down she was there. Closing his eyes to intensify the feeling, he drew in a long slow breath as she let out a deep sigh. But now entwined in her, instead of feeling satisfied, the whole of his body came alive in a way he had never known before. He desperately wanted to kiss her but dared not hope that was possible. Unwilling to let go of her or break this spell, he really didn't want to scare her in case all she needed was his comfort as she continued to cry in his arms.

When she slowed to a stilted sob, her shoulders lifting as she tried to catch her breath, she slowly drew away and searched his face intently. He swallowed down his brimming desire as he looked into her beautiful green eyes, so sad and red from crying. God, he wanted to kiss her so badly.

'Nikolai.' She whispered, 'There is something else, something important I need to tell you.'

His chest started to tighten. He didn't want to break this moment between them, prayed she wasn't going to reject him somehow. But what if something had happened? Had someone seen her? Had something been uncovered? They'd both been so careful. His mind raced with a thousand thoughts as he fought his need to throw caution to the wind and kiss her anyway. Somehow within the avalanche of emotions that was coursing through his body he found a calm tone, though his voice was tight.

'What? Tell me.'

'It's about you, Nikolai,' she whispered.

He pulled back. 'Me?' Oh no, here it came. She was going to say this was wrong, that she needed more distance.

But instead of pulling away she took his shoulders and pulled him towards her until their faces were so close he could feel her breath on his lips.

Her eyes narrowed with her intensity. 'I want you to answer

me one question, and I want you to be honest with me. Nikolai, can you do that?'

He nodded apprehensively as his stomach clenched with the tension.

'Do you love me?'

Releasing his breath in a low hiss, he was taken aback. So taken aback, all he could do was tell her the truth.

'I do. I have been in love with you for a very long time.'

A look of relief swept across her face. She sucked in a breath then teased it out slowly with relief, and then, placing her forehead against his own, closed her eyes and whispered, 'That's good, because I love you too.'

Before he had time for her words to really sink in, she kissed him so passionately he didn't get a chance to catch his breath. As Anya pulled him close and intensified the kiss, blood pounded through his head and his chest with such ferocity he was scared it might actually stop his heart. And as she began to run her hands down his body, every single nerve ending inside him came alive, his skin prickling with ecstasy. It was so heightened by her touch that the desperate need to make love to her became so acute it was almost painful, as the desire he had been holding back for months seared through his whole being.

35

LONDON, PRESENT DAY

Laura

On the train back to Norfolk, Laura decided to be courageous and text Jamie once more.

Hi, Jamie, I just wanted to let you know I am on my way back to the manor. The friend I went to visit in hospital passed away so it has been a roller coaster of a couple of weeks and I'm looking forward to the peace and quiet of a walled garden. I thought I might take a trip to the beach tomorrow just to clear my head before I start work. Would you like to join me?

She pressed 'send' and waited with bated breath. It showed he had read it, but there was no response. So, she added:

I know the last time we saw each other was awkward, to say the least, but I have no plans to return to the flat in London and I have packed up all my things. Liam has finally come to terms with the fact this is over, and I'm ready for a new start in my life and would love to explore our friendship and where that was going. No pressure. Either way, it would just be nice to have coffee with a friendly face. Your choice of location. What do I need to do to make this up to you?

She pressed 'send' and her hand reached up to cover her mouth as she held her breath.

Text bubbles rippled and then there was a pause, then a short response.

So sorry about your friend. I will be at Beach Cafe at 9 a.m., if you need to talk.

She teased out the breath she had been holding and felt a jolt of excitement at the prospect.

———

The next morning, she made her way out early to Cromer. The sun was just starting to rise in a lazy haze of morning cloud over the water, its fingers stretching forth to illuminate idyllic white-washed cottages and their slate-grey roofs. As she drove slowly through the town, she took a moment to enjoy the early morning scene, complete with a milkman clattering along on his cart and two well-fed cats stretched out on a red brick wall enjoying the first rays of warmth. Turning her car onto the beach road, her heart was stirred by the emerald-green water that lapped gently at the grey seawall that was coated in a soft green moss. In the harbour, boats bobbed in contentment as the sunlight glinted off metal awnings and the edges of their red hulls.

Parking her car, Laura stepped out and took in a full breath of the cool salty air. She was drawn from her reverie by the high-pitched call of a squabble of seagulls that swooped down in frantic spirals, being fed crumbs of bread by an elderly woman at the water's edge. Tucking her hands into her pocket, Laura strode to the coffee shop where she had agreed to meet Jamie. Beach Cafe, with its five-star rating, she had noted on her phone, was tucked in a side street, a tad up a short hill, from where it had an extensive overlook of the harbour. She nodded to a man in a flat cap walking his dog as she ducked inside the coffee shop. Apparently, Beach Cafe was known for its lovely ambiance, and as she opened the large heavy wooden door, she could see why. The aroma of rich coffee and sweet pastries welcomed her in.

Her eyes adjusted to the darkened room, bathed in a warm golden light. Inside, the early morning trade was a bustle of what looked like regulars huddled in corners laughing and sharing stories, hands clasped around thick pottery mugs, and in front of them plates of the remnants of flaky delicacies. A quick survey of the shop confirmed to her that Jamie wasn't there yet. So, she found a cosy nook nestled into the thick whitewashed stone walls next to the window where she could watch for his arrival. A pleasant young woman wearing a traditional black-and-white waitress outfit bounded up to the heavy oak table and, speaking in a strong Norfolk accent, took Laura's order.

Laura's hand was shaking slightly as she scrolled through her phone, needing something to occupy her mind until Jamie arrived. She realized, noting her fast-beating heart, that she couldn't wait to see him, but she was also nervous after their last encounter.

She didn't have long to wait. And her heart jumped a little in her chest as she saw him approaching from the far end of the village, making his way down the seawall steps. She would have known him anywhere. His easy comfortable stride, one hand stuffed in a jean pocket as he smiled and connected with the locals he knew along the way. He entered the coffee shop just as the waitress arrived back at the table with Laura's coffee.

'Hi, Jamie!' the waitress called out to him as he entered through the door.

Jamie beamed back at the pretty face. 'How are you, Emma?'

'Better now, after seeing you,' she joked.

Laura felt the grip in her chest, not quite sure what to do with herself now he was here. Suddenly she felt very small and insignificant. As he continued to chat to Emma for a minute, she felt her nervousness rise up inside of her. Gripping hold of the coffee cup, she was grateful for its heavy pottery base, because if it had been any more delicate, she might have snapped it in two with the tension she was feeling. She took a sip and swallowed it down hard while she waited.

Jamie turned to her, and there was that smile, the one that melted her heart. Should she hug him? Should she kiss him on the cheek? She felt flustered. He made up her mind for her. Striding towards her, he pulled her up into his arms and gave her an incredibly warm hug. It made her feel safe, and the memory of their time in the garden floated back to her. Finally releasing her, he gazed down.

'It is good to see you, Laura.'

Laura was feeling a little overwhelmed with their closeness, so she just nodded.

Emma was suddenly by their side.

'Will you be wanting some coffee, Jamie?' she inquired. 'And maybe a little pastry or something? Or have you got all the sweetness you need right there?' She laughed.

Brushing off her insinuation, he responded with, 'I'd love just a cup of coffee, please, Emma, thank you.'

Emma bustled away to do her job, and Jamie sat down opposite Laura and let out a contented sigh. Had it only been a couple of weeks? It had felt like they'd been apart for years. They both laughed then, with the awkwardness and with the joy of seeing one another again. She felt coy, nervous, and blurted out the first thing that came into her head. 'How is your day going?'

He raised his eyebrows. 'Well, it's only just started, but it has great potential.'

She decided to plunge right in. 'I'm so sorry. I'm so sorry about what happened at the cottage. I had no idea that Liam was going to come and he had no right to tell you that we were engaged or that I was his partner.'

Jamie brushed it away with a bat of his hand, but she saw hesitancy in his eyes even though he was acting nonchalant. She remembered again the shock she'd seen on his face when he had met Liam.

'You do believe me, don't you? You do believe me that there's nothing between us, now?'

Jamie's body language shifted, and he sat back in his chair, and she sensed he wasn't sure about either of them. He swallowed hard before speaking. 'I'm sure you've been together a long time. You were together a long time,' he corrected himself. 'It must be hard for both of you.' What he said sounded rational, but the tone under his voice reflected a carefulness. She could tell he was trying to weigh it all up. She wished she could have eroded what had happened, and hoped they could get past it.

'It's over,' said Laura decisively. 'Me and Liam, it's over for sure.'

He nodded. 'I was just surprised you didn't say anything about him. I'm just a little wary of secrets, even in a friendship, Laura. I need to know our relationship is based on honesty. I dealt with far too much deceit in my marriage. So, it is important to me that there is honesty no matter how hard it is to face. No secrets, Laura, if we are to be friends. Let's start as we mean to go on.'

'Okay,' she whispered.

She saw the pain then, and realized how fortunate it had been that he had given her a second chance, and, swallowing down a gulp of coffee, she decided that she needed to tell him her biggest secret. She owed him that, so he would believe she had heard him.

'If we are to have a clean slate, there is something I need to tell you about me right away, because it affects everything in my life. Everything is tainted by this one past event. It is the reason that I stayed with Liam for so long. It is also, I think, the reason I feel compelled to continue this search for Annie.'

Jamie was going to respond, but Emma suddenly appeared with his cup of coffee and the moment was gone. While she placed down his cup and bantered with him in a friendly way, Laura waited and felt the familiar quiver begin in her chest that always accompanied a retelling of her childhood nightmare.

When, finally, they were alone, he took a sip of his coffee, and, sucking in breath, she began her story.

'When I was twelve, my sister died, and it was my fault.'

He froze, his cup in his hand suspended in mid-air with disbelief.

'My sister was seven, and we'd gone to visit relatives, and had been playing in some woods close to the house. It was not dense or dangerous – just a small copse of trees near a little brook, perfect for playing. Then after a short time, I was hot and tired. I wanted to go back to the house and read, and I was angry I had to look after her, but Katie was adamant she wanted to continue to play.' Laura's breath caught in her throat, preparing herself for the strongest feeling of guilt of her confession as it had been her idea.

Jamie's eyes moved from wariness to filled with concern as he began to register the seriousness of what she was telling him.

'I suggested she play a game of scavenger hunt while I sat and read my book. It was a sunny day, and I was tired and if I had to stay, I just wanted to enjoy the sunshine. I remember to this day that it was *Charlotte's Web*, a worn pink paperback, dog-eared at the corners, the picture of a smug-looking pig dominating the front cover.

'Reluctantly, Katie agreed, and I told her a list of things to find in the little wood to hunt down. It was the usual things for a hunt, an acorn, a white feather, a brown leaf, and then I added a blue robin's egg, knowing that would be really challenging for her to find, and it would take her a long time to get back to me. Then I sat on the kerb of the quiet street, which I hadn't seen one car come up and down while we'd been there. As I watched her run through the trees, searching the ground, excited to be playing a game, I settled down to read my story. When she would find something, she'd call out to me.

'"An acorn. I've got the acorn" and so on. I would just wave half-heartedly, and then I'd bury my head back in the book.

'I'll never forget the last thing I heard her say, with a child-like squeal in her tone: "I've got it. I can't believe it. I have found it." I didn't look up because, inwardly, I groaned, hoping it didn't mean that she'd got everything and that she'd come and bother me to play with her again. But I was so engrossed in what I was reading I didn't even hear or see the car until it was almost upon us. All I heard was the screech of brakes. The sunlight was dazzling, but I can still see clearly the shadow of Katie's childish frame in the lemon-yellow dress with the miniature white daisies that she loved, billowing in the wind as she ran. Then it was as though everything happened in slow motion; I was frozen, watching it unfold in front of me, unable to stop the inevitable. Her tiny body racing into the road, her fist clenched shut with her treasures, her face so excited and then the knowledge of what was about to happen, the sickening thud of her body hitting metal and her being tossed into the air, above the car, landing on the roof like a rag doll and sliding down onto the road.

'I jumped up, racing towards her. Willing her to be okay, knowing my mother would be angry with me if she was hurt. As

I got to her tiny, lifeless body, I could see the thing that she had in her little hand, the last piece of the treasure hunt, the fragile pieces of a blue robin's egg. But she was so quiet and still, and so pale, and with utter shock I knew. Even before I touched her, I knew that Katie was gone and that I'd never see my sister again, but in that moment, I couldn't believe it. It had happened too quickly. I tapped her hand, shook her shoulders, willing her to open her eyes.

'Even though somewhere deep inside I knew it was fruitless, I continued to cry out her name over and over again. Racing back to the house I remember my legs were shaking so violently I could barely run and I felt so sick I thought I might actually throw up before I even got to the house. I will never forget the look on my mother's face as I broke the news to her. She had been roaring with laughter when I entered the kitchen to tell her, and I would always remember that, because I never heard her laugh like that again.'

'Oh, Laura,' Jamie whispered, taking her hand in his own, an apparent reflex, without even realizing he was doing it, though she was glad of it.

'What followed were the longest and shortest hours of my life. Moments when it went so fast I couldn't catch my breath, and when it moved so slowly it was excruciating. A blurred montage of harrowing moments. Ambulance sirens and paramedics racing to help, a policeman talking to a pale fragile version of my mother, being held upright by her sister. Another policewoman removing her hat and sitting next to me asking gentle questions, which I answered mechanically, as I stared down at the cover of my book on the ground with a picture of a smiling pig as it flapped open and closed, its pages fluttering in the breeze. And the most painful memory of all that finally made the truth real, catching sight of the driver of the car, the elderly gentleman, his shoulders shaking as he sobbed across his steering wheel. It was like a nightmare come to life, frantic activity and people trying to do what they could to help, coupled against the total shock and motionless of others. In a split second, my life went from the carefree thoughts of school, friends, and holidays to guilt, sadness, and endless tears.

'It was so hard on my family. And though nobody said it, there was a sense that they felt I was responsible. So, I just took on that guilt, too. Then, five years later, my father was dead. And my mother never really recovered from either of their deaths, and she became a shadow of her former self. I took responsibility for all of it, and on top of it all, I missed Katie terribly.'

Laura took a minute to drink her coffee as tears streamed down her cheeks and Jamie silently continued to wait, holding her hand.

'It was the deepest and hardest pain, and it was the loneliest time in my life. And I'll never forget it. It's always with me, just a breath away. I think the shadow of that twelve-year-old walks beside me sometimes, still heartbroken, still filled with the pain and guilt. It took a while to process but when I was twenty-four I had a complete breakdown. Days of not really knowing who I was and not wanting to go on. I would replay Katie's last minutes in my memory over and over again, wanting a different outcome.'

'So you think that's why finding out what happened to Annie is so important to you?' Jamie asked slowly, apparently putting all the pieces together.

'I know it's a wild hope, as she is probably dead and the person she left the message for is probably dead too, but when I found the box in the secret garden, on the top of the soil there was a tiny blue robin's egg.' Laura's voice hitched with the painful confession but she pushed through the tightness in her throat to continue, 'And I felt it was a message from Katie that I had to find whoever hid the box, and now you see why I have to know for sure.'

'Laura, I'm so sorry that happened to you,' he whispered, gently stroking her hand as she pulled out a tissue and blew her nose.

She hadn't intended this conversation to go in the direction it had, but it felt good to tell him. And even to clarify her growth to herself. 'It was hard, but I am definitely healing. Being able to let go of my relationship with Liam proved that. Liam was brilliant during my breakdown, organizing all of my medical care, and it is the reason we moved in together. You see, underneath all that bravado he does have a heart and I will never forget what he did for me. He was the right partner for the person I used to be, but not the person I am becoming. Like shedding a skin of the past, I am becoming a whole new me, and the new skin is raw and tender, but it is real. Which is why I wanted you to know. To at least understand why a person with a character such as Liam's could have been such an important part of my past, but not my future. And to also show you I intend to be honest with you, as you said, "no matter how hard it is to face."'

'Then we will do this together,' he said quietly, 'follow the clues to the end, no matter how long it takes.' She took in a long slow breath and nodded.

Now her darkest secret was out, she felt the relief, and as they ordered a second cup of coffee Laura settled herself, moving her thoughts from the past to her present, and, drawing in a new breath, she updated Jamie on her most significant step forward so far.

'I have an idea of what the importance of the book means. Are you up for an adventure today? If what I think is right, we will need to go on a journey.'

A smile crossed his face as he raised his eyebrow and, taking another swig of his coffee, he nodded his head.

36

HATWORTH MANOR, AUGUST 1941

Anya

The next few months were the happiest Anya had ever known. She may have still been in a war. She may still have felt the fear that was all around them, but she was so in love it seemed to soften all the rough edges of her life. It was hard keeping the secret of her love affair to herself, even though she suspected that Millie sensed it, and would look quizzically over at her sometimes.

Now their love was confessed, Anya gave way to all the feelings she had been keeping buttoned down while she had been trying to maintain a seriousness to their work. Nikolai was her first thought on waking and last thought when she finally fell to sleep. In between she spent the whole of her days hoping to get a glimpse of him, counting down the minutes until she would be in his arms again. She could hardly wait to go down for breakfast in the morning, and as she and Millie would enter the main kitchen with their cheerful 'good mornings' she would quickly scan the room to locate him as her heart would start to thud.

They both worked hard during breakfast not to catch each other's eye, in case they revealed their true feelings. But once she was settled at the table and the buzz of conversation resumed around the room she would give herself a minute where she would just enjoy looking over at him for a long moment. She couldn't draw attention to their relationship though; this had been stipulated before the assignment in case one of them was caught. Even so, she would still give herself that special time to enjoy looking at him. Despite their lack of eye contact she would often sense his eyes upon her as she spent the whole of breakfast fighting the uncontrollable urge to rush over to him, run her fingers through his washed damp curls, cover his cleanshaven face in kisses, or feel the heat of his body wrapped around her own. Instead of responding to any of those impulses, Anya would swallow down her emotions that robbed her of sleep and her desire to eat and would try to force down her breakfast so no one suspected what was going on inside her. Whenever she would catch sight of him in the day, her stomach would flip-flop with joy because just being away from him was painful and made her ache. It actually physically hurt her, as if her heart were being crushed in a vice. As soon as it became dark, her excitement started to mount. Once all the staff were in bed, she could barely wait for Millie's breath to slow to a deep sleep before hastily putting on her clothes and moving quickly through the house and out the back door to the garden. The anticipation of seeing him was almost as exciting as seeing him itself. She would imagine the first time their eyes would meet and the effect that would have on her whole body. The first time she could touch him, their first kiss, and the thoughts of all of that would exhilarate her as she rushed through the warm night air, keeping to the shadows so she couldn't be seen on the way to the secret garden. Sometimes he too couldn't wait and would be pacing underneath the wisteria bush, looking for her.

Arriving, Anya would fumble nervously with the key as he would slip his arms around her waist, his fingers pressing gently into the soft skin above her hips as he drew her body towards him, flattening her against his own. As he did, he would cover the back of her neck and shoulders with kisses, sending shivers down her spine. Pushing open the door, she would kick it closed and lock it quickly, desperate to touch him and for their first kiss. Then pressing him against the wooden door she would allow all of her pent-up passion to be released as their hands and lips hungrily found one another. When, finally, they came up for air, panting to catch their breath, their clothes often untucked, they would laugh with the pure joy of just being with one another. Only then would her body, which had tightened throughout the day like a wound-up string, finally relax. Once they had satisfied that first urge, they would hasten to the safety of the willow tree, removing their clothes as they went, then safely under canopy they would start making love. Other times they would just hold each other close, interweaving their naked limbs together. As they held and kissed one another they would talk about their love and how much they'd missed each other. And no matter how close their bodies were, she never felt close enough to him.

Sometimes they made love slowly, with his intent gaze conveying all of his care and desire for her as he gently caressed her and covered every inch of her body with kisses as she shivered with exhilarated pleasure. Other times it would be urgent and passionate, both of them breathing deeply and moaning with deep carnal pleasure. Either way, she didn't think she would ever get enough of the joy and intensity of their lovemaking. They still swapped information once their desires were met, but in between their work, the secret garden became the place they explored their love. She hungered for him in a way neither of them had ever hungered before, and no matter how many times they made love, it never felt enough for her. Sometimes they made love in every part of the garden, under the stars every night as though it was their last time.

She loved how sensual it all was. The smell of evening jasmine mingled with the roses. The way they were serenaded by the gentle hoot of the barn owl and the frogs, and how their exhausted naked bodies glistened in the moonlight as they lay side by side on the cool damp grass. The garden was magical and they felt its love surround them and protect them. But even with these brief moments of pleasure, there was still the realization that this was a life captured in a bottle, borrowed time, and she wondered when the day would come when it would come to an end. Then, one evening when they had just finished making love, they lay naked as Nikolai drew light fingers along her skin; tracing gentle circles on her stomach, he watched her face and seemed to sense something was wrong.

She had hoped to hide what had preoccupied her all day from him, but when he asked her, she attempted to brush it off.

'I'm just being stupid, that's all,' she insisted when he pressed her.

She tried to roll away from him, but he stopped her and turned her to face him.

'Tell me what is wrong. I can't bear to see you so sad.'

She sighed and gave in as he sat next to her and cradled her in his arms.

'It's ridiculous,' she said. 'You will laugh at me if I tell you.'

'I'd never laugh at you,' he whispered into her hair as he kissed the tip of her ear. 'Tell me what is wrong.'

She turned to face him again. His eyes looked full of concern.

She asked him bluntly, 'Do you love me?'

He looked relieved. 'Mishka, you know I love you. I think I fell in love the minute you pushed me down into the mud.'

She smiled at the memory. 'You were horrendous during our training,' she said defensively. 'I should have pushed you down in that mud every day.'

He chuckled and pulled her close again. 'I wanted you to fail. I was scared of my attraction to you and didn't want you to come here and your life to be in danger. Why don't you think I love you?'

'It's not that I doubt it. It's just all so pointless, isn't it? Look at our lives. Every day we have a chance of being caught and killed. The only time we can meet is here in the garden, under the cover of darkness. This is not really what I expected when I fell in love. I hoped to announce my love to the world, telling everybody, my friends, my family...' Her breath caught then, thinking about her mother.

He propped himself up on one elbow and caressed her cheek, seeming to sense her thoughts. 'She would have been so proud of you, Anya. She would have been so proud of the fact you walked away from that evil man. You stood up to him. And even though we're caught in whatever this is now, this crazy web of deceit, not knowing who we're working for, it doesn't mean that we are terrible people. You were in a desperate situation and I was so blinded by my need to find out about my father and still feel eaten up by not knowing what happened. I wish I could go back though. I truly do. I would have made different choices. But then I never would have met you...'

Pulling around her shoulders the blanket she kept hidden in the garden, Anya stood up and walked away from him. Then, running her hands through her hair, she turned. 'I just wanted more for my life, Nick. I wanted it all. A love affair, a wedding, a child, maybe two.'

A smile crept across his face. 'With your beautiful green eyes,' he continued her train of thought.

'I wouldn't have cared,' she said, shaking her head. 'I just wanted a normal life. I never really thought about all of this before. I didn't think I had another option at the time. I thought it was my only way out. Now I'm regretting everything. I was stupid to think this was the only way, and there is no way back.' She got down on her knees and pulled him close. 'I love you so much. All I want to do is be your wife and give you children, and instead we are probably both going to die as spies.'

'Then let's get married.'

She rocked back on her heels and laughed.

He took her hands in his own and kissed the tips of her fingers. 'Anya Baranov, would you do me the greatest honour of being my wife?'

'Why not?' she laughed, mocking him, thinking he was joking. 'I'm sure there's a Russian Orthodox church around here somewhere we could use and we'll just go and get our birth certificates, shall we?'

He pulled her to her feet, his gaze so intent she began to think he meant it.

'Marriage is more than that. Marriage is a connection between two people who are in love on a much deeper level. We can get married between ourselves.'

'Without witnesses? What are you talking about?' She still didn't understand what he was trying to say.

'The trees in here can be our witnesses. The flowers and the owl right there in the tree. Let's get married right here in the garden.'

Shaking her head, she started to laugh again.

'I'm serious, Anya.' He pulled her close. His warm, naked arms held her as he whispered into her ear, 'I want to be your husband, and just because we can't do it officially doesn't mean that I don't want to have a ceremony with you right here.'

She pulled away and studied his face, which was alive with his suggestion. 'You're serious. What, with me wrapped in this blanket?'

'Yes. Exactly like that, beautiful and natural with your hair all tousled from making love. Let's do it right now. We will make up our own vows. We will promise ourselves to one another. I will give you something, and you can give me something. Then in our heart of hearts, we'll know that we're married.'

'You're incorrigible.'

'Seriously,' he said, pressing the point and squeezing her hands. 'I want you to know I'm serious about us.'

'Okay,' she responded coyly, starting to warm to the idea. 'Where should we get married? Over here under the apple tree? With the fountain and the frogs as our musical accompaniment?'

'No, over here, where we can see the moon the best.'

She looked across to where he was pointing, just beyond the rose arch, and she agreed. The pink roses fragranced the air with their perfume, mingling with the night jasmine, and together they created an intoxicating scent. He then slipped on his trousers, but continued bare chested to help her gather flowers to interweave traditional Russian flower wedding crowns. Then Anya, still wrapped in her blanket, placed her hands in his and walked him to the rose arch. As they turned to face one another, she ran a hand down his firm muscular chest, now freckled and darkened from the summer sun. He had been helping the gardener build a stone wall earlier that week, not really part of his job, but he had volunteered. 'I like your wedding attire,' she said, placing a kiss in the centre of his chest and making him shiver.

'You have never looked more beautiful either,' he said, placing his lips on her bare shoulder and making her shiver too.

Pulling her close, he whispered into her ear in Russian. 'Are you ready? There is no going back, Anya. You are the only one for me.'

In the moonlight she studied his face, lingering on the circle of tiny sun-darkened freckles that she loved so much that encircled his intense blue eyes as he scanned her face for assurance.

Slowly she nodded, feeling her stomach tighten with the seriousness of their decision.

Carefully, placing the flower crown on her head, he drew his face so close to hers she could feel his breath warm her cheeks as he spoke in their native tongue with deep conviction.

'I, Nikolai Petroff, take you, Anya Baranov, as my wedded wife and I promise you love, honour, and respect, to be faithful to you, and not to forsake you until death do us part.'

He said it with such intensity she shuddered in his arms.

She looked up into his face, and then placing his crown also spoke, also in Russian. It was the first time she had spoken to him in Russian in a long time, and he appeared to enjoy the familiar way it sounded on her lips. It made all this feel real to her, after months of hearing each other speak only English.

'I, Anya Baranov, take you, Nikolai Petroff, as my wedded husband and I promise you love, honour, and respect, to be faithful to you, and not to forsake you until death do us part.'

'And I promise,' he said, whispering into her ear, the smell of their floral crowns between them intoxicating, 'I promise I will always love you no matter what. You will always hold my heart. My life didn't start until you arrived in it, and it would stop if ever you were gone. So, all I want is to be by your side, enjoying every minute we are granted.'

He leaned down and kissed her tenderly and she noted that he smelt of fresh air and roses.

She then responded, her tone as earnest as his own. 'And I promise if for any reason we are ever parted, I will wait for you every day until the day I die. Only you shall have my heart. Only you shall have my love.'

Then as he held her there in the moonlight, she marvelled at how much it felt different, just proclaiming their vows in such a profound way; she did actually feel married to him, even though there was no one to witness them but the owl and the trees.

'What shall we give one another?' she said, giggling.

He reached into his pocket, and in there was the heart-shaped shell she had given him, the one she had collected on the beach with Millie. He pulled it out, kissed it, and placed it in her hand. 'I am giving you this back. All my love goes with it.'

'I shall love it forever,' she said.

In return, she raced over to her pile of clothes and, laughing, pulled out her lucky penny, the one she kept with her always – a gift from her mother's home country.

She placed it in his hand. 'With this coin, I give all my love to you, my betrothed, my lover, my husband.'

He smiled and turned it over in his hand. 'A penny, huh? Not the biggest of dowries. But I will take it,' he said, kissing it and slipping it into his pocket.

'Now we must do something to commemorate our love, so the garden remembers,' she said.

'Okay,' he said, 'I have an idea. Don't look while I do something.'

Anya studied him with a puzzled expression as he bounded toward the apple tree. In response to his request she moved to the swing and rocked gently while she waited – a cool breeze chilling her bare shoulders as she stared up at the golden moon surrounded by the starry night's sky.

When he had finished, he took her over to the base of the tree, guiding her hands, letting her fingers run along the trunk so she could feel his work with the small knife he always carried. She smiled as she felt small ears and the round face, and by the light of the moon, she could just make out the shape of a baby bear.

'For my Mishka,' he said with a smile. 'So the garden will never forget you.'

Then lying in one another's arms under the apple tree for

the first time as husband and wife, they looked up through the twisted branches to the full moon, believing nothing could ever rob them of this joy. But also both knowing that a real world lurked outside their walls of safety, and it was only a matter of time before they would have to pay the price for their part in this war.

37

HATWORTH MANOR, OCTOBER 1941

Anya

As the carefree days of summer turned to autumn, the harvest was finished and the Land Girls prepared to get the soil ready for the spring plantings. In October, Charlie turned eighteen and got his call-up papers, and they all gathered in the kitchen for a party to say goodbye. Becca brought down the gramophone player from her family rooms. Anya looked over at Charlie, who had put on his uniform to show them all. It had only been eight months since she'd arrived, but she felt close to him, as if it were a younger brother who was leaving them. He was always ready to tell her a joke or make her smile. He was a simple sort of person but with a tender and kind heart. And as she watched him joking with them all, he looked so grown up in his new uniform of khaki brown, his hair neat, now cut to the regimented length. Mrs Barton had cooked him a cake with some of the house rations, and she cut him a large slice.

''Ere, watch out,' he said, blowing out air when he saw the size of it. 'If you feed me up too much, I won't be able to do my belt up on my uniform.' He tapped his slender frame, and Anya smiled. It would take more than a slice of cake to put any meat on his bones.

The head gardener with his young son by his side gave a rousing toast, and they all echoed their good wishes, reassuring him of how proud they were of him. The only person who was very withdrawn and quiet was Millie. Over the last few months, Millie and Charlie had become quite close. Even though he was younger than her, they had formed a tight bond, and she'd confessed to Anya how much she was going to miss him.

As they finished their tea, Becca wound up the gramophone record, placed on the latest Glen Miller hit and then encouraged them all to dance. Anya watched as Charlie glided around the room with Millie, blowing raspberries on her neck to make her laugh and spinning her in fast circles as she admonished him. Nikolai, so as not to draw attention to him and Anya, had asked Christine to dance but would constantly flash Anya tiny glances that would send a shiver down her spine. Finally, one of the other footmen asked her to dance, and they talked politely as they moved around the room together. He constantly apologized for standing on her feet, and she played it down with a smile through gritted teeth. She mused about how much she missed dancing with Nick.

The music finished, and Christine organized them all into a circle for some crazy new dance sweeping the nation called the Hokey Cokey. It seemed to be some sort of raucous novelty dance where you move body parts in and out of a circle and then, grabbing hands, cavorted together. They soon got the hang of it, but Anya was again reminded how unusual the British people were. In some ways so straightlaced but able to be silly and fun at the drop of a hat. And since she had arrived, not one of them had done any of the things she had been told about, and she wondered how propaganda had swept her into a world of danger and espionage. She had grown very fond of her new country and felt so sad that Charlie would be leaving their little family.

At the end of the evening, they all gathered around the table and Charlie opened up little letters and cards that they'd created for him. Anya could see tears in his eyes as he thanked them all. He kept joking with them as he opened them up and, tipping each one upside down, showed mock disgust with the lack of money inside. 'Call yourselves friends?' he said, shaking his head. 'Not a penny in any one of these cards.'

They danced and laughed till late and Anya was sad to leave the party, but when she found Millie in the room later crying, she put her arms around her friend.

'I'm so scared for him, Annie. He seems so young, and I've got used to him being around.'

Anya hugged her. 'I'm sure he'll be fine. We'll all write to him. This war will be over before you know it.' As Anya held her friend in their darkened bedroom looking out at the moonlight, she hoped more than anything that was the case. She wasn't sure how long she could go on being an enemy, an enemy to these wonderful people.

38

HATWORTH VILLAGE, NOVEMBER 1941

Anya

In the village one morning, Anya spotted Nikolai across the street as she walked by Millie's side. Millie called out to him, 'Nick!' She waved and he came towards them.

'Hello, girls,' he chirped, and automatically butterflies began their usual dance in Anya's stomach.

He looked so gorgeous as he made his way over to them. He was wearing his footman's uniform, a warm coat over the top, one hand in his coat pocket. She knew that in that pocket was no doubt the microfilm camera with pictures of notes from the meeting Lord Sinclair had a few nights before.

'I have a few errands to run,' he answered with one of his dazzling smiles that made her want to melt. Once again, Anya noticed his English was impeccable. Boarding school had been good for him. He was also a good spy. He didn't even look at Anya as he interacted.

'Annie and I are going to the bakery to get some goodies. They had some flour delivered, and they have cakes,' stated Millie, the excitement obvious in her tone.

Nick nodded. 'Sounds lovely. Don't forget to save one for me.' He started to move away and shouted back to them, 'Enjoy your cakes, ladies. Nothing can be as sweet as you are though, Mill,' he said, glancing back at her with a wink.

Anya knew what he was doing. He was trying to divert attention from him and her, and he was doing such an excellent job of it, it was actually making Anya a little jealous.

He moved away swiftly in the opposite direction, and she knew he would probably circle around before he did his drop at the photographer's.

Millie carried on down the hill to the bakery.

'Oh, I wanted to go in and see if they had that book I ordered,' said Anya, pretending that she had only just remembered. 'Why don't you go ahead and I'll meet you in the bakery?'

'All right,' shouted back Millie. 'I'll try not to eat them all before you get there.'

Millie sauntered off down the hill. As Anya rushed quickly into the bookshop, the bell tinkled as she closed the door. But as she approached the counter, she was almost stopped dead in her tracks when she saw the usual man wasn't behind the counter. An older woman looked up through her half-moon glasses and peered at her. Anya's heart started to thud. Something was wrong. She didn't know this woman, and no one had said that there would ever be anybody else in the shop.

'Can I help you, my dear?' she said with a smile.

'I'm just looking around,' said Anya, trying to sound nonchalant.

'Is there anything particular that you're looking for?'

Anya shook her head as she walked down one of the aisles and pretended to look at the books there. The woman stayed at the counter, looking down, but she seemed unnaturally still, as though she was waiting, occasionally looking up to watch her. Something was definitely wrong. Anya's heart started to pound in her ears now as she made her way down the next aisle, trying not to show how terrified she felt. The woman turned her back for a second and Anya rushed down the correct aisle. Was it safe to grab the note? If she didn't, she may not find out what was going on. Turning her back to the counter, she picked up the book, and suddenly she heard footsteps coming towards her. Without thinking about it, she shoved the book into her handbag and reached up and grabbed a completely different book from the shelf.

'Jane Austen,' the woman said, rounding the corner. 'Can't beat Jane. Are you looking for something to read?' The woman peered down at her with an intense stare.

'I think I've read this one,' she said, hoping the woman couldn't hear the quiver in her voice. She was trapped at the end of the aisle against the wall. There was no escape from where she was standing. She started to pretend to read the opening page of *Pride and Prejudice* and the words swam in front of her. The woman was so close now, Anya could feel her breath on the back of her neck. She reached up to put the book back onto the shelf and the woman grabbed Anya's elbow. Anya hitched her breath with surprise. All of a sudden, the bell on the door jangled out urgently, disturbed by the way someone had sped in the door.

'Annie, come quickly!' It was Millie's voice.

Startled, the woman let go of Anya's arm, and it gave Anya just enough of a chance to push past her, handing the Jane Austen to her as she left. 'Sorry, I have to go,' she shouted, over her shoulder, running to the door. 'What is it, Millie?' she gasped, trying to steady her breath as they both bounded outside.

'Look,' she said, 'across there at the photographers. Something's going on.'

Anya's heart started to race even harder as her head started to spin.

Oh my God, that's where Nikolai was. She watched as a dozen men rushed into the shop. It appeared they'd been compromised.

All at once, a muffled shot rang out from inside.

'That sounded like a gunshot,' said Millie, clutching Anya's arm.

Men poured out onto the street and rushed around to the back of the shop down a small alley. Raised voices could be heard. Then all at once someone came hightailing out of the back of the shop. It was Nikolai, running hell for leather down the alley, being chased by a group of men.

'Oh my God, they're chasing Nick,' said Millie in disbelief. The parade of men turned a corner and raced onto the street at the bottom out of sight. Then, all at once, there was another crack in the air, another gunshot, and Anya thought her heart was going to stop, it was beating so fast.

'Oh no, I hope they didn't just shoot Nick,' cried Millie mournfully as she tried to make her way down the alley to see.

Anya would have followed but was paralyzed with fear. Her training told her to run in the opposite direction. But her heart needed to know if the British had just shot her husband. All of a sudden, she felt ill, really ill, her head spinning. The last thing she remembered was hearing Millie scream as everything around her went black. When she came around, a group of people were all staring down at her.

'Look, she's all right,' said one of them. 'Just a bit overcome.'

Feverishly, Anya stared from one face to another, desperate for someone familiar. Desperate to see Nikolai.

'You okay, love?' said a concerned voice, and the baker's face swam into view.

She nodded her head, wanting to speak, wanting to say anything. Then, all at once, Millie was there.

'It's all right. She's with me,' she said, taking control, getting down beside her. 'She just needs a bit of air, that's all.'

'What's happened?' Anya managed to gasp out.

'I don't know. It's all a bit crazy down there. But the man who used to run the photographer's shop, he's been shot dead. Can you believe that? Apparently, he was some sort of informer for the enemy. That was what one woman heard one of the military police saying. Who would have thought it, a real-life German spy right here in our little village? God, you just can't trust anybody, can you?'

Anya did not want to ask her next question but she had to know. 'What about Nick? Has anyone seen him?' she asked in a halting tone.

'I don't know. I'm not sure if that last bullet was for him. I'm not sure if he got hit or not. I can't see what he has to do with it or why he was running – probably scared by all that commotion, no doubt. I went down there and I told them. I said, "Leave him alone, he works for the manor. He's a good sort. He isn't anyone you're looking for." But whoever is in charge there just ignored me and pushed me away, saying, "Go back to your work, this is government business." Come on, Annie,' she said, helping Anya to her feet, 'we should get you home for a lie-down.'

Anya clambered up, her head still spinning as she tried to take it all in. As they walked back, she continued to reassure herself over and over again. Nick would have gotten away; he had become a good runner and would be back as soon as he could. He had to be, because the alternative was just too horrible to comprehend.

39

HATWORTH MANOR, NOVEMBER 1941

Anya

Back at the manor, Millie insisted on settling Anya into bed. After Millie went down to make her a cup of tea, Anya raced to the toilet they all shared down the hallway from her room. Locking the door behind her, she laid her back against it and tried to catch her breath. The gunshot sound repeatedly echoed in her head, causing her heart to race and her stomach to cramp. 'Please, God, please don't let Nikolai be dead,' she whispered to herself. Her head spun, but she had to think straight. What did she need to do? What had she been trained to do? She desperately tried to think. She had to calm down.

Sitting on the top of the toilet, she pulled out the book that she'd thrust into her handbag. She still didn't know why she'd taken it. But with shaking fingers, she pulled open the pages to the middle where the note would be. Taking out a pencil, she wrote quickly along the top of the note, decoding the message. Perspiration misted her eyes as she tried to focus on her codes. Finally, she finished decoding it, and, sitting back against the damp stone wall that cooled the heat of her body, she couldn't believe what she was reading. *Network compromised, trust no one, go GM tonight, new assignment.* Then, there was a code that she realized was a new map coordinate.

All the maps were hidden in Nikolai's room, in his bag under the false bottom, along with a locked box their information had been in. It would be too strange if she went to the library in the house and started looking at maps, plus she had to recover his bag. If he was still alive, and she couldn't even contemplate the alternative, it would be damning for him if the British authorities uncovered it. *Go to GM*, which she imagined meant Gracemere. It was so vague, though. *Trust no one.* Did that mean the agent at Gracemere as well? Why were they sending her there if it told her to trust no one? She had to be hypervigilant. If somehow Nikolai had gotten away, how would he know where she was if she was to trust no one?

She tore up the message and flushed it down the toilet. If she left him this one, he would not know whom to trust. She had to write something from her so he would know. She had to find a way to get a message to him that he would understand just in case. As she sat there with the book in her hand, she suddenly remembered what they had talked about doing, and quickly she put it into action. Then, she splashed water onto her face in the tiny sink in the corner and peered at herself in the mottled mirror. She looked terrified; she had to look calm.

Drying her face, she picked up the book and stuffed it back into her handbag and made her way back to her room.

After Millie had brought her a drink and Anya had said she was going to sleep, she waited and watched Millie moving off across the grounds before she ventured back out into the corridor. As it was the middle of the day, most people would be downstairs working in the manor or out in the garden. This may be her only chance to get into his room. But it would be tricky getting to the other side of the house and into the male quarters. She drew in a deep breath as she crept down the back stairs, through the kitchen, then up another staircase and along the corridor where all the men's rooms were. She prayed none of them were in their rooms. If she was caught, she'd be in a lot of trouble. She knew where his room was, as he had told her before, and she counted the doors as she crept towards it. All at once, Anya heard laughter coming up from the kitchen. She stopped to wait for a second, then continued.

Coming to Nikolai's door, she knocked quietly just in case. No one answered, so she crept inside. The room was dark, and the smell of his shaving soap and boot polish greeted her. It took a minute for her eyes to adjust, but inside there were two beds, the same as her and Millie's room. Which was Nikolai's? By the side of one of the beds were photos of a woman, the other footman's sweetheart, so she headed for the other.

Hanging on the outside of the tiny wardrobe was Nikolai's spare footman's uniform, and her heart hurt. He had looked so smart in those clothes, and already she missed him with an unfathomable pain. She pulled herself together. She had to find the bag before she was discovered. He wouldn't leave it in plain sight, so she started to search through the wardrobe. Nothing. She looked underneath the bed. Not there. Then she noticed something on top of the wardrobe hidden behind some boxes – a sliver of canvas, the bag. Standing on the bed, she managed to move the boxes across and pull it down.

Inside, as a decoy, he had left a few of his sweaters and some of his personal things. She couldn't help picking up the sweater, holding it to her nose for a second and inhaling him in. 'Nikolai,' she whispered out into the world, 'please still be alive.' She pushed the clothes aside and, working her fingers into the tiny hole, pulled up the false bottom. She'd remembered their plan, and everything she needed was in there.

Taking the bag, Anya made her way back to the toilet.

Locking herself in again, she put her plan into action. Finishing what she had to do, she hurried back to her bedroom, hurriedly packed her case and quickly stuffed the bag underneath her own bed. Cutting some of Millie's wool, she tied the key to it and slid it down inside her trousers. She ran her fingers through her hair and made her way down into the kitchen.

'There you are,' exclaimed Millie. 'Are you still feeling unwell?'

'I was feeling a little bit sick, but I'm okay now,' she lied as she joined the table.

'We made you a cup of tea, but it will probably be cold by now. Looks like we won't have any work tomorrow, Annie. Look.' She pointed to the kitchen window. Outside, flakes of snow were starting to fall in long cold streaks and her heart sank. She would have to make her move tonight, and through this snow that had been threatening for days, she could see it was already coming down quite heavy, coating all the garden.

She looked around the table at the women as they laughed and talked about how unusual a snow was this time of year and about having a lie-in and reading the next day, and her heart felt sick. She was leaving them. She studied every one of them carefully. Jennifer's slender frame and pale eyes glistening with tears as she doubled over laughing at a joke Christine had just told them all. Christine, with elbows on the table, a cup of tea clasped in her hands, took command of the conversation. And Millie, listening carefully, a sweet smile on her face caught Anya staring at her and reached across the table and squeezed her hand. Her reassuring touch brought tears to Anya's eyes that she quickly swallowed down. As much as she knew she had to do this, her heart hurt with the feeling of loss she knew was ahead of her. They'd been a little family in this house, and she would miss every one of them. That evening, she would visit the walled garden for the last time and leave her message for Nikolai. Then she would have to go. She couldn't wait. Millie was exhausted as they started to climb the stairs hours later. 'I'm going to get a drink for bed,' Anya informed her friend. 'Why don't you go on ahead?' Millie nodded her head, her eyes closing. It was now or never. Even though the snow was thick she had to take a chance for Nikolai and couldn't leave without leaving him a trail.

40

CROMER, NORFOLK COAST, PRESENT DAY

Laura

As they both ordered their second cup of coffee, Laura pulled out her copy of *The Old Curiosity Shop* that she had in her bag, the one they'd found in the canvas bag. Eyeing it again, Jamie smiled.

'Did you get a chance to read it yet?'

'Not past the first page, but that's all I needed to do.' She slid the book across the table and asked him to open it.

He flipped open the top cover and noted the pretty ink drawing on the left and the information about the book on the right.

'Do you see anything unusual about this page?' she asked.

He looked it over from top to bottom. Then, shaking his head, he recited what he saw. 'There's the title, *The Old Curiosity Shop*, in a charming older font, and the words "by Charles Dickens," then what I guess is the address of the publisher, London Chapman and Hall Limited, and then the set of numbers you see on all books.'

He looked up and shrugged his shoulders.

She drew her fingers to the bottom of the page.

'What about here?'

'Isn't that just another mark from the publisher?' he asked as he frowned, looking at the line of numbers written in tiny digits underneath the address.

'I did some research. It's called the publisher's key.'

He stared at the list of numbers, with some abstract Roman numerals mixed in.

'Is there something wrong with it?'

'We didn't have the publisher's key in 1940. We didn't have a publisher's key until mid-century. So, these numbers have been added to this page.'

His eyes widened as he tilted the book to the side. 'Oh, yes,' he said. 'Look, it's slightly raised. I would never have known if you hadn't said. How did you figure it out?'

'While I was in London, I went to visit the Charles Dickens Museum. It had an exact copy of this book. I noticed straight-away that the numbers were missing.' She pulled out her phone and scrolled to the photograph and showed him. 'Look at the difference.'

'Well done, Watson.' He smiled.

Grabbing a napkin, he took a pen and started to work out the Roman numerals.

'According to this, he wrote this book in 1485.'

'Exactly. It doesn't even make sense. Even if, for some reason, this was printed later somehow, or somebody put the key in afterward, this implies it was published before he was born. This set of numbers means something different.'

'I take it you're going to tell me what, by the look on your face.'

'They're map coordinates. It took me a few hours to figure them out. Simon had a great book on World War Two code-breaking. But that's what they are. When the person left, she must have had to do something very quickly. So, she put the map coordinates into this book. That's why she locked it into the box and hid it in the bottom of the bag. She didn't want it to get into the wrong hands. And whoever this book was intended for must've known the code.'

'Map coordinates and codebreaking,' said Jamie, his eyes growing large as he pondered that thought. 'This doesn't sound like a love story or a game. This sounds like espionage.'

'Exactly,' said Laura, her face aglow. 'I think what we're looking at here is a code sent from one spy to another.'

'So, you think Annie was a spy?'

'It actually makes sense.'

'I take it you've already looked it up. Where this is?'

'I have,' she said proudly. 'As soon as I figured it out last night. These map coordinates take you directly to another stately home called Warmly Manor, about twenty miles from here. Which, after a quick internet search told me, also had Land Girls during the war. So, this message was to tell somebody else where she was going to be.'

'Fascinating,' said Jamie, narrowing his eyes. 'Are you thinking there may be something there of interest?'

'Simon knows the estate manager who works at Warmly. I asked him if he would do me a favour and give him a call last night. And he did. The guy there has agreed to see us. Want to come?'

'Always,' he said with enthusiasm.

'Good, because I told him I would be coming over there today, and I might be bringing a friend.'

They made their way out of the coffee shop and into her car.

Before they drove off, he turned to her and placed his hand on her arm.

'Laura.'

She looked over at him quizzically.

'I'm glad you told me about your sister. It means a lot that you were honest with me and were willing to share something so personal.'

She drew in a breath with the mention of Katie before she spoke. 'And thank you for agreeing to see me after that incredibly embarrassing situation. I genuinely want us to be friends.' He smiled and nodded. Then they set off in the car to Warmly Manor, talking animatedly about following the trail of a spy set seventy-five years before.

41

NOVEMBER 1941

Anya

As soon as Anya got back to the house from the secret garden, she rushed to her bedroom. She'd already packed her case and she tiptoed into the room to retrieve it. Millie was already in bed, her back turned to her, her hair bound in curlers, her soft whiffling snore betraying the fact she was in a deep sleep. Anya would miss her new friend so much it hurt. She hated how she couldn't even tell Millie that she was leaving. She scribbled a quick note saying she had a family emergency and had to go. As she signed it, she felt sad. Millie was the first real friend she had ever known and she hated that their whole friendship had been built on deceit.

Quietly she tugged out her case and the canvas bag from under the bed, and put on her jacket and hat; she crept back out of the bedroom, making her way stealthily along the hallway.

Opening the back door, Anya walked back out into the chilly night, her body shivering as she avoided the windows in the house where she knew people would be. She would have to go quickly, make her way by foot. Walk in the darkness. It would take her a couple of hours, maybe even longer with the snow, to get to the safe house. By the time she reached the beach, first light had surrendered to a golden dawn. The sun was climbing high in the sky in a golden glow, making the whole world glisten white in front of her.

She quickly moved through the streets, keeping her head down, avoiding eye contact. At that time in the morning and with the inclement weather, there were not many people to be seen.

She arrived at the front door just as the large clock somewhere in the town chimed 6 a.m. Dithering because her feet were freezing, she gently knocked on the door, looking up and down the street to make sure no one had been alerted to her presence. It took a while for her handler to answer, and when he did, his eyes showed great concern. Pulling her in, he also looked up and down the street.

'Why did you come here in the daylight?' he snapped at her.

'I didn't have a choice. I had to leave the house last night. It was my only opportunity. The other agent may have been caught.' She felt the pain in those words as she continued.

Once she was inside, Anya suddenly felt so incredibly alone without Nikolai. They had travelled the whole of this journey together. Now she was alone. And here she was, not even knowing whom she could trust and whom she couldn't trust. Especially this man with a day's worth of beard growth and greasy hair. Could she trust him?

He begrudgingly offered her a drink and brought her a cup of lukewarm tea in a chipped mug and then shuffled about the room complaining to her about how he was risking his neck for them.

Putting on his heavy overcoat, he grumbled to her that he had to go and make a phone call and would be back soon. And if she needed to sleep, there was a room upstairs. But the way his eyes roved over her body, she didn't fancy being found asleep in a bed when he returned. So after he left, she lay on the settee, fully clothed, her eyes becoming heavy with no sleep and her long walk.

The sofa was hard and lumpy, and the room smelt of mildew. And as she tried to rest, tears stung her eyes. She already missed Nikolai so much it hurt. She must have dropped off because she dreamed about him. She saw him in the street one more time, just like the last time she'd seen him the day before, his newly washed hair, wearing his pressed footman's uniform, his gentle blue eyes being careful to avoid hers. Then, in her dream, she threw her arms around him and held him so tightly she could hardly breathe, not even caring about how strange it seemed in front of Millie.

Anya woke up with a jolt as she heard the echo of the gunshot in her memory. Her heart was pounding with fear, her mouth bone-dry. Then she heard the handler moving around in the hallway; he must have slammed the door, creating the sound she thought was a gunshot in her mind. Her eyes flicked open, and he was back hovering over her – his rancid breath in her face.

'I need to call them again in two days. They will let you know when it is safe to move. Until then, you have to stay here and stay out of sight. Do you understand?'

She nodded despondently. The last thing she wanted to do was stay in this tiny house with this strange man. At least the view of the water was pleasant outside the window.

He ran his hand through his hair. 'I don't have a lot of money for food and guests.'

Sighing, Anya understood and, pulling open her bag, found some money and gave it to him.

He smiled, showing blackened teeth and a glint in his eye. 'Well, that's good for starters,' he said. 'We can have a nice breakfast at least.'

He went out to buy what was needed, and she wandered

from room to room, waiting. And that was her experience for the next two days. She never used the dirty bedroom he offered her upstairs. Instead, when she was sure he was fast asleep, she would close her eyes on the sofa, fully clothed, and constantly dream over and over again about Nikolai.

When he made a call on the third day, her handlers had confirmed the plans for the new assignment were all in place at a new stately home. When he had gone later that day, she pulled out the bag.

Now, she had to hope this handler would give it to Nikolai. Of course, she couldn't risk drawing attention to it in case he wasn't to be trusted, but this was her only hope that she could see.

The next day, she made her way to her new posting, leaving the bag at Gracemere, telling the man there were just some extra clothes in there for Nikolai that he needed to give to him. As he was a completely different size to her husband, she hoped he wouldn't try and use them or sell them. She hoped Nikolai would get her message.

She made her way to the train station that day and felt lonelier than she'd ever felt. She had nowhere to go with her heartache; she felt as if she was in constant emotional limbo, not knowing how to feel until she knew for sure what had happened to him.

42

WARMLY MANOR, NORFOLK, PRESENT DAY

Laura

Laura and Jamie arrived at Warmly Manor about eleven o'clock. Laura pulled her car to a stop in front of the main door and sighed as she looked around. The manor was indeed beautiful but was definitely in need of substantial repair. Its walls were crumbling, its garden was overgrown, and creeping ivy lurked in all the corners. Though it was still magnificent to behold, with its portcullis and exquisite gables, even if they were lined with clinging grey moss crawling out all along the cracked stone.

'The estate manager, who's called John Randal, said he would be willing to meet with us,' Laura said. 'Simon informed me that, though the house is undergoing a massive renovation, Mr Randal has offered to talk to us.'

Walking to the grand panelled front door, they pulled on the ancient bell and listened to its ringing echo down the hallway. A cacophony of barking dogs accompanied hurried footsteps, and the entrance to the manor flew open. Four retrievers flew out to greet them, and the man who stood in the doorway was tall and willowy, probably in his early fifties, with lively eyes, a broad smile, and reddened cheeks. He stepped out onto the steps to welcome them, and a stray wind lifted his hair into a mass of grey curls that rose in the air like little question marks. He stretched out his hand.

'Please call me John.' He smiled warmly. 'And I take it you are Simon's friend Laura?'

She nodded and then introduced Jamie.

'Lovely place, Hatworth. I was there just a few weeks ago. I look forward to seeing your work on the walled garden. We are always on the lookout for good gardeners who have your expertise.'

He beckoned them inside as he rounded up the dogs, and Laura looked around the large dark-panelled hallway, which housed a small suit of armour in one corner, a beautiful candelabra above them, and paintings of finely dressed ancestors. John's voice echoed off the walls as he talked about the manor's state of repair, escorting them to his office on the ground floor.

'We had a significant problem with the roof and a flood that created a lot of water damage. Unfortunately, it takes a while to get everything repaired with a house this old, so we don't estimate being open to the public this season.'

Once they were all inside his warm little office, Laura told him the story of their search from the beginning, showing him the book with the coordinates. And his eyebrows rose in fascination when she insinuated that a former member of their household may have been a spy.

After she had finished her story, John massaged his chin as he thought.

'I believe we still have some records from that time. We did indeed have Land Girls here for the whole of the war.' He disappeared into another room and returned with an ancient-looking ledger that took up most of his desk. 'This is a record of all the staff working here throughout the last century. Let's see if your young spy was indeed here.' He opened the book to the 1940s as Laura held her breath.

Running an index finger down a list, he beamed as he turned the page to show Laura and Jamie what he had found. In a spidery script was 'Annie Stone, Land Girl, November 1941–January 1942.'

'Doesn't look as if she was here very long. But there are no other Land Girls called Annie who came during the war.'

'Annie Stone.' Laura tested their mystery woman's full name for the first time as, finally, their Land Girl started to feel like a real person.

'I wonder why she left so quickly,' pondered Jamie.

'Maybe the Brits were onto her,' responded John, obviously enamoured with uncovering this part of the house's history.

'Or the person who was tracking her found her,' Jamie suggested.

'But if that was so, why was the key still buried in the garden?' Laura reminded them. 'My bet is that the person never found her, and she maybe had to move on, but to where?'

Suddenly, Laura had an idea.

'I know this is a long shot, but if she left one clue in a book, why not try the same tactic again? Whoever was tracking her may have had access to stately homes as well.'

'It's worth considering,' responded Jamie.

'Do you have any books that may have been around in that period?' Laura asked.

'Interestingly enough, I suspect the lord of this estate probably let the Land Girls borrow books from the library. We have a photo somewhere of several of the girls sitting in there knitting and reading. Let me find it.'

He disappeared again and returned with a shabby photo album, and inside were some photos from the early '40s of Land Girls sitting in their uniforms, reading, playing board games, and knitting. Laura quickly scanned the image for the striking young woman she had a picture of, but Annie wasn't there.

'I suppose if she did have to move on, she might have left another clue in a book if the library was available to the staff. She could leave something coded like that in plain sight because only somebody looking for it would know what to look for.'

'Unfortunately, everything in the library is in sixes and sevens,' stated John reluctantly. 'The water damage from the flood affected that side of the house. And there was a severe leak in there. But you are welcome to look.'

The library was indeed in a shamble, books piled high, higgledy-piggledy away from damp walls and the floor, and the smell of mildew was strong in the room. There were couches covered in dog hairs and an old coffee cup with a greening drink in the bottom of it.

It wouldn't be easy to find what they were looking for, especially as they didn't even know where to start.

'Maybe we should look for books by Charles Dickens,' Jamie suggested. 'Maybe that author was significant.'

John smiled. 'Well, the best thing to do is just begin searching. I'm going to let the dogs out; come by my office and let me know how you get on.'

He disappeared off, and Jamie looked at Laura in bewilderment. 'I didn't realize when you invited me along on this adventure that I might need a hazmat suit,' he joked.

Laura sighed deeply, adding, 'It's much more romantic in the movies, isn't it?'

They started to wade through the many piles of books that went back generations. Eventually, Jamie found a copy of *The Old Curiosity Shop* sandwiched under a pile of maps and a heavy medical encyclopaedia.

'I've found it, Laura,' he said, holding it up for her. She walked over, relieved; the smell of mildew was starting to bother her, and the dust was making her sneeze. The cover felt damp from being in the room, but it seemed in good condition. Apparently, with the staining, it had suffered a little water damage, but its spine was intact, and the pages were still pretty dry.

She opened up the book and looked up with excitement towards Jamie. 'I've got something,' she said.

After showing it to him, Laura felt buoyant. She took several photos with her phone.

They stopped by John's office on the way out, reporting what they had found, and handed him the book to look at. He seemed excited to know this new part of the house's history and told them to keep him updated as they continued their search.

Back out on the driveway, Jamie turned to her. 'Do you want to go and get some lunch? We can explore what we've found while having something to eat.'

She readily agreed, and, bidding the manager goodbye with a wave, they made their way out of the estate.

43

AN ARMY HOSPITAL, LONDON, NOVEMBER
1941

Nikolai

Nikolai blinked open his eyes and tried to focus. Where was he? Instantly his heart started to pound with fear as he realized he wasn't in the dimly lit bedroom of the manor and he was staring at a white ceiling, the pungent smell of antiseptic filling his nostrils. He tried desperately to remember. Since he had come to England, anything out of the ordinary was terrifying, signifying something had gone wrong. He tried to move his body, but it was impossible. He was weighted down somehow, as if pinned to the bed. As he attempted to raise his head and get his bearings, searing pain shot through his temple, taking his breath away. Panting to try and bear the pain, he ran his tongue across his lips, which felt dry and swollen. His throat burned with an incredible thirst. All at once, everything came back to him, accompanied by a tidal wave of emotion. The British had chased him through the streets; there had been the sound of a shot, then agony, then nothing. Oh God, he'd been shot.

He had to get up. He had to get away. Gritting his teeth, he forced himself up, and it took all of his effort just to get up onto his elbows. Forcing breath in and out of his body, he tried to bear the pain as he glanced around him, looking for an escape. He was in some sort of a hospital. Beside him, a line of empty white metal beds. A starchy nurse approached him.

'Steady on there, cowboy,' she said in a cheerfully admonishing tone. 'You took quite a blow to your head. We don't want you to get up just yet. You need to lie flat.'

She laid her hand gently on his shoulder, and even that light pressure was enough to force him back down onto the bed, exhausted. He had to remember to speak English. He was still in England.

'Where am I?' he gasped.

'You're in a hospital. Do you remember anything?'

He stared into her questioning eyes and didn't know how to answer. He felt vulnerable, exposed. His mind was moving slowly, as if it were through treacle. If he told her he remembered, would he divulge some deep secret he was not supposed to tell? He couldn't put it all together in his mind.

She nodded, assuming his silence was the answer.

'Do you need some water?'

'Yes,' he gasped, not wanting to move his head again, and in response, she lifted a glass to his lips.

They were so cracked and dry. Even this tiny amount of water felt painful as he swallowed it down, passing through his parched lips and down his throat. She continued to talk to him.

'Someone will be along to talk to you shortly. They told me to let them know when you were awake, but until then, you need to lie still. That wound is pretty serious. You'll need time to recover.'

He stared up at her as he tried desperately to pull the pieces of his life together. All he knew was he was a spy and he was in love with someone called Mishka. The rest of it was a jumble in his mind.

About two hours later, two army officers appeared at the side of his bed.

'Hello there,' said one with a plummy British accent and a half-cocked smile. 'We're glad you're awake. You'll be staying here for a while at the invitation of his majesty's government, I'm afraid. We have some work for you to do.'

Nikolai swallowed down the dryness in his throat one more time. 'What happened?' he asked.

'We were hoping you'd be able to tell us that,' the man said, removing his cap and placing it under his arm.

'Why am I alone on this ward?' Nikolai asked warily. In Russia that would have been significant. Maybe a hint of something more sinister intended for him.

'Because what we're going to talk about is highly sensitive. We know a little of your history. We know you're Russian – *zdrastvooytye* – and we know you came here with the Germans. We uncovered a lot of the information from the owner of the bookshop, the now-deceased Mr Peter Samuelson, whom I'm sure you're familiar with. We've been following Samuelson for a while and keeping account of, shall we say, his rather diverse activities. So, we have records of who you are and what you have been passing to him. Now you will be working for us.'

'I don't want to work for you. I don't want to do this anymore,' Nikolai sneered.

'Well,' responded the officer, tapping his stick rhythmically on his thigh as he strode up and down. 'It's that or I'm afraid the alternative is that we would have to shoot you for being a spy. And I'm thinking that might interest you less.'

'I have nothing I want to share,' spat out Nikolai.

'Maybe so,' said the commander as he strode to exit the room. Before leaving he dealt a final blow. 'There is one other thing that might help motivate you. From our sources, we have reason to believe your real name is Nikolai Petroff, and if that is so, we have highly sensitive information on your father's death that you may be interested in knowing.'

Nikolai's heart jumped into his throat. It had been so long since he'd thought about his father, the journey that he'd been on in the first place, the answers that he'd been seeking for so long. He stared at the man to assess if he could trust him or not. The man's face portrayed nothing. The fact that he had even mentioned his father had to be something, didn't it?

The officer gave him a smug smile and strolled towards the door. 'We will go and let you get well now and speak soon when you are feeling stronger.'

He was about to leave the room when Nikolai called out, 'Did you only catch... me?'

The man turned on his heels. 'The female agent got away, but we'll talk more about her tomorrow, shall we?'

After he exited the room, Nikolai lay back on his pillow and let out a ragged breath. At least Anya was still alive. At least she wasn't dead or caught. As he settled back down, he was in turmoil, his mind whirring, moving between potential information about his father's death and fear for Anya, whom he couldn't even warn or let know he was alive.

44

WICKHAMFORD MANOR, EVESHAM,
JANUARY 1942

Anya

Anya had started work at the new stately home and continued to feel nervous every day, waiting for any word from Nikolai. She couldn't entertain the alternative. Surely if he'd been shot and killed, there would be word, but there was nothing sent to her through the handler. So, he had to be somewhere out there. She imagined he was somewhere in hiding, laying low, waiting for the time when he could go back to Hatworth and pick up the trail. He would be arriving any day soon. But as the days went on, she became more and more discouraged.

The Land Girls at this new stately home were less friendly than the ones who had been at Hatworth. They tended to keep to themselves, and the lord of the manor was quite strict, creating a curfew for them and giving them rules about boyfriends and drinking, which seemed to add to the melancholy feel about the place. Though he did let them use the library in the evening to read. To help discourage them from dances and courting young men.

She had only been there for two months when she got a

mysterious note in the post. She had no idea who it was from; it was just signed 'a friend.' She opened it up in the toilet and was shocked to see that it was a newspaper clipping. A story in the news about her handler at Gracemere and how he had been arrested on suspicion of espionage. Her heart started pounding as she read all the details. And suddenly she thought about Nikolai and the trails she had set for him. How would he find her if the handler had been arrested and Nikolai never got the bag? She also felt afraid for herself. The net was closing in around her and she didn't know how to survive. That was three in her cell who had been caught now: the bookshop owner, the photographer in the village, and now the handler at Gracemere.

The networks were set up so that the agents only made contact with the minimal amount of people. That way, if something went wrong, fewer agents were affected if people were captured. But now her cell was completely blown and she had no one else she could turn to. Whoever had sent her this article obviously knew about her but hadn't given her any way to trace them. There was only one more thing written in code on the top of the article, the name of another stately home outside of Birmingham. Though she wasn't sure she wanted to go there. But could she stay here now that her main handler was uncovered? She just didn't feel safe. She felt like a sitting duck just waiting to be discovered. If the handler at Gracemere was gone, it may only be a matter of time before they'd start looking at all the local houses for her. She had to do something and she had to do it fast. She knew she needed to leave a message for Nikolai just in case he was somehow able to follow her last coordinates. It only had a sliver of a chance, but she had to try. She lay awake all night trying to figure out how to get a message to him, and there was only one tiny hope. With no walled garden or anything else that he might think of to connect with her here, she hoped he would think of this.

The next evening after the girls had finished relaxing in the library, she lingered until they'd all left and quickly slipped the book out of the bookcase and carefully wrote the code in the front of it. She hoped not only would he get a chance to find it, but would also be able to find a reason to be in the house. She just couldn't think of another way to let him know where she was.

Leaving the next day, she made her way to the new stately home on the outskirts of Birmingham.

Anya had barely unpacked at the next house when somebody came to find her. She'd only been there for a day. And the young woman looked at her quizzically.

'Are you Annie Stone?' she asked. Anya looked up and nodded. 'Oh, there's some men downstairs that want to speak to you. They look like they might be police. They look kind of official.'

Anya felt her stomach cramp as she nodded and said, 'I'll be down in a second,' trying to keep her voice really even.

Once the girl left, she quickly pushed everything into her bag and raced along the corridor. How had they found her so fast? They must be searching all the stately homes, all the Land Girls. She could no longer stay in this line of work. It was too dangerous, now that she knew that they were looking for her. She desperately needed a new identity, but who would she go to for it? There was no one left. Running down the stairs, she rushed out into the night and caught a bus to the train station. She didn't know what she was going to do. Nowhere was safe for her now. She was beside herself. It was midwinter, freezing, and she had nowhere and no one to go to. As she boarded the train into the city centre, the sleet that chilled her reminded her of Russia, and she wondered if she would ever see her home country again. She felt so alone. She decided she would wander the streets, rationalizing if she went somewhere that was more crowded, it might be easier to stay safe. The biggest challenge she had was that her papers still had her listed as Annie Stone and she wouldn't put it past the Gracemere handler to sell her short in order to save his own neck. So, it was very possible that the authorities were already looking for her. She would have to go on the run and maybe look for a completely different type of work. She had wanted to stay as a Land Girl because she believed it was the easiest way for Nikolai to track her, but they would just have to find each other another way. Her heart hurt with how distant she felt from him already and how long it had been since she had been in his arms.

She arrived at New Street station, which was alive with servicemen and women all getting ready to do their duty, and she stepped off the train ready to disappear until she could figure out where to go next.

As she made her way to the exit of the train station, she heard someone call out her name and thought it must be a dream until she turned, and caught her breath when she saw who it was.

45

NORFOLK, PRESENT DAY

Laura

Heading into a local town, Jamie did a search and located a little bistro that had a high rating. Stepping inside, Laura instantly relaxed. Low-hanging black beams and a whitewashed wall welcomed her in as she stepped down onto the grey flagstone floor.

'It's Elizabethan,' Jamie informed her as they were escorted to a small table at the back. There was soft jazz music playing, and even though it was lunchtime, it was still quite dark. A droopy-eyed waiter lit a candle in a wine bottle as they sat down.

Laura perused the menu. It had a good selection of local produce, including plenty of yummy-looking seafood and local fruits and vegetables. They both ordered and then settled down to talk.

'Okay, let's look and see where we're going next,' said Laura with a sense of excitement.

She pulled out her phone and read the numbers.

Using the code cracking strategy that Simon had taught her,

she finally got the right coordinates and Jamie searched on Google Maps. Finding the location, he swivelled the phone towards her.

'Wickhamford Manor in Evesham,' Laura gasped. 'That's miles away. It would take at least four hours to get there.'

'Imagine how long it took her in the 1940s during the war,' Jamie added, as he took a sip of his wine. 'We could take a drive up, the weather is so nice right now. Maybe we should make a day of it?'

Laura's stomach flip-flopped a whole day with Jamie excited her.

Jamie sat back in his seat and looked at her across the candlelight.

He paused then, looking for the right words.

'Laura, I want you to know something. I really enjoy spending time with you.'

'Me too. You're so easy to be with. Liam was often so... difficult.'

Jamie nodded his head. 'Every relationship has its challenges, but I'm enjoying this adventure we're on together.'

She smiled her agreement, then looking down at her phone again, said, 'It seems to be open every day. It's now a stately home that you can visit through National Trust, and it's open at ten in the morning till five.'

'Okay, so we could start off early. That gives us plenty of time to see if there is a clue there.'

'This is just so exciting,' said Jamie. 'I can't believe it. I can't believe that we're following a trail that's seventy-five years old.'

'I know,' said Laura, sitting back.

The waiter brought the food to them, and they started eating, falling into easy conversation.

'Okay, so what time should we set off on Saturday?' Jamie asked over dessert.

'How about I pick you up at nine o'clock?' suggested Laura.

'Okay, we should make it there by one-ish.'

After the meal, they headed back to Gracemere and walked the beach together. After eating dinner out, they lingered, enjoying one another's company and it was late when they stood in the moonlight on his doorstep, talking for a few minutes, when she could tell he was stalling. Did he want to kiss her? She found she wasn't against the idea, but after what had happened with Liam, she felt she may need to initiate the first move.

She reached forward and gently kissed him on the lips. It was a little bit longer than a friendly kiss, but not long enough to be anything more. But just his touch sent a shiver through her entire body, and her limbs quivered with the exhilaration. Attempting to disguise it, she hugged him quickly and moved towards the car.

'See you on Saturday,' she chirped, hoping he couldn't hear the slight quiver in her voice.

'Nine o'clock!' he added as he waved at her and she drove away.

When she arrived home, she decided to call Walter and update him on her progress, as he had asked for Laura to let him know if she found out the full name of the mysterious Land Girl. He was delighted to hear about her progress and commended her for her thorough research. He also offered to help locate a possible death certificate.

Laura went to bed that night and allowed her thoughts to linger on their day. She really liked Jamie, but would she be brave enough to consider a new relationship so soon after Liam? The honest answer was she wasn't sure. It had all been very light up to now, but if she was confronted with the chance of something more, she wasn't sure she was ready to commit her heart again at this time.

46

WICKHAMFORD MANOR, EVESHAM, PRESENT DAY

Laura

They drove to the next house and as they moved through the large iron gates, Laura had a feeling of great excitement.

'I tried to call ahead of time, but I just got the answering machine,' she told him. 'Though it is open for visits today. So hopefully there will be access to the library.'

As the car pulled up, they noticed a bus of tourists and a couple more cars, apparently all coming to take the tour. Laura hoped that she'd be able to talk to somebody about the book before it started.

Unfortunately, on entering the foyer, the tour was ready to start straightaway, and so Laura didn't get an opportunity to talk to the guide before. An elderly gentleman dressed smartly in a blue blazer and red tie, he spoke in low respectful tones as he described the history of the house from William the Conqueror to the present day. She looked around the foyer; it was medieval, a line of faded standards hanging from the walls. The wind ruffled the banners, which looked as crisp as paper and as if they might deteriorate into dust at any moment. The manor smelt of wood, dried paint, and the highly waxed floor.

As they moved from room to room listening to the tour guide, she looked at the pamphlet she had been given on the way in to read. It talked about each of the rooms in detail.

Finally, they wound around to the library. Jamie looked across at Laura in anticipation and whispered to her, 'When we get inside, let's look and see if we can see any Charles Dickens. That way we can talk to the tour guide about it afterwards.'

The library was vast. The walls, that were at least twelve feet high, were decorated with rich mahogany bookcases ingrained with ornate carvings. Jamie and Laura scanned the shelves looking for that one title, or anything by Charles Dickens. There were many books, but many were locked behind wired doors, so they were impossible to see. But there was no Dickens on the open shelves.

Jamie looked crestfallen. Laura felt so disappointed too.

After the tour was over, she approached the tour guide and introduced herself and the work she was doing.

The elderly man nodded. 'Yes, yes, I actually know of Hatworth Manor.'

Then she went on to tell him briefly of Annie's story.

The tour guide looked surprised and a little taken aback. 'What year would this be?'

Laura swallowed before she said the date. 'January 1942.'

He shook his head in disbelief. 'We can look, though I must tell you, you won't be able to take anything with you.'

'Oh no, we don't want to take it with us. I just want to look inside it.'

The tour guide looked bemused, but, jingling his keys, he walked upstairs, saying to the other guides, 'I'll be back in five minutes.' Leading them back into the library, he moved into the room. 'Can you remember who the book was by?'

'*The Old Curiosity Shop.* Charles Dickens.'

'I do remember some Charles Dickens shut away in one of these locked shelves.'

All three of them moved towards the bookshelf. The smell of leather and paper greeted her as she got closer. He opened the wired doors and there was indeed a whole set of Dickens novels.

He pulled out all the books and laid them carefully on the desk.

Like children trying to look for a treasure, both she and Jamie tentatively opened up the first pages of each book, but they were clean, without the usual feeling of wear, and there were no numbers in the front of any of them, including *The Old Curiosity Shop*, and Laura's heart sank.

They handed the books back to the curator.

'Anything of help?'

Laura shook her head.

He put them back on the shelf, and they thanked him for his time.

As they drove away, Jamie looked across at her. 'What do we do now that we don't have another clue?'

She took in a deep breath. 'I could do some research about this area, Walter offered to help too, and now that we have her full name, maybe we can find a death certificate. At least now I've got more of an idea of where she may have been before she died. I'll keep looking. There may be something more.'

But Laura couldn't keep the disappointment from her tone. It felt without the shadow of a doubt that Annie had been showing her where to go and now the next clue wasn't here, what had happened to her?

'Oh, Annie, we need your help for the next step.' She hadn't realized she spoke it out loud and Jamie looked across at her and smiled.

47

NEW STREET STATION, BIRMINGHAM,
JANUARY 1942

Anya

Anya fell into the arms of her best friend as Millie sobbed on
her shoulder.

'I can't believe it's you, Annie. I can't believe you're here.
No one could believe it when you left,' she said, wiping the back
of her hand across her damp cheeks. Then, pulling out a handkerchief, she blew her nose. 'I was so upset when you went
without even telling me what was going on in the middle of that
snowstorm. What were you thinking?'

Anya just shook her head, not knowing how to respond. 'I
had to leave,' she finally said. 'There was something I had to
take care of.'

Millie smiled then. 'It's so good to see you. Let's go and get a
cup of tea.'

They made their way from the station and into a lovely little
tea shop, where they settled themselves down. Millie smiled
again at her friend, but Anya saw something else in her eyes; she
looked tired and sad. It had been two months since she'd laid

eyes on Millie, and Millie seemed to have aged years from the last time she'd seen her.

'Why are you in Birmingham? Are you here to see your family?' asked Anya as they sat huddled around a hot teapot.

Millie's eyes clouded, and she took a moment to answer, sucking in her breath before she spoke. 'I've been here to attend their funerals,' she whispered, her chin trembling with the gravity of her confession.

Anya felt so deeply sad for her friend as she relayed that both her parents had been killed overnight in an air raid a week before. Millie looked so fragile; she'd lost her whole family, her brother in the skies, and her parents in what they had thought was the safety of their own home. She reached out and grabbed Millie's hand.

'I have no one now, Annie,' she continued. 'I missed you when you left. That's why it's so good to see you. Promise me that we'll always make the effort to stay in touch?'

Anya nodded without thinking about it. It was almost as though her heart could split itself into two. The Anya who was a Land Girl and part of her sweet little manor family, and the spy who was running for her life.

'But Millie, there are many things about me you don't know. I don't think you could love me if you knew the half of it.'

Millie eyed her curiously. 'That's how love works, Annie. We love the person we know even with their darkness. I know you, Annie. I see your heart and I also see your loneliness.' She gripped Anya's hand tightly. 'I will always be here for you no matter what happens or whatever you have done.'

Anya felt the strength of her grip and wished she could feel the same way about herself.

Millie continued, 'I can't even tell you about the sadness that I've been through in the last week. You are the only good thing I've seen.'

'How is everyone else?' asked Anya, attempting to lighten the mood. 'Everyone back at the manor? Are they all well?'

Millie nodded, but there was something she was holding back, Anya could tell. 'The other Land Girls are doing well, and believe it or not, Jennifer is engaged. She was seeing one of the footmen on the sly. Not the one who got shot at. Do you remember that, Annie? He never came back, you know. We never heard hide nor hair from him after that. There were so many rumours going on about what happened there. And then after you left, people speculated that maybe you'd been lovers and that you were pregnant. I never believed any of it and told them all so.'

Anya blushed with the thought. 'Oh no,' she mumbled. Yet, in her heart, she so wished that was true. 'I didn't even really know him,' she lied as her throat tightened. 'And what about Charlie?' Anya asked, moving the subject away from her and Nikolai.

Millie pulled out a handkerchief again and blew her nose. Then she shook her head slowly. 'Oh, Charlie,' she said wistfully. 'He didn't even last a month. He was dead before Christmas. Killed in the line of duty. So, when I say I'm alone, I mean really alone. I took some time off from the manor to gather myself, and I'm not even sure I will return. I was just here at the station to see if I could get my money back on my return ticket.'

Anya felt her stomach tighten. Charlie was gone. Millie's parents were gone. Why had she ever agreed to be a spy? The cost was so high. These were the people she cared about most in the world, apart from Nikolai, and they were being affected by her actions. She decided then she would never go back to spying. No matter what happened, she would find a way to have a normal life and live here in England and be close to Millie. She could never go back to Russia because of Nikolai. She wouldn't give up until she found him. She knew now there was probably a good chance he may be dead. But she would continue to live in hope.

Just as they were finishing their tea, air raid sirens screeched out, and they jumped up, looking for somewhere to take cover. People were running towards the station, where there was a huge shelter. But they didn't have time to get there; the bombs already started to drop. Grabbing hold of her friend, Anya pulled her inside a now-empty shop so they could take cover. The two of them crouched below a counter as bombs rained down all around them.

The sound was incredible. Anya gripped Millie so tightly she was afraid she would lose feeling in her arms. A huge bomb detonated right overhead and the sound was deafening as Millie screamed in terror. All at once above their heads the ceiling started to crumble and a huge piece of masonry crashed down on them. Anya scrambled to pull her friend under the counter as far as she could. But then there was an enormous cracking sound as the whole ceiling gave way. As the sound of stone crashed down all around her, Anya felt a moment of intense pain and a feeling of being pinned down, and then all she knew was darkness.

48

LONDON, 1946

Nikolai

Nikolai stepped out into the sunshine and felt the tears brimming in his eyes. It had been so long since he'd been out in the free world. He had spent the rest of war working for the British, unable to communicate with anyone in the outside world, and they'd decided to let him go at the end, as he'd spent most of the war spying for them. The only thing that had kept him going through the whole time were his thoughts of Anya, his little Mishka. Did she believe that he was dead? Surely, she would have waited for him. He had been unable to contact anyone while working for the British secret service. He just hoped she had escaped. Maybe she was even back in Russia. He was full of so many questions. He knew there was only one way to find out all he needed to know. And that was the first thing he was going to do.

Leaving London, where he'd been sequestered, he got the first train he could out to Hatworth Manor. He would inquire at the house about her and find a way to slip into the garden and see if Anya had left him a trail.

As he looked out of the window, he reflected on his years working for the British government.

As soon as Nikolai had been well enough to work for them, MI5 had pressured him into becoming a double agent. Daily, they would taunt him with his father's file telling him if he worked for them, they would let him know what happened to Anton Petroff. So, to keep alive, he had continued to relay false messages to Russia via a radio he built and translated documents for the British. But as the war came to its climax, the work he did began to intensify.

'There is only one way I would do this for you,' he said after one particularly gruelling interrogation, when they had a very important ruse they wanted him to be a part of; then he offered his trump card. The one he had been holding on to all these years, waiting for the stakes to be this high.

'If you promise me that the other agent, the one that I was with, will go free. If you show me an official document that you have given her immunity, then I will do whatever you want me to do.'

The agent had looked at him speculatively as Nikolai had continued.

'If she is still alive after all this time, then she's running scared. She won't be a threat to you, I promise you. She hated what she was doing, but it's the only way I'll do this.'

Eventually, they agreed on the understanding that if she kept out of trouble and stayed under the radar, as she had up until then, they would let her remain free.

Now as he looked back to that time, two years before, that had been not long before the D-Day landings, and it appeared that they were getting all the turned agents to send false information back to their governments about the landings and where they would be taking place. He was more than happy to do it, though he didn't tell them that. He didn't have loyalty to the Soviet Union anymore, just as much as he didn't have any loyalty to England. He only had loyalty to her, wherever she was.

When they showed him the official documents with her name on them, he hoped they would keep their word, and he had done what they asked of him.

At the end of the war, one agent came in and threw a file down on a desk he was sitting at. He looked at the wording on the top of it, and there was his father's name, Anton Petroff. He felt the pain in his stomach and the lurch in his heart as he opened the buff file and started to read down it. The British had been monitoring all that Stalin had been doing for years. And as Anton Petroff had been to England, the British had files on him. As he read through the documents, it was as he had suspected. His father had been part of the purge, Stalin's way of getting rid of all the people who weren't loyal to him. It outlined how his father had been killed and how he had been loyal to his country and not Stalin right to the end. These words struck Nikolai in his heart as he read them. Could Nikolai say the same thing about himself? After reading the file, he put it down on the desk and wept.

But now as he watched the countryside rush by outside the window, that was behind him, now he had better days to dream about.

At the house he was greeted by Becca, who was now married, and she and her husband were running the estate.

'It is so wonderful to see some of the staff who were here during the war; we thought you had been shot as a German spy. That was the rumour,' she laughed.

Nikolai smiled, not confirming anything. He changed the subject by asking about the different staff. Becca gave him a rundown of all the old members. Talking about Jennifer's romance and the fact she was expecting her first baby.

'And Millie unfortunately lost her parents as well as her brother and is now living back outside Birmingham somewhere,

I believe, though I haven't had a letter from her for a long time. And do you remember Annie?' she asked as she offered him a cup of tea.

His heart started to beat wildly in his ears as Becca continued, 'Sadly, she was killed in an air raid in Birmingham.'

Nikolai's world stopped. He knew Becca was still speaking. He could see her lips moving as she explained all the details of Anya's death. But he was only receiving bits and pieces as all he could hear in a loop in his head were the words 'killed in an air raid.'

He must have paused for too long as Becca looked concerned.

'I'm sorry, did you know Annie well?'

She was my wife; my life; she is the reason I wake every morning and the last person I think of before I go to sleep, was what he wanted to say. But years of being a spy had taken its toll and instead he just shook his head.

'Only a little,' he muttered. His voice sounded tinny and pathetic, as if there was not any energy left inside him to speak. Everything had been taken from him in that moment, all his hopes, his dreams, the reunion he had visualized for years, gone in those few words. He pulled himself together enough to ask, 'Where is she...?' He wanted to say 'buried,' but couldn't bring himself to utter that word. It sounded too final, something that happened to other people's loved ones. Not his Mishka, so vibrant, so beautiful, so full of life.

Becca eyed him with concern and softened her tone, seeming to sense his vulnerability. 'No family could be found and Millie had confirmed who she was to the authorities, so we paid for her to be buried there.' Becca then gave him the name of the cemetery in Birmingham where her body had been laid to rest.

Nikolai didn't stay long. After that, he caught a train to Birmingham. His journey was a blur. It wasn't until he stood in front of her headstone, without even her real name etched into it, that it finally sank in.

Sinking to his knees, the tears fell freely down his cheeks. 'Oh Mishka, my Mishka, why you and not me?' He thought of their nights in the garden, where she would tell him stories of her childhood in the little treehouse or make daisy chains she would force him to wear. Her laugh, her eyes when they sparkled with a secret. The way she would hold her chin in defiance when she wanted her own way. The time in Russia she had fallen in the mud and then pushed him in as well. How would he live another day without the hope of ever seeing her again? He wanted just one more second in her arms, just one moment to hold her gorgeous body tightly and tell her how much he loved her. Instead there was this lump of dirt and this stone epitaph that didn't even have the right name on it.

He wasn't sure how long he stayed there weeping. But as he finally got to his feet his knees were aching with the cold. His hands and face were numb. He would get her some flowers, some roses like she had gathered from the garden for their wedding crowns. A hundred of them to cover this grave and take away the hollow emptiness that was this harsh cold space. He walked out onto the busy Birmingham streets. He was so preoccupied, he wasn't thinking straight, hadn't been out in the world before, had been away for so long. So many people, so many things going on around him. He was distracted by the cry of a child and his thoughts about Anya.

He stepped out into the road, foolishly looking the wrong way; even after all these years in Britain, certain things were still Russian about him. He didn't see it coming. The last thing he remembered hearing was a squeal of brakes, a scream from a woman behind him. Then as he turned his head, there was a flash of steel, a crack, his body in agony, and nothing more before he blacked out.

49

WITTON CEMETERY, BIRMINGHAM,
PRESENT DAY

Laura

Laura and Jamie stood reverently in front of the simple grave. The words 'Annie Stone, born 1920, died 1942' were etched into the mossy grey stone, with the exact dates, no hint of her occupation, family, or even her work during the war. In front was a permanent stone vase with the words 'And from the death of each day's hope, another hope sprang up to live tomorrow. I miss you always.'

'A beautiful quote,' Jamie remarked. Laura looked it up on her phone and caught her breath. She showed the screen to Jamie. '*The Old Curiosity Shop*,' he said incredulously. 'That is too much of a coincidence.'

'But what can it all mean?' Laura asked, trying to put all the pieces together. Jamie shook his head.

It had been a few days before that Laura had received a call from Walter, saying that he thought he had located the death certificate of the mysterious Land Girl, not far from her last placement. And it had only taken a small amount of detective work to find out where she'd been buried.

A light drizzle had started to fall, settling in droplets on Laura's hair and on her collar and cuffs. It was not wet enough to be a shower but moist enough to dampen her face.

'It's so sad,' sighed Laura, looking down wistfully at the overgrown grave, the tiny box clenched in her hand. 'I so wanted a happy ending. I always hoped that we would find her. I know that sounds silly after seventy-five years, but I was hoping that somehow we could complete the circle of the story. I was so sure that this time...' She couldn't finish the words as emotions bubbled up into her chest.

Jamie placed his arm around her shoulders and pulled her close. He gently kissed her hair. 'I know, but at least you saw it through to the end, and it was an amazing adventure.'

She smiled. 'Isn't it strange to think that there once was this woman who was a spy who left clues for someone to find her? Though we will never be able to ask her who that was now.'

Laura knelt to place the small tin at the base of the grave when something caught her eye. The grass was somewhat overgrown but there was something there.

It was a bouquet of dead flowers, still wrapped in cellophane. Curiously, she tugged it out of the grass.

'Look, Jamie, somebody left flowers on her grave. How odd. Who would leave flowers for a woman who was a spy during the war? I'm sure if she came from abroad as a spy, she wouldn't have had any family here in England.' She brushed off the mud on the bouquet that now looked to have once been roses, the colours faded to a shabby chic yellow. As she cleared the dirt, her hand brushed against something. 'Oh,' she exclaimed, 'there's a card attached.' Pulling it free, she rubbed away the mud caked on it. And even though the ink was faded to a light brown with the sun and the rain, she could just make out the words.

*To my dearest, sweetest friend, even in the seventy-five years
since I last saw you, I have never forgotten our friendship, and
your sacrifice and forgiveness will live on in my heart forever.*

Millie

Laura's breath hitched.

'Oh my God, Jamie, do you think it's from another Land
Girl? Or maybe the person whom the clues were left for? Do
you think someone from that time is still alive, and she left these
flowers?'

'I'm not sure, but look at this.' He continued pointing at the
address at the bottom of the card. These were from a flower
shop.

The two of them scrutinized the tiny address until Jamie
looked up with assurance.

'Chipping Campden. It's from a florist in the Cotswolds.'

'What does that mean?' asked Laura, daring to hope.

'It means that, not long ago, this Millie, someone who knew
Annie, was still alive, and if she was well enough to come up
here to place these flowers, then we have a good chance that she
is still around, maybe living right there.'

'How long do you think the flowers have been here? Can't
be longer than a year, can it?'

'I don't know, but we have to find her; she may be able to tell
us the whole story. I would also like to give her this cigarette
case.'

Jamie nodded enthusiastically. 'I think it will start with a
phone call to the florist.' He pulled out his mobile phone and
tapped in the number on the card. The phone rang out, and he
explained who he was and what he was looking for.

Even from where she stood, Laura could hear a very irate
woman explaining in a high-handed manner how she didn't give

out information about her customers. And before he had time to say anything further, she'd hung up on him.

'We have to go, Jamie. We have to go to the Cotswolds. We have to make this lady understand how important this is.'

Jamie nodded.

Laura felt a sense of expectation and excitement. Could she finally meet someone who knew the woman she'd been following for months? She hoped that, in her heart of hearts, she could finally bring the story to an end.

———

The journey to Chipping Campden was magical. The weather was balmy as the summer sun played hide-and-seek through the trees and the hedgerows. There was something really fun about being with Jamie. As they travelled together, listening to music, they fell into an easy conversation. Laura had mapped the journey on her phone, and they started out early in the morning.

Pulling into the little Cotswolds village, they were both enchanted. Mellow golden-coloured buildings lined the little high street. Jamie crawled down the tiny road until they found a brown and white awning with the words *Village Flowers* emblazoned above a small shop. Inside, a pleasant-looking older woman in a bright green-and-white-striped apron met them.

'Can I help you?' she asked with a polite smile.

'We're trying to solve a mystery,' said Laura.

'A seventy-five-year-old one,' added Jamie.

And the woman looked bemused as she listened to the whole story. She still showed an amount of reluctance until Laura showed her the photo of the Land Girls she had on her phone. She screwed up her eyes as she stared at the photo but something she saw there and their earnestness must have convinced her to help them.

'Do you know if she is still alive and where we can find her?'

The woman nodded. 'Well, she was alive yesterday when I saw her in the high street, and yes, I can tell you where she lives. Let me call her and see if it is OK for me to give you her address.'

Jamie and Laura looked at one another, the excitement obvious on both their faces. They were finally going to talk to someone who had not only known Annie but seemed to have been a very close friend, and Laura wondered if Millie had known that Annie had been a spy.

50

CHIPPING CAMPDEN, PRESENT DAY

Laura

They stood nervously on the doorstep after ringing the doorbell of the quaint thatched cottage. It didn't take long for the door to open, and a slender older woman stood before them. Laura was taken aback at first, wondering if maybe this was a daughter or relative. Millie would now possibly be in her mid-nineties, and this woman looked a full ten or twenty years younger, with her lively green eyes and thick grey hair.

'Can I help you?' she said with a smile.

Laura felt like she had when she'd first stood on Jamie's doorstep. Where to begin? In her hand, she was gripping the little cigarette case that she intended to give to her. Jamie sensed her hesitation and spoke first.

'We have a mystery that we're hoping you can help us with.'

Her eyes danced with the thought. 'What makes you think I can help?'

'We've been tracking a young woman whom you may have known during the war. Her name was Annie Stone.'

Millie's face changed from a pleasant smile to a look of

sadness. For a moment, Laura was afraid she was going to close the door on them, but then her smile returned, and she said quietly, 'She's dead. Annie died during the war.'

Laura nodded her head. 'Yes, we know that, but we wonder if you could tell us something about her. We've been trying to track her for a long time now. We would love to know the whole of her story. Anything you can help us with would be wonderful.'

The woman looked nervously from one to the other and then, apparently giving in, invited them inside. The house was charming, clean, and full of light, and they made their way into a chintz-covered sitting room. Millie busied herself in the kitchen making tea before she finally came in and dropped floral teacups, a teapot, and creamer onto a highly polished table.

'I know this is strange just to come out of the blue, but we know that Annie's dead – we visited her grave – so you may be the only person who can help us with her story.'

The woman drew in a deep breath. 'That was such a long time ago. Are you sure you want to dig up the past?'

Laura went on to tell her the story of how she'd found the box. She watched the woman's face go from interested to intense as she held the box forward for Millie to see. Finally, the older woman caught her breath and grabbed her necklace for comfort for a moment before tentatively reaching forward with a shaking hand and taking it from Laura.

'I haven't seen this for seventy-five years,' she said wistfully.

Laura couldn't believe it. Had she known about what Annie had been planning? Maybe Millie had been a spy as well.

Carefully, as tears filled her eyes, Millie opened the box and looked inside. Her fingers grazed the note, and then she looked puzzled. 'Was there a key with this?'

Laura smiled and pulled the book out of her bag and showed it to her.

'So, he never found it,' she said quietly to herself.

'Who never found it?' asked Laura. 'Can you tell us more about the story?'

She slowly drew in a long slow breath and walked to the windows as if she needed more air and, taking in two more deep breaths, whispered out towards the garden, 'Nikolai, the man I was in love with.'

Laura felt confused. Millie was in love with a man whom Annie had left a message for? She didn't understand, so she asked for clarification.

The woman turned and walked back and sat down. 'I suppose it doesn't matter anymore. No one's going to care. My name was Anya Baranov. I married and became Anya Petroff and my undercover name was Annie Stone. Millie was my best friend. I took her identity during the war because I needed to escape. And I became a new person during the night of a Birmingham air raid.'

She went on to tell the story from so long ago.

51

NEW STREET STATION, BIRMINGHAM, JANUARY 1942

Anya

Anya opened her eyes and tried to remember where she was. Her head was throbbing, her ears were ringing, and dust was clogging the back of her throat. All around her, wood and stone pinned her body down, and as she moved, she felt every bone ache with the searing pain. Then she remembered. They'd been in an air raid. The shop must've been hit. She felt so cold. How long had she been lying here? Then, all at once, she thought of Millie. Millie had been right next to her. As the dust started to clear, she began to tug at the wood and masonry that covered her body. She noticed she had lots of cuts and bruises, but nothing seemed to be broken. She didn't care, though, as she dug away at the debris looking desperately for Millie. She finally found her, lying across the room, on her side. Millie's eyes were closed.

'Millie,' she croaked. 'Millie, can you hear me?'

She coughed as the dust continued to make her choke.

'Millie!'

She dragged herself over to her friend and started pulling

away at some of the masonry that covered her friend. Millie was so still, it scared her.

'Millie. Can you hear me?'

Then, gently, she cleaned away tiny specks of glass that were all across Millie's face, noticing how cold she seemed.

'Millie, please, can you hear me?'

She suddenly had an awful thought. She put two fingers to Millie's throat. It was still. She must've made a mistake. She tried again, taking Millie's hand and holding her wrist between her fingers, but Millie's hand was lifeless, and once again, she remembered her mother. Her hand had looked just the same, white and like a ragdoll's.

The pain started in her stomach and ripped up through her throat into a cry.

'No, Millie! Not you!' She couldn't believe she was living through this again. She pulled her up and held her dearest and only friend to her chest and sobbed. 'No! No! It's so unfair.'

Millie was dead, and she didn't deserve it. She had been through so much. Why did she have to die like this, alone in the world with no family to bury her or go to her funeral? Anya rocked her friend in her arms, kissing her hair and stroking her cold face.

Then, through the darkness of her thoughts, something jarred in her. Millie had no one. Millie was totally alone in the world, and from Millie's constant chatter, Anya knew everything about Millie's life.

She suddenly heard the sound of ambulances outside. They were coming to dig them out, and she could hear someone shouting out from above them.

'Is anybody alive? Is there anybody down there?'

She suddenly knew what she needed to do. Undoing Millie's coat, she searched the pockets until she found them. Millie's papers. Above her, people started to dig, and a flashlight flickered through the rubble, bouncing off the walls.

'Is anybody down there?' another voice called out.

She hastily took out Millie's papers and, swapping handbags with her dearest friend, placed her own documents in Millie's pocket. She kissed her best friend gently on her forehead and whispered into her hair, 'I will never forget you, my dear sweet friend, and your kindness. I'm glad you are with your family now.'

'Is anybody down there?' the voice called out again.

'Yes,' Anya finally croaked back. 'I'm down here. I've been hurt, but I think my friend Annie's dead.'

They dug their way down to her, and soon they were with her. After examining Anya, it was determined that she was unharmed, although she had many cuts and bruises.

'You say your friend's name is Annie?' asked the air raid warden.

'Yes, my friend's name is Annie, Annie Stone. We used to work together at Hatworth Manor in Norfolk as Land Girls.'

The men looked down sadly at the young woman and wrote down the details.

'Don't worry. We'll make sure to let those people know. You get yourself home. We'll take care of her.'

Anya stumbled out of the building in shock and relief. Her heart ached for the loss of her dearest friend. But Annie Stone, the spy, was dead, and no one would ever be looking for her again.

52

CHIPPING CAMPDEN, PRESENT DAY

Laura

Jamie and Laura sat in shocked silence as Anya finished her story from the past. She took a sip of tea as she continued.

'I was sent here during that time under the Russian government spying for them. Arriving off the coast of Scotland, I was dropped off by a German submarine.'

Anya went on to tell them her whole story, how she'd had to leave Russia, how she'd met Nikolai and fallen in love with him, how he had called her Mishka and why, and how she'd loved all the people whom she had worked with and desperately hadn't wanted to spy anymore. And then how she had assumed Nikolai had been caught and shot and how she'd managed to get away. She held out the necklace she was wearing to show Laura.

'This shell here.'

Laura looked at a beautiful heart-shaped white shell mounted in gold on a chain around her neck.

'This is the shell that Nikolai gave to me on our wedding night. We exchanged vows in the walled garden at the manor.'

Laura's heart caught in her throat. 'I'm working in there now. I'm restoring it.'

Anya smiled and continued. 'It was a magical place infused with our love. It protected us, kept our love safe, held our secrets. We loved and laughed in that garden. It was a tiny piece of heaven in a world gone mad. He even taught me to play chess in there. He was brilliant at the game. Nikolai was a wonderful man, and during our wedding vows, I promised to find him if ever we were parted, but it was impossible. I tried afterward but there was no way of locating him. And I know that if he had still been alive, he would've found me. I even added a quote he would know to Millie's grave years after the war just in case.'

'From *The Old Curiosity Shop*?' Jamie remarked.

Anya nodded. She sounded melancholic as she continued. 'But I'm grateful to see this again,' she said, brightening as she rubbed her hand across the cigarette case. 'It brings back so much sadness but also some great memories of being young and in love.'

'Did you ever look for him?' Jamie asked gently.

She drew in a deep breath. 'After Millie's death, I laid low for a few years until the war ended, taking work where I could under Millie's identity, hoping that he would find me.

'When I did not hear from him, I started to inquire. But right after the war, there was a lot of confusion. It was difficult to find out what had happened to prisoners. Everything was still very painful, and England was rebuilding. Even so, I continued my search for him for years afterward; it was challenging, especially as I didn't want to draw attention to my own dubious identity. And I could never return to Hatworth without exposing that truth, because everyone there knew me as Annie. But even when I finally gave up my official search, I never gave up looking for him in my heart.'

Laura felt the older woman's pain and desperation as she continued.

'Constantly looking for him, hoping to bump into him around every corner, praying to see just one face in every crowd.' She took a sip of her tea as she reflected on her words. Then she continued with great sadness, 'Eventually, life caught up with me and our love started to slip from my thoughts, fading to just a beautiful memory.'

'You never married?' Laura whispered.

A gentle smile played on her lips. 'I was *already* married. The vows I exchanged under an incandescent moon in a homemade flower crown in a walled garden were always so present in my life. It was impossible to contemplate breaking those vows without betraying the man I loved. In my vows, I promised never to stop looking for him if we were parted. I didn't know then as I spoke those words the cost of that promise.'

She looked wistfully towards them as she topped up their teacups. 'I tried courting a few people after the war, but it was as though the door to my heart was sealed, trapped inside the garden, within the midst of an endless summer of a perfect love affair. And nobody whom I met seemed to hold a candle to the intensity of that experience.' She stared at them both, her piercing green eyes becoming very serious. 'Make sure when you find true love like that, you hold on to it with both hands. Falling in love is easy. Holding on to it can be much more elusive than we think.'

Laura's eyes met Jamie's, as Anya carried on telling the story of her love and her life until two pots of tea were finished and she became tired.

She asked one last question. 'What made you decide to pursue me? You're a young person. This seems like a strange thing to spend your time doing.'

After the bravery of her story, Laura suddenly felt she wanted to tell her, so she opened up about Katie. Anya seemed to instantly understand Laura's pain, taking Laura's hand and holding it tightly as her voice quivered through the story.

At the end of it, she said quietly, 'You seem to have a lot of guilt. I know a lot about that. The trouble with guilt is it stops you loving and living.'

Laura nodded.

'I normally take a walk about now in Stratford. Would you like to join me?'

53

STRATFORD-UPON-AVON, PRESENT DAY

Laura

Laura, Jamie, and Anya walked beside the Avon, passing the famous Swan Theatre and the church where Shakespeare was buried, and Anya gently took Laura's hand.

'When I lost Nikolai, I had so much guilt, it crippled me. It crippled me so much that it filled my whole life. That's all I saw, all the guilt and all the questions. Why didn't I stop him longer that day when I saw him? Why didn't I hug him one last time? Did I do something to uncover us? Was it something that I did that exposed him? Why did we even leave Russia? Or we should have gone on the run when we got here. And even harder, guilt about my friends. Would Millie or Charlie still be alive if I hadn't spied for the enemy? I was so consumed with all that guilt that in 1956 I finally decided to give myself up to the authorities. But when I did, there was information in my file stating that I had been granted immunity – no reason why, with no more details. I had walked in, ready to be incarcerated or even killed for my crimes. And the only hope of feeding that monster of guilt was to be punished. But even that experience was snatched from me. In the eyes of the law, my wrongdoings didn't even exist, and it seemed a cruel twist of fate that I would have no remedy for the pain I was in. Then I had an experience that I want to share with you.'

Anya stopped, closed her eyes, took a deep breath to ground herself, and then opened them again. The wind whipped around Laura's face, and she struggled to hear the older woman's words, her voice thready with age.

'Look out along the river. What do you see?'

Laura looked out ahead. 'Water?'

'Be more specific,' encouraged Anya with a smile.

Laura peered out to take in the view more closely. 'I see ducks and swans. I see the banks of the river ahead of us with trees.'

'What that is, Laura, is your future. We're heading towards it. We're not there yet. We can only glimpse it. We have an idea of where we're going. As you say, you can see the trees and the land, the swans. If we were to stop walking right now, we would never get there. All it is is a dream of a future, a glimpse of what can be possible.' She turned to face her. 'What about here? Tell me what you see and feel here.'

'I see your face. I can smell your perfume. I can feel your hand holding mine.'

'This is what you have. This is your present. This is the only thing that you can really count on. Now follow me, Laura.' The older woman moved to the edge of the river as one of the narrowboats passed by them. 'Look out there, Laura. Look at the water and tell me what you see.'

'Reeds, plants. I also see the water being churned up by the boat as it moves.'

'That is called the wake. That is your past, Laura. That wake, it's not real. It's not a tangible thing. It is only an echo of what was. When we are on a boat we can see the disturbance of the water as we pass through it, but it is no longer part of our present unless we make it so. We were there. We're not anymore, and as we moved through the water, we created our past like that. It's not solid. It's not even real. It's only a glimpse of what it was. It has no power. It has no substance. And the farther away we get, the less it holds its shape.'

She turned to Laura to face her as she looked at her directly and spoke gently.

'When you look back at that time with your sister, you think of it as something solid, something you could've changed, but look at the wake, Laura. You couldn't have changed anything because it's already happened.'

Laura felt a sob rip through her throat, and her legs began to buckle as Jamie pulled her close to support her. All of her guilt spilled out of her in a long stream of words.

'I should have been watching her closer. I should have suggested another game. I shouldn't have suggested the woods. We could have played hopscotch right outside the door. I shouldn't have been angry with her for wanting to play with me. I should have gone for help quicker. I was her big sister. I should have been able to save her.' Finally, she couldn't speak anymore as the pain of her past overwhelmed her, and she let the tears flow freely.

The woman spoke gently, stroking her dampened cheeks. 'Every one of those things you just said to me is just part of that wake. There is no substance in it. It has already happened, and you feeling guilty cannot change that. We cannot change how that wake looks. What we need to understand is that we're not responsible at this point. All you have is this moment, Laura. All you have is now.'

Laura sobbed on the woman's shoulder as Anya held her tightly, and for the first time in her life since she had last seen her sister, she felt some understanding, a little relief from the guilt she had felt for so long.

'The wake is always there,' Anya whispered as she stroked

Laura's hair. 'But it will only appear as real if you choose to put all your focus on it. You have to choose to look in a different direction: you, me, and Jamie. The feeling of wind in our hair, the smell of the river, and the sounds of the ducks talking to one another are all real in this moment. And the future hasn't been written. But as you can only look in one direction at a time, don't spend all your time staring back at the wake of your life. Otherwise, you will never see the sunshine of this precious moment. Treasure today. You can glance back – it is what made you who you are – but don't dwell there, because what you are looking at is just an illusion of what was. Look now, Laura,' she said, signalling back to the water that was now still, 'the wake from the boat is already gone, it doesn't even exist anymore, only in our memory.

'It took me many years to learn to understand the power of living in the present and that remembering my past was only an echo of what was unless I made it more.'

54

HATWORTH MANOR, PRESENT DAY

Laura

After they arrived home from visiting Anya, Laura felt different about everything. Something had changed for her after meeting her, and she found herself opening up in a new way.

The following month on midsummer's eve a huge party with a bonfire was organized at the manor. She had invited Jamie to join in with the celebrations and enjoyed watching him socializing through the light of the flames as she took a sip of her wine. As the reds and golds of the fire danced under the full moon, they bathed the manor in a warm red glow and illuminated his features, causing his ebony eyes to glow like black onyx.

He looks gorgeous tonight, she mused as she took in his whole frame. He was wearing blue jeans and a blue cotton shirt that enhanced his early summer tan. He was talking to the groundskeeper, one hand pushed deep into a pocket, the other wrapped around his glass. He caught her looking in his direction and her stomach flip-flopped responding to his warm smile.

As people started to leave, he finished his conversation and walked around the bonfire to talk to her.

'It's been an amazing night, best midsummer party I've ever been to.'

She nodded, trying to control the electricity that always seemed to run between them. As they stood close together in a companionable silence, they sipped their wine and looked out over the estate.

Finally, she took a deep breath and plucked up the courage for what she had been planning.

'Would you like to go for a walk?' she asked.

He looked down at her and smiled. 'Sure.'

'There's something in the garden I want to show you. Just wait here for a second. I want to grab something first.'

He sipped on his wine while he waited for her to return. In her hands she had her glass, a half bottle of leftover wine, and a couple of woollen blankets. They fell into easy conversation as they walked through the estate to the secret garden.

Slipping the heavy key into the lock and turning it twice, she pulled gently on the door and they moved quietly inside. He followed her in and stood for a moment taking in the beauty of what was before him as she locked the door behind them.

As their eyes adjusted to the dark, she turned to him.

'It's finished,' she said with a great sense of satisfaction. 'The garden is complete.'

He drew in a deep breath by her side. The summer night was intoxicating. The gentle clean scents of spring had given way to the heavier fragrances of summer in the form of roses, nicotianas, and lilies. The garden was awash with rich hues of colour, including the two different roses that were in full bloom over the arbour.

'This is incredible,' he said as she led him through the arbour and past the fountain. He stood to take in every detail. Everything was exquisite by the warm light of the moon, which bathed it in such a way it made it feel mystical, magical some-how. As he continued to look around the garden, she was glad she had locked the door. She wanted this moment to be just the two of them. She did not want to be disturbed by the last few people who were milling around on the estate.

'You've done a beautiful job,' he said, admiring the peren-nial beds clear of weeds and full of overflowing multicoloured flowers.

'Thank you,' she said as she took him to the lawn and laid out one of the blankets. She sat down on it and he joined her and closed his eyes to enjoy the ambiance.

Laura studied his face, his dark eyelashes on his cheeks as he concentrated on the sounds around him. She closed her eyes too. In one area of the garden, she could hear the frogs and the crickets that were now lively around the pond. In the corner, something scurried to find a hiding place. Laura opened her eyes just in time to catch the tail end of a tiny hedgehog as it buried itself in the undergrowth.

Opening his eyes, he looked over at her.

'Thank you for bringing me here. This has been the high-light of my day.'

She poured him another glass of wine and they drank quietly together as their senses enjoyed everything around them.

Finishing his drink, he lay back on one of the blankets and, looking up at the sky, tucked his hands behind his head. 'That is the most incredible moon,' he mused.

Lying back on her elbows, she too looked up. It was huge and hung heavy in the clouds.

He turned and gazed at her. 'Are you happy, Laura?'

She was startled by his directness, was about to burble something offhandedly when she felt her heart stir. She had promised to always be honest with him.

'I am when I'm with you,' she said, meaning it. 'After Katie's death, I felt like there was a whole part of me that was closed down, padlocked behind the guilt. And even though I spoke to therapists and doctors, I could never really get past that. But talking to Anya and knowing how great her guilt was and how her actions may have lost her friends and the love of her life, and knowing she had found her peace with it all, opened the door to my heart in a way I didn't think was possible. Before, I could never really fully love someone, not even Liam, because it didn't feel right if Katie would never get that chance, but now I feel so different. I not only feel I could truly love someone now, but I want to.'

She glanced over at him and saw such compassion on his face.

'I want to go forward into something new,' she continued, 'and if you are open, I would love to explore that possibility with you.'

He slid his arm beneath her, and, gently cupping the back of her head, he drew her slowly towards him and kissed her. It was sensual and warm and once again lit her up inside. She briefly opened her eyes to enjoy watching him as he kissed her. A stray curl had escaped onto his forehead, his eyes intent and closed beneath his thick dark lashes. He slid his hand from her neck to rest lightly on her face and rolling onto her side Laura teased her fingers slowly through his thick curly hair. She moved her body closer and following her lead he rolled onto his side so he could get closer to her as well and deepen the kiss. Running his fingertips down her arms, which made her shiver, he found her waist, and pulled her gently towards him, till their bodies were pressed tightly together. She felt completely surrounded by him, her tiny frame melding into his large one. They were so close she could feel the tautness of his body below his clothes, and the long length of his legs as she wrapped hers around his.

Finding his shirt slightly untucked, she allowed her hand to travel up and down his broad back, feeling him shiver slightly at her touch. Their limbs entwined as they continued to kiss and the world around them in the garden became timeless. It could have been ten minutes, it could have been two hours – Laura had no clue, she was so lost in the experience. As he rolled her onto her back and their kisses became more urgent, she felt her body moving in a rhythm with his own, her heart pounding, her breath moving rapidly through her lungs. She undid the buttons on his shirt and caressed the soft hair on his chest as he moaned above her. He unbuttoned her top as well and finally she felt the warmth of his body against her own. They continued exploring and slowly removing items of clothing until finally they were both naked, and she shuddered as their bodies tangled together and their lovemaking started to intensify. He pulled away and his eyes found hers.

'Are you sure about this?' he asked her breathlessly, his desire acute in his eyes.

She vigorously nodded, not wanting to be apart from him and pulled his lips back towards hers to show him just how sure she was. His hands caressed her whole body then, sending tiny shudders down her spine before they succumbed fully to their desire and their lovemaking became more passionate. Laura found herself surrendering to the experience in a way she had never done before. She felt so vulnerable yet so safe in his arms. She found herself connecting with Jamie on a much deeper level than she had known before. It was also something to do with being in the garden. Not just the sensual pleasure of every-thing around her, but also knowing that this was a safe place, that it had nurtured love in the past and knew how to keep love's secrets. He made love to her with such tenderness, yet in a deeply sensual way, as if he wasn't just interested in his own pleasure but also in hers. His eyes barely left her face as he watched her respond to what gave her pleasure, putting his whole heart and soul into what he was doing. It reminded her for a moment of the passion she had seen in his art, so alive and vibrant and yet so intimate and tender, like a beautifully choreographed dance of touching and pleasure.

Afterwards, as they lay spent in one another's arms, catching their breath, she looked up at the moon and turning to Jamie whispered, 'I have the oddest sensation.'

'That is exactly what a man wants to hear after making love for the first time,' he mumbled with a wry smile as he drew her to his side.

She dropped a kiss on his naked chest. 'No, not about you, us. This was... wonderful.'

Jamie responded by kissing her gently on the forehead and pulling her even closer to him as she continued.

'I feel as if the garden wants to help us find out what happened to Nikolai. When I lie here, surrounded by its nurturing presence, it's as though I hear the trees and plants talking to me. Please don't laugh, I know it might sound weird, but it's as though they're saying that we have to keep moving forward, that we have to find out all the answers, uncover all the secrets. I keep thinking back to that first day when I arrived and how the key just turned up for me. Lifted from the ground by a storm and the roots of that old willow tree. Since then, it's led me on such a wild journey: finding Anya, all the changes in my own life, and... meeting you,' she added quietly. 'I feel wrapped in its love, as though it's trying to draw us closer and encourage us forward to keep looking for the end of the story: find Nikolai.'

'I don't know how we could do that. We know nothing about him.'

Laura closed her eyes. A gentle breeze rustled the leaves in the apple tree, and a way off, an owl hooted as if the garden were answering her.

'Can't you feel it? Can't you feel all the love and all the lives that have been touched in this space? It wants us to keep looking for Anya's sake. It wants us to find him.'

'Well, I hope it sends us a postcard.' Jamie smiled, sitting up. 'Because I sure don't know where we would go next.'

She stood up, tied the blanket toga-style around her chest, and lifted her hands like an act of worship towards the garden.

'Okay, garden, show us the next step. If you want us to find Nikolai you need to show us.'

The wind picked up again through the trees and whispered its response through the branches as the leaves rustled. Then, after she knelt down to kiss him one more long and lingering time, they both dressed and made their way back to the cottage.

As he walked with his arm around her, he spoke gently to her.

'I know this may not be the right time, but I want us to be honest with one another, and there is something I have to tell you.'

She turned and studied his face; he looked serious.

'Laura, I know you talked about going back to London after the garden was complete, but I think I'm falling in love with you, and I would love it if you would consider staying here so we could get the opportunity to spend more time together to see where that takes us.'

She felt her heart quicken with his confession and, brushing his lips with a fleeting kiss, offered him the honesty he had asked her for.

'I think I am falling in love with you too, though that really scares me so soon after coming out of a long-term relationship. As far as where I will go next, let me think about it and let you know.'

He nodded as they continued to walk back to the cottage. Laura thought of the weight of his confession and for the first time really pondered what a future might look like with Jamie.

55

HATWORTH MANOR, PRESENT DAY

Laura

In late summer the night before the grand opening of the walled garden, Laura was woken from her sleep by a crack of thunder, followed rapidly by the patter of raindrops that built in intensity until they lashed against the pane. Sitting up in her bed, she listened with concern as lightning filled the sky and the rain intensified. Jumping out of bed, she rushed to the window and looked out. It was coming down in heavy sheets, twisting in wind-whipped spirals all around the estate.

She sighed despondently. The garden. What sort of state would this leave the walled garden in? The door to the secret garden would be open for the first time to the public at midday. Would she have time to clean it up? As soon as it was first light, she grabbed the key and made her way across the estate, and as the wooden door creaked open, her heart sank. It was a mess. She rushed back to the house to get herself equipped for the day.

Alicia found her in the kitchen, grabbing a piece of toast

and putting on her boots. 'The garden?' she asked. 'Did it survive the storm?'

'It's in a terrible state.'

'Simon and I will help,' said Alicia as she then called to her husband, and they all put on their wet-weather gear and boots to go to work.

The three of them worked tirelessly in the garden all morning, raking leaves and fallen twigs, tying up plants, and clearing away storm debris. Fortunately, even though many smaller branches had blown from the apple tree, the newly planted willow tree was still in place and the bedding plants didn't look too bad once they were straightened up. And there was no damage that couldn't be fixed.

As she made her way around the garden, she noticed that one of the apple tree branches had flown right through the window of the little treehouse and was sticking up in the middle of the floor. Climbing up the ladder, Laura went to it and started to heave it up. As she did, she noticed something strange below it. She pulled the branch out of the way and went down to examine the floor.

A floorboard was loose. She'd have to nail it down. She was just about to go and get a hammer when she noticed there was a little tiny indent in the wood with just enough room for a finger. When she pulled it up, there was a hidden compartment below it. Somebody had created a little space under the floor in the wood.

Down inside, it was just big enough to hide a small bundle. Clearing a few cobwebs away, she pulled the bundle out. It was a small canvas package. She unfolded it and was amazed to see a makeshift chess board painted onto a brown canvas cloth and a whole set of chess pieces inside it. She took them out to show Alicia and Simon.

'Any idea where these came from? Maybe one of your children?'

Simon shook his head and took one of the pieces from her. 'This looks unusual,' he said, holding it up to the light and turning it in his fingers. 'It looks like it was hand-carved. Our children wouldn't have anything like this. This may be older than us. Look at it. It's so unusual. It has a Slavic name carved here?'

Laura's heart caught in her throat. Could this be something to do with Anya and Nikolai? She had asked the garden for a sign. Was this it? She decided to call Anya and ask her about it. If it had been Nikolai's, at least it would be something she could give her back, something that had belonged to her husband.

———

The opening was a resounding success and even the older gardener she had met and Walter Bartholomew came to see all the work. The next day Jamie came to paint in the garden and they talked about the previous weeks as Laura cut some fresh flowers for the cottage.

'Incredible to think that the roses she cut for her wedding bouquet are still growing over the arbour. They listened to the ancestors of the same owl, stared at the same moon through the branches of the same tree, and here we are sharing the same experience, seventy-five years later. Her story was amazing,' said Jamie, concentrating on his brushstrokes. 'I'm so glad we found her.'

As she brushed off the ladder to the tiny treehouse, she remembered her earlier find and showed it to Jamie. He held the little wooden pieces in his hand.

'Anya thinks they may have been Nikolai's. I called her last night, and she told me that was where he taught her to play chess. I will send them to her.' Laura placed them back in their hiding place as she ruminated. 'It makes me sad that we couldn't find Nikolai, even his grave, for her. I invited her to the garden opening, but she told me she thought it would be too hard without Nikolai by her side.'

Taking a break, the two of them sprawled out on the lawn and enjoyed the garden in high summer. It was beautiful now, and her work was done. Laura thought she would stay into early autumn to make sure the plants were bedded down for winter, then it would really be time for her to move on, and her stomach twisted with that thought. She wasn't quite sure what this was with Jamie yet. It was so new and beautiful, but she had to figure out the rest of her life.

Jamie interrupted her thoughts. 'Why can't we find Nikolai?'

'Anya said she looked everywhere for him after the war.'

'Maybe he changed his name too, or perhaps he was killed for his crimes and put in an unmarked grave. There are ways that we could look,' said Jamie.

'Without a name?'

'What about his chess?'

'When I called to invite her to the opening, I told her what I had found and she told me a funny story of him playing chess on the submarine with the Germans on the way to England and beating them all for their money.'

Jamie jumped up and started pacing. 'People can change their identities, but they can't change who they are. And what they love.'

'What do you mean?'

'If he was a chess player before he arrived and he was a chess player when he was here, it only stands to reason that he carried on playing chess.'

Laura started to feel some excitement. 'You're probably right. He may still even be playing if he's still alive, which I highly doubt. He would be in his nineties.'

'Then there is no time to waste,' Jamie responded as he pulled out his phone and began to search for chess competitions and competitors. 'If he was as good as you said he was, he might have won a competition or two.'

There were hundreds to look at, and it was long after he left and she was getting ready for bed when she got a phone call.

'Laura, it's Jamie.'

She still got a warm feeling whenever she heard his voice, and she smiled just listening to him on the phone.

'I think I found something to do with Nikolai. There's a man who won a competition a few years ago. There was a story about him in his local paper. His name is different, but initially, he came from Russia. He jokes in the interview about how he was shot in the head during the war by the British, and he thinks that he would be an even better player if it weren't for that.'

Laura's breath caught in her throat. 'Do you think it could be him?'

'I'm sending you the article right now.'

She went to her laptop and opened it and waited for the email to arrive. When it did, she pulled open the article. There was the older man, probably about the right age, smiling, holding a trophy. And on his head, there was indeed a scar where he may have been shot with a bullet.

'We should try and contact him. Let's not say anything to Anya just yet. This may be nothing, and I don't want to get her hopes up, but let's try and at least find him.'

'If he's alive, why did he never try and find her?'

'Maybe because she changed her identity too? Or he couldn't locate the first clue? It seems so strange and so sad though. Two people that were so in love could be apart and yet still maybe even live in the same country. It says here he lives on the Isle of Lewis up in Scotland. I'll do a search first thing in the morning – there can't be that many Russians there and we'll see if we can meet with him.'

56

ISLE OF LEWIS, SCOTLAND, PRESENT DAY

Nikolai

Nikolai had the dream again, the one that caused him to wake up in a sweat, his heart pounding so rapidly that at his age he was afraid it might stop. It had been seventy-five years since his time during the war, and yet still, the same memories came jumbling back as though it all happened yesterday.

He had managed to piece together much of his life during those turbulent years, but still, that first year that he was in England had never returned. He'd remembered training in the Soviet Union. He'd remembered working with an agent called Olga, but that was it. The rest was a blur.

He had tried in the early days to find out more information about the woman of his dreams, but it was hard without the memory. Now he just lived through these dreams when they came, the jumble of pictures, the sound of someone's voice, and that face – the face that had haunted him for all of his life. If only he knew who it belonged to instead of it being embedded in his past, caught in time like a dragonfly in amber. And after all these years it appeared she was destined to remain there.

Screwing his eyes shut, he held on as long as he could to the feeling, the overwhelming feeling of love and completeness he felt in her presence, until the real world, sounds from downstairs and outside, drew him back into his present.

Fully awake, he shuffled out of bed and made his way to the window, passing the unmade side of the bed, which still stung him. He missed Margaret, her vivacious laugh, her thick chocolate-coloured hair that he had watched fade to a downy grey. She had loved life and given him two beautiful children. He'd been very fortunate to be married to such a wonderful woman, and it wasn't that he hadn't loved his wife; he had just loved her differently. There was something about this mystical missing first love that was part of his soul, buried deep into his heart. It held captive a part of him that he was unable to give to anyone else, even his own wife.

It seemed ludicrous to know that there was a woman somewhere from his past who had held his heart in such a way that it had never been completely available to give to anyone else.

Opening the curtains, he looked out over the water. He'd lived on the Isle of Lewis now for over seventy years, since not long after his accident, the one that had robbed him of his memory. His wife had been working as a nurse in Birmingham when he'd been taken to the hospital and she had helped nurse him back to health. Her warmth and kindness won his heart until they married, eventually moving back to her home in Scotland to be close to her parents.

Nikolai looked out and thought about his day ahead. His daughter would be arriving soon. He would look forward to that to help distract him from the memories of the mysterious woman, whom they nicknamed Nell after the character from his favourite book, *The Old Curiosity Shop*. Closing his eyes, he allowed the memory of the dream to wash over him one more time, enjoying the feeling of being with her, even in this elusive way, even though it wasn't physical. His heart didn't know the

difference. It still pounded, and the memory was so real he
could feel her in his arms.

57

HATWORTH MANOR, PRESENT DAY

Laura

Laura managed to find an email for a woman who might be Nikolai's daughter; she had her own business, and after they explained that they may have some information about her father's life during the war they were invited to Lewis for a visit.

As they seated themselves in Nikolai's home, Laura scanned the room. Her eyes wandered to the top of the mantelpiece, and her breath caught in her throat. She could barely get the words out as she looked across at Jamie and saw he hadn't noticed yet.

'Excuse me, who is the picture of?' Laura asked before they had barely exchanged pleasantries with their new host.

Now she'd drawn attention to it, Jamie's eyes drifted to the mantelpiece too, and she felt him tighten beside her.

Rula barely glanced at it before she answered, 'Ah, that. That is Nell, the unknown beauty. You will see her a lot while you're on your visit here.'

'Where did you get it?' inquired Jamie, his voice almost at a whisper.

Rula eyed them quizzically, apparently trying to understand the unusual intensity from the pair of them.

Attempting to cover up the awkwardness, Laura followed up with, 'Jamie is a painter, you see, and we know a woman who looks very similar.'

Rula dismissed the idea.

'She is not real. My father paints her. He took up painting after my mother died. And one day after a dream he had, he just started painting her. He tells me he dreamed about her for years but doesn't know who she is. I believe it is a woman he knew in a past life, maybe a princess from the dark ages or a Russian fairy-tale beauty.'

Laura couldn't take her eyes from the picture. There was no doubt. She'd been looking at the same eyes just a few weeks before. The woman in the portrait was much younger, and the hair not grey, but the way she held her chin, the piercing green of the eyes, the shape of the mouth, this was Anya. Rula continued making small talk, and Laura barely answered. She didn't want to say anything until she had spoken to Nikolai himself. It sounded a little bizarre. Rula stood up and made her way out of the room.

'I will go and see if my father has woken from his nap. He likes visitors.'

As soon as she was out of the room, Jamie and Laura jumped to their feet and walked to the mantelpiece. Laura gripped his arm as if to confirm this was real. Jamie couldn't resist drawing his fingers down the painting.

'It's her,' he said, 'isn't it?'

Laura nodded. 'I don't doubt it. He's the one. He's the one she was searching for all these years.'

Before they could say any more, Rula was back in the room and only barely showed her surprise at the two of them standing inches from the portrait.

'He is awake,' she said, 'and looking forward to your visit.'

They followed her out into the hallway, where she opened the door into a small but brightly lit room. Inside, an older broad-shouldered man, surprisingly upright despite his age, was leaning across an ancient desk. Wearing a pair of bright-coloured reading glasses, he was writing something with a fountain pen. It was a comfortable room. But as soon as they stepped into the centre, their attention was struck by the decor.

On every wall, on every shelf, every available space, was a picture of Anya: Anya lying on a bed, Anya laughing with a drink in her hand, Anya standing, and – Laura caught her breath – under an apple tree. She was standing in the walled garden. Laura was sure of it. Even though the plants were so much younger than she knew, the shape of the brickwork, the unusual doorway, and the apple tree in the background... She tugged at Jamie's arm and showed him. He, too, nodded his confirmation.

Before they could say anything, the older man was on his feet, his hand extended.

'My daughter tells me that I have visitors.'

Laura nodded, unable to speak as she took his hand and looked into the eyes of this man. She had a feeling she was about to change his life forever. He seemed oblivious to the momentous moment that was happening between them and signalled to some patio doors, which he went towards.

'It is just such a lovely day. Now I have finished my correspondence, maybe we could go and sit outside. It is good to meet new people. It has been a long time,' he said, smiling as he made his way out into the warm day.

They sat down on the patio.

'My daughter tells me you are interested in my life during the war. I was a guest of your secret service for most of it,' he said.

As he turned his head, Laura saw a scar above his right eye. It hadn't been visible when he'd been seated at the desk with his head away from her. As if reading her mind, his fingers stroked the tiny concave hole in his head.

'This is the only souvenir they decided to leave me with.'

Laura couldn't speak. She was glad that Jamie asked a question.

'When did you arrive during the war?'

He sat back in his chair and looked into the sky, as if contemplating that very thought. 'I believe I was here for a year before I was captured. And then, once the war was over, they let me go. I had to change sides in order to win my freedom. I worked alongside them for most of the war years, helping them translate Russian documents, sending coded messages, anything that would keep me out of prison. I did spend an extended time in one of your hospitals.'

'Did you ever work at a place called Hatworth Manor, probably in your first year?' Laura asked him directly. The nonchalant expression on his face changed to intense concentration.

'To be honest with you, I don't know. All I know is what I've been able to piece together from released MI5 documents. I remember working in the Soviet Union. I remember preparing for a mission. I have a vague recollection of playing chess on a submarine. Then there is nothing. Nothing until I woke up in a hospital bed after I was knocked down by a bus right after the war. They said I'd been unconscious for two months. They didn't believe that I was going to pull through. I had to learn everything again. How to walk, how to talk. It was ironic that I managed to survive easily being shot in the head, but not walking across a road. It was very disconcerting not to know my history. Anyway, enough of these old stories... Tell me what brings you to Lewis?'

Laura didn't know where to begin. She could tell by the look on Jamie's face, he was in the same boat.

'We came to see you... because...' said Laura haltingly, trying to find the words.

Nikolai quirked an eyebrow.

Jamie continued where she'd left off. 'We may be able to help you a little bit with that time gap. We think you may have been at a place called Hatworth Manor during that time you don't remember.' The man shook his head slowly, as though trying to understand this information but it didn't mean anything to him. 'We have reason to believe that you may have been a footman there.'

'This is amazing,' he said in almost a whisper. 'How would you know that?'

Laura looked across at him. Dare she tell him? Anya had been a dream for him for so long, a fantasy, a figment of his imagination. He was elderly. What would this kind of truth do for him? But unless she told him why she was here, it would all sound like nonsense.

'We found a trail, a trail set between two agents. And we believe one of them might've been you. It looks like it was set up to inform you of the journey the other had taken.'

His eyes widened with surprise. 'Why would you think it is me? Surely there were more agents in England at the time?'

There was no avoiding it. 'The pictures you paint...' Laura said gently. 'All the pictures on your walls... We have met the woman in them.'

It was as though the words didn't register at first. He stared at her, stared back at his walls, and stared at her again. 'Nell is real?'

She nodded and leaned forward. 'Her name is Anya.'

A look of disbelief crossed the elderly man's face.

'Anya?' he repeated, trying to get used to it.

'You may have known her as Mishka.'

Suddenly something registered, a flicker of recognition in his eyes. He hitched his breath and held it. Then slowly, with great care, he repeated the word as though it was precious on his tongue. 'Mishka. Mishka, "little bear" in Russian.' He said it a little louder and then jumped to his feet, walked into his room, and stared at one of the pictures. The large one that was dominant on the wall, the one with her laughing, drinking from a glass. 'Mishka?' he asked, almost as if he was asking a question to it. 'Is that who you are?' He stood for a long time staring at the picture, not saying anything as Laura and Jamie joined his side.

'We have met her,' Jamie said.

The man turned to them and shook his head. And she noticed tears were streaming down his face.

'When you said that name, something struck me in my heart. And even though my mind doesn't remember or even know anyone with that name, it was as though something deep inside of me did. The name resonated intensely. I don't know how to really describe this in English. It was like déjà vu but with an emotional element. Are you really telling me this person is real?'

Laura instinctively took his hand. She felt like he needed support. 'As true and as real as you are to me, and she's been waiting a very, very long time to see you again. She has a story to tell you: her story and your story.'

He nodded in understanding and then he turned to look at the portrait again, as tears continued to stream down his face.

CHIPPING CAMPDEN, PRESENT DAY

Nikolai

Nikolai sat nervously fingering the bouquet of pink roses that he held in his hand. It seemed awkward giving them to a stranger, but if she was the answer to a lifelong puzzle for him, he already felt a connection with her. Would she feel the same? Noticing his reflection in the window, he sighed. He was so much older than she would remember him. Would she even recognize him? As he watched the unfamiliar countryside rush past his window, he felt out of his depth and he missed his island.

His daughter beside him on the back seat took his hand and squeezed it. 'It's going to be all right, Dad,' she whispered, loud enough for him to hear but quiet under the hum of the engine so that Laura and Jamie didn't hear in the front seat. They had made arrangements to pick the two of them up from the train station once Nikolai had agreed to see Anya.

He drew in a breath and whispered the name they had told him to see if it had the same effect on him. 'Mishka.' It rolled around his tongue, and there was still a familiarity to it, almost as if his mouth knew how to form the word. It was familiar to his tongue, even if his mind was vacant.

'We spoke to Anya on the phone,' said Laura, breaking into his thoughts, 'and informed her we'd be bringing someone to see her. She goes by another name now and has for many years. Apparently, she was looking forward to having visitors. I didn't say too much about who you were. I wasn't sure what to say. It's been such a long time.'

He swallowed down the dryness in his throat and nodded. He was as nervous as a bridegroom as he fingered the bouquet, yet there was an anticipation and an excitement as well.

It didn't take them long to get to the village from the train station, and Jamie pulled the car to a stop. Stepping out, Nikolai stretched his legs and straightened to his full height. It seemed strange coming to visit her as an older woman, as all his memories of her face were young and vibrant. But of course, so was he in his dreams.

They knocked at the door, but the woman who answered was young with a dewy complexion, her hair tied in a low ponytail.

'You must be Millie's visitors,' she chirped. 'I'm Melinda. I help clean now and again. She wanted it to be nice for you.'

They all walked into the front room and Anya was sitting looking out of the window towards the garden. A shaft of morning light streamed across her face. As Nikolai stood in the doorway, he caught his breath, his heart thudding violently with the sudden familiarity. Yes, she was older. Yes, her hair was grey. But it was her, the woman of his dreams, and tears misted his eyes.

She turned and their eyes met for the first time in seventy-five years, her beautiful green eyes that he could paint with his own closed, he knew them so well. She looked confused, then her eyes lit up as she gasped, drawing a hand to her mouth in shock.

They all moved towards her, and she stood up. She closed her eyes and opened them again, as if trying to make sure that this wasn't a dream. Laura introduced them.

'Nikolai, Rula, this is Millie. She was also known as Anya.'

Anya walked towards him and as he handed her the flowers, she whispered, 'You will remember me as Mishka.'

There was that voice, the voice that had haunted his dreams, and the eyes that he'd looked upon so many times while he'd been asleep, a walking, talking person in front of him.

'Mishka,' he whispered back.

She spoke to him in Russian. 'I thought you were dead, Nikolai.'

He shook his head, the words familiar and unfamiliar at the same time. It was so long since he'd spoken in his native tongue.

'I was kept by the British,' he answered in English. 'All through the war, they kept me until they let me go, and then I had an accident, and I don't remember anything about that first year in England.'

She stepped towards him and, reaching forwards, brushed the curve of his cheek with her fingertips then circled his eye, tracing a line where he knew he had a cluster of freckles, as though in touching him he would become real to her. He shuddered at her gentle touch, and something around her neck caught his attention. She was wearing a heart-shaped white shell.

'Do you remember it, Nikolai? The shell that you gave me?' She held it out to him, and he took it in his hand and rubbed his thumb across the smoothness of it.

Her face was so expectant, but he didn't remember. He didn't remember anything. Slowly he shook his head. 'I'm so sorry, Anya. I don't.' And then, almost reflexively, he pulled her close to him and held her in his arms. And as he closed his eyes and felt her body entwined in his own, she fit perfectly, as if his body already knew every curve. She was as light as a feather and as she sank into him she let out a deep slow sigh, followed by a sob. She tightened her grip, pulling him closer as she wept and he responded by holding her tighter too, wishing he could remember, wishing something would come back.

59

CHIPPING CAMPDEN, PRESENT DAY

Anya

The night after Nikolai came to visit, Anya barely slept. She tossed and turned until 3 a.m., then came downstairs to get herself a cup of tea. The house was so still and quiet as she wandered into her front room. Next to her chair, now arranged in a vase was the bouquet of pink roses, the only actual evidence that Nikolai had even been here. Her husband had *been here* in this very room, and her breath caught in her throat with that thought. She still found it hard to believe it wasn't a dream. As she stared at them she realized the flowers he had given her were the exact shade of the roses from their wedding crowns. Had it been unconscious or was it just a coincidence?

Staring out of her window, she sat for hours reflecting on everything that had happened. They had talked until they had both become tired, and Rula and Nikolai had gone to the hotel that Jamie and Laura had booked for them. It had been heartbreaking to find out he had no memory of their life together, but when Rula had showed her a small portrait he had painted, she had wept with the unbelievable likeness and the realization that somewhere inside him he still remembered her.

As the sun came up Anya looked out into her garden at the tangible world she'd created for herself and tried to mesh it with a world where Nikolai was still alive. A tiny part had never given up hope that somehow she would see him again. But the rest of her, the practical side of her, had reminded herself many times that Nikolai had to be dead. What was important was remembering what they had and who he had been to her, her beloved husband.

But now he was here. The man she had waited for, for seventy-five years, the man who had never really left her. Anya relived over and over again her feelings when he'd entered the room – the shock, the surprise, the relief. As he had filled the doorway of her little chintzy cottage, her heart had actually skipped a beat. Anya had thought for a second that she had imagined him, this white-haired man with striking blue eyes who looked so much like a man she had once known.

But as he'd walked towards her, her heart had known. And in that moment, she had been whisked back to the first day she had met him, as he had thrust out his hand and introduced himself. His body had aged – the thick wavy hair now white and wispy, wrinkles, where there had been taut skin – but the presence he brought into her home was as she had remembered it that day in Russia, his blue eyes still draining all the colour around her into greyness. But as she reflected, there was something more. Without his young looks and youthful bravado, Nikolai's spirit had been more present, more alive. And as she closed her eyes and dwelt on that thought, her heart ached as she realized how much she'd missed him, just the person he was, for so many years.

Whenever she had looked back, she'd often been caught up in her memories of their passion, the emotion, the beauty of love in a midnight garden. Yet, somehow in all of that, she had forgotten how he could fill a room and her heart with the very essence of himself.

Anya opened her eyes and looked back out the window again. It had started to rain, a feathery, damp kind of rain that made the roses glisten with droplets of shimmery wet diamonds and encouraged gentle streams of raindrops to roll gracefully down the pane.

She marvelled at the gift she had been given. Nikolai was alive. She drew in a long breath as she caressed her shell necklace and allowed that truth to sink in. Her husband was alive. As fresh tears of gratitude began rolling down her cheeks, she gently whispered words out to a grey day she never thought she would ever get to say. 'Oh, Nikolai, at last you came home to me.'

60

HATWORTH MANOR, PRESENT DAY

Laura

Laura pulled out the large brass key, and, placing it in the heavy brown door, enjoyed the anticipation of opening it, as she did every day. She turned it twice to the right, and twisted the round iron handle. It swung open easily and without a sound now that Laura had oiled its hinges. The height of perfect seasonal beauty and the freshness of the summer breeze wafted out to greet them all, bringing with it the delicate fragrance of the abundance of flora.

Nervously, Laura turned to look at Anya, rooted to the spot at the garden gate. As she waited, the older woman's eyes filled with tears, and instinctively, Anya reached out and grabbed Nikolai's hand. Prompted by the feel of her touch, he caught his breath too, swallowing down his own emotion. It took them both a moment to collect themselves, but Laura waited, not wanting to rush something that had been seventy-five years in the making.

Then, without a word and apparently perceiving her need to be brave, Anya rolled back her shoulders and slowly moved into the garden, Nikolai by her side. Jamie and Laura followed. Inside, the magic of nature greeted them. Even if she said so herself, the garden was at its most precious today to welcome two of its oldest visitors. The pink roses were fully blooming across the arch. The fountain, now cleaned out, was flourishing as ripples of silver sparkling water rolled down the stone tiers. The swing swayed gently in a carefree breeze; it was freshly painted in a robin's egg blue, and so was the little treehouse. A couple of starlings took flight as they moved inside, jarred from their home in the apple tree by the intruders. Around the garden, bumblebees and butterflies danced merrily from plant to plant, enjoying the abundance of nectar.

Following Laura's lead, the four made their way into the centre of the garden, where Anya turned nervously to Nikolai.

'Do you remember any of it, Nikolai? Is anything coming back?'

A look of pain crossed his face as he concentrated very hard, but finally, despondently, he shook his head.

'It is like remembering a dream in pieces. There are feelings, impressions, but nothing that is conclusive. As if I know I may have been here once before, but none of it feels real.'

Anya slowly nodded and bowed her head. Laura could tell that she was praying that this would be the miraculous healing that she'd been hoping for, the moment when he would remember their lives together, and her heart ached for Anya. Seeing the mounting sadness welling up between the couple, she decided to distract them by taking them on a little tour. She showed them around the garden, pointing out her restoration work. Anya would comment, informing Laura of the changes that had been implemented during the war.

As they rounded the corner towards the apple tree, a breeze picked up and rustled the leaves. The smell of apples ripening on the branches was rich and poignant, sweetened by the early windfalls already on the grass. It was as they moved past it, all at once Nikolai stopped dead and, releasing Anya's hand, he slowly walked towards the tree and, placing both his palms on it, he closed his eyes.

It was barely above a whisper, but they all heard it.

'I remember something.' They held their breath as they watched him; Anya's hand moved slowly to her mouth.

He knelt down on the floor. And at first Laura thought he was overcome, and moved forward to help him but Anya grabbed her arm to stop her.

A breeze rustled the leaves again, as slowly, with his eyes still closed, Nikolai ran his hand down the bark and around the back of the tree. He found what he was looking for. Turning to Anya, there were tears streaming down his face as he blinked open his eyes.

'I remember, I remember this.' His voice was deep and husky with the weight of his emotion. 'I carved a bear into the trunk of this tree. I remember it clearly now. And you were sitting there on the swing, your back turned to me, the starlight framing you like diamonds on black velvet and your beautiful naked shoulders were bathed in the soft creamy moonlight.'

Anya's breath hitched in her throat; she moved slowly to his side, and, helping him up, she gently took his hands in hers.

'The night we were married. That night, you carved that bear into the tree to commemorate our love, so the garden would not forget and would hold our secret,' she whispered.

And, remembering something, he pulled her hands to his lips and kissed them gently as they both closed their eyes with relief and drew in a long slow breath.

The memory of it was such a small thing, and yet somehow it was everything. As Anya opened her eyes and looked up at him again, Laura noticed that the years seemed to melt away from her face. As though up until this point, Anya had still not been sure Nikolai was real, and Nikolai in turn not sure about the truth of his bride. But with that one act, the air changed between them. She reached her arms out to him, and he enveloped her.

'Oh, Mishka,' he said. 'My Mishka, I'm so sorry that I've been away from you for so long. I'm so sorry I don't remember all of our love. My heart and body seem to remember what my mind cannot. Now, all I want to do is spend as much time with you as I can, so you can tell me the story. Tell me the story of us so I can relive it again.'

EPILOGUE

After they were reunited, Anya and Nikolai could not bring themselves to be apart. They decided to spend some more time in Norfolk to be together at the manor in the walled garden. As Laura watched them arrive every day, something began to dawn on her. Anya's words of warning struck her heart about how love can be snatched away so easily, and she decided that even though she wasn't sure of where it was going, she couldn't risk losing Jamie as Anya had lost Nikolai.

One morning, Jamie brought Anya and Nikolai to the manor with him, and as the older couple walked hand in hand into the walled garden, Laura held him back.

'If I'm not in London full-time, I may have to travel with my work all over the country.'

He looked at her with expectant eyes as she continued.

'I think that there will be enough room in my car for an easel or two in case an artist might like to keep me company on those cold nights wherever I am working though.'

He pulled her into his arms and held her close. 'What an amazing adventure. I'm sure that might work if you can find the right artist,' he joked, and then with the scent of garden flowers surrounding them, he kissed her gently on the lips.

Then, hand in hand, the two of them walked into the garden to find Anya and Nikolai, who were sitting on one of the stone benches, just as they'd done every morning since they had been reunited. Nikolai with a pen and his journal, and Anya with her memories. And under the shade of the apple tree, she told him a story of love, their story, the story that had been kept nestled in the arms of the garden for over seventy-five years – waiting for them to return and uncover all of its secrets.

A LETTER FROM SUZANNE

I want to say a huge thank you for choosing to read *Garden of Secrets*. If you enjoyed it, and want to keep up to date with all my latest releases, just sign up at the following link. Your email address will never be shared and you can unsubscribe at any time.

www.bookouture.com/suzanne-kelman

For as long as I can remember, I've wanted to create a love story that was set in a walled garden, ever since I first read *The Secret Garden* by Frances Hodgson Burnett in my childhood. I can still remember being enthralled with that classic at a tender age, captivated by the safety I found inside the garden walls, surrounded by the magical rebirth of nature.

Since that very first reading, I've always believed in the power of nature to heal and renew and have experienced its magic over and over again in my own life.

So, with that idea in mind I toyed with the possibility of creating a story where the garden would become a character in its own right, playing an essential role in the storytelling. Alongside its enduring quality, it seemed the perfect environment for a love story that spanned seventy-five years where secrets could be captured within its walls like a message in a bottle.

So, from start to finish, writing this book was a sheer labour of love for me.

Garden of Secrets also holds a special place in my heart

because, although not my first historical fiction book published, this book was actually the first in this genre I attempted to write. I still remember sitting down with a trembling ego as I tried out a new genre, opting to place it in a world that felt safe and nurturing to me as I unfurled my budding wings in this new form of writing. As I took my first tentative steps, it was as if the garden and I grew together – she from her desolate winter wasteland into a paradise and me into a new type of storyteller.

I never realized when I first put pen to paper, or fingers to keyboard, to be precise, so many years ago, what an important story this would become for my own journey through a pandemic. A time when the safety and endurance of nature has felt like the only impervious place in a world that is turned upside down. Through the past two years, I have been encouraged daily by the natural world as it unfolds through its seasons and continues silently on its way, unperturbed by the world that is changing around it.

With that hope in my heart as we continue to move through this season in our world, I choose to believe that just like a neglected garden, no matter how dire it gets, all things can be made new again – wishing you all good health and gentle blessings as you navigate this season yourselves. As for me, I will keep filling my pages with stories, hoping for better days, choosing to remember that even the weeping willow grows upwards.

I hope you loved *Garden of Secrets*, and if you did, I would be very grateful if you could write a review. It'd be great to hear what you think, and it makes such a difference helping new readers to discover one of my books for the first time.

I love hearing from my readers – you can get in touch on my Facebook page, through Twitter, Goodreads, or my website.

Thanks,
Suzanne

KEEP IN TOUCH WITH SUZANNE

www.suzannekelmanauthor.com

 facebook.com/suzkelman
twitter.com/suzkelman

ACKNOWLEDGEMENTS

First, as always, I want to thank my phenomenal publisher, Bookouture. It is wonderful to be supported by such a passionate and talented team. To my amazing editor, Isobel Akenhead, your enthusiasm and commitment to my writing inspires me every day to get up and create stories and I couldn't wish for a more talented editor to work alongside me to make my books shine.

Also, to Jenny Geras, Peta Nightingale, Alexandra Holmes, and Alex Crow, and the many others who shepherd my books, thank you all for your skills, vision, and enthusiasm. To Kim Nash, Noelle Holten, and Sarah Hardy, the fabulous team that promote my book with such passion you would think it was one of their own, thank you for all your hard work.

A huge thank you, as always, to my wonderful husband, Matthew Wilson. Thank you for all your work on this book. Your constant support and research skills were invaluable and saved me so much time and energy. Also, I'm so grateful that you have always been there for me, supporting me through the many ventures that make up the life of a storyteller. I only get more and more in awe of the depth of our love as the years go on. To my amazing son, Christopher, every day I have the privilege of being in your life I see as such a gift. I am so proud of you, son, and so grateful for your amazing love and infinite kindness. I love you with all my heart.

As well as my own little family, I am so blessed to be cradled and loved by a family of the heart, honorary sisters and a brother, which forms the circle of love that is my world. To my dearest friend, Melinda Mack, thank you for a friendship that continues to grow and nurture me as the years go on. I'm so glad you are by my side supporting me. Thank you for being there during the darkest times of the past two years. Also, heartfelt thanks to my brother of the heart, Eric Mulholland. I have been so grateful for the privilege of sharing our stories over the past year. Those times have been invaluable to me and only continue to deepen my love for you as my friend. Thank you, as always, for being there for me. To my other wonderful sister of the heart, Shauna Buchet, I can't imagine this journey without you too, and I treasure the time we get to laugh, talk, and share together, my 'bezzie mate' for over twenty-five years. Also, to my number one writing buddy, K.J. Waters, I love that we have travelled together through our writing careers and I have so valued your constant support and look forward to many more years of friendship and storytelling together.

Lastly, once again thank you to you, my reader. In writing this book, I am always so touched by your reviews, stories, kind words, and lovely emails, especially during a time when connection has meant so much. I am grateful and indebted to every one of you for enriching my life.